Irresistible Greeks

Red-Hot & Rich

Irresistible Greeks COLLECTION

May 2016

June 2016

July 2016

August 2016

September 2016

October 2016

Irresistible Greeks

Red-Hot & Rich

CAROLE MORTIMER   EMMA DARCY   MAISEY YATES

MILLS & BOON

First Published in Great Britain 2016
By Mills & Boon, an imprint of HarperCollins*Publishers*
1 London Bridge Street, London, SE1 9GF

Irresistible Greeks: Red-Hot & Rich © 2016 Harlequin Books S.A.

His Reputation Precedes Him © 2012 Carole Mortimer
An Offer She Can't Refuse © 2012 Emma Darcy
Pretender to the Throne © 2014 Maisey Yates

ISBN: 978-0-263-92237-0

24-1016

Harlequin (UK) Limited's policy is to use papers that are natural, renewable and recyclable products and made from wood grown in sustainable forests. The logging and manufacturing processes conform to the legal environmental regulations of the country of origin.

Printed and bound in Spain
by CPI, Barcelona

HIS REPUTATION
PRECEDES HIM

CAROLE MORTIMER

To absent friends

Carole Mortimer was born and lives in the UK. She is married to Peter and they have six sons. She has been writing for Mills & Boon since 1978, and is the author of almost 200 books. She writes for both the Mills & Boon Historical and Modern lines. Carole is a *USA Today* bestselling author and in 2012 was recognised by Queen Elizabeth II for her 'outstanding contribution to literature'.

Visit Carole at www.carolemortimer.co.uk or on Facebook.

CHAPTER ONE

'I thought the meeting earlier with Senator Ashcroft's aide went well…'

Markos Lyonedes took one last look at the late afternoon New York skyline from the eightieth-floor window of his office before turning to look at his PA, his expression rueful. 'Yes?'

Gerry gave him a quizzical glance as he stood on the other side of the imposing mahogany desk. 'Didn't you?'

Markos moved back into the spacious room. His dark suit was tailored to fit perfectly across muscled shoulders and chest, lean waist and long, powerful legs. He honed that fitness at the moment with early-morning runs in one of New York's parks. Aged thirty-four, he was a couple of inches over six feet, with dark, slightly over-long hair, and shrewd green eyes set in a swarthily handsome and chiselled face indicative of his Greek heritage.

He gave the other man a steady glance. 'That depends upon whether Senator Ashcroft would have sent his aide or come himself if Drakon were still in charge of the New York office.'

Just a month ago Markos had been based at the

London offices of Lyonedes Enterprises, the company he owned with his cousin Drakon, with a full and busy business and social life, and no thoughts of moving to New York. That was before Drakon had met Gemini, the London-based Englishwoman he was to fall in love with. Drakon and Gemini had become engaged and were married just two short weeks later. The two of them were even now on their honeymoon on the Aegean island owned by the Lyonedes family.

Luckily Markos and Gerry had instantly found a rapport, and Drakon had already expressed his approval of the PA Markos had taken on at the London office, following a rather embarrassing episode for Markos with the young woman who had been his previous PA. Just thinking of the way she had thrown herself at him during the last business trip they'd made together was still enough to make Markos shudder.

'Drakon had already accepted the Senator's invitation. He must have forgotten to mention it with all the wedding arrangements,' Gerry dismissed. 'Senator Ashcroft obviously wished to make sure that the new head of Lyonedes Enterprises, New York, was aware of the invitation. And he didn't send just *any* aide to extend the invitation—he sent his only son!' Gerry gave a grin. He was a tall, rangy man in his late thirties, with sandy-coloured hair and a pleasant rather than handsome face.

Markos raised dark brows. 'That's good?'

Gerry's smile widened. 'The Senator is grooming Robert Junior to take over when he retires in a couple of years. And invitations for the event on Saturday evening are being coveted like bars of gold by New York society. My wife would kill to get one. I thought your offhand acceptance of the invitation was pitched about right,' he added approvingly.

'It was actually caution on my part—because I wasn't sure if I was being insulted or not.' Markos gave a grimace as he sat down behind the desk. 'I'm afraid American politics remain a complete mystery to me.'

'All you need to know about most of our politicians is that re-election is their main goal, along with gathering up the necessary finances to run a successful campaign. That's why the Senator's schmoozing the New York head of Lyonedes Enterprises. This company employs several thousand New Yorkers, and thousands more all over the world.' Gerry gave another grin.

'That's a pretty strong incentive for the Senator—' He broke off as a knock sounded on the door before Markos's executive secretary entered the office.

Lena Holmes was yet another invaluable employee Markos had inherited from his cousin. A woman in her late forties, slightly plump and motherly in her plain dark business suits, she nevertheless succeeded in running Markos's office with the precision of a sergeant-major in the English army.

'Sorry to interrupt, Mr Lyonedes, but I thought I should let you know straight away that Ms Grey has cancelled her five o'clock appointment.'

Again, Lena's disapproving tone implied.

Evangeline Grey, interior designer extraordinaire— if her reputation was to be believed—and the woman Gerry's wife had recommended for redesigning the rooms in the penthouse apartment above them, had already cancelled one appointment earlier in the week.

'What was her excuse this time?'

Lena's mouth tightened. 'An emergency appointment with her dentist.'

Markos glanced at the plain gold watch on his wrist and saw that it was already five minutes to the appointed time of five o'clock; if Evangeline Grey had intended being here for their appointment this evening then she should have left her downtown office some time ago, not cancelled five minutes before she was due to arrive.

'It must have been a very sudden emergency...'

'I wouldn't know, Mr Lyonedes.' Lena expression remained disapproving. 'She asked if she might re-schedule for Monday evening at five o'clock instead.'

'What did you say?'

'I told her that I would return her call on Monday morning and let her know if that time was convenient for you,' Lena reported with satisfaction.

'And is it?'

'You currently have no other appointments at that time,' she conceded.

Markos smiled ruefully. 'But it won't hurt to let her think about it over the weekend?'

'Exactly.' Lena nodded.

'Thanks, Lena.' Markos waited until his secretary had left the office and closed the door firmly behind her before turning to look questioningly at Gerry. 'That's the second time Evangeline Grey has cancelled on me in a week.'

The older man turned up his hands. 'I have absolutely no idea what's going on there. Kirsty thinks the sun rises and sets on the woman's interior designs. And I have to admit I thoroughly approve of the innovations she made in our bedroom six months ago...'

Markos quirked mocking brows. 'Do I want to know what they are?'

'Probably not, as Kirsty is now four months pregnant!' Gerry chuckled before sobering. 'Do you want me to see if she can recommend someone else?'

Lyonedes Tower, both here in New York and in London, had a penthouse apartment occupying the whole of the top floor of the building. Markos had never taken up residence in the apartment in London during the ten years he had been based there, preferring to live away from his place of work—just as Drakon had preferred to own an apartment in Manhattan for the time he had lived and worked in New York: an apartment he and Gemini had decided to keep for the times when they visited.

Having only arrived a week ago, and finding the apartment above this office to be both convenient and spacious, with fantastic views over the skyline of New York, Markos had thought it best to make it his home until he felt more settled. He had decided to call in an interior designer with the intention of having it decorated more to his personal taste. Evangeline Grey was that interior designer.

The apparently elusive Evangeline Grey.

He gave a dismissive shrug of his shoulders. 'Let's wait and see what happens on Monday.'

'Phew, am I glad you said that!' His PA grinned good-naturedly. 'I would really hate to disappoint Kirsty. She likes the woman so much that before you even asked for the name of an interior designer she was thinking of trying to arrange a dinner party so that she could get the two of you together,' he explained at Markos's questioning glance.

'If she cancels the next appointment that may be the only way the two of us ever meet!' Markos leant back in his high-backed leather chair. 'For some reason the name Evangeline gave me the impression she was an older woman…?'

Gerry shook his head. 'Late twenties, I think.'

'Really?' His brows rose. 'Isn't that young to have built up the professional reputation she has?'

The other man shrugged. 'If you haven't made it in New York by the time you're thirty then you're never going to!'

Markos smiled slightly. 'Is she attractive?'

'I was always out at work when she came to our apartment, so I've never actually met her.' Gerry frowned. 'But I'm presuming so, if Kirsty wanted to introduce the two of you.'

Markos gave an appreciative grin. 'In that case let's hope that she actually manages to get here on Monday evening!'

Gerry nodded. 'If only to save me from suffering the brunt of Kirsty's disappointment! Although there will be plenty of beautiful women for you to meet at the Senator's party tomorrow evening.'

He gave a weary shake of his head. 'I think I've probably already been introduced to every beautiful woman in New York over the last four days!'

'You haven't met Kirsty yet!'

Markos grimaced. 'Being surrounded by all this love and romance is bringing me out in a rash!' First Drakon and Gemini, and now Gerry had made no secret of the fact that he was very happily married. 'As I now unexpectedly have an hour free, why don't we go through the last of these contracts?'

The elusive Evangeline Grey was already dismissed from Markos's thoughts as he instead concentrated his attention on the work he wanted to get finished before beginning his weekend.

A weekend which now seemed to include spending his Saturday evening at Senator Ashcroft's drinks party.

For some reason Markos had felt slightly restless since moving to New York. Of course the two weeks before the wedding had been frenetic, followed by his lethargy after flying to New York only a day later. His arrival had been quickly followed by one meeting after another as Markos introduced himself to the company's extensive business associates, and there had been a social function of some sort for him to attend every evening as New York society opened their homes and welcomed him to their city in place of his cousin Drakon.

Maybe the change-over had happened so quickly that Markos still felt slightly wrong-footed by the unfamiliarity? This office. The apartment on the penthouse floor above this one. The new people Markos worked with every day, and the others he socialised with every evening.

Whatever the reason for his restlessness, Markos knew that attending yet another party tomorrow evening was the last thing he wanted to do...

Eva had never enjoyed cocktail parties, having been forced to attend far too many of them in the past. She enjoyed those given by US Senators even less. All of the city's rich and beautiful were filling to capacity the huge reception room at one of New York's most prestigious hotels. The chatter was loud, the laughter even more so, and the jewels adorning the elegantly clad ladies' wrists, throats and ears glittered and sparkled in the light given off by the dozen or so crystal chandeliers hanging overhead. At the same time Eva's senses were being assaulted by the smell of dozens of expensive perfumes filling the air-conditioned room.

But, as her mother had been so fond of saying, 'What can't be cured must be endured.' It had certainly been true with regard to her marriage to Eva's father...

It was taking all of Eva's endurance to grit her teeth and get through this cocktail party hosted by none other than visiting Senator Robert Ashcroft. Not because she thought there was a risk of meeting any of her ex-husband's family—she knew from mutual friends that Jack had taken over the family's Paris office just over a year ago, and her ex-father-in-law, Jack Senior, didn't support Senator Ashcroft's political party. No, there was no possibility of her meeting any of Jack's family this evening.

Even so, Eva doubted she would have bothered accepting the Senator's invitation if she hadn't known how much it would appeal to the man who was her date for this evening. It was exactly the sort of social function Glen enjoyed. Which was fine. It just wasn't the real reason she had wanted to see him again.

In truth, Eva had no idea how Glen was going to react when she found the opportunity to explain that she had absolutely no intentions of going to bed with him—ever—or with any other man, for that matter. Instead she was thinking of asking him if he would be the sperm donor if she went ahead with the IVF she was considering. A subject so delicate, so personal, was something she felt she had to lead up to slowly, rather than blurting it out at their first—or even second!—meeting.

Senator Ashcroft's drinks party was turning out to be every bit the crush of people Markos had expected it might be. Most of them were already known to him after this past week of socialising, and a lot of the men wanted to renew their acquaintance with him. Their wives, daughters or girlfriends were making no secret of the fact that they found his dark and brooding looks attractive.

Not that Markos had any complaints about that last part. He had enjoyed a healthy sex life during his years of living and working in London, and he sincerely hoped to continue doing so now that he had moved to New York.

Nevertheless, even surrounded by beautiful women as he was, all seemingly vying for his attention, Markos still noticed the woman in the figure-hugging red gown, standing across the room...

Probably because she stood out from the rest of the 'beautiful people' present in as much as she was making no effort to respond to the flattering conversation of the half a dozen men currently surrounding her, but instead seemed totally bored—both by them and by her surroundings.

But it wasn't just that air of uninterest which had captured Markos's attention. Nor was it the fact that she was young—probably in her late twenties—and extremely beautiful. Ebony hair cascaded lushly over her shoulders and halfway down her spine, and her eyes were light in colour—possibly grey or blue?—and sur-

rounded by thick dark lashes. Her skin was the colour
of pale alabaster, her features delicately lovely, and the
fullness of her lips was glossed the same tempting red
as that utterly decadent gown. Her only jewellery was
a pair of delicate gold filigree earrings which dangled
almost to the bareness of her shoulders.

All of that would certainly be enough reason for
any man to give her a second glance, but still it wasn't
what had caught and held Markos's attention, what had
caused his body to harden in instant arousal the moment he looked at her.

Every other woman in the room wore masses of expensive jewels at their ears throat, wrists and fingers
and, whether tall or short, they were all fashionably
slender—a look that wasn't flattering to some of the
younger women, and even less so to most of the older
ones. The woman in the fitted red strapless gown wore
only those earrings, and her figure was…

There was a word for her type of figure. An old-
fashioned word that described her exactly—one that
had often been used to describe movie stars of the
golden age… Voluptuous! That was it! The tall woman
in the red fitted gown was voluptuous. Not fat—her
body was too obviously toned for that. She simply had
an hourglass figure: curvily, lushly, sexily voluptuous.
The sort of body, in fact, that most men preferred but
so rarely found in this fashionable age of slender and
willowy.

Her shoulders were bare, that expanse of skin the
same smooth alabaster as her face, and that wickedly
enticing gown enhanced the fullness of breasts that
were obviously bare beneath the silky material that
swept over her narrow waist before clinging lovingly

to the sweet curve of her hips. The material finished a couple of inches above her knees to reveal long and shapely legs, with three-inch heeled red strappy sandals on her elegantly slender feet.

Markos's breath now caught in his throat as she looked over the top of the heads of the men surrounding her, glancing around the room in obvious uninterest—almost as if she was aware of someone watching her, but had no idea who or why. His earlier impression of her complete boredom with her admirers and her surroundings was confirmed as she repressed a yawn. At the same time as their glances met.

Met and then, as the woman's gaze shifted slowly back to his, held.

Markos quirked a questioning brow—only to receive a blank stare and then a uninterested shrug in reply, before the woman in the red gown, as Markos was already calling her in his mind, turned away to accept a fresh glass of champagne from one of the men surrounding her, to all intents and purposes as if she had already forgotten Markos's existence.

While it might be a refreshing change after the past week and this last couple of hours of having women throw themselves before him like sacrificial offerings, this certainly wasn't the reaction Markos was used to receiving when he showed an interest in a beautiful woman.

As one of the two Greek-born Lyonedes cousins, with business interests worldwide, and wealthy beyond imagining, Markos had never been naïve enough to believe it was his looks alone which attracted women to him. Nor did he believe that every woman he met had to find his height and dark looks attractive.

But still, it irked him that the woman in the figure-hugging red gown—a woman who made him hard just from looking at her!—had dismissed him so easily and completely.

Maybe she was married?

Or engaged?

Or perhaps in a serious relationship?

No, it certainly wasn't either of the first two; the hand holding the glass of champagne she had just raised to those lush red lips—her left hand—a long and slender hand Markos could all too easily imagine moving caressingly over his much darker skin in a pastime his arousal also approved of as he felt his shaft throb in anticipation!—was as naked of jewellery as her throat and wrists. And if it was the latter then where was the man she was involved with?

If a woman as beautiful as that had belonged to Markos then he certainly wouldn't have left her alone for a minute, at the mercy of the pack of hyenas currently in for the kill.

If a woman like that *belonged to him*…?

What the hell?

Markos didn't do belonging. Or even long-term. And definitely not permanent.

A few days, in some cases a few weeks, of enjoying each other's company—and bodies—was the limit of any interest he had shown in the women he had been involved with over the past eighteen years.

Liking—yes.

Sex—definitely yes.

Love or belonging—definitely no.

His cousin Drakon—a man who had been even more averse to permanent relationships than Markos until he'd met Gemini a month ago, and fallen so quickly in love with her—might have succumbed to commitment to one woman, but Markos certainly wasn't interested in doing the same.

He *desired* the woman in the red gown. He was more than a little annoyed at the ease with which she had dismissed him just now. At the same time as he was aroused and hard just from looking at the way that fitted red gown clung so lovingly to all those voluptuous and below the gown naked curves. It was an arousal Markos knew he would prefer *her* to satisfy, rather than another woman's willing body.

It was with that thought in mind that Markos distractedly made his excuses to the women crowded about him before crossing the room towards the woman in the red gown.

CHAPTER TWO

GOLD.

Markos had been wrong about the eyes of the woman in the red gown; they were neither blue nor green, but so light a brown they appeared a deep shade of amber gold.

A deep, glowing and unfathomable amber that swept over Markos in cool uninterest even as the men gathered about her took one glance in his direction before parting to allow him to reach the woman's side.

Like Moses parting the Red Sea, Eva noted ruefully as the men around her instinctively stood aside for the tall, dark and arrogantly handsome man who had deliberately caught her gaze a few minutes ago before making his way so determinedly across the room towards her.

She had noticed him before, of course. And recognised him. What woman wouldn't notice this dark and broodingly handsome man? Or not recognise him as being one of the wealthy and powerful Greek Lyonedes cousins? Certainly Markos Lyonedes's photograph had been all over the New York newspapers this past week as he attended one social function or another.

His looks didn't hurt, of course. Eva stood five

eleven in her three-inch-heeled red sandals, but Markos Lyonedes was still several inches taller. Tall enough that he could look down at her with warm and broodingly sensual green eyes.

His dark hair was inclined to curl over his ears and nape, and his emerald-coloured gaze was now narrowed and assessing, set in an arrestingly handsome face that looked as if it might have been carved from mellow gold stone: high and hard cheekbones, a long blade of a nose, chiselled lips, and a square and determined chin. The perfectly tailored black evening suit did little to hide the fact that he was also powerfully built—wide and muscled shoulders and chest, flat and tapered abdomen, lean hips, and long, long legs.

No doubt about it. When it came to charisma and good-looks, Markos Lyonedes had it in spades!

It was perhaps unfortunate—for him—that Eva knew Markos Lyonedes to be exactly the sort of man she wanted nothing to do with. Personally or professionally. Which hadn't precluded her having a little fun at his expense this past week…

'I hope you'll excuse my coming over and introducing myself?' He quirked dark, questioning brows over enigmatic green eyes. 'I'm Markos Lyonedes.'

Even his voice was sexy, Eva acknowledged. Deep and husky, with an undertone of dark and sensual. The sort of voice guaranteed to send a shiver of delight down women's spines.

Other women's spines, Eva corrected firmly. Fortunately she was totally immune to conceited men like Markos Lyonedes. Most especially to Markos Lyonedes himself. 'I know who you are, Mr Lyonedes,' she said. Just as she knew exactly *what* he was.

The dozen or so men who had been vying for her attention seemed to have recognised that he was a man to beware of—if for different reasons than Eva's—and had now drifted off to a safe distance, leaving the two of them completely alone in a room full of the richest and most fashionable people in New York.

'You do?' His brow arched questioningly.

She gave a smile of rebuke. 'All of New York society—and most especially the women!—is agog with the fact that Markos Lyonedes has recently arrived in our midst!'

Markos studied the voluptuous woman in the clinging red gown through narrowed lids as he detected the mockery beneath her smoky tone.

Her beauty was all the more apparent now that Markos was standing next to those deep amber-coloured eyes, the perfect nose, the full and sensuous lips above a pointed chin. Her alabaster skin had the fine smooth appearance of porcelain in the bareness of her shoulders in the strapless gown.

And she was most definitely naked beneath that gown!

Well…her breasts certainly were. The berry-like nipples were temptingly outlined against the silky material, the perfect fit of the gown over the fullness of her hips surely only allowed for a pair of gossamer-thin panties. Panties the same vibrant red as her gown? And would they be made of lace? Or silk?

Markos drew in a deep breath as his already hot and aroused shaft gave a throb of response just at the thought of his seeing this shapely woman wearing only a pair of brief and silky red panties.

'And you are…?'

'Eva.'

His smile was teasing. 'Just Eva?'

She gave a light inclination of her head. 'Just Eva.'

The coolness in her voice, as well as her demeanour, was really starting to irritate—and arouse!—the hell out of him. 'It's a pleasure to meet you, Just Eva.'

The sensual fullness of her lips curved into a chiding smile. 'Shouldn't you get to know me a little better before deciding that?'

'Well, I already know that you're English,' Markos murmured slowly as he finally heard her speak more than two words together.

That enigmatic smile widened, revealing white, even teeth. 'Obviously.'

Yes, definitely mockery, Markos noted wryly, even as he wondered at the reason for it. It usually took a beautiful woman a lot longer than two minutes' acquaintance to decide he might be dangerous.

He nodded. 'Having just lived in England for ten years, English is an accent I've become familiar with.' An accent, he now realised, that he had sorely missed this past week.

Eva gave an acknowledging inclination of her head. 'And how are you enjoying New York?'

He shrugged broad shoulders. 'Well, so far I've realised that it truly is a city that never sleeps.'

That was one of the things Eva had come to love about New York since she had moved here seven years ago. At the time she had been twenty-two, fresh out of university and newly married to a native New Yorker. Her career had instantly blossomed, and the city of New York had 'taken'—but unfortunately the marriage hadn't. She and Jack had separated after only four years, and divorced not long after. That experience, and her own parents' less than happy marriage, had left Eva with the viewpoint that once bitten was twice shy—and with the intention of never marrying again.

She shrugged. 'Oh, come on. If nothing else you have to appreciate the fact that you can buy a decent cup of coffee here any time of the day or night.'

Smoky green eyes warmed in sensual invitation. 'I've found that the percolator in my apartment makes an excellent cup of coffee. Day or night...'

'Wow.' Eva looked at him admiringly. 'It took you... what...? All of five minutes' acquaintance before inviting me back to your apartment.' She went on dryly at his enquiring look, 'Surely that has to be a record, even for you?'

Markos stilled, now positive that he hadn't been mistaken about the sharp edge of derision that seemed to underlie every word this woman said to him. '"Even for me..."?' he prompted softly.

She shrugged those bare shoulders, the movement drawing attention to the full and creamy swell of her breasts above the neckline of the silky red gown. 'I'm afraid your reputation has preceded you, Markos.'

'And what reputation might that be...?'

Amber-coloured eyes looked up into his unblinkingly. 'Why, that you're as lethally single-minded in your pursuit of a woman you desire as you are cold and calculating when it comes to ending a relationship.'

Markos straightened, his lazy humour fading in the face of her attack. 'I beg your pardon...?'

Had she gone too far? Eva wondered with an inward grimace. After all, circumstances might be such that she was predisposed to dislike and disapprove of

Markos Lyonedes, but having now met him there was no doubting that he was a force to be reckoned with in New York—both professionally and socially. Just as his cousin Drakon had been before him.

She had met Drakon Lyonedes twice, both times only briefly, and had found him to be a much different man from his slightly younger cousin. Just as handsome as Markos, Drakon had had a demeanour that was arrogantly remote—whereas she already knew that Markos possessed a latent sensuality capable of wrapping its tentacles about a woman's senses.

Even hers?

Perhaps...

But the fact that Markos Lyonedes now appeared every inch the powerful and arrogant Greek billionaire businessman that he was, instead of the flirtatiously seductive man of a few seconds ago, would seem to indicate that she had indeed overstepped the line. As far as he was concerned, at least.

Eva had only wanted to let him know that she had no intention of being so much as flattered by his marked attention, let alone falling for his seductive and no doubt practised—charm.

She gave a light and deliberately dismissive laugh. 'I'm only repeating what the gossips are saying about you.'

'Indeed?' That green gaze was hard and unyielding. 'And do you always listen to rumours rather than forming your own opinions of people?'

She shrugged. 'It's an unwise woman who ignores gossip completely.' Just as it was an unwise woman who chose to ignore the fact that Markos Lyonedes's voice had hardened in the last few minutes. Those clipped tones now betrayed the fact that English was not his native tongue.

'No doubt allowing you to decide that there is no smoke without fire…?'

Oh, Eva was pretty sure there was a *lot* of fire when this man chose to turn his lethal charm on a woman. 'Not exactly,' she dismissed dryly. 'There have been dozens of photographs of you with beautiful woman in the newspapers over the years. And articles in glossy magazines. Those things aside, I do have eyes and common sense with which to make up my own mind.'

His nostrils flared. 'And yet you had already decided to distrust me, from what you had heard of my reputation, before we had even met?'

Eva had decided so much more than that! 'I knew enough to be wary, yes.'

Markos Lyonedes's jaw tightened. 'You are not prepared to give me the benefit of the doubt?'

'In what way?'

'In that photographs in newspapers can often be deceiving, and gossip misleading.'

'Probably not, no,' she answered without hesitation.

'That's a pity.'

'Is it?'

His mouth tightened and he gave a stiff inclination of his head. 'I trust I did not interrupt your enjoyment of the evening?'

She grimaced. 'I wasn't enjoying it much even before you came over and spoke to me.'

'And my conversation has added to that lack of enjoyment?'

Eva shrugged. 'I shouldn't let it bother you, Markos; it's really nothing personal.'

'On the contrary. I believe your comments in regard to me to have been *very* personal,' he responded tersely.

Eva looked up at him, realising that although he appeared outwardly controlled, inwardly Markos Lyonedes was quietly, chillingly angry—as the tightness of his jaw and the angry glitter of those green eyes testified. Maybe playing this silly game of cat-and-mouse with him over this past week had not been a good move on her part.

She gave a dismissive shake of her head. 'I just thought I would save you wasting any of your time in attempting to charm me.'

'Would it be wasted?'

'Most definitely,' Eva confirmed with feeling.

His eyes became glacial. 'In that case, I will relieve you of the necessity of suffering my company a moment longer.'

Was that disappointment Eva now felt at this man's acceptance of her scathing dismissal of him? Surely it couldn't be—not when she knew from her cousin Donna how callous this man could be?

Donna should have known better than to become involved with a man like Markos Lyonedes in the first place, of course. But then, her cousin had never had the most discerning of tastes when it came to her choice in men—a family trait on the female side, if Eva's mother and Eva were any example. Having now met the man herself, Eva could perhaps better understand Donna's attraction to him. A fatal attraction and, in Eva's opinion, one that applied to *any* woman Markos Lyonedes became involved with. The man was far too powerful and attractive for his own good. He had only to click his fingers to have any woman he wanted.

Except Eva.

She and Donna had often stayed with their maternal grandparents when they were children, and during those visits they had developed a healthy competitiveness towards each other. A competitiveness which had become less healthy in adulthood, unfortunately, resulting in their rarely meeting as they pursued their separate careers and lifestyles, particularly once Eva had married Jack and moved to New York. But when Eva's marriage had finally come to an agonising end Donna had been the only one in her family to bother telephoning Eva to commiserate.

In fact her cousin had been ecstatic when she'd first called and told Eva of her relationship with Markos Lyonedes. She's been able to talk of nothing but how wonderful he was, and how much she longed to become his wife. When Markos Lyonedes had suddenly dumped Donna, just over a month ago, it had seemed only fair for Eva to listen sympathetically when her cousin called almost every day to talk endlessly of how much she was still in love with him.

Even if Eva hadn't been warned off by Donna's unhappy experience with Markos Lyonedes, she knew she would still have been wary of him. He was everything her broken marriage had taught her to stay well away from. Too rich. Too handsome. Far too powerful. And, as she now knew, too immediately and lethally sensual!

It was perhaps the latter trait that Eva found most disturbing. She knew that she wasn't as immune to that inborn sensuality, the way this man looked, or the hard leanness of his body, as she might have hoped or wished to be.

She had met dozens of handsome and charming

men during the three years since her separation and divorce—had even tried dating some of them. But not a single one of those men had touched her emotions, and nor had they dispelled the cynicism of feeling she now felt in regard to relationships.

Markos Lyonedes was such a forceful presence, even in a room full of equally powerful men—one of them was a US Senator, for goodness' sake!—that Eva had become aware of him the moment he had entered the room a short time ago. When he had looked at her a few minutes ago she had felt a shiver down the length of her spine as she'd recognised the admiration in his heated green gaze.

'I will leave you to enjoy the rest of your evening,' Eva finally replied derisively. 'I'm sure all the other ladies present will be only too happy to entertain you.'

Markos looked down at her piercingly. 'Is it possible the two of us have met before?'

Those amber eyes widened. 'Not that I'm aware, no.'

Not that Markos was aware, either—he was sure he would have remembered if he had ever met this voluptuously beautiful woman before. Even so, he sensed there was something more to Eva's comments regarding his reputation than her offhand dismissal implied. As far as he was aware, none of the women he had been involved with had ever walked away broken-hearted.

Or could it be that he was just too used to having women falling over themselves to attract his attention rather than the other way around? That he had believed Eva would feel flattered at his marked attention? If that was indeed the case then it was worse than arrogant of him, and he deserved the scorn she made no effort to hide.

Markos forced the tension from his shoulders. 'You—'

'Ah, there you are, Eva baby.' A tall, blond-haired man in his late thirties moved in beside Eva. His blue gaze was curious as he turned to smile at Markos, his teeth very white and straight against his slight tan. 'Great party, isn't it?'

'Great,' Markos echoed, as he inwardly acknowledged that he wasn't pleased at seeing the other man's arm draped possessively about Eva's waist. This was ridiculous of him, when Eva had made it so obvious that she had no interest in him. Perhaps the other man's proprietorial attitude explained that lack of interest?

Maybe. Although Eva hadn't looked particularly pleased at being called 'Eva baby'.

She straightened away from that possessive arm about her waist before making the introductions. 'Markos, this is Glen Asher. Glen, meet Markos Lyonedes.'

'Really? *The* Markos Lyonedes?' Glen prompted warmly as the two men shook hands.

'Yes, really,' Eva confirmed, irritated that Glen was so obviously bowled over by meeting him.

Admittedly the man was as rich as Croesus, but he was too handsome and charming for his own good. And Lyonedes Enterprises was one of the most powerful business organisations in the world, owning a private jet, as well as properties all over the world—including, Eva believed, their own private island in the Aegean. But did Glen *have* to look quite so impressed?

'Lyonedes Tower is a monument to beautiful architecture,' Glen added admiringly.

In that, Eva did have to agree with him. Standing

at least eighty floors high, and built of a pale, rose-coloured marble, with tinted sun-reflecting windows, Lyonedes Tower was one of the most beautiful buildings in New York, rivalling the Empire State and the Chrysler Buildings.

Even so...

'It's just another tall building blocking the view, Glen,' she dismissed impatiently.

Markos Lyonedes looked amused rather than annoyed by her comment. 'But I thank you anyway,' he told the other man dryly.

Eva's irritation deepened. 'I believe it's time we were leaving, Glen.'

He looked crestfallen. 'But we only just got here...'

Markos's previous annoyance at Eva's scathing comments about his reputation had dissipated totally in the face of her increasing irritation with the man who had accompanied her here this evening. If she *was* in a serious relationship, it wasn't with Glen Asher, and Markos couldn't see how a man Eva was involved with would be happy about her attending a party with another man—particularly one as handsome and obviously successful as Glen.

So, no serious relationship.

But what did it matter? The woman he knew only as 'Just Eva' couldn't have made her complete lack of interest in him any more obvious. Contrarily, it just made her all the more intriguing to Markos.

He had never thought of himself as being a masochist before, but maybe this move to New York, and the over-abundance of beautiful women vying for his attention this past week, was turning him into one—because if anything his attraction to Eva had only deepened in the last few minutes.

He looked down at her from between hooded lids. 'I would be more than happy to escort Eva to her home if you would like to remain at the party a while longer, Glen.'

Amber-gold eyes widened in what looked like horror at the suggestion, even as bright spots of colour brightened those pale alabaster cheeks. 'If Glen wishes to stay, I'm perfectly capable of ordering a cab and taking myself home, thank you,' she replied tightly.

He continued to look down at her. 'There's no need when my car is parked downstairs.'

Eva wanted to tell Markos Lyonedes what he could do with his car!

But, even more important than that, she now deeply regretted having invited Glen to accompany her here this evening in the first place.

They had met the previous week, at a party similar to this one. Eva had studied him dispassionately, finding that she approved of his blond hair and blue eyes, and the fact that he was tall and appeared healthy.

On the basis that she couldn't just march up to a complete stranger and ask him to be the donor for her IVF baby—once tests had proved he was fertile, of course—Eva had decided it might be better if the two of them got to know each other a little better before she dropped the bombshell on Glen. That was the only reason she had gone to his office early yesterday evening and asked him to be her escort to Senator Ashcroft's cocktail party tonight.

Although Glen seemed to have a very different idea of where their relationship was going...

She gave Markos Lyonedes a brightly insincere smile. 'It's very kind of you to offer, Markos, but—'

'But there's absolutely no need when I'm happy to leave with Eva,' Glen cut in with smooth confidence, his arm once again moving about Eva's waist. 'I booked dinner for the two of us at nine-thirty,' he added temptingly.

A dinner that he was no doubt hoping would result in the two of them sharing the bed in his apartment later on this evening, or possibly in Eva's. But Eva knew that sharing Glen's bed—or any other man's, come to that—simply wasn't going to happen.

Nor, in this day and age, was it necessary. It had all seemed perfectly logical when Eva had made her decision several months ago. She was desperate to have a child of her own, but not another marriage or relationship with a man who would ultimately let her down. One failed marriage was surely enough for any woman.

She had it all planned out. She would become pregnant before her thirtieth birthday in six months' time, move her offices to her apartment and continue working from there until her eighth month, have the baby, and then resume working once the baby was three months old or so, hiring a nanny who could take over on the occasions Eva had to go out and visit with her clients.

Logic. Not emotion.

Except it wasn't logic which drove Eva but an aching, driving need. Jack had wanted to try for a baby as soon as they were married, and as a family of her own was what Eva wanted too she had been only too happy to agree to the suggestion. Month after month she had waited to see if *this* was going to be the month when she could excitedly tell Jack she was pregnant. Except it hadn't happened. Not the first year. Nor the second. Until in the end they had decided to see a specialist and find out if either of them had a problem—and, if they did, what to do about it.

The results of those tests had been devastating and, although Eva hadn't realised it at the time, they had also sounded the death knell to her marriage.

Jack was sterile. One hundred per cent, no room for error, sterile.

Oh, they had told each other that it didn't matter, that they had each other. It had only been when Eva suggested that maybe they could adopt that the chasm had widened even further between them. Jack had adamantly refused to consider adoption, stating that his blue-blood New York family would never accept as heir a child who wasn't biologically Jack's.

Eva had tried to believe that having each other really *was* enough. While each day she had died a little inside at the knowledge that there would never be any children in her marriage. No babies to love and nurture, her own or adopted. No happy house full of the children, she had longed for all her life after growing up an only child in the war zone that had been her parents' marriage.

She and Jack had stayed together for another two years after the specialist had delivered his devastating news. Years during which they had drifted apart as they both buried themselves in their individual careers rather than face the ever-widening rift in their marriage. Years when Jack became involved in affair after affair—possibly as a sop to his dented virility?—only to break them off each time Eva found out about them, with tears and declarations of love on his part, and promises of future fidelity. Until the next time. And the next.

Eva's love for Jack had died a little more with each of those affairs. Until there had been nothing left but the shell of their marriage. A marriage Eva wouldn't have wanted to bring a child into even if it had been possible.

Another three years of being on her own after the divorce, of building her interior design business into one of the most successful in New York, and Eva had realised there was still something missing from her life. The same something that had always been missing from her life.

A baby of her own.

Lots of professional women had babies on their own nowadays—so why not Eva? She certainly had enough money to be able to provide for them both comfortably, and her career was of a kind that could be worked around a baby's needs.

So the plan was to find herself a man who was healthy, explain to him what it meant to be an IVF donor, and present him with the legal contract she would expect him to sign. Both of them would be protected from any financial demands being made on the other after the baby was born.

Putting that idea into practice had proved much harder than Eva had imagined. Broaching the subject, asking any man to coldly, clinically donate his sperm for IVF, had proved difficult.

'That's very thoughtful of you, Glen.' She smiled warmly, more for Markos Lyonedes's benefit than Glen's. Her smile faded as she turned to look at the Greek businessman. 'If you will excuse us?'

'Of course.' Markos gave a slight inclination of his head, wondering what thoughts had been going through Eva's head these past few minutes to form that frown between those golden eyes. Whatever they had been, he certainly didn't hold out a lot of hope for Glen Asher's chances of sharing her bed tonight. 'It was a pleasure to meet you both.'

'And you,' Glen assured him warmly.

It was a warmth that was in no way reflected in Eva's incredible gold eyes, and she made no effort to echo her escort's enthusiasm. 'We'll wish you a good evening, then, Mr Lyonedes.'

His eyes laughed down into hers. 'I believe you called me Markos earlier.'

'Did I?' she dismissed coolly. 'How over-familiar of me!'

Not familiar enough for Markos. He turned to watch Eva and her escort cross the room to make their excuses to their host before leaving. All without those amber-gold eyes giving so much as a glance back in his direction.

Markos continued to watch the sensuous sway of those curvaceous hips so lovingly outlined in that clinging red gown, and made a silent promise to himself as the doorman closed the door behind Eva's departure.

A promise that one day—or night; it didn't really matter what time it was!—he would hear Eva scream his name as he made love to her.

CHAPTER THREE

'WELL, well, well—if it isn't Ms Evangeline Grey come to call at last!' Markos observed dryly from where he sat in his high-backed leather chair behind the mahogany desk in his office.

Lena had shown the interior designer in at exactly five o'clock on Monday evening, before quietly closing the door behind her as she left them alone together.

Markos and the interior designer Evangeline Grey.

The same Evangeline Grey who had introduced herself to him as 'Just Eva' on Saturday evening, in the knowledge that she had cancelled two appointments with him earlier in the week.

Markos had wasted no time after she and Glen had left the party on Saturday in asking one of Senator Ashcroft's many aides about the identity of the woman in the red dress. Only to be informed that she was the interior designer Evangeline Grey.

Those amber-gold eyes flashed her displeasure now, as she marched into the centre of the spacious office, allowing Markos to see that she managed to look sexy even wearing a business suit—a fitted black jacket and knee-length black skirt, the latter revealing long and silky-smooth legs. Her silk blouse was the same unusual colour as her eyes; her long ebony hair neatly gathered and secured at her crown.

'Your telephone call this morning made it clear you expected me to be here promptly at five o'clock, whether it was convenient or otherwise,' she reminded him with barely concealed impatience.

'Indeed.' Markos stood up and moved slowly round his desk to lean back against it as he looked down at her between narrowed lids. 'And the fact that you are here would seem to imply that you were no happier than I was on Saturday at the possibility of having a slur cast upon your reputation?'

A frown appeared on that smooth alabaster brow. 'That's hardly a fair comparison, Mr Lyonedes, when the threats you made to me this morning were in regard to my professional reputation, not my personal one.'

'I believe the saying is "payback can be a bitch"?' He gave an unrepentant shrug. This woman had wilfully—deliberately!—played with him on Saturday evening by not revealing her true identity, and no doubt been highly amused at Markos's expense because of it.

Markos had thought about it long and hard over the weekend, finally deciding that if Evangeline Grey wanted to play games then he was happy to oblige her. With that in mind he had telephoned her office himself that morning and demanded to speak to her personally. After a short delay there had been a more or less one-sided conversation during which Markos had informed her that there would be no more cancelled appointments. If she didn't want him to tell anyone and everyone who cared to listen just how unreliable he had found her professional services she would come at five.

Her only answer had been to end the call abruptly,

causing Markos to chuckle wryly as he slowly placed his mobile down on his desktop.

Nevertheless, he had been sure that Eva *would* be here at five o'clock. He knew that she was now aware that it was well within his power to seriously damage her professional reputation if he chose to do so.

'You're unusually quiet today,' he remarked, lifting his dark brows mockingly.

Oh, Eva had plenty she wanted to say to this man. She was just erring on the side of caution—for the moment.

She had realised after leaving Senator Ashcroft's cocktail party on Saturday— her feelings of anger on behalf of her cousin aside—that it probably hadn't been a wise move on her part to antagonise a man as powerful as Markos Lyonedes by making appointments with him which she'd never had any intention of keeping. Unwise and not a little childish, she now accepted reproachfully. As if it would *really* matter to a man as powerful as Markos Lyonedes if some little interior designer chose to snub him by not keeping her appointments!

Except, having met her on Saturday evening, it obviously *did* matter to him. It didn't help, having duly arrived at Lyonedes Tower at five o'clock, that Eva was now totally aware of the way in which Markos Lyonedes managed to exude a predatory air—despite the expensive elegance of his tailored dark grey suit and paler grey silk shirt, with matching tie knotted meticulously at his throat.

'Did you and Glen enjoy your late dinner on Saturday evening?' he prompted softly.

Eva's mouth tightened at this reminder of the time

she and Glen had spent together at an Italian restaurant after leaving the Senator's party. Several hours during which she had desperately tried to dredge up some of her former approval of Glen as an IVF donor, only to find that, rather than appreciating Glen's healthy good looks, she was comparing them to the hard and chiselled features of the man now standing in front of her.

A man she wouldn't even *consider* putting on a shortlist of potential donors for her baby.

Oh, Markos Lyonedes was definitely handsome, and obviously he was healthy and intelligent, but there all suitability as the possible father of her child ended. Markos might have more than earned his reputation for avoiding serious relationships, but Eva knew there was no way that a man as powerful as one of the Greek Lyonedes cousins would ever agree to clinically, calculatedly father a child by donating his sperm for IVF.

In fact her experience with Glen now made her wonder if it might not be better to opt for an anonymous donor after all. In the meantime, she had to cope with knowing she was physically responsive to Markos in a way she hadn't experienced in the three years since her divorce—if ever!

Jack had been several years older than her when they'd married, and more experienced. Their lovemaking had been fun to explore at the start of their marriage. That interest, for obvious reasons, had eventually faded. To the point that by the end of their marriage, they hadn't made love in months.

Eva's self-esteem had been at a very low ebb after the divorce, her confidence in her desirability even lower, and it had taken months for her even to go out on a date with another man—only to discover that her emotions were completely numb, and the most she could feel for any of those men was a distant liking.

But it wasn't anything as lukewarm as *liking*—distant or otherwise!—she felt in regard to Markos Lyonedes.

Eva had been convinced—with the experience of her disastrous marriage behind her, and after listening for hours to Donna's broken-hearted meanderings down the telephone as her cousin mourned her lost love—that she was destined to be the one woman who wouldn't *ever* be stupid enough to fall under the sensual spell of all that lethal Lyonedes charm and charismatic good-looks.

Which only went to prove what an arrogant fool she had been.

Because Eva now knew she only had to be in the same room as Markos Lyonedes to be aware of every single thing about him. She could feel the tug of that desire even now, causing her hands to tremble slightly, her breasts to feel hot and swollen, and a dampness between her thighs.

She could see the same desire reflected towards her in the warmth of those dark green eyes. It was a physical attunement that seemed to make the very air between them crackle and dance.

'It was fine,' Eva dismissed abruptly. 'Now, if we could—'

'Have you and Glen been together long?'

Eva frowned slightly. 'I'm not sure that it's any of your business, but we haven't "been together" at all.'

Eva had gently but firmly refused Glen's suggestion, before they parted on Saturday evening, that the two of them might go out together again this week, having lost all interest in him with regard to approaching him about IVF.

Markos raised questioning brows. 'Yet…?'

'Really, Mr Lyonedes—'

'Markos.'

'Markos.' She gave a brief, meaningless smile of acknowledgement. 'I really didn't come here to discuss my personal life—so if we could we just get down to business?'

Markos settled more comfortably against the front of the desk and folded his arms across his chest. He considered Eva with narrowed but appreciative eyes. Her features really were extremely delicate: those gold-coloured eyes, high cheekbones, slender jaw, those full and sensuous lips glossed a deep peach today. With her hair secured at her crown it was now possible to see the slender arch of Eva's delicious throat, with skin as delicate as pale china.

It was a delectable delicacy that Markos found himself aching to taste. Presumably that wasn't completely out of the question, if Eva and Glen really weren't together.

He straightened slowly. 'That's a pity, because the only thing that I'm in the least interested in talking about this evening *is* your personal life.'

Those gold eyes widened warily. 'I don't understand.'

'No?'

Markos found himself watching intently as she moistened those peach-glossed lips before speaking again.

'I understood from our telephone conversation earlier today that you wanted me here at five o'clock so that we could discuss possible new designs for the décor in your apartment.'

Markos smiled slightly. 'I don't remember so much as mentioning any designs for my apartment during our brief conversation this morning.'

'Well…no,' she conceded slowly, after a few seconds' thought. 'But that was the reason for our two earlier appointments.'

'Two appointments which you didn't ever have any intention of keeping.'

'No.'

'Why not?'

Eva felt about two inches tall as she realised she had behaved like an idiot. But it had just been so tempting, when she had received the call the previous week from Markos Lyonedes's secretary, asking if she would come to his office to discuss the possibility of redesigning the interior of his apartment. Tempting to accept and then cancel as a small way of showing him that not *every* woman jumped at the click of his fingers.

She should have realised—given more consideration to the repercussions of her behaviour if the powerful Markos Lyonedes decided to make an issue of it.

Her gaze didn't quite meet his now. 'I really did have to be somewhere else on Monday evening.'

'And Friday?' He quirked dark brows. 'Did you really have an emergency appointment with your dentist?'

'Er—yes.'

Markos eyed her warily. 'Would you care to explain?'

She grimaced. 'Perhaps when I introduced the two

of you on Saturday evening I should have mentioned that Glen *is* a dentist.'

His mouth thinned. 'I see.'

She winced. 'Do you...?'

'Oh, I think so.' Markos nodded slowly, his interest well and truly piqued by the woman now standing in front of him. More than piqued, if he were honest. Markos had no idea why it should be, but he found everything about Eva Grey intriguing. From her lippy conversation to her desirable hourglass figure. 'You obviously felt an urgent need to have a cavity filled.'

Those golden eyes widened in blank shock, her cheeks filling with colour as she gasped her indignation.

Now it was Markos's turn to chuckle at Eva's expense. And for that chuckle to develop into full-throated laughter as he saw that he really had succeeded in rendering this complicated woman speechless. 'My God, Eva, you should see your face!' he finally managed through his laughter. 'Or maybe not; you look a little like a fish out of water at the moment.'

Probably because Eva *felt* like a fish out of water at that moment. Mouth opening and shutting, her chest rapidly rising and falling as she gasped for breath, her eyes wide and staring. 'I can't believe you just said that!'

'Actually, neither can I.' He sobered. 'My Aunt Karelia would consider my conversation most ungentlemanly. Unfortunately for you, I'm more than happy to risk her disapproval if I've succeeded in rendering you speechless for once!'

'Really?'

'Really,' Markos confirmed teasingly, aware that

Eva was still having trouble regaining her usual spiky confidence.

She gave a disbelieving shake of her head. 'Your Aunt Karelia would be perfectly correct in her assessment of your behaviour just now.'

'She usually is,' he acknowledged ruefully.

A frown appeared between those golden eyes. 'Who is your Aunt Karelia, exactly? And why does her opinion matter to you?'

Markos gave an affectionate smile. 'My cousin Drakon's mother. She's also been a mother to me since I was eight years old—after I went to live with her and my Uncle Theo when my parents were killed in a plane crash.'

Eva drew her breath in sharply as she heard the pain underlying the practicality of Markos's tone. She hadn't known that about him—hadn't cared to know that about him—and she frowned slightly as she acknowledged that his confiding that information to her had introduced a different sort of intimacy between the two of them from their previous physical awareness, which had seemed to sizzle and crackle in the air only minutes ago. An intimacy that was emotional rather than physical.

'I'm sorry for your loss,' she murmured finally.

'Thank you,' he accepted gruffly.

Eva shifted uncomfortably. 'Did you like living with your cousin and his parents?'

His grin warmed his eyes to the colour of emeralds. 'Eventually. I was pretty traumatised the first year or so, and probably gave my Aunt Karelia a few grey hairs. But eventually I settled down, and I really couldn't have asked for a better surrogate family.'

'You and Drakon are close?'

'As brothers,' he confirmed without hesitation.

Eva raised dark brows. 'I met him a couple of times when he was in New York. I didn't find him a particularly warm man.' Tall, dark and gorgeous, yes—just like his cousin Markos—but there was a single-minded ruthlessness to Drakon Lyonedes that he made no effort to hide.

Was it a trait his cousin also possessed...?

Probably, Eva concluded, remembering how Markos had changed on Saturday evening, his manner going from lazily charming to coolly precise, after she had made the comment concerning how he ended his relationships. In fact, apart from the heat of desire that glinted in Markos's eyes when he looked at her—something that had certainly never been present on the two occasions when Eva had met the coldly remote Drakon Lyonedes—the cousins were very much alike: heart-stoppingly gorgeous and lethally powerful.

Markos's grin widened. 'That's probably because you aren't a blonde with sea-blue eyes named Gemini!'

'Gemini is your cousin's new wife?'

'It's been very much a case of "how the mighty are fallen"!' Markos nodded. 'One look at Gemini and Drakon was knocked off his feet.'

'I somehow can't imagine *anything* knocking your cousin off his feet.' Eva eyed him disbelievingly.

Markos shrugged. 'Neither could I until it happened.'

This conversation had become altogether too personal for Eva's liking. 'Interesting as this conversation is, it's getting late, Markos,' she said briskly.

He raised those dark brows. 'Do you have yet another appointment to go to this evening?'

She could so easily have said yes. But instead…
'Well…no. But—'

'But what?'

'But it's Monday evening, and I always clean my apartment on Monday evenings,' Eva rallied weakly.

He eyed her mockingly. 'I thought that was what the weekends were for?'

She gave a disbelieving snort. 'Admit it, Markos, you've never had to clean your own apartment, or anywhere else you've lived, at the weekends or any other time!'

'Not true. I had to keep my own rooms clean when I was at university in Oxford.' He grimaced. 'Admittedly I couldn't see the bedroom carpet for the clutter after the first few weeks, and I ran out of clean clothes on a regular basis, but I coped.'

'By ignoring the clutter and buying new clothes, probably,' she guessed derisively.

'Guilty as charged,' Markos admitted with an unrepentant grin.

'That is so— Oh, *wow*…!' Eva gasped as she noticed the view from the huge picture window behind him for the first time—surely testament to exactly how powerfully attractive she found Markos, because the view from the window was amazing. New York City in all its glory.

Eva continued to look at the New York skyline as she slowly walked over to the window, dazzled by the combination of the tall, gleaming buildings and the lush green park.

'I seem to recall you said you thought of Lyonedes Tower as just another tall building blocking the view,' Markos reminded her as he joined her at the window.

Eva gave a wince at this reminder of the bluntness of her conversation when they first met. 'I may have been a little…impolite to you at the party on Saturday evening.'

'May have been?' he taunted softly.

'I *was* impolite,' she conceded.

'Any particular reason why…?'

'Does there have to be a reason?' Eva glanced sideways at Markos, totally aware of how close he was now standing to her. Close enough for her to inhale the heady combination of the lemon soap and sandalwood aftershave. Close enough that their arms were almost touching. Close enough that Eva was now fully aware of the heat emanating from Markos's body.

Close enough that Eva could barely breathe for wanting to close that short distance between them and lose herself to the feel of those sensuously chiselled lips devouring her own.

Instead she rushed into speech. 'I behaved badly—unprofessionally—and I apologise.'

He arched dark brows. 'Does that mean you've reconsidered and are now willing to give me—and my reputation—the benefit of the doubt…?'

'I'm not sure I would go that far,' she said warily.

'Liar,' Markos murmured huskily. He'd seen the way those luscious golden eyes had darkened to amber, the slight flush appearing in Eva's porcelain cheeks. Her lips were slightly moist and parted. As if waiting to be kissed.

As if she realised that was Markos's intention, Eva took a step back and away from him. 'I really do have to go now. If you've changed your mind about considering my designs—' She broke off as Markos took another step forward, until they were now once again standing so close they were almost touching. She gave a determined shake of her head. 'Markos, if you're trying to intimidate me then I think I should warn you—'

'Warn me of what...?' Markos murmured throatily, even as he raised one of his hands to cup the warmth of her cheek, before moving the soft pad of his thumb over the softness of her lips, feeling the warmth of her breath against his fingers as he parted those lips in preparation for his kiss.

His own arousal intensified at the feel of that sensual warmth against his skin. His shaft was hard and pulsing, demanding...

Eva's eyes were wide, deep amber pools as she stared up at him. 'I should warn you—'

'Yes...?' Markos prompted softly, holding that wide and startled gaze with his own as his head began to lower towards hers.

She breathed softly. 'I really should warn you—'

'Warn me later, hmm?' he dismissed gruffly, before finally claiming those full and pouting lips with his own.

Eva totally forgot what it was she wanted to warn Markos about as his other arm moved firmly about her waist and he pulled her in tightly against the heat of his body, angling her face up to his before his mouth finally took possession of hers.

Markos's kiss was everything that Eva had known it would be—not in any way a gentle exploration, but an instant explosion of the senses, taste, smell, feel, and it felt so good to be against the hard heat of his body as they kissed hungrily, deeply, lips devouring, tongues duelling.

Eva tightly gripped Markos's shoulders, her legs feeling weak as he crushed the ache of her breasts against his chest. Heat pooled between her thighs as she felt the hard throb of his arousal pressing insistently against her.

The sky could have fallen at that moment, the building collapsed around them, and Eva wouldn't have noticed, too lost in the heat that consumed them both as Markos's hands moved down to cup her bottom and pull her in more tightly. He ground his erection against and into her even as their mouths drank greedily of each other.

Eva was on fire, her inner ice melting, and her fingers became entangled in the dark hair at Markos's nape as she returned that heat, needing, wanting—

She *wanted* Markos Lyonedes…!

CHAPTER FOUR

'Oh, I'm terribly sorry! I had no idea…!'

Eva wrenched her mouth free of Markos's to push against the hardness of his chest in an effort to free herself as she heard that startled gasp from the other side of the room. Her cheeks were aflame with embarrassed colour as she turned to see the middle-aged woman who had shown her into the office earlier—obviously Markos's secretary—now standing in the open doorway, her eyes wide with shock at having interrupted them in a moment of intimacy.

Eva's efforts to free herself proved totally ineffective as Markos's arms tightened about her. 'Let go of me!' she said fiercely under her breath.

His only answer was to give her an amused glance before turning to look at the woman still standing in the doorway. 'Are you ready to leave for the day…?'

The woman looked flustered. 'I was about to, yes. I— Yes.'

In stark contrast, Markos appeared completely at his ease as he nodded. 'Thanks, Lena, I'll see you in the morning.'

'Mr Lyonedes. Ms Grey.' The woman Markos called Lena didn't meet either of their gazes before she quickly turned and left the room, closing the door briskly behind her.

'I asked you to let go of me!' Eva instructed, agitated as she once again pushed against the solid muscle that was Markos's chest. That particular moment of madness was definitely over.

'Do I have to?'

'Yes!'

'Why?'

Eva glared up at him. 'Because I asked you to.'

He regarded her with amused green eyes. 'And do you always get what you ask for?'

Sometimes Eva got a lot more than she asked for! For instance, she hadn't asked to be attracted to this man. Just as she hadn't asked to enjoy his experienced lips moving so surely and sensually against and over her own. Or to feel her heart almost leap out of her chest as she recognised her own desire to feel and taste the hardness of Markos's obvious arousal throbbing against the heat of her thighs. All of them were emotions Eva had believed herself to be incapable of feeling. Emotions she didn't *want* to feel!

Her eyes narrowed. 'Don't say I didn't warn you...' she murmured, before reaching behind her to grasp one of his hands, bringing it forward before bending the wrist up at a painful angle as she slipped deftly out of his arms before releasing him.

'Ouch!' Markos frowned as he grasped his pained wrist. 'Where did you learn to do that?' He eyed her with bemusement once he was sure nothing was broken.

'Self-defence classes.' She briskly straightened her jacket before checking that her hair was still neatly secured at her nape, sincerely hoping that Markos couldn't see that her hands were trembling as she did so. 'A necessary evil since I moved to New York.' She shrugged unapologetically.

'Hmm.' Markos grimaced as he once again leant back against his desk. 'You never did tell me the reason you moved to New York.'

She raised dark brows. 'Probably because that's another one of those things I consider personal.'

Markos regarded her from between narrowed lids for several long seconds. 'There was obviously a man involved,' he finally murmured speculatively.

She gave a derisive laugh. 'What a typically arrogant male conclusion.'

He shrugged broad shoulders, unconcerned. 'That's probably because I *am* a typically arrogant male.'

'And obviously proud of it,' she scorned.

Markos wouldn't say he was proud of it. It was just the way it was. His father and uncle had founded Lyonedes Enterprises before he was even born, and he and Drakon had added considerably to the success of the company's businesses worldwide since taking over completely when his Uncle Theo died ten years ago. There would be little point in Markos denying that this success, and the power that came along with it, had resulted in a certain assured arrogance in both himself and Drakon.

He grimaced unapologetically. 'It is what it is. And you, Ms Evangeline Grey, are deliberately trying to change the subject from my original question,' he added knowingly.

Yes, she was. Because Eva was uncomfortably aware she didn't want to answer Markos's original question.

Divorce, the ultimate admission of the failure of a marriage, was something that not even Eva's parents had succumbed to—even if they should have done so years ago, rather than slowly destroying each other with the bitterness of their disappointment. Eva wasn't in the least proud of her failed marriage, and nor did she wish to talk about it.

Her chin rose determinedly before she turned Markos's earlier comment back on him. 'It is what it is.'

Which told Markos precisely nothing. 'I can easily make the necessary enquiries that would give me the answer to that question...'

Her mouth tightened. 'That's your prerogative.'

'But I won't,' Markos concluded dryly. 'I would so much rather wait for you to tell me about yourself than listen to inaccurate gossip,' he added, in answer to her questioning look.

Her face flushed. 'If that was a dig at me for the things I said to you on Saturday—'

'It wasn't,' he assured her softly. 'I would just rather wait for you to confide in me.'

She gave a dismissive snort. 'Then you'll be waiting a long time.'

Patience had never particularly been a part of Markos's character, but he had a feeling that where this intriguing woman was concerned it might well be worth the wait...

'I have no plans to leave New York for the foreseeable future, Eva,' he said huskily.

Eva was well aware of that—which was why, after the mess she had made of things with this man, she was seriously considering relocating her office to

Outer Mongolia, or possibly Antarctica—anywhere but New York!

Because this second meeting with Markos Lyonedes had shown her that he wasn't at all what she had assumed he was after listening to Donna bemoan how callously he had brought an end to their relationship. He was arrogant, yes, but it wasn't the over-bloated self-aggrandizement Eva had expected to find—more an inborn confidence in who and what he was. Markos had demonstrated that he was capable of dealing with, and returning, any challenge she might care to give him. He also had a wicked sense of humour, which he was just as likely to turn on himself as he was anyone else. There was something very appealing about a man who could laugh at himself.

And Eva defied any woman to remain unaffected by that heady combination of charming self-assurance and devastating good-looks.

That brief and thankfully interrupted kiss they had shared had certainly proved to Eva that *she* wasn't immune to anything about Markos Lyonedes.

A man whose wealth and charm was everything and more than Jack, her ex-husband, had been...

Which was more than enough reason for Eva to take herself out of Markos's insidiously seductive company. *Right now!*

'Then I hope you enjoy the city,' she told him lightly. 'Now, if you will excuse me...'

'Haven't you forgotten something?'

Eva paused before turning back reluctantly to answer that softly spoken query. 'Have I?'

He gave a mocking inclination of his head. 'You haven't been up to look at my apartment yet.'

She tensed warily. 'Up…?'

Markos gave a husky chuckle even as he glanced pointedly towards the ceiling above them. 'Up.'

Markos's apartment was on the floor above this one? All this time there had been a bedroom—probably several—right above them? Oh, good Lord…!

Eva drew in a deep breath before speaking. 'I think you're right. It really wouldn't be a good idea for me to work for you—'

'Coward.'

'I beg your pardon?' she gasped softly.

Once again he shrugged those broad shoulders. 'I called you a coward.'

'Because I don't want to work for you?' She eyed him incredulously.

Markos shook his head slowly. 'Because we both know the reason you don't want to work for me.'

Her jaw tightened. 'Which is?'

'You're afraid.'

'You think I'm *afraid* of you?' she said disbelievingly.

'I think that you're afraid of how you feel when you're with me,' Markos corrected softly. 'You're more comfortable in the company of a man like Glen Asher because you know you can manipulate and control him in a way you would never be able to do with me.'

All the colour drained from Eva's cheeks. She knew that every word Markos spoke was the truth. Oh, not about Glen. But she *was* frightened—of Markos, and of what he made her feel when she was with him.

She didn't want to feel that way about any man. After her divorce she had been relieved to feel so numb, to know that she would never again have to go through the pain of a broken relationship.

To now realise that Markos Lyonedes had penetrated her emotions, if only on a physical level, was *not* a welcome revelation.

'Has anyone ever told you that you have an ego the size of Manhattan?' She snorted disgustedly.

'Not that I recall, no.' He gave a slow and confident smile. 'Was anything I said to you just now untrue?'

Her mouth thinned. 'I'm not afraid of you.'

'Then why not prove it by agreeing to redesign the interior of my apartment?'

Eva gave a disbelieving shake of her head. 'I'm twenty-nine, Markos, not nine, and as such I'm not about to be goaded into a juvenile game of dare with you. Especially when I don't think it's a good idea for me to accept a commission from you.'

'Kirsty is going to be *so* disappointed about that,' he murmured regretfully.

'Kirsty?' she repeated warily.

'Kirsty Foster. Her husband, Gerry, is my PA, and she was the one who recommended your work to me,' he added pleasantly.

Ordinarily Eva would have been pleased to have her work so appreciated by one of her previous clients that they had chosen to recommend her to their friends. And she liked Kirsty Foster. The two women had remained friends even after Eva had completed the work on Kirsty's bedroom, often meeting for coffee and a chat. Not so much recently, Eva recalled guiltily, as the other woman's blossoming pregnancy was a painful reminder of her own aching hunger for a baby.

But Kirsty was the one who had recommended her

work to Markos Lyonedes. The same Markos Lyonedes who employed Kirsty's husband, Gerry…

Eva's eyes narrowed. 'Are you threatening me, Markos…?'

He eyed her innocently. 'I was merely commenting that Kirsty's husband works for me.'

'Which sounds suspiciously like a threat to me!'

His lips twitched with repressed humour. 'That's *your* prerogative, of course.'

Eva didn't know whether to admire him for his audacity or lambast him for his arrogance. Either way, she couldn't work for a man she didn't even like…

Lying to herself wasn't going to make this situation any easier, Eva immediately chastised herself. The problem was not that she didn't like Markos Lyonedes, but that a single kiss had shown her that physically she liked him too much. Eva had been convinced she would never—*could* never—feel again. She was determined not to feel physical desire for any man when she knew it would ultimately lead to more pain and disillusionment.

'What are you thinking about…?' Markos had watched Eva's expressions during the last few minutes of silence between them.

Had seen the dismay. The confusion. Followed by the doubt. And then what had looked like pained anguish. All of them emotions he would never previously have associated with the prickly and confident Eva.

She shook herself out of that mood of despondency with obvious effort. 'I was just… Obviously if Kirsty recommended me—perhaps we could reschedule another meeting for later in the week?' She gave a tight smile as she saw his sceptical expression. 'I promise not to cancel this time.'

Markos regarded her through narrowed lids. 'You never did say what the emergency was last Monday.'

Her smile turned to a look of exasperation. 'A client was having hysterics when the curtain material I had ordered, which I duly took round for her to approve before the curtains were made up, turned out *not* to be exactly the same colour as her husband's eyes after all.'

Markos's eyes widened. 'People really do things like that?'

She laughed softly. 'You would be surprised. I had a client a couple of years ago who matched the colour of her carpet to her Golden Labrador.'

'Must have made it difficult to find him when it came time to go for a walk!' Markos murmured—only to watch in satisfaction as Eva's laughter deepened, causing her eyes to glow a deep gold. 'Have dinner with me tomorrow evening,' he prompted abruptly.

'To discuss the changes you'd like in your apartment?'

'To discuss any damn thing you please.'

'I was trying to tell you earlier...' Eva frowned. 'I make a point of never mixing my professional life with my personal one.'

'So it's one or the other?'

Eva instantly added stubborn determination to the list of things she was rapidly discovering about Markos Lyonedes. 'I believe I've already taken you on as a client by agreeing to look at your apartment.'

'And if I would prefer to have dinner with you tomorrow evening instead?'

Eva's breath caught in her throat as her eyes widened. 'Would you...?'

He frowned darkly. 'Why don't we compromise and

make our next appointment in my apartment tomorrow evening at seven-thirty? That way I can arrange for us to have dinner together immediately afterwards, so that we can discuss any suggestions you might have.'

Manipulative determination. Eva wryly corrected that earlier addition to her ever-growing list of Markos's character attributes. 'I'm starting to see how you gave your Aunt Karelia grey hair!'

Markos gave a grin. 'Does that mean you accept my invitation?'

Did it? There were so many reasons why Eva shouldn't have dinner with Markos tomorrow evening—this man's callous treatment of her cousin being only one of them. But—and she inwardly apologised to Donna—that certainly wasn't the *main* reason Eva would prefer not to have dinner with Markos—tomorrow evening or any other time.

She straightened briskly. 'I don't think so, but thank you for asking.'

Markos eyed her frustratedly, knowing it wasn't just the desire to have Eva in his bed that made him so determined. He also enjoyed her company. He appreciated the spirited way she stood up to him. The way her dry sense of humour was more than a match for his own. And he couldn't help feeling curious as to what Eva had been thinking about earlier when she'd looked so wistful.

He raised dark brows. 'And if I intend to keep on asking…?'

She shrugged. 'Then I'll just have to keep on refusing.'

'And if I manage to wear you down…?'

'You won't.' She smiled.

'You sound very sure,' Markos said knowingly.

'I am.' She nodded.

Had any woman turned him down so emphatically before? Markos wondered with a frown. Not that he could ever remember, no. And, again, that wasn't arrogance talking—it was just a fact. Nor did he believe it was only Eva's reluctance to see him again that made her so attractive to him.

Everything about Eva intrigued him. Even her obvious boredom on Saturday evening with the other guests at the cocktail party—including him—as if she had attended one too many parties just like it and met one too many arrogant men to be impressed by yet another one.

That behaviour had been completely nullified by her heated response to him a few minutes ago—before she had shut down that response with the finality of a steel trapdoor closing about her emotions.

And what had seemed like an expression of sadness, even anguish, only added to the mystery and contradiction that was fast becoming Evangeline Grey.

Markos sensed Eva had secrets hidden behind those beautiful golden eyes. Several of them. Secrets he was longing for Eva to share with him.

'Okay.' He straightened to move and check the diary on his desktop. 'I'm busy tomorrow and Wednesday, but six o'clock on Thursday evening looks good.' He looked up at her enquiringly, wondering if it was wishful thinking on his part or if that really was a look of disappointment on her face because he was seeming to back off.

And he was only seeming to back off. Markos had no intention of giving up where Eva was concerned.

'Thursday at six is fine with me too,' Eva accepted abruptly, pretty sure that if she designed a colour scheme of pink and white, and ultra-feminine, it would ensure that Markos no longer wished to employ her. It would do absolutely nothing for her professional reputation, of course, but it might be worth it just to see the look on Markos's face when she presented the sketches to him!

'I'm learning to be wary of that particular look of amusement...' He eyed her suspiciously as he straightened.

Eva laughed softly. 'Just a private joke.'

'Design-wise, you should know that a harem theme or an explosion of pink ruffles is definitely out,' he commented dryly.

How had he guessed what she was thinking? 'Now you're ruining all my fun!'

'When I would so love to be the cause of it...' he came back huskily.

Eva gave an exasperated sigh. 'Do you *ever* give up?'

'Where you're concerned? No.'

Now it was Eva's turn to look wary as she heard the finality in his tone. A warning, perhaps, that Markos's lazy good humour was merely a front, an illusion. As if she needed any warning!

'Why are you even continuing to bother pursuing me when there are dozens of women in New York who would be only too flattered to receive the attentions of Markos Lyonedes?'

He smiled ruefully. 'Because it doesn't work that way.'

She frowned. 'What doesn't?'

He shrugged those broad shoulders. 'I can't speak for other men, of course, but as far as I'm concerned, desire is exclusive to one woman at a time.'

Eva moistened lips that had become suddenly dry. 'That isn't what I've heard…'

Markos scowled. 'Just who the hell have you been listening to, Eva?' he prompted impatiently.

Her gaze avoided meeting that piercing green one. 'It's public knowledge—'

'It's malicious gossip—accompanied by unreliable articles and photographs in newspapers,' he corrected harshly. 'None of which can or should be believed.'

That might be true, but Donna's experience with this man was indisputable—set in stone. Wasn't it?

But no doubt Jack's version of the breakdown of their four-year marriage would differ greatly from Eva's own. There were always two sides to an unsuccessful relationship…

No!

Eva couldn't afford to have any doubts about Markos Lyonedes's callous reputation with women. The physical desire she felt for him already made her feel more vulnerable than she was comfortable with. She had a plan for the rest of her life, and it was a sensible plan— one which did not include an affair for a few weeks with Markos Lyonedes!

'Whatever,' she dismissed uninterestedly. 'I really do have to leave now.'

'But you'll be back on Thursday at six o'clock?'

Eva sighed at his dogged persistence. 'I said I would, yes.'

Markos nodded his satisfaction. Eva might not know

it yet—might not want to know it—but that single kiss they had shared had told him that she wanted him too.

And Markos had every intention of pursuing her until he had her exactly where he wanted her. In his bed.

CHAPTER FIVE

'I totally agree.' Markos grimaced as he saw the look of horror on Eva's face on Thursday evening as the two of them entered the sitting room of what was now his penthouse apartment on the top floor of Lyonedes Tower. He had received a call from Security a few minutes ago, informing him of her arrival downstairs. Most if not all of the Lyonedes employees had gone home now—including Markos's secretary.

'I think bland must have been the middle name of the previous interior designer.'

'I was thinking it's just plain ugly...'

Eva couldn't think what on earth had possessed the previous designer to choose cream and beige as the colour scheme in this beautifully appointed room. The furniture, though obviously expensive, was unattractively square and minimalist, and the only saving grace to this room was the impressive one hundred and eighty degree view of New York, visible from the huge picture windows that covered two of the walls.

Not only was the colour scheme insipid in the extreme, it didn't suit the man who now lived here. Markos's swarthy complexion, dark hair and piercing green eyes required that he be surrounded by the warm colours of the Mediterranean: terracotta, with touches of green and blue, maybe the palest hint of yellow...

Eva brought her thoughts up short as she realised her interior designer instincts had taken over from her common sense. It was two days since she had last seen Markos—two days and two restless nights—during which time Eva had become even more determined that she did not want to spend any more time in this man's company than she absolutely had to. To do so would be opening herself up to all sorts of disappointment. As such, knowing how this room should look was one thing. Being the one to effect those changes was something else entirely.

Of course it didn't help Eva to remain detached and professional to see that Markos was dressed as casually as she was this evening. The darkness of his hair was still damp from the shower, and he had obviously changed out of the formal suit he had worn to work today. He was now wearing a black shirt, the collar unbuttoned at his throat and the sleeves turned back to just below his elbows, with a pair of faded blue denims clearly outlining the leanness of his waist and his perfectly taut bottom and long legs.

She straightened briskly. 'Are the rest of the rooms as awful?'

'Worse.' He grimaced.

Eva found that hard to believe. 'How many rooms are there?'

'Four *en-suite* bedrooms, kitchen, breakfast room, formal dining room, a gym—'

'Okay—a lot.' She grimaced, rummaging through her capacious shoulder bag for her sketchbook and pencil as she continued to look about the room with

narrowed, assessing eyes. 'It looks more like an imper-
sonal hotel suite than a private apartment.'

'That's probably because that's what it was designed
to be.' Markos shrugged. 'Drakon has his own place in
Manhattan. This apartment was used only to entertain
business associates in less formal surroundings than
the offices downstairs.'

'Do I want to know in what *way* they were enter-
tained…?' Eva eyed him derisively.

'Just drinks and the occasional dinner,' he assured
her dryly.

'I'll believe you—thousands wouldn't!'

Markos eyed her ruefully. 'Your opinion of the
Lyonedes family isn't very high, is it?'

Eva felt the warmth of colour enter her cheeks. 'I
don't know any of you well enough to make a sound
judgement.'

'Yet.'

'Ever,' she stated with finality.

'I'll go and make us some coffee while you look
round,' Markos suggested lightly.

'Okay.' Eva was relieved to be able to turn her attention to her surroundings as she began to sketch in
her pad.

Markos stood for several moments and admired
the way Eva's denims clung so lovingly to her curvaceous hips and thighs. The firm swell of her breasts
was clearly visible beneath a fitted green blouse, her
long dark hair brushed back and secured in a ponytail
that made her look younger than her years.

Markos smiled wryly as he realised she had become
so absorbed in her work she seemed to have forgotten
he was even there. 'Cream and sugar?'

'Fine.' The tip of her tongue was caught between her teeth as she frowned in concentration.

Markos felt his shaft stir at the thought of all the more sensuous uses the moistness of that tongue could be put to. 'Or alternatively I could lie naked on the bed and wait for you to join me?' he said huskily.

'Fine.' Her eyes had a faraway look as she continued to sketch in her pad.

'Or maybe swing naked from the chandelier?' he added with amusement.

'What did you say?' She looked up sharply, her cheeks blushing a fiery red.

'Never mind.' He was still chuckling softly to himself as he walked down the hallway to the kitchen.

Eva felt the warmth of the colour in her cheeks as the rest of Markos's conversation now penetrated the concentration that always enveloped her at the start of a new project.

Except she wasn't going to start a new project.

Was she…?

That certainly hadn't been what she had intended when she'd arrived promptly for this evening's appointment—but one look at the blandness of what should have been a magnificent penthouse apartment and she had instantly been assailed with visions of how wonderful it could and should look.

Still, that didn't mean *she* had to be the one who instigated those improvements…

'Mmm—you were right the other night. Your percolator *does* make a delicious cup of coffee.' Eva gave a satisfied sigh half an hour later, having taken her first sip of the strong brew.

The two of them were now sitting on stools across

from each other at the breakfast bar in the sterile black and white kitchen.

'Now you know where to come the next time you want a decent cup of coffee in the middle of the night.' Seductive green eyes looked across at her in challenge.

Eva straightened, her expression rueful. 'Seems a little extreme when there's a coffee shop directly across the street from my own apartment building.'

'I doubt it has the same fringe benefits,' he drawled.

'Oh, I don't know—the young guy who serves behind the counter at weekends is pretty hot.'

It was Eva's turn to laugh as Markos growled low in his throat, but that laughter faded as she became aware that it was the first time for a very long time that she had felt so relaxed in a man's company she was actually allowing herself to flirt with him. And Markos was the very last man she should be feeling relaxed or flirtatious with!

She straightened on the barstool. 'He's about nineteen years old, and probably not into older women who could do with losing a few pounds,' she said dryly.

'Are you serious?' Markos gave her a disbelieving look.

She gave a perplexed frown. 'Sorry?'

He gave a shake of his head. 'Eva, that nineteen-year-old in the coffee shop probably has his tongue hanging out the whole time he's serving you your coffee!'

She scowled. 'Don't be ridiculous!'

He gave a pained wince. 'Eva, exactly *what* do you see when you look in the mirror?'

'I don't understand...'

Her puzzlement was so totally without guile or artifice that Markos was left in no doubts as to it being genuine. His expression softened. 'Maybe if I were to tell you what I see when I look at you…?'

Eva eyed him warily. 'This conversation isn't going to get insulting, is it?'

'Hardly!' Markos grimaced as he recognised that's exactly what *he* currently was: hard and hot and throbbing, as he always seemed to be when he was in Eva's company. And when not in her company too, if the last two days were any indication. 'Can it be that you really don't know—don't see—how stunningly, incredibly gorgeous you are?'

She shifted uncomfortably. 'Could we get back to discussing a colour scheme for your sitting room—?'

'Let's see.' Markos chose to ignore her change of subject as he looked across at her consideringly. 'Your hair is the colour of midnight—black with a blue sheen—and your eyes—oh, God. I could talk about your eyes all night! They are the colour of the purest gold. Hot—'

'Markos—'

'Molten gold I could happily drown in,' he continued remorselessly. 'And your skin is as pale and unflawed as alabaster. And your mouth!' His voice darkened smokily. 'Would you like me to tell you the things I have imagined those softly sensuous and pouting lips doing to me these past two days?'

The blood in Eva's veins was now pounding as 'hot and molten' as the way Markos had seconds ago described her pale brown eyes, and she shifted uncomfortably as she felt an echoing heat between her thighs, dampening her panties.

Her denims chafed against the arousal nestled there.

An arousal that, until meeting Markos Lyonedes, she hadn't believed herself capable of feeling. An arousal she didn't want to feel. Not for Markos. Not for any man!

Jack had been only too eloquent in his criticisms of her on the day they'd parted for the last time. He had scathingly told her how it was *her* fault he had turned to other women, that she had let herself go since learning they wouldn't have a baby together, that she had always lacked the social graces necessary in his wife, that her hair needed professional styling rather than being left to grow naturally, and that her fuller figure wasn't only unfashionable but a total turn-off sexually.

Oh, Eva hadn't been so without self-esteem by that time that she hadn't known some of his remarks had been made out of pique, deliberately designed to hurt her because she had finally had enough of Jack and his affairs, but that didn't mean his criticisms hadn't hurt, or remained as a vulnerability buried deep inside her.

Which was perhaps the reason why she had decided she didn't need another man permanently in her life.

There was no perhaps about it: her unhappy marriage to Jack and the hurtful things he had said to her that last day were *precisely* the reasons Eva had made the drastic decision not to remarry and to have the baby she craved on her own, through IVF.

And yet she couldn't seem to find the words to stop Markos as he continued gruffly, 'I've imagined you licking and kissing my chest and nipples, your lips and tongue hot and moist as they move down my stomach to my—'

'Markos, please…!' Eva groaned in breathless protest, even as she felt her own nipples ache beneath her blouse. Just from listening to Markos describe having her make love to him? Oh, God...!

His eyes were dark now, burning with the same desire that coursed through Eva. 'But I have not yet finished telling you how beautiful you are.' He gave a self-derisive shake of his head. 'First let me say that you do not need to lose even one pound in weight. You are perfection just as you are,' he added firmly, his voice once again clipped and precise, but this time with forceful decisiveness rather than anger.

She gave a rueful shake of her head. 'I—'

'Eva, there are very few men who actually prefer women with no breasts or hips,' he continued determinedly. 'That is a myth which has been perpetrated by dress designers and by women themselves, I believe.' The darkness of his gaze swept over her appreciatively.

'The fullness of your breasts is exactly the right size to fit perfectly into the palms of my hands.'

'That's only because you have large hands.'

'And all of me is in proportion,' Markos assured her as he reached across the table to clasp one of Eva's smaller hands in his. 'Eva, who told you that you are not sexy and beautiful? What ungrateful, stupid man could ever have told you such lies?'

Eva couldn't breathe. Markos's sensually descriptive words had aroused her to the point where she had briefly dropped the safeguards that had got her through the past five years—the last two years of her marriage to Jack, suffering his numerous affairs, and the past three avoiding any relationship that even *looked* as if it might touch her emotionally.

But Markos was a man who had refused from the first to take no for an answer. A man who was now demanding answers to questions that were too painful for Eva to answer.

She pulled her hands free of his before getting abruptly to her feet. 'Has it occurred to you that maybe it was a woman?' she challenged scornfully, deliberately. 'That maybe the reason I'm not interested in a relationship with you is because I'm not into men?'

Markos sat back on the stool. 'No.'

Eva blinked. 'Just...*no*?'

'Just no, Just Eva,' he drawled dryly.

She eyed him scathingly. 'Is that male arrogance talking?'

'Or the knowledge that seconds ago you were as aroused as I am?'

Her gaze slid down from his, across the rapid and shallow rise and fall of his chest, the flatness of his stomach, down to—

Eva's breath caught in her throat as she saw the thick hard length of Markos's arousal clearly outlined against the press of his jeans.

He hadn't been exaggerating when he'd said that everything about him was in proportion.

'You are so beautiful you make my chest ache, and so desirable you obviously make another part of me ache.'

'Please, Markos—did your years of living in England teach you nothing about our reserve?' she cut in to prevent him making what she was sure was going to be another embarrassing—arousing!—statement.

'Oh, yes.' He walked slowly towards her. 'But fortunately I am Greek, and we Greeks are far less reserved in our appreciation of a woman.'

He was standing so close to her now—just a heartbeat away—that Eva could feel the heat of his body, smell that lemon soap and sandalwood aftershave. That heat and the male smell that was uniquely Markos was now curling about her, invading her senses until she could no longer think straight.

If she had been thinking straight then she would never have allowed this situation to get so completely out of hand. So charged with sexual awareness she could almost reach out and touch it…

Markos drew his breath in sharply at the first touch of Eva's hands against his chest. Her palms seemed to burn through the thin material of his shirt to sear the flesh beneath. His first instinct was to reach out and pull her into his arms before lowering his mouth to claim hers.

His first instinct.

His second instinct warned Markos against moving at all as he allowed Eva's hands to tentatively seek out and touch the hard contours of his chest and the muscled width of his shoulders, sensing that the slightest movement on his part would result in her once again erecting those barriers around her emotions and needs. Barriers some other bastard had instilled in her, which Markos now realised had resulted in Eva hiding her vulnerability behind a mask of spiky cynicism.

It quickly became an agony of self-control for him to withstand the caress of her fingers and palms against and over him. His teeth were gritted, his jaw clamped shut, and his hands were clenched tightly at his sides as he resisted the impulse to reach out and take her into his arms. It was an impulse that became even more painful still as her fingertips ran lightly over the front of his denims, against his thickened length.

Eva's caresses grew bolder as she felt the pulsing response beneath her fingertips, and she knew a deep and compelling need to release that aroused hardness from the confines of Markos's jeans and—

She snatched her hand away before moving back abruptly. 'I think this has gone quite far enough!' Her voice came out husky and breathless rather than conveying the firm resolve she had hoped it would.

Markos groaned low in his throat, wanting, needing so much more, but instead he allowed himself to be guided by those instincts that warned against pushing Eva too far too fast. 'Will you come to a party with me on Saturday evening?'

Startled, she raised her lids. 'What...?'

Markos gave a pained smile in acknowledgement of the fact that his obvious arousal made this the last thing Eva had expected him to say. But he knew that the invitation he *wanted* to make—for her to stay on here now, so that the two of them could cook dinner together—would be met with a blunt refusal. As would his plans for what happened after dinner...

'I have been invited to a party on Saturday evening, and I would very much like it if you would agree to be the guest included on my invitation.'

She blinked. 'You're asking me out on a *date*?'

Markos chose his words with care, having realised in the past few minutes that he still needed to go slowly with this particular woman, that to do anything else would only drive her away. 'I am asking you to accompany me to a party on Saturday rather than leaving me to spend the evening alone in a room full of strangers.'

She shook her head. 'You must know your host to have been invited in the first place.'

'He is a business associate. Nothing more.' Markos shrugged dismissively.

Eva smiled wryly. 'There are sure to be dozens of beautiful women there, so I doubt you'll remain alone for long—'

'And I would prefer to take my *own* beautiful woman,' he interrupted firmly.

Her cheeks warmed. 'I am not your—'

'Eva, please.' Markos cut off her protest gruffly. 'For business reasons I have to attend this party, and for personal reasons I would like *you* to accompany me.'

When he put it like that...

Every instinct of self-preservation Eva possessed told her to say no to Markos's invitation. To stand by her earlier decision to recommend he use another interior designer, and then refuse to see him again.

She should say no. She had to say no. She *must* say no.

'In that case I would be pleased to accompany you. Thank you for asking me,' she heard herself say softly.

Markos chuckled huskily when he saw the chagrined expression appear on Eva's face immediately after she had accepted his invitation. 'Sometimes instinct can be stronger than logic, hmm...?' he suggested mischievously.

'And sometimes instinct can be a complete pain in the—!' She broke off with a grimace. 'I'll meet you here, if that's okay?'

'Because you do not wish me to come to your apartment?' Markos guessed easily.

'Not at all.' She frowned her irritation. 'I'll probably have some preliminary sketches and colour charts to bring over for you to look at by then, anyway,' she added briskly.

It was in an effort, no doubt, to put their relationship back on a businesslike footing. A businesslike footing Markos felt sure Eva had previously decided they wouldn't even be having. Her visit here this evening had been in response to Markos's threat of two days ago rather than any real intention of working for him.

'Bring them, by all means. I had intended to arrive at the party at about nine o'clock, so if you were to come here at eight, that should give us time to look at your sketches before we leave.'

'Fine,' Eva agreed tersely—and realised she had just committed herself to the redesigning of his apartment.

She looked so annoyed with herself for doing so, so irritated, that Markos didn't know whether to laugh or kiss her.

'It is no good, Eva, I have to kiss you again!' He groaned as he moved to put his arms lightly about her waist. 'Just once, hmm?' he encouraged throatily, lowering his head slowly towards hers. She seemed too surprised to protest.

Markos was determined not to send Eva hurtling off into the night this time, so he restrained his need to devour her and kissed her slowly, lightly, tasting her lips as she stood stiffly in his arms rather than giving in to the desire to swing her up into his arms and carry her off to his bedroom.

He kept a tight rein on his control until he felt the first quiver of Eva's response and she began to return that kiss, her lips parting hesitantly as her hands moved up to rest lightly against his chest. It was the most erotic and yet at the same time most frustrating kiss of Markos's life, as he allowed Eva to set the pace of their passion rather than take control as he usually did.

He was finally rewarded for his restraint as he felt Eva relax in his arms and she began to kiss him back in earnest.

Markos groaned low in his throat as he felt the press of her breasts against his chest, the softness of her hips nestling against his arousal. Her hands moved up over his shoulders until her fingers became entangled in the thickness of hair at his nape and the kiss turned hungry.

Markos wrenched his mouth from hers in order to seek out the dips and hollows in her bared throat, his breath moving across her skin in a fiery caress as his hands moved restlessly up and down the length of her spine, igniting trembling desire wherever they touched.

Eva's breasts felt full and hot, and between her thighs she was aching in need for the touch of Markos caressing hands— 'No!' She pushed her hands against his chest and held herself away from him, her breathing ragged and deep as she stared up at him in increasing horror. 'This is not what I want, Markos.'

His arms remained like steel bands about her waist. His eyes were dark green pits of hell, his breathing as ragged as her own as he obviously fought for control. 'What is it you want, Eva? Tell me and it shall be yours,' he promised fiercely.

What Eva wanted was to go back to her previous numbness, to the place where her emotions had been as colourless as the décor in this apartment rather than the blazing colours of fire!

She breathed shallowly. 'I want to collect my things and leave.'

'But you will come back on Saturday?'

Eva knew that she shouldn't—that she should consider running instead, as far and as fast as her car and credit card would take her. Which, considering the money currently in her bank account, was a very long way.

But, having finally stood up to Jack three years ago and put an end to the torment of their marriage, and then remained living and working successfully in New York despite the fact that Jack had made it clear he would rather she returned to England—probably so that he could forget he had ever made the mistake of marrying her in the first place—she had no intention of being forced to leave now just because Markos Lyonedes was making life uncomfortable for her.

She straightened determinedly. 'I'll come back on Saturday.'

'That is good.' Markos's smile was still strained as he indicated she should precede him out of the kitchen to collect her things from the sitting room.

What was good about it? Eva wondered slightly dazedly once she was safely back in her car, driving back to her apartment. It couldn't possibly be 'good' that minutes ago she had been so physically aroused by Markos that she wouldn't have cared if he had laid her down on the coldness of the black and white tiled kitchen floor and taken her right then and there...

CHAPTER SIX

'Oh, no…! Markos, turn the car around!'

'What—?' Markos turned his head to give Eva a startled glance from where he sat behind the wheel of his car on Saturday evening, driving them both to the party.

She clutched at the arm of his black evening jacket. 'Turn the car around—*now*—and get us out of here!' she repeated fiercely as she released his arm to stare up in horror at the brightly lit house at the end of the short gravel driveway.

There was already a car in front of them, and one had just turned into the driveway behind them too, effectively blocking any move on Markos's part to do as Eva asked and turn the car around.

'What's wrong, Eva?' He reached out with his free hand to clasp one of hers, instantly aware of how cold that hand was, considering the warmth of the summer evening.

What was *wrong*? Eva had just realised that the party Markos was taking her to was at the home of her ex-father-in-law—that was what was wrong!

Why hadn't she realised sooner?

More to the point, why hadn't she asked Markos on

Thursday whose party it was and saved herself—and Markos—all this embarrassment? As it was, Markos's black Ferrari was now effectively trapped between two other cars, making immediate escape impossible.

Maybe she should just get out of the car and walk back to the city?

Oh, yes, very practical—considering she was once again wearing three-inch-heeled sandals, black this time, to match with the black tube of a dress she wore, in which the length of her legs was very visible beneath the short hemline. Not only was it impractical, but if she tried to hitchhike a ride back into the city she was more likely to be taken for a hooker than a hitchhiker; she doubted too many drivers would recognise the black dress for the expensive designer label silk that it was.

So she couldn't walk back to the city, and she couldn't accompany Markos into the party either. She moistened the dryness of her lips before speaking, still staring at the crowded mansion house in front of them. 'I can't go in there, Markos.'

'Dissatisfied customer?' Markos teased.

Eva smiled faintly at his attempt at humour. 'Not exactly.'

'Then why can't we go to the party?' Markos had parked the car now and turned to look at her in the bright lights of the busy driveway, frowning as he saw how pale her cheeks had become.

The evening had been going so well up until this point. Eva had arrived promptly at Markos's apartment at eight o'clock and, remembering how sceptical she was about compliments, he had deliberately kept his comments as to how stunningly beautiful she looked to a minimum. That figure-hugging black dress, her hair once again loose in blue-black waves about the bareness of her creamy shoulders… Instead he had decided to pretend an interest in the designs she had brought with her.

One look at Eva's designs and he'd no longer had to pretend that interest. They were so vibrant with colour—not a hint of pink in sight, thank goodness!—that Markos had had no qualms whatsoever about allowing Eva free rein with all the rooms in his apartment.

Those initial designs proved that she knew exactly what he needed to feel comfortable in his own home. Perhaps, without realising it, she was coming to know him? Markos certainly hoped that was the case. And he'd been hoping to get to know her better later on tonight…

Consequently they had both been relaxed on the drive over here—only for this to happen. Although at the moment Markos still had no idea exactly what 'this' was!

'Eva, talk to me,' he urged gruffly.

She blinked, those golden eyes having darkened to a deep, deep amber. 'I didn't say *you* couldn't go to the party—'

'I'm not going anywhere without you,' Markos assured her firmly.

'There's no reason why we both have to miss the party—' She broke off as the door beside her was suddenly opened.

'May I help you, ma'am?' One of the young car valets, no doubt hired for the evening, stood outside on the gravel.

Eva's look of panic deepened. 'Markos…!'

He leant over to look out at the smiling teenager. 'Just give us a minute or two, okay?'

The youngster's smile faltered slightly. 'Of course, sir. Except I really need to move your car to the back of the house, with so many other guests still arriving…' he added awkwardly.

Markos sighed his frustration with this situation. Eva was his only concern at the moment. 'You *will* wait—'

'It isn't his fault, Markos.' Eva reached out and put a placating hand on his arm. 'It's okay,' she assured him shakily. 'I'm okay now.'

Which wasn't exactly true. But her initial feelings of wild panic seemed to have settled down to less troubled ones, and now that the initial shock was over Eva knew that most of her residual feelings of unease were only because she had arrived at her ex-father-in-law's home with the powerful and handsome Markos Lyonedes.

She had chanced to meet her ex-father-in-law several times socially in the past three years—it was impossible not to do so when they both remained part of New York society. The difference tonight was that this party was actually in Jonathan's home—the home where Eva had once been welcomed as his daughter-in-law—and also that Eva had never been in the company of another man when the two of them had met in the past.

Not that she thought Jonathan would be in the least unwelcoming—he was far too charming for that to happen, and Markos was his guest after all. Eva was the one who felt distinctly uncomfortable about attending a party at her ex-father-in-law's in the company of a man as powerful and charismatic as Markos Lyonedes.

In the company of *any* man who wasn't Jonathan's own son!

'Eva...?'

She turned to give Markos a reassuring smile. 'I'll be fine now, Markos. Really.' She picked up her black clutch bag before turning to get out of the car.

Eva looked far from fine to him. Her face was still pale, and her eyes still that deep amber and wide with apprehension. But other than making a scene—something Markos was pretty sure Eva would not appreciate—he had no choice but to join her outside on the driveway before handing his car keys over to the obviously relieved young man waiting to park his car.

Markos took a firm hold of Eva's elbow as they walked towards the mansion house ablaze with lights, the rooms visible to them obviously already filled to capacity with other guests. 'Is there anything you want to tell me before we go in?' he prompted softly.

There was a faint sparkle of humour in Eva's eyes now as she gave him a sideways glance. 'Such as?'

Markos had absolutely no idea.

Their host for the evening had been a widower for some years, and was a man in his sixties—surely not someone Eva had ever been personally involved with.

'Don't let your imagination run away with you, Markos,' Eva drawled derisively as she gave him another teasing glance.

'Ah, Markos—so pleased you could make it!'

The smoothly charming voice of their host interrupted them.

Markos instantly felt Eva's tension, and he maintained a proprietorial hold on her elbow even as he turned to face the older man. 'Jonathan.' He nodded stiffly. 'Can I—?'

'Evangeline!' The older man appeared momentarily stunned as he instantly recognised Eva, but that surprise was quickly masked as he once again turned on a politely charming smile. 'How lovely to see you again, my dear.'

'Jonathan,' she returned softly, and the two of them kissed each other lightly on the cheek. 'You're keeping well, obviously.'

'Very much so, thank you,' Jonathan said smoothly, his eyes narrowed shrewdly as he assimilated the fact that Eva was here with Markos Lyonedes. 'Evangeline, I feel I should warn you that the party this evening is— We'll talk again shortly, if that's okay?' he added distractedly as yet more guests arrived noisily behind them. 'Please, go through to the drawing room for champagne and canapés.'

Eva turned instinctively towards the blue and cream drawing room—a room which she had designed for Jonathan four years ago, before her marriage to his only son had come to such an acrimonious end—all the time aware of Markos's brooding preoccupation as he walked beside her, his hand still lightly on her elbow.

He was deservedly preoccupied. Despite Eva's advice to the contrary a few minutes ago, she knew that Markos's thoughts must be running riot as he considered all the possible scenarios for her being acquainted with a man like Jonathan Cabot Grey.

Jonathan Cabot Grey *Senior*.

Because Jack, Eva's ex-husband, was Jonathan Cabot Grey Junior...

'Are you going to tell me what's going on?' Markos

prompted softly once he and Eva were standing beside the unlit Adams fireplace a minute or so later, the two of them having been supplied with glasses of champagne by one of the many attentive waiters circulating the crowded and noisy room. 'Why didn't you want to come in? And exactly what is—or was—Jonathan Cabot Grey to you?' he added harshly.

'Jonathan Cabot Grey was my father-in-law.' Eva was still too distracted by Jonathan's unfinished warning even to attempt to prevaricate, wondering what it was Jonathan had wanted to warn her about. He hadn't sounded in the least threatening, so it obviously had nothing to do with the fact that she was here with Markos. So what—?

'Your *father-in-law*?' Markos repeated incredulously, totally stunned by this unexpected revelation.

She nodded abruptly. 'Cabot Grey was my married name.'

'Of course. Evangeline Grey—Jonathan Cabot Grey…' Markos realised with a pained wince, inwardly kicking himself for not having added two and two together before now.

She shrugged bare shoulders. 'I established my business under the name Cabot Grey Interiors, but dropped the Cabot part after my divorce.'

'So you were married to Grey's son?'

'The one and only,' Eva confirmed, aware that several of the other guests had seen and recognised her now. Their gazes were speculative as they also saw the identity of the dark and handsome man standing beside her. Even in a roomful of other men dressed in evening clothes, Markos stood head and shoulders above them all, in both looks and autocratic bearing.

Eva realised she was grateful for his presence; if she was to be forced to meet any of Jonathan and Jack's friends again then she was glad it was in the company of a man as impressively handsome and wealthily powerful as Markos Lyonedes!

She turned to smile at him regretfully. 'I really am sorry about this, Markos.' She placed her hand lightly on his arm. 'I would never have put you in this embarrassing position if I had known it was Jonathan's party you were inviting me to.'

Markos was still coming to terms with the fact that Eva had been married and divorced. Not that he had anything against divorce; he was of the opinion that it was far better to end something that wasn't right than spend a lifetime of unhappiness with the wrong person. No, it was the thought of Eva having been married at all that disturbed Markos. That left him with so many questions unanswered...

When, and for how long, had Eva been married? Why had the marriage ended? Who had ended it? Eva or Jonathan Cabot Grey's son? And if it was the latter, did she still love the man who had once been her husband?

He drew in a ragged breath. 'Eva, what—'

'Hello, angel.'

Markos found himself as irritated at hearing Eva addressed as 'angel' by another man as he had been the previous week when Glen Asher had called her 'baby'. But even without Eva's hand tightening to a painful grip on Markos's arm at the first sound of that man's voice, a single glance at the man standing behind her would have immediately identified him as being Jonathan Cabot Grey's son.

The hair was golden-blond, where Jonathan's was turning silver-grey, but other than that the family resemblance was unmistakable: blue eyes in similar boyishly handsome faces, both men lean and elegant in black tailored evening clothes.

There was no doubt in Markos's mind that this was the man who had once been Eva's husband.

This was what Jonathan had been going to warn her about a few minutes ago, Eva realised numbly, even as the full force of Jack's presence hit her with the force of a blow.

He shouldn't be here. Shouldn't even be in the States. He had moved to France over a year ago, when he'd taken over the Paris offices of Cabot Grey Enterprises.

Yet it was most definitely him standing just behind her. Even if Eva hadn't known his voice as well as she knew her own, there was no one else on earth who called her 'angel'.

What was she supposed to do now? What was the protocol for introducing your ex-husband to the man you were now…now *what*? She couldn't claim to be dating Markos when this was the first evening they had gone out together, but she knew they weren't only business acquaintances. So what *were* they?

Well, she had better make her mind up—and soon—because the three of them couldn't continue standing in this frozen tableau for much longer.

'Angel?' Jack prompted dryly, obviously coming to the same conclusion.

Eva gave a pained wince as once again he used the name he had once affectionately called her by. A long time ago. A lifetime ago. A different lifetime ago…

She drew in a deep breath and finally looked up into

Markos's rigidly set features. He stared past her at the
other man with eyes as hard as the emeralds they re-
sembled, his mouth thinned, jaw tight.

His harshly etched features softened slightly as he
finally looked down and saw her expression of mute
appeal. 'Introduce us, will you?' he prompted huskily
even as his arm moved possessively about her waist.

The gentleness of Markos's tone, and that supportive
arm about her waist, instantly reassured Eva that whatever his inner feelings were about this strange situation
Markos was there for her now—even if the warning
gleam in his eyes also told her that he would expect answers to his numerous questions once they were alone.

Eva turned slowly to face Jack, her expression deliberately non-committal as she took in the subtle changes
in his appearance since the two of them had faced each
other across a divorce court.

He was now in his mid-thirties, and there were
touches of grey at Jack's temples that hadn't been there
three years ago. His face was thinner too, with lines
etched beside his nose and mouth. Other than that he
was still as lean and boyishly handsome as he had always been, and looking every inch the wealthy Cabot
Grey heir in his tailored black evening suit and snowy
white shirt.

'Markos, this is Jonathan Cabot Grey Junior.'
She made the introduction stiffly. 'Jack—Markos
Lyonedes.'

Eva knew there was just a hint of satisfaction
in her clipped tone as she stated Markos's name.
Understandably so, she inwardly defended herself,
when the last time she and Jack had spoken for any

length of time he had taken great pleasure in telling her all of her faults.

Jack's eyes widened in obvious surprise as the other man's identity registered. 'Mr Lyonedes,' he greeted him smoothly as the two men shook hands.

'Cabot Grey.' Markos coolly returned both the handshake and greeting.

'Please call me Jack,' the other man invited lightly, the smile fading from those narrowed blue eyes as he turned to look critically at Eva. 'You're looking well, angel.'

'Eva looks beautiful,' Markos corrected coldly.

Eva's continued tension against his encircling arm left him in no doubt that this was the man who had somehow succeeded in convincing Eva that she was neither beautiful nor sexy. The very same man who had once been her husband.

Markos wondered under what circumstances Jack Cabot Grey could have made those hurtful and demeaning comments to Eva. Obviously they had not been happy ones, or the two would not now be divorced.

'That's what I meant, of course,' Jack Cabot Grey agreed, with the same smooth charm as his father.

'I'm afraid Jack and I are well past the stage of being insincerely polite to each other, Markos,' Eva dismissed with noticeable brittleness. 'Speaking of which—shouldn't you be cosying up to your father's other guests rather than wasting your practised charm on the uncharmable?' She raised mocking brows and looked challengingly at her ex-husband.

The hardening of those deep blue eyes was Jack Cabot Grey's only noticeable reaction to the taunt. 'I believe Mr Lyonedes *is* one of my father's guests…?'

But Markos was no more inclined to be charmed by this man than Eva was. Basically because he had never particularly liked men with the smooth and, as Eva had already stated, *practised* charm of a politician, but mainly because Markos resented the fact that this man had once been married to Eva. Lived with her. Known her longer and more intimately than any other man ever had.

Or possibly would again.

The tension between Eva and her ex-husband went a long way towards explaining her cynicism about men and relationships. Especially if their marriage had ended as badly as their attitude towards each other would seem to imply.

Markos straightened determinedly. 'A politeness only,' he clipped. 'For obvious reasons Eva and I will not be staying long.' He looked challengingly at the other man.

'Jack, darling...'

Jonathan Cabot Grey Junior avoided meeting Markos's challenge as he turned to smile warmly at the tiny blonde-haired woman who slipped her hand possessively into the crook of his arm as she moved to his side. 'Come and say hello to Markos Lyonedes and Eva, Yvette. Markos, Eva—this is my wife, Yvette.'

Those blue eyes glittered with malice as he deliberately looked at Eva as he made the introduction.

If Markos had thought Eva pale before then she now turned an ashen grey, obviously shocked as she looked at the woman who was Jack Cabot Grey's second wife. Yvette was a little over five feet tall, with glowingly

lovely features and shoulder-length blonde hair. The
rounded swell at her waistline showed that she was
also very pregnant.

CHAPTER SEVEN

'IF you will all excuse me...' Eva turned and hurried blindly from the crowded drawing room as the felt the nausea rising at the back of her throat, only just managing to make it into the ladies' powder room down the hallway and lock herself into one of the two marble-tiled cubicles before she was violently ill.

This couldn't be happening!

On top of every other humiliation Eva had suffered at Jack's hands, his second wife was obviously at least six months pregnant, with a baby that Eva, at least, knew couldn't possibly be his!

Unless—

No, it simply wasn't possible that it was Jack's baby. Jack was totally incapable of fathering a child of his own. And yet Yvette Cabot Grey was undeniably pregnant...

How? By another man? Or by the IVF that Eva was contemplating for herself? If that were the case, the baby Yvette carried wouldn't be Jack's...

That was perhaps the thing that hurt Eva the most. After tests had shown that Jack could never have a child of his own Eva had begged and pleaded with him to adopt, or for him to allow Eva the possibility of becoming pregnant by an anonymous donor. Tearful pleas Jack had always denied, with the disclaimer that he could never love a child that wasn't truly his.

'Eva?

'Markos...' She straightened abruptly as she recognised his voice on the other side of the cubicle door... *inside* the ladies' powder room!

'Are you all right?'

Was she all right? Of course she wasn't all right! Not only had her ex-husband remarried, but his second wife was pregnant with the baby Eva had so longed for herself!

No, she certainly couldn't claim she was 'all right'. But what seemed more pressing right now was that Markos shouldn't be in the ladies' powder room in Jonathan Cabot Grey Senior's house...!

Markos looked at Eva searchingly when she unlocked and opened the door, her gaze quizzical as she stepped out into the carpeted area where ladies usually freshened up. It was now empty of all but the two of them. Deliberately so, Markos having turned several of those ladies away before he stepped into the room and locked the door behind him to prevent anyone else from entering.

'You really shouldn't be in here.' Eva gave a derisive shake of her head as she moved past him to one of the porcelain sinks to wash her hands and face before filling and drinking a glass of water. Her face was still that sickly grey colour.

He raised dark brows. 'You are obviously unwell.'

'That's still no reason—'

'The door is locked, and I will go where I want

whenever I deem it necessary,' Markos declared harshly.

Eva gave a pained wince. He now appeared every inch the arrogantly forceful Markos Lyonedes, joint owner of Lyonedes Enterprises. 'And you deemed it necessary tonight to lock the two of us in a ladies' powder room in my ex-father-in-law's home?'

His jaw tightened. 'Yes.'

That was what Eva had thought he would say. And he was right, of course; she could imagine nothing worse than that anyone else should witness her humiliating reaction to being introduced to Jack's very pregnant second wife. It was enough that Markos must now be wondering why she had reacted so strongly...

She took another sip of water and deliberately avoided meeting Markos's gaze in the mirror above the sink. 'I'm sorry about this. I suddenly felt ill—I must have eaten something earlier that disagreed with me.'

'Or met someone...?' he suggested dryly.

Eva gave a humourless smile. 'Or met someone,' she acknowledged self-derisively.

Even in her distress Eva couldn't help noticing how out of place Markos looked in this ultra-feminine room, with its rose and green floral wallpaper. Even the soaps next to the sinks were the same deep rose colour, and several bottles of expensive perfume and pale pink towelling squares were arranged neatly on the onyx marble top. There were also two comfortable chairs covered in rose-coloured velvet.

'Could we possibly leave now, do you think?'

He nodded tersely. 'I have already asked for the car to be brought round.'

Eva's tensed shoulders slumped with relief. 'Have I mentioned before how wonderful you are?'

'I do not believe so,' Markos answered dryly. 'But I will be happy for you to tell me so once we are well away from here.' His face darkened grimly.

Eva couldn't even begin to imagine how awkward this situation was for Markos. How awful to have brought her here, expecting to spend a pleasant evening at the home of a business colleague, only to learn that business colleague was in fact Eva's ex-father-in-law—and, even worse, that her ex-husband was also here with his second and very pregnant wife...

'Markos, I really am sorry.'

'As I said, we will talk about this once we are well away from here.' He continued to frown grimly as he took a firm grip of her elbow to hold her firmly at his side as he unlocked the door. 'We will leave now.'

She blinked. 'Without saying goodbye?'

Markos nodded abruptly. 'Without speaking to anyone.'

Eva sensed the anger burning beneath the surface of Markos's outwardly calm demeanour as they stepped out into the huge hallway, but she didn't know him well enough yet to know who that anger was directed at: this uncomfortable situation or her.

'Markos—'

'Ah, there you are, angel. Feeling better...?'

Eva's heart skipped a beat at the sound of Jack's voice. Markos's fingers squeezed her elbow reassuringly before the two of them turned to face the other man in the otherwise deserted vestibule of the entrance hall. Eva breathed an inward sigh of relief as she saw

Jack was alone; she wasn't sure she could bear to see the pregnant Yvette again this evening.

'Markos and I are leaving now,' she said coolly.

Jack raised blond brows. 'You only just got here.'

'And now we are leaving,' Markos bit out coldly. 'Please inform your father than I will telephone and speak with him some time next week.'

The other man's cheeks became slightly flushed. He obviously resented Markos's authoritative tone. 'It would be more polite if you were to tell him that yourself.'

'As I am sure you are only too well aware, the current situation is beyond politeness.' Markos looked at the other man with coldly glittering eyes.

'Markos—'

'Stay out of this, angel!'

Markos released Eva's arm and strode quickly across the hallway until he stood only inches away from the other man. He was slightly taller than Jack Cabot Grey. He was not touching him, but was still intimidating nonetheless.

'Her name is Eva. And you will not speak to her in that way. Ever again! Do I make myself clear?' he grated softly.

The other man's jaw tightened. 'You can't just come into my father's home and threaten me—'

'I believe I just did,' Markos purred softly. Dangerously.

'I call her angel because her name is Ev-*angel*-ine.' Jack Cabot Grey met his gaze challengingly for several seconds before those deep blue eyes slid away and he instead looked at Eva. 'It would seem that your marriage to me gave you a taste for powerful men, angel,' he drawled insultingly.

Markos drew in his breath sharply. 'You—'

'I only see one man who fits *that* description, Jack,' Eva cut in scathingly. 'And it isn't you!'

'Why, you little—' Jack Cabot Grey broke off warily as Markos placed a hand against his chest.

'I believe I have warned you never, ever to insult Eva in my presence again,' he reminded him in an icily soft voice.

'What on earth is going on here?'

Eva turned a stricken face to see her ex-father-in-law, Jonathan Cabot Grey, stride forcefully into the vestibule.

Shrewd blue eyes narrowed on his son and Markos Lyonedes as they faced each other challengingly. 'Is there a problem...?'

Markos gave Jack Cabot Grey one last contemptuous glance before slowly stepping away from him to stroll back to Eva's side. He faced his host. 'Eva and I were just leaving.'

'So soon?'

Markos might have been more impressed with the older man's attempt at regret if he hadn't seen the look of relief in Jonathan's eyes before it was quickly masked by polite query. It was a politeness Markos was too displeased to indulge at this moment.

'I am of the opinion that it would have been better if we had left some time ago,' he said dismissively, giving Jonathan a disapproving look as he took a hold of Eva's arm, his mouth tightening with displeasure when he realised she was trembling again as she leant into his side.

What could have happened between Eva and Jack Cabot Grey in the past to have caused this severe reaction in her? For her to be physically ill just from seeing him again?

Except…

Unexpected as it might have been, it *hadn't* been seeing Jack Cabot Grey which had made Eva ill. That had only happened when the other man's second wife had joined them.

Was it because Eva still had feelings for the man, and the existence of that second wife now made reconciliation impossible?

Her scathing attitude towards her ex-husband whenever she spoke to him would seem to imply otherwise. And yet… There was no denying that *something* had made Eva ill just a short time ago. The same something that was still causing her to tremble.

Markos had no idea what Eva was reacting to any longer, and that irritated him as much as everything else about this evening displeased him; he had believed earlier that they were coming to know each other, to like each other—and now this!

'We will speak again later in the week, Jonathan,' he assured the older man stiffly before turning to leave.

'I'll be in touch, angel.'

Eva stiffened as Jack called after her softly, not fooled for a moment by the pleasantness of his tone, and pretty sure she knew the reason Jack intended contacting her again…

Almost as soon as Eva and Jack had married, and had moved to New York to live, Jonathan had started talking of the possible arrival of his grandson—Jonathan Cabot Grey the Third. It was something which Eva and Jack had eventually realised was never going to happen, but Jack had never, at least to Eva's knowledge, confided in his father. The fact that Yvette Cabot Grey was now pregnant, supposedly with Jack's child, was either a medical miracle or something that Jack did not wish Eva to discuss with his father.

Eva didn't know whether to be insulted, because Jack thought she would tell his father that the child Yvette carried couldn't possibly be his, or angry, because Jack thought she would feel vindictive enough towards him that she would deliberately hurt the man who had once been her father-in-law.

The latter emotion won out as she turned to look coldly at Jack. 'We have nothing to talk about,' she assured him scathingly.

He quirked blond disbelieving brows. 'No?'

'Absolutely not,' she snapped, before turning to her ex-father-in-law. 'Goodbye, Jonathan. It was nice seeing you again.' Her voice warmed slightly as she spoke to the man she had always rather liked.

Jonathan must have been surprised when Jack had returned from working in London for two years with Eva as his wife—a young Englishwoman who wasn't in the least wealthy or of the same social strata as the Cabot Greys. But never by word or deed had Jonathan ever shown her anything but the respect and liking due to her as his son's wife. The future mother of his grandchildren...

'Take care,' she added huskily, not sparing Jack so much as a second glance as she and Markos finally left together.

'Not here and not now,' Markos advised gruffly as Eva tried to speak once they were outside.

She shot him a fleeting glance. 'I was only going to say thank-you.'

Markos's tension eased slightly and he relaxed his grip on Eva's arm. The last few minutes had been far from pleasant. For any of them.

'If you insist, you may offer me suitable thanks once we are alone together in my apartment,' he assured her gruffly.

She looked uncertain. 'Your apartment...?'

He shrugged broad shoulders. 'We have to return to Lyonedes Tower in order for you to collect your car. Once there, we might as well go up to my apartment and talk in comfort.'

An argument to which she had no rebuttal, Eva acknowledged ruefully. Her car *was* at Lyonedes Tower, and she did owe Markos a suitable thank-you—although she had a feeling her idea of suitable and Markos's might differ greatly in content! He had been so supportive of her this evening and she owed him an explanation as to the reason he had needed to be so.

'Coffee, wine or brandy?' Markos offered dryly once they were once again in the anaemic sitting room of the penthouse apartment at Lyonedes Tower.

'Oh, I think this situation calls for brandy all round, don't you?' She sighed wearily as she sank down in one of the boxy cream armchairs.

'I am unsure as yet exactly what this situation is.' He shrugged out of his jacket and draped it over a chair, before moving to the bar situated at the other end of the room and pouring brandy into two glasses.

Eva grimaced as she took the glass Markos held out to her before moving to stand a short distance away from her. 'It isn't every day that you meet your ex-husband by accident!' She sipped the brandy, instantly

feeling the effects of the fiery alcohol as it slid easily
down the back of her throat. 'The last I heard of Jack
he was living and working in France.'

'Which is obviously where he met and married
Yvette.'

'Obviously,' Eva echoed non-committally as she
stared down at the beige carpet.

'Are you still in love with him?'

She gave Markos a startled look and the glass shook
precariously in her hand. 'What?'

His smile lacked humour. 'In the circumstances it is
a relevant question, I would have thought.'

Eva drank down the rest of her brandy before answering him, in the hopes that its warmth would melt
the block of ice that seemed to have formed in her chest.
'What circumstances?'

Markos kept his expression deliberately bland. 'You
did not appear to become ill until after the appearance
of Grey's second wife. Do not cry, Eva.' All attempts to
remain detached fled as he saw the tears shimmering
in Eva's huge gold-coloured eyes, and Markos quickly
placed his brandy down on the glass-topped coffee table
before moving onto his haunches beside the chair where
she sat, to take her icy cold hand in his. 'Talk to me,
Eva. Tell me why you are crying.'

'I'm not,' she denied, even as those tears began to
fall down the paleness of her cheeks. 'I just… You're
right. Seeing Yvette…it was a shock—' She broke off
and began to cry in earnest.

It was as if a dam had burst inside Eva—the dam
that had held back all the grief and pain she had buried
deep inside her when her hopes and dreams of having a
family of her own, a baby of her own, had been dashed

five years ago, when the specialist had told them that Jack could never father a child.

A child Jack now appeared to be having with his second wife.

It didn't matter by what means Yvette Cabot Grey had become pregnant, only that she was. With the baby Jack had denied Eva five years ago.

Markos was completely at a loss as to what he should do or say as Eva buried her face in her hands and sobbed as if her heart were breaking. Which perhaps it was.

Over Jack Cabot Grey?

Having no experience upon which to draw, it wasn't for Markos to criticise whom others might choose—or not choose—to love. Except that Jack Cabot Grey was everything Markos disliked in a man: shallow, selfish and, where Eva was concerned, in Markos's opinion cruelly vindictive. None of which changed the fact that Eva could not seem to stop crying as if her heart were breaking.

Markos reached out and gathered Eva up into his arms, lifting her and cradling her tenderly against his chest before sitting down in the chair himself. Her tears quickly dampened the front of his shirt. Markos ran his fingers soothingly against her temple, considering the irony of holding the woman he desired in his arms as she cried over another man.

If his cousin Drakon could only see him now.

'It was the baby,' Eva finally choked out painfully. 'I—we—we tried for so long to have a baby of our own, and—we finally had tests. The specialist told us it wasn't possible,' she sobbed.

Oh, dear God! And that cold-hearted bastard Cabot

Grey had stood there and calmly introduced his pregnant second wife to Eva, all the time knowing that Eva wasn't able to have a baby herself. The absolute bastard!

Could this also be the reason Eva's self-confidence was so fragile beneath her veneer of derision? The reason she was so determined not to become involved with another man? Possibly also the reason she and Jack Cabot Grey had divorced?

Markos could certainly believe the latter. Even on such short acquaintance Markos knew that Jack Cabot Grey was the sort of vindictive bastard who would never have let Eva forget she was unable to give him the Cabot Grey son and heir.

'It's all right, Eva,' he assured her softly, speaking into the silky softness of her hair. 'Everything is going to be all right.'

She gave a choked laugh. 'Of course it isn't.'

No, as far as Eva was concerned perhaps it wasn't... 'You are a beautiful young woman, with all your life still ahead of you. Not all men are like Jack Cabot Grey—'

'Thank goodness!' She gave a shiver of revulsion.

Markos looked down at her quizzically. 'You really do not love him still?'

Eva straightened before attempting to stand up, but she was prevented from doing so as Markos's arms tightened about her to keep her firmly sitting on his knee.

Which was pretty embarrassing, now that Eva thought about it. In fact the whole of this evening had been embarrassing, she realised, now that she had got over her shock and calmed down a little.

First of all she had completely flipped out when they'd arrived at Jonathan's house. Then she had almost collapsed with surprise when she had realised Jack was also at the party. Even worse, she had run from the room and been violently ill in the ladies' powder room once she had seen that Jack's second wife was pregnant. An embarrassment that Markos had witnessed when he followed her. And now she had cried all over Markos's white shirt, probably ruining it, no doubt giving him completely the wrong impression as to why she had become so upset in the first place.

Not the best first date she had ever been on.

She doubted Markos had ever had one like it before, either.

She gave a shake of her head. 'I'm not sure that I ever did love Jack,' she answered him honestly. 'Not really.'

'And yet you married him...?'

Eva nodded. 'I was a student when we met at a party given by one of my father's friends. Jack was six years older than me, and he seemed so mature and self-assured in comparison with my other friends— taking me out to the theatre and wining and dining me at expensive restaurants.' She grimaced as she saw Markos's raised brows. 'I've had plenty of time to think about this, and I know now that I allowed myself to be dazzled by Jack's easy charm and self-confidence. I mistook being dazzled for being in love.'

Markos looked down at her quizzically. 'It was a big thing to move to New York with him—away from your family and friends—after you were married.'

'I'm afraid that was probably in an effort to get away from most of my family. My parents aren't the happiest married couple in the world,' she explained at Markos's questioning look. 'They should probably never have married each other, and they certainly shouldn't have had a child together. My childhood was like a battle-field.'

Markos gave a pained frown as this further knowl-edge of Eva's life only added to those reasons why she now felt so cynical towards love and relationships. His own childhood hadn't been without trauma, when his mother and father had died so suddenly when he was only eight, but when he'd gone to live with his aunt and uncle he had been lucky enough to find another set of parents who had loved and cared for him as their own. Whereas Eva didn't seem to have had even one set of parents to love and nurture her.

'You haven't had an easy time of it, have you?' Markos observed.

Eva smiled bravely. 'No worse than a lot of people.' She drew in a deep breath. 'Markos, I seem to be doing this a lot recently where you're concerned—but I really am sorry for blubbing all over you just now.'

'No apology is necessary.'

'What if I were to make it a "suitable" one...?' Eva quirked her brows at him as she pulled his bow tie undone, before starting to unfasten the buttons down the front of his shirt.

Markos regarded her warily. 'I am not sure this is a good idea—'

Eva didn't allow him to finish as she moved to lean into the hardness of his bared chest before pressing her lips against his.

Markos sat completely unmoving, his arms still lightly about Eva's waist as those deliciously sensual lips moved softly against him, as light as butterfly wings. The lightness of her perfume was invading his senses, and he felt the heaviness of her breasts pressing against the hardness of his chest.

She moved back slightly, her palms hot against his chest, her breath warm against his lips as those golden eyes looked directly into his. 'Make love with me, Markos…'

His body reacted instantly to that husky invitation, his pulse racing, heart pounding, and his shaft becoming rock hard and throbbing in seconds. It was impossible for him to deny how much he wanted to accept that invitation.

But he wasn't going to do so.

Eva might have stopped crying, but there was no forgetting how upset she had been earlier. And the reason for that distress wasn't going to go away any time soon—which probably meant she wasn't completely responsible for her actions right now. For Markos to make love with her under these circumstances would surely make him as much of a bastard as her ex-husband. Even if he *did* literally ache to just pick Eva up in his arms and carry her to his bed!

CHAPTER EIGHT

'WHERE are you taking me?' Eva's arms moved up about Markos's neck as he stood up with her still cradled firmly in his embrace.

His eyes were a deep, dark emerald as he glanced down at her. 'Where would you like me to take you?'

'You know...I don't think I really care,' Eva answered, surprising herself with her own honesty as she realised she really *didn't* care where she was going, so long as Markos was going to be there too.

Something had happened to her when that dam of emotion had burst inside her earlier and she had cried in Markos's arms. Somehow—miraculously—she had been released from all past hurts and disappointments, leaving her emotions as light and free as they had been when she was a university student. She felt that same bubbling sense of anticipation inside her now that she'd had then—what might happen in her life next?

What *might* happen—not what had Eva been *planning* to happen? Because she no longer felt that determination to decide her life. She had let go of the past. All of it.

So Jack's wife was going to have a baby? So what? Jack probably wouldn't believe Eva if she were to say the words to him, but it no longer upset her that Yvette was pregnant. She simply wished the two of them every happiness with their future son or daughter, and she had no doubt that Jonathan would be over the moon when his grandchild was born—boy or girl.

One day Eva might even have that for herself—a man and a family of her own to love—but until and if that day came she would feel a contentedness, a calmness, and just wait and see what happened next.

And she really hoped that Markos was going to be part of that more immediate 'next'. She had already known he was as charming and self-assured as Jack had ever been, and Markos was certainly more powerfully charismatic—he'd had to be to have persuaded her to go out with him at all this evening! But after tonight she also knew Markos was kind and considerate, with a quiet strength, caring for her in a way her ex-husband never had. For a brief moment earlier tonight she had really thought Markos was going to pick Jack up by his shirtfront and shake him like a rag doll!

But Markos's strength of character was inborn, not acquired or a veneer—and Eva had never physically wanted a man so badly in her life as she now wanted Markos.

Her arms tightened about his neck as she gazed up at him admiringly. 'You really are pretty wonderful, you know.'

He gave a half-smile. 'Because I am capable of carrying all these extra pounds you believe you possess into my bedroom?'

'It's all perfectly proportioned and in the right places!' Eva gave him a playful punch on the arm, realising as she did so that she still carried her black silk clutch bag.

He gave a disarming grin. 'I believe I have already assured you that I am well aware of that.'

Yes, he had—which was another plus in his favour. Markos seemed to be accumulating pluses in spite of Eva's previous prejudice against him. Too many more of them and she could be in serious danger of falling—

Whoa!

Wanting, aching to make love with Markos was one thing—a big thing, considering he was the first man Eva had wanted to be intimate with since the disintegration of her marriage. But allowing her emotions to become involved was something else entirely.

Markos was a Lyonedes. From a family that was powerful and rich beyond her imagining. More to the point, Markos was a man known for having short and meaningless relationships—not a man that a woman might pin her future hopes and dreams on. A lesson her cousin Donna had learnt only too well...

Donna!

Damn it, with everything else that had happened this evening Eva had forgotten all about her cousin's unhappy experience with Markos!

Had she really forgotten? Or could she just no longer quite accept her cousin's version of what had and hadn't happened between them?

Donna had described him as being wonderful when they were going out together, but turning into a cold and ruthless stranger when he had decided he no longer wanted the relationship. Oh, Eva believed Markos was more than capable of being cold and ruthless—she had seen him being exactly that with Jack earlier this evening—she could just no longer see Markos behaving that way towards a woman. No doubt that was another no-no his Aunt Karelia had instilled in him!

Besides which, the cruel and callous Markos her cousin had described him as being at the end of their relationship would never have had the patience or the inclination to deal with Eva's tears tonight. He would have run a mile in the other direction.

Which left Eva precisely where?

Trusting her own intuition?

She had done that in her life once before, with dire results.

No, that wasn't quite true of the events of seven years ago. At twenty-two, her marriage to Jack had seemed to her like a good way of escaping the vicious circle of her parents' relationship. But she was twenty-nine now, with a successful career and a life of her own. This attraction she felt towards Markos was based on that maturity and success, not on an imagined youthful idealism.

'What are you thinking about?' Markos had been watching the play of emotions across Eva's expressive face for the past few minutes after switching on the bedroom light, realising that she was so lost in thought she hadn't even noticed they were now in his bedroom and he was standing beside his king-sized bed, still holding her in his arms.

She gave him a startled glance as she took in the intimacy of their surroundings, and then that surprise was replaced by a warm and inviting smile. 'Nothing of any importance,' she assured him huskily.

'Sure?'

'Very sure,' she confirmed determinedly.

It sounded to Markos as if she had made her mind up to something—to *do* something—and was determined not to allow anything to make her change it.

All of which confirmed to Markos that the decision he had made a few minutes ago in regard to making love with Eva tonight was the right one.

'Could you pull back the bedcovers?' He lowered her slightly so that she could turn back the brocade cover and the duvet, before lowering her completely onto the bed. Her arms fell from about his neck as he straightened slightly to look down at her. Her hair was an ebony tumble against the cream silk sheets. 'Roll over,' he encouraged gruffly as he took the black bag gently out of her hand and placed it on the bedside cabinet.

'Roll…?'

Markos allowed himself to chuckle softly at the doubtful expression on Eva's face. 'Do not look so worried, Eva; my only intention is to unzip the back of your gown, not to force some strange sexual practice on you.'

Her cheeks were slightly flushed as she glanced at him over the bareness of her shoulder once she had rolled slightly away from him. 'Maybe force wouldn't be necessary.'

Markos drew in a sharp breath even as he bent down to slowly lower the zip at the back of her black gown. That breath stayed caught in his throat as he took in the creamy perfection of Eva's long, naked spine, and revealing the top of a pair of silky black panties.

Markos clenched his hands into fists in an effort to stop himself from touching the creamy length of Eva's bared flesh now so temptingly revealed to him, and a nerve pulsed in his jaw as she rolled over to face him once again, allowing him to lower the gown down

over her breasts and the slenderness of her waist, curvaceous hips and long silky legs, before discarding it
completely.

Those black silky panties were now the only item of
clothing she wore—a perfect foil for the creamy naked
swell of her breasts. Full and pert breasts, tipped with
rose-coloured nipples, which were swelling, hardening,
under the heated intensity of Markos's gaze.

Eva was beautiful everywhere—so very beautiful—
and in a way that made Markos ache just from looking at her, from breathing in the sensuous perfume of
her skin.

'Markos?' Eva looked up at him uncertainly.

His nostrils flared as he breathed out deeply, before
bending slightly so that he could pull the covers gently
over Eva's tempting nakedness.

Her eyes widened. 'What are you doing...?'

Markos sat on the side of the bed, securing those
bedcovers beneath her arms as he reached up and
smoothed the silky hair back from her temples. 'I would
very much like to kiss you goodnight, if that is agree-
able to you?'

'Goodnight...?'

Markos gave a gentle smile. 'I believe you have already suffered enough excitement for one evening,
don't you?'

Eva would hardly call the time she had spent at
Jonathan's house earlier this evening exciting—nor
the bursting dam of emotions that had followed it! Nor
would she compare either of those things to the thrill
of just imagining making love with Markos...

'I don't understand.'

He gave a shake of his head, his eyes dark. 'This

evening was a less than happy one for you, and I believe it would be wrong of me to now take advantage of you. As such—'

'But I'm perfectly okay now,' she protested.

'You are *not* okay, Eva,' he insisted flatly, his fingers still lightly soothing against her brow.

But she *was* okay—more than okay, actually—so much so that she couldn't even begin to describe the euphoria she felt at being free from the past. 'Perhaps you're the one that's changed your mind about wanting to go to bed with me after I made such an idiot of myself earlier this evening?'

'I have not changed my mind in the slightest in regard to wanting to make love with you, Eva,' he assured her. 'But, as I have already stated, I would prefer not to take advantage of the fact you are feeling less than your usual feisty self.'

Eva looked up at him searchingly. The sincerity of the expression in his eyes and face was unmistakable. 'Such gallantry isn't doing a thing for your reputation as a womaniser, you know,' she teased huskily.

His expression hardened. 'The thing to remember about reputations is that they are formed by people other than the person whose reputation is under discussion.'

Yes, they were. And the man Donna had described to Eva wouldn't have shown a moment's hesitation in taking 'advantage' of her.

Which left Eva feeling more confused than ever in regard to the enigma that was Markos Lyonedes.

She gave a baffled shake of her head. 'If you have no intention of making love with me then why did you undress me and put me in your bed?'

His expression softened again. 'I believe, if we are to be exact, that I put you in my bed first and then undressed you. And I did so because you are emotionally exhausted and need to sleep.'

'I could have gone home and slept.'

'And tomorrow is another day...' Markos continued softly as if she hadn't spoken at all.

Eva chuckled softly. 'You're supposed to be Rhett Butler, not Scarlet O'Hara!'

He shrugged those broad shoulders. 'It is the sentiment which is important, no matter who says it.'

Yes, it was, and Markos's thoughtfulness in not making love with her tonight had succeeded in throwing Eva's emotions into even further turmoil. As well as making her ache for his touch!

'Where are you going to sleep?'

He shrugged. 'There are three other bedrooms in the apartment that I can use.'

'And if I would rather you stayed here with me...?'

Markos drew in a ragged breath. 'I would ask what I have done to deserve such torture!'

'You've been a perfect gentleman,' Eva assured him firmly. 'And if I ever chance to bump into your Aunt Karelia, I'll be sure to tell her what a credit you are to her.'

'I am gratified to hear it,' he replied dryly. 'And now I believe it is time for you to kiss me goodnight and then get some sleep,' he added huskily.

Eva was only too eager to kiss Markos goodnight, but at the same time as she was totally unsure that sleep would be possible once she had.

'And I am going to return to the sitting room to finish my glass of brandy before taking a very long, very cold shower!'

The grimness of his smile revealed the depth of self-control he was having to exert *not* to make love with her as his head lowered towards hers.

Eva curled her arms up about his neck as their mouths met. She put every shred of emotion she was feeling at that moment into a long kiss. The fondness she felt for Markos. The desire. The aching yearning. Most of all the joy in at last being free of the past and able to feel all of those things...

For Markos.

Markos wrenched away from Eva's tantalising lips, breathing hard as he gently but firmly pulled her arms slowly down his shoulders and chest. 'Enough,' he breathed raggedly, shaking his head as Eva's fingers lingered on the bareness of his chest. 'Please, Eva, I sincerely hope that I am a gentleman, but I know I am not a saint!' A nerve pulsed in his tightly clenched jaw.

Her lips were swollen from the heat of their kisses, her eyes a dark languid gold as she looked up at him. 'Goodnight, Markos.' Her voice was as sultry and inviting as the unhidden longing in those extraordinary eyes.

Markos rose quickly to his feet, so as not to give in to the temptation to throw back the bedcovers and taste those deliciously naked breasts. 'I think I may be in need of more than a single glass of brandy to help me get to sleep!' He stepped away from the bed—away from Eva.

Eva gave an enigmatic smile. 'You know where I am if you don't succeed.'

Markos ran an agitated hand through the thickness of his hair. 'You are not helping, Eva!'

She laughed huskily. 'I don't believe I was trying to…' Her breasts were thrust forward and up as she stretched languidly before once again settling down beneath the covers, those golden eyes gleaming with mischief as her gaze lingered on the obvious bulge in Markos's trousers.

'Temptress!' he murmured achingly.

'Spoilsport!' she came back challengingly.

Markos gave a rueful shake of his head. 'I will take great pleasure in reminding you of that taunt in the morning.'

'Promise?'

Markos sucked in a sharp breath and stared down at her for several long seconds more before turning to walk determinedly across to the bedroom door. He paused in the doorway to turn and look at Eva once more. 'You might want to barricade this door with any of the bedroom furniture you can move!'

Her eyes shone back at him teasingly. 'I'm not the one walking away…'

No, Markos was. And he had more than enough reason to regret it once he had returned to the sitting room. Not even two large glasses of brandy were enough to dispel the knowledge that an almost naked and apparently willing Eva was just a short distance away down the hallway.

'You look—'

'Awful,' Markos finished dryly as he looked across the kitchen the following morning to where Eva stood framed in the doorway. 'Whereas you look…' *Sexy as hell,* Markos acknowledged achingly as he took in her appearance in his black silk dressing gown, which reached almost down to her ankles, and with her hair an ebony tangle about her shoulders. 'Rested,' he substituted wryly.

'Did you sleep in those clothes?' Eva eyed the crumpled white evening shirt and black trousers he had been wearing last night.

'I didn't sleep at all!' Markos grimaced.

Having realised once he had taken a shower the night before that all of his clothes were still in the bedroom where Eva was—hopefully—sleeping, he'd had to put back on the same clothes he had worn to go out that evening. Only to then return and sit in one of the armchairs and stare sleeplessly out at the night sky as it changed slowly from black to grey and then orange as the sun came up and the new day began.

'Perhaps you should go to bed now...?' Eva suggested throatily.

'Coffee?' He stood up now from where he'd been sitting at the breakfast bar, moving across the room to the place he had made a much-needed pot of coffee a few minutes earlier. 'Cream?'

Eva paused for only a heartbeat to look at the broad expanse of Markos's back, turned towards her, before crossing the tiled floor on bare feet, knowing from his avoidance in answering her and his guarded expression before he turned away that any move towards intimacy this morning was going to have to originate from her.

She slid her arms about his waist from behind and leant her head lightly against his suddenly tensed back. 'That was an invitation for you to come back to bed with *me*, Markos.'

He breathed in deeply but didn't turn. 'Are you sure?'

'Very sure...'

'If I go to bed with you now I should warn you it would not be with the intention of sleeping!'

'I'm sincerely hoping not.'

The spoon he had intended using to stir the cream into her coffee landed on the marble worktop with a clatter as he turned quickly and gathered her up into his arms. His mouth came down forcefully on hers.

Hungry didn't even begin to describe the fierceness of the passion that flared instantly between them as Markos's hands became entangled in her hair as they kissed: lips devouring, tongues duelling, their breathing hot and ragged in the silence of the apartment.

Eva ceased to breathe at all when she felt Markos's hand cup beneath the fullness of her breast, the soft pad of his thumb moving in a light caress across the hardened tip. Pleasure instantly spiralled through her and she arched into that caress, causing her to groan low in her throat as it pooled, moistened that already aching apex between her thighs.

His lips left hers to trail across her cheek, moving down the column of her throat, inciting fire wherever they touched. A low moan escaped her as Markos gently pushed aside the black silk robe to take the throbbing tip of her naked breast into the heat of his mouth.

Eva clung to the hard heat of his shoulders as she stumbled back to lean against the kitchen unit. Her knees threatened to buckle beneath her, pleasure coursing through her hotly now, as Markos cupped her other breast. She looked down at Markos's darkness against the paleness of her skin, his dark lashes fanned across his swarthy cheeks as he drew her nipple hungrily between his parted lips. Feeling, watching, as Markos paid homage to her breasts, was the most erotic thing Eva had ever done.

She slipped the unbuttoned shirt from his shoulders and down his arms and he allowed the garment to slip to the marble floor. His shoulders were so wide—much wider than they looked beneath his shirt and tailored suits, and deeply muscled. Proof that Markos didn't spend all his time behind a desk. The muscles in his back flexed with pleasure as Eva's fingers lightly caressed down the length of his spine.

'You're beautiful, Markos…' she purred.

He chuckled softly, the reverberations from that chuckle travelling from Eva's nipple to the pulsing heat between her thighs before he reluctantly released her. The warmth of his breath felt cool against her dampened breast as he spoke softly. '*These* are beautiful.' He took his time kissing each of her swollen and sensitised nipples in turn before looking up at her, his eyes gleaming a dark, deep emerald. '*You* are beautiful, Eva. All over.'

'You haven't seen all of me yet…'

'But I am going to.' It was a fierce promise of intent.

'Here?' Eva looked about at the sterile practicality of the black and white kitchen.

Markos gave a mischievous smile as he also became aware of their surroundings. 'The temptation to drape you decorously on top of the breakfast bar and make you the feast is appealing, but, no, I think I would prefer to be comfortable in bed the first time we make love together,' Markos said with gruff intent.

'The first time…?' Eva echoed throatily.

His eyes glowed that deep emerald. 'You can have no idea in how many locations and in how many ways I have imagined making love with you during my long and sleepless night!'

Her cheeks warmed. 'Show me,' she invited huskily.

'Oh, I intend to!' Markos assured her decisively, and he slid one arm beneath her knees and the other about her shoulders before lifting her up into his arms and marching out of the room.

Eva draped her arms about his neck, not in the least self-conscious when her breasts and thighs were laid bare as the black silk robe fell open, knowing she had been longing for Markos to make love to her since last night.

Possibly since the moment she had first looked across that hotel reception room and seen him looking right back at her...

CHAPTER NINE

MARKOS slowly lowered Eva's feet to the carpeted floor before untying the silk belt about her waist and sliding the robe off her shoulders to allow it to pool at her feet. His breath caught in his throat as he looked down at her lusciously naked body: slender shoulders, full and sloping breasts, narrow waist, lush hips covered by that single scrap of black silk and lace, legs long and shapely…

His heated gaze returned to her face, eyes narrowing as he saw a return of that uncertainty in her expression. Her shoulders had tensed, as if she was waiting for a blow to fall.

'You are beautiful, Eva,' Markos assured her huskily. 'And anyone who has told you otherwise is nothing but a fool!' he added harshly, having no intention of saying Jack Cabot Grey's name and allowing the other man to intrude into their intimacy, while at the same time well aware that the other man had to be the reason for Eva's insecurities about her body. 'An idiot and a fool,' he repeated firmly. 'And I intend to worship every delicious inch of you!'

Eva glowed, feeling beautiful under Markos's admiring gaze. 'Can I finish undressing you now…?'

Markos seemed to cease breathing for several seconds before nodding abruptly. 'Please...' He stepped back.

Eva had never thought of herself as a *femme fatale*—how could she when she'd only ever made love with one man in her life, and even that had become more of a chore than enjoyment?—but there was something deliciously wicked about slowly unbuckling the belt at Markos's lean waist. The bulge pressed against the zip as she slowly lowered it to reveal black boxers beneath. Eva sank down onto her knees in front of him as he stepped out of his trousers.

'Eva!' Markos reached out to tightly grip her shoulders. 'I am not sure—'

'Oh, my...!' She had now stripped off those black boxers to reveal the heavy weight of his jutting arousal, moistening her lips with the tip of her tongue before her head slowly lowered.

Markos gave a strangled gasp, his knees threatening to buckle as he felt the moist rasp of her tongue run the length of his shaft before slowly taking him fully into her mouth.

It was torture. Agony. Of the most exquisite kind!

An exquisite ecstasy that Markos enjoyed for as long as he could without releasing.

'Next time, Eva!' he groaned between gritted teeth as he reluctantly pulled away from her. 'Right now I need to be inside you, before I go quietly and completely insane!'

He reached down to lift her before placing her against the covers and following her down onto the bed, his thigh draped across hers as he claimed those wickedly sensual lips with his own.

Markos claimed her mouth again and again as he cupped and caressed her breasts. Their passion was raised to fever-pitch, their pleasure even more so, before he pulled his lips from hers and once again claimed her nipples with his mouth, kissing and biting as Eva gasped her own pleasure.

Her skin felt like velvet as his hand caressed the curve of her hips, slipping beneath the silk material of her panties. His fingers sought and found her sensitive spot, and Eva's response was instantaneous as he caressed that throbbing clitoris, before dipping one finger into the moistness of her channel and trailing that moisture over and around that fiercely pounding arousal in an ever-increasing rhythm.

He gave a low groan even as Eva purred deep in her throat, as she began to thrust her hips up and into that rhythm, her breathing becoming rapid and laboured as her pleasure rose.

Had Eva ever known such hot, mindless pleasure before? She didn't think so. She felt truly beautiful in Markos's arms as he had worshipped every inch of her, and her pleasure had spiralled out of control the moment she felt his mouth and tongue on her, her own movements instinctive as she rose up to meet those moist thrusts.

'Oh, God, Markos…!' She cried out her need as his hands moved up to cup her breasts, squeezing her nipples with just the right amount of pressure between pleasure and pain. The volcanic heat of her rapidly approaching climax was coursing through her like molten lava.

Markos looked down at her with hot and heavy eyes. 'I want to taste you as you come…' He slid down the length of her body until he lay between her parted and silken thighs, claiming her with his lips.

'Markos!' Eva cried out as her pleasure intensified to an unbearable degree. Wave after wave of pleasure washed over her, and she closed her eyes as she gasped and trembled, her fingers curled like talons into the sheet beneath her as Markos refused to release her from that plateau until he had extracted and given every last vestige of pleasure.

'Dear Lord...!' Eva collapsed back against the pillows, her smile dreamy as she held out her arms to him. 'Come up here.'

Markos kissed his way slowly up her body. 'Now I can say with full authority that you are truly beautiful all over,' he assured her gruffly.

'I want you inside me, Markos. I *need* you inside me,' Eva invited huskily. 'Please.'

Markos chuckled his satisfaction as he moved over her, his smile fading as Eva's hand moved down between them and he felt her fingers close about him before she guided him in. He groaned as he slowly entered her, inch by pleasurable inch, until he was sheathed to the hilt.

Which was the moment when Markos's already shaky control broke completely, and he captured her mouth with his as he began to thrust into her with long, claiming strokes, her tightness rippling and clenching about him as he drove into her fully again and again.

He wrenched his mouth away from hers and cried out as her hands caressed the length of his back. Her fingers suddenly dug into the flesh of his backside, and the intensifying ripples of her body told Markos that she was about to climax for a second time.

And Markos intended going with her this time.

He thrust harder, longer, allowing his control to slip completely, shooting hotly down the length of his shaft in a long and satisfying release that shook him to his very soul—and his pleasure was intensified by knowing he had taken Eva with him as her cries matched his own.

'Wow.'

Eva gave a satiated chuckle at the understatement. Markos's head lay pillowed against the fullness of her breasts, and both of them were breathing raggedly in the aftermath of their earth-shattering lovemaking.

It had certainly been earth-shattering for Eva, and Markos's exclamation gave her every reason to believe he had been equally affected. 'Was it worth suffering a sleepless night for?' she teased.

'Most definitely,' Markos assured her with feeling, knowing there had been no ghosts from the past standing between them this morning—just the two of them making exquisite, perfect love. It had been a lovemaking of such tenderness of feeling, with an intensity of pleasure Markos had never experienced before...

Eva tensed in his arms. 'Markos—'

'I believe, if I wish us to spend the rest of the day in bed together, that it is time I fed you.' He lightly interrupted the uncertainty of her tone, sitting up and swinging his legs off the side of the bed and standing up.

'The rest of the day...?' she repeated slowly.

Markos chuckled at the contrasting emotions of surprise and anticipation he could see in those expression golden eyes. 'You did not think that I would allow you to leave after making love with you only once?' He bent down to collect his black silk robe from the bedroom floor.

'I haven't been able to think at all for some time...' Eva trailed off as she gazed up unabashedly at the nakedness of Markos's back, ceasing to breathe as he stretched, the muscles in his back flexing and relaxing with the effortless ease of a jungle cat.

'Good.' He nodded with satisfaction as he turned, his gaze once again becoming hot and heavy as he saw the open hunger she knew must be in her expression. 'Food first,' he repeated firmly, and he laid the black silk robe down beside her before striding determinedly—still naked—from the bedroom.

Eva lay on the bed for several minutes longer, luxuriating in a feeling of total physical satisfaction as she stretched, feeling the pleasurable ache of muscles long left unused.

Making love with Markos had been unlike anything Eva had ever felt or known before. More erotic, more pleasurable than anything she had ever experienced with any man.

There was no point in not being honest with herself at this point in her life. The only other man she'd ever had sex with was Jack. And sex with him had been more centred on his pleasure than hers. Whereas Markos—

She mustn't allow herself to blow this time with Markos out of all proportion.

Not unless she wanted to be left as heartsick as her cousin Donna when whatever this was with Markos came to an end...

She was an independent, sophisticated twenty-nine-year-old woman. They were the things that had attracted Markos to her. No matter how wonderful their lovemaking, he certainly wouldn't want that independent, sophisticated twenty-nine-year-old woman making a fool of herself over him!

Accept this for what it is, Eva told herself firmly as she finally got out of bed to go into the bathroom and tidy herself: wonderful sex, teasing banter and a good time had by all. For her to expect anything else from Markos was totally unacceptable.

Having feelings for Markos certainly wasn't an option...

'So as a child you spent most of your summers on the family's private island in the Aegean?'

Markos nodded, having returned to the bedroom long enough to pull on faded denims and a black T-shirt, totally relaxed as he and Eva sat at the breakfast bar eating warmed croissants with honey and drinking coffee. 'Drakon and Gemini are there now—on their honeymoon.'

Eva gave a wistful sigh. 'It sounds idyllic.'

Markos quirked one dark brow. 'I believe you mentioned your own childhood was less so?'

She shrugged narrow shoulders, the movement instantly drawing Markos's gaze to the way the firm swell of her breasts was revealed as the black silk of his robe parted slightly. 'My parents should never have married each other, and they probably wouldn't have done if my mother hadn't been expecting me.' She grimaced. 'Needless to say they didn't make that mistake again, which is why I'm an only child.'

Markos frowned. 'But you have other family...?'

Eva lowered her gaze as she began to crumble a

croissant on her plate. 'An aunt and uncle…a couple of cousins. And we aren't exactly big on family reunions; I haven't been back to England once in the last seven years.'

Unlike the Lyonedes family. There had been over three hundred guests at Drakon and Gemini's wedding the previous month, and almost all of them had been related to the Lyonedes family in some way.

'I can't even begin to imagine what it must be like not to have a huge extended family,' he said.

'It isn't so bad.' Eva gave another shrug. 'Not enough people to have a big family fallout, for one thing!'

'The Lyonedes family can certainly be volatile,' Markos acknowledged dryly.

She smiled. 'Must be all that hot Mediterranean blood!' Her cheeks coloured hotly as she seemed to realise what she had just said. 'I meant—'

'I know what you meant, Eva.' Markos chuckled at she blushed. It was an endearing and unexpected quality in a woman in her late twenties who had been married and divorced, had lived in New York for the last seven years, and ran her own very successful interior design company. 'And I believe you once implied that you thought Drakon cold when you met him?'

Eva was beginning to wish she had never continued this particular conversation! 'You must have realised after last night that my judgement of a man's character isn't all that good—oh, good Lord!' She winced as Markos raised one mocking brow. 'I obviously wasn't referring to *you* when I said that—what I was really trying to say was—' She broke off with an irritated frown as Markos began to chuckle. 'It isn't funny!'

'I couldn't agree more.' He was still smiling as he

stood up slowly to move around the breakfast bar until he stood beside her. 'Obviously I need to take you back to bed and refresh your memory as to how *un*-cold my own character is…'

He held out his hand, very dark and handsome with his dark hair still slightly ruffled, his jaw unshaven, and the tight-fitting black T-shirt outlining the muscles of his chest and flat abdomen.

'So soon…?' Her eyes were wide.

Markos eyed her quizzically. 'You would rather not…?'

'I didn't say that!' she protested instantly, her nipples having noticeably tightened beneath the black silk robe, and that moist warmth once again heating between her thighs. 'I just— I'm just surprised that you— well, that—'

'That I would, or could, want you again so soon?' Markos finished huskily, his eyes dark with intent. 'Come back to bed, Eva, and let me show you how much and in what ways I want you!'

Eva felt slightly shy as she placed her hand in Markos's and stood up to accompany him to the bedroom. A ridiculous feeling after the intimacies the two of them had shared earlier.

The intimacies they were about to share again…

'You may just succeed in killing me with pleasure, Eva!' Markos groaned as she collapsed on top of him a long, long time later.

'Not intentionally, I assure you.' Eva chuckled weakly as she lay against the dampness of his hair-roughened chest, having totally lost count of the number of times and in how many ways Markos had brought her to climax—before she had gently pushed him back against the pillow and made love to *him*, first kissing his chest and the flatness of his stomach, before moving lower to take him into her mouth. Her fingers had encircled him as she'd licked that responsive length, until Markos had begged her to stop and she'd moved up to straddle his hips, taking him deep inside her, inch by pleasurable inch, before riding him—riding them both—to explosive pleasure.

His arms encircled her as he rolled to one side and took her with him. 'What *are* your intentions towards me?' he prompted gruffly.

Eva's heart gave a leap even as she opened one wary lid to look up at him. 'Entirely dishonourable, I assure you,' she said softly.

Markos felt a sense of disappointment in Eva's answer, even though he held her in his arms and had every intention of doing so for the rest of the day. And tomorrow…? Tomorrow, as he had already stated, was another day…

'Markos?'

He gave a relaxed smile. 'We will sleep now and talk later,' he encouraged huskily, and he rested her tousled head more comfortably against his shoulder before settling back against the pillows.

'Talk about what?' she prompted, that earlier wariness now back in her voice too.

'Whatever needs to be talked about,' Markos dismissed lightly, and he closed his eyes, Eva still held firmly in his arms.

Eva lay awake for a long time after she knew by the soft and even tenor of Markos's breathing that he had fallen into an exhausted sleep—hardly surprising when he'd confessed to having had no sleep the night before, and then embarked on two athletic bouts of exquisite lovemaking.

Amazingly wonderful lovemaking, during which Eva knew she had lost all and every inhibition she had ever had as Markos touched and kissed her in places she had never been touched or kissed before...

She felt...*wonderful*. Deliciously satiated. Every part of worshipped. And for once in her life Eva intended to let tomorrow take care of itself.

She had no idea whether it was day or night when she woke up, although the brightness of the sun shining through the bedroom window would seem to indicate it was probably late on Sunday afternoon.

Amazing.

She had never ever spent the whole day in bed with a man. And this was not just any man, but Markos Lyonedes.

She turned her head sideways on the pillow to look at him, smiling warmly as she saw that Markos was doing exactly the same thing. Those green eyes gleamed appreciatively, and the stubble was darker on his square chin, his hair tousled on his forehead, his muscled shoulders bare above the bedcovers.

'Good afternoon,' she greeted him huskily.

His eyes crinkled at the corners as he returned her smile. 'Did you know that you purr in your sleep?' he asked.

'You're making that up!' Eva refuted indignantly, her cheeks warming as she turned fully to face him.

'No, I'm not,' he assured her indulgently as he

reached out to touch the hair at her temple. 'You sounded like a contented kitten.'

That was probably because she felt like a contented kitten: warm, intensely satisfied and safe.

Safe?

How could she possibly feel safe when she now knew that Markos was capable of breaching every barrier she had ever placed about her bruised emotions?

And yet that was exactly how Eva felt—safe, cared for, even cherished. So unwise when it came to this particular man! Eva knew better than most how ephemeral Markos's relationships had been and always would be, and she had no intention of falling for a man who chose to fill a woman's life before leaving it—and her—totally empty when he chose to walk away. She had already been burned so very badly once in her life. She certainly didn't need—

'You are thinking again,' Markos rebuked gently, as his fingers moved to smooth the frown from Eva's creamy brow. 'Perhaps it is time for more food...?'

'Good idea.' Her smile didn't reach those golden eyes as she turned away to throw back the bedcover. 'If you don't mind, I think I'll go and take a shower while you look for something to eat.'

She picked up the black silk robe and shrugged into it in such a way that Markos couldn't see her nakedness, before standing up to tie the belt tightly around her waist.

'I can't say I exactly like the idea of going home in a black silk evening gown in the middle of the afternoon!' She wrinkled her nose in distaste.

Markos lay relaxed against the pillows as he looked at her from between narrowed lids, one of his knees bent and raised as a shield to the rampant hardness of his arousal. One look at a tousled Eva when he woke up, along with listening to those soft little purring noises she made in her sleep, and that part of him had immediately perked up and taken an interest!

'Who said anything about your going home in the middle of the afternoon...?'

Eva frowned as she looked across at him uncertainly. 'I think I've already been here long enough, don't you?'

Markos gave a shrug. 'I have no other plans for the rest of the day. Do you?'

'Well...no, not exactly.' She shifted uncomfortably, obviously having no idea how the silk material of robe once again outlined the fullness of her breasts. 'I do have to things to do before work in the morning, though.'

'Such as?'

Eva frowned. 'How about I take a shower and we talk about this again afterwards?' she said briskly. 'I'd really like to freshen up now.'

As it was almost twenty-four hours since Markos had last taken a shower, he could perfectly understand Eva's need to freshen up; he could do with a shave and a shower himself.

'You'll find a spare toothbrush in the bathroom cabinet.'

Eva raised dark, mocking brows. 'Really?'

Markos could almost see the cogs of her imagination turning. 'There's also a spare razor in there—but you really shouldn't infer anything from that!' he drawled dryly.

Colour flared in her cheeks. 'Very funny!'

Markos gave another shrug. 'Just in case you were wondering.'

'I wasn't!'

Oh, yes, she most definitely had been. And Markos knew it hadn't been in a good way. 'What have I done since we met to give you the idea I make a habit of bringing women home to spend the weekend with me?' He moved up on one elbow to look at her from between narrowed lids.

Nothing since the two of them had met, Eva accepted. His pursuit of her this past week or so had been completely single-minded. But she couldn't allow herself to forget his reputation of coldness towards a woman once he had decided he no longer wanted them in his life. As with her cousin Donna.

'Nothing at all,' she dismissed lightly. 'Is this the bathroom over here?' She indicated the closed door on the right of the bedroom.

Markos shook his head. 'The dressing room. Where you will find several of my shirts hanging up if you don't want to put your dress back on.'

Eva tensed at the idea of the intimacy of dressing in one of Markos's shirts. 'Er—no. I'll be fine in the dress, thank you.'

Markos continued to look at her for several long seconds before giving an abrupt nod of his head. 'In that case, that's the bathroom over there.' He nodded at the closed door to the left of the room.

Eva avoided meeting that piercing green gaze as she grabbed her dress up from the carpeted floor, where it had been dropped the night before; no doubt she was about to go home in a very crumpled black silk evening dress!

'Thanks.' Her chin was high as she hastily left the bedroom.

Markos remained laying in bed for several minutes longer, listening as Eva turned on the shower. A large part of him—that hard and rampant part of him!—wanted to get out of bed and join her in the shower to make love with her again, but the more cautious part of him warned that Eva needed a few minutes alone, that—incredibly—her embarrassed awkwardness earlier this morning, and again just now, gave every indication that spending the day in bed with him had been completely out of character.

Reading between the lines what Eva *hadn't* said last night, Markos could well imagine that her marriage to Jack Cabot Grey hadn't been what the English called 'a bed of roses'. So much so that Eva had fought shy of becoming intimately involved with anyone since her divorce.

Markos frowned as the music of Mozart interrupted his train of thought. The sound was coming from inside Eva's evening bag, where it lay on the bedside cabinet, and was obviously the ringtone of her mobile phone.

He glanced towards the bathroom door, wondering briefly if he should go and tell Eva that she had a phone call, and then dismissed the idea as he thought of how she had almost run from the bedroom—from *him*. The sound of water still running told him that Eva was still in the shower. If the call was important then whoever it was would either leave a message or ring back.

Markos's thoughts came to an end as the music stopped just as abruptly. As he'd thought—whoever it was would call back.

Mozart began to play a second time.

The caller was either very persistent, or the call was an emergency. After Jack Cabot Grey's parting comment to Eva last night Markos could easily guess who the persistent caller might be, and having Eva talk to her ex-husband now was guaranteed to hasten her departure. But if it *was* an emergency—

Damn it, he'd answer the call and take the flak from Eva later for doing so!

The name of the caller on the lit screen of Eva's mobile phone made his eyes widen in surprise.

CHAPTER TEN

Eva felt more than a little awkward when she entered the kitchen half an hour later. Her hair was still damp from the shower and she wore no make-up, although she had accepted Markos's invitation and borrowed one of his shirts from the dressing room—a cream silk. She felt less conspicuous wearing the shirt over her figure-hugging evening gown like a jacket, the sleeves turned up to just beneath her elbows.

Markos had obviously been busy in her absence. A salad and a selection of cheeses were laid out temptingly on the breakfast bar, and she could see from the dampness of his dark hair and clean-shaven jaw, as he turned to look at her from beneath hooded lids, that he had also taken a shower and freshened up in one of the apartment's many other bathrooms. He was wearing black denims and a fitted white T-shirt which emphasised both his muscled chest and the natural tan of his skin. Markos looked more edible than the food!

This was not what Eva wanted to feel after deciding earlier on today that she was going to be sophisticated and casual about all this, and not try to make it into something it wasn't. As far as Markos was concerned, anyway. Eva would have time to sit and decide how she felt about it once she was safely back in her own apartment.

The guarded look in Markos's expression as he put a basket of freshly baked bread on the breakfast bar before sitting down on one of the stools only served to confirm that Eva needed to act cool as well as sophisticated.

'This all looks delicious!' she complimented him brightly as she sat on the stool opposite him. 'I'll just eat a little something and then I really do have to leave.'

His expression was still guarded. 'I thought we could talk first.'

Eva avoided his piercing green gaze as she concentrated on breaking open a piece of the crispy bread. 'I'm not really one for post-mortems, are you?' she dismissed lightly. 'We had fun together. Let's just leave it at that.'

Markos looked across at her. 'Can we do that?'

She gave him a startled look. 'Sorry...?'

Markos leant his elbows on the breakfast bar and continued to stare across at her. 'You had a telephone call earlier when you were in the shower.'

Her eyes widened, her thoughts racing at Markos's continued aggression. 'And you answered it...?' If Jack had carried out his threat to 'be in touch...'

'No.' His eyes glittered through narrowed lids. 'I decided not to after seeing the identity of the caller on the display.'

Eva moistened suddenly dry lips. 'And...?'

'And it would seem that you forgot to mention we have a mutual acquaintance,' he commented mildly. Too mildly.

Eva gave up all pretence of putting food on her plate and straightened warily. 'We do…?'

'Yes,' Markos rasped.

She gave a puzzled shake of her head. 'I'm afraid you're going to have to be a little more explicit than that if you expect me to know what you're talking about.'

Markos stood up abruptly, too filled with impatient restlessness to sit at the breakfast bar any longer. 'I am curious to know why you have not mentioned that you are acquainted with Donna Cresswell—the woman who you surely know was my PA in London until a few weeks ago?'

'Ah.'

'Yes—*ah*,' Markos bit out evenly, not in the least comforted by the way the colour had leeched from Eva's cheeks.

To say that Markos had been surprised to recognise the name of the Englishwoman making the call to Eva's mobile phone earlier was putting it mildly. It was the same Englishwoman who had once been his PA—a PA he had been forced to dismiss some weeks ago under less than pleasant circumstances.

Eva's obvious dismay now only seemed to confirm his earlier suspicion that perhaps this was the reason behind those two cancelled appointments made by interior designer Evangeline Grey, and behind her dismissive manner towards him the evening Markos had introduced himself to her at Senator Ashcroft's cocktail party. He also strongly suspected there was a distinct possibility Donna Cresswell might have told her friend Eva a different version of those events of six weeks ago.

'The two of you are friends…?' he prompted evenly.

She swallowed before answering. 'Cousins.'

Cousins? Eva and the machinating Donna Cresswell were *cousins*?

Markos's thoughts were now in such disarray he had no idea what to think about this less than welcome revelation. 'I thought you said yours was not a close family.'

She flinched. 'It isn't.'

'With the exception of yourself and your cousin Donna, it would seem?'

Her gaze avoided meeting his. 'We aren't exactly what I would call close, either. We saw a lot of each other when we were children, but not so much any more.'

'But you are still close enough that you exchange regular telephone calls?'

'Occasional telephone calls,' she corrected distractedly.

His nostrils flared. 'And your cousin never mentioned to you the name of her current employer during these "occasional" telephone calls?'

'Well, of course she mentioned you!' Eva eyed him exasperatedly.

'And what, exactly, did she say about me? From your earlier attitude towards me nothing complimentary, I would guess.' His mouth twisted scathingly.

'Considering the way things ended so badly between the two of you—'

'Badly?' he repeated harshly. 'I had to dismiss your cousin for behaviour that was not only unprofessional but also less than acceptable to me personally!'

Eva frowned. 'Admittedly Donna should have had more sense than to fall in love with you, but I would hardly call that—'

'Eva, I have no idea what your cousin has told you

of our past...association, but I somehow doubt, from your comment just now, she can have mentioned that I was less than pleased the evening I returned to my hotel suite and found her naked in my bed!' His eyes darkened angrily at the memory.

Eva's frown was pained. 'If that really happened—'

'Oh, I assure you it did!'

'Then I agree. It wasn't the wisest move on Donna's part.'

Eva grimaced, having had no idea until that moment of the extremes her cousin had gone to in order to try and revive her relationship with Markos. Although it *did* sound like the sort of thing Donna would do...

'But it was hardly grounds for dismissal, when she was obviously only reacting to the fact that she was so unhappy you had ended your personal relationship.'

His brows rose into his hairline. 'We did not *have* a personal relationship.'

Eva stilled at the vehemence of his tone. 'Sorry?'

'Your cousin and I did not have any relationship other than the fact that she was—briefly—my employee,' Markos repeated evenly.

Eva looked at him searchingly. The angry glitter of his eyes and the tension in his jaw were enough to assure her that Markos was telling the truth. The truth as he saw it, at least...

'Markos, you aren't the first man to make the mistake of having an affair with an employee which results in awkwardness once that affair is over—'

'Eva, what did you not understand about my previous statement?' he cut in exasperatedly. 'I have not been, and will never be in the future, personally involved in any way with Donna Cresswell.'

Eva blinked. 'But Donna said—'

'After the things she screamed at me the night I had to dismiss her from my employment, I can all too easily imagine what your cousin said about me, Eva.' Markos began to pace the kitchen restlessly. 'I can only say—once again—that my feelings towards your cousin were never anything other than the polite regard of an employer. And even that ceased the moment she decided to put herself naked in my bed!'

Eva swallowed hard. She'd begun to feel nauseous. 'But…'

'Yes?'

Could Donna have lied…?

The possibility of that having been the case was so strong that Eva felt as if the ground had just dropped out from beneath her feet. Eva had seen Markos arrogant, even haughty on occasion, but never coldly, chillingly angry—as he undoubtedly was now.

So much so that he bore little or no resemblance to the man who had treated her so gently the night before, or made love with her such a short time ago.

But what possible reason could Donna have had for lying to Eva about having a relationship with Markos Lyonedes?

Eva thought back to her childhood, to the family occasions when she and Donna had been together—those weekends they had both spent with their grandparents. Eva hadn't thought of them for years, but now she belatedly recalled how Donna had always had to have a bigger or better toy than her, or have attended a more fun or glamorous birthday party.

Better. Bigger. More glamorous.

And a relationship with the charismatic Markos

Lyonedes would no doubt have sounded so much more than even Eva's marriage to the wealthy American Jonathan Cabot Grey Junior...

'Donna lied,' she stated flatly.

'Oh, yes, she most certainly lied if she claimed the two of us were ever intimately involved,' Markos confirmed softly. 'What I wish to know is how, and to what extent, those lies have affected your own behaviour towards me?'

Eva gave him a startled look. 'I don't understand...'

'Oh, I think you do, Eva,' Markos bit out grimly. 'And I think your family connection to Donna Cresswell more than explains the little game you played with me at the beginning of our acquaintance.'

She moistened her lips with the pink tip of her tongue. 'I was predisposed not to like or trust you, yes—'

'A fact you made more than obvious!' Markos frowned as he recalled the way Eva, as interior designer Evangeline Grey, had made and then cancelled two appointments with him in a week. She had been scathingly dismissive of him, even insulting, on the evening the two of them had met at Senator Ashcroft's cocktail party, and had made that cryptic comment concerning his 'reputation'. Believing the lies her cousin had told her about him would certainly explain that remark!

'The question is, Eva, how do you feel about me now that we have come to know each other better?'

She gave him a startled glance before focusing that wide golden gaze somewhere over his left shoulder. 'How do I feel about you?'

'Yes!' A nerve pulsed in his tightly clenched jaw. 'Now that we have spent time together—talked, made love—what are your feelings towards me?'

Eva gave a pained frown, knowing she couldn't deny that she had initially behaved in exactly the petty way Markos suspected she had. Quite when her feelings towards Markos had changed from scathing dismissal to a grudging liking Eva had no idea, but she had known last night, when he'd behaved so protectively towards her in regard to Jack, that she not only liked him—a lot—but also that she desired him too. It was a desire the two of them had acted on earlier today—several times.

But the chances of Markos believing that, now that he knew of her family connection to Donna—the woman who had not only completely invented a relationship with Markos, but had also lied to Eva about the callous way Markos had brought that non-existent relationship to an end—were exactly nil!

At least they were if Eva didn't want to totally humiliate herself and tell Markos how much, and how deeply, she now liked him—perhaps more than liked him. Which was *definitely* something she needed to think about once she was alone in the privacy of her own apartment.

Eva forced a rueful smile. 'I believe I told you earlier my intentions are entirely dishonourable!'

He gave a humourless smile. 'In exactly the way you have imagined my own were in regard to the women who have shared my bed in the past? Women who would, if asked, confirm that I have never deliberately, knowingly, hurt any of them. No matter how much the gossips or newspapers might have chosen to sensationalise those relationships. Certainly I have never behaved towards a single one of those women in the cruel and heartless way that your cousin appears to have claimed I treated her.'

'I believe you—'

'Do you?' he questioned sceptically. 'Do you *really* believe me, Eva? Or do you still think your suspicions in regard to me to have been justified? Enough, perhaps, for you to have decided to give me a dose of my own medicine?'

Her eyes widened. 'Are you implying that I might have *deliberately* gone to bed with you with the intention of—of—?'

'I have absolutely no idea what today was about.' His eyes glittered intently. 'Why did you go to bed with me, Eva?'

'I don't—' She gave a dazed shake of her head. 'You were kind to me last night—'

'And do you always spend the day in bed with men who are *kind* to you?'

Her face was very pale as she answered him quietly, 'There really haven't been that many.'

'Men in your bed? Or men who have been kind to you?'

Both, as it happened, Eva acknowledged heavily. Just as she acknowledged that this conversation had now deteriorated to such a level there was surely no hope of the two of them continuing a relationship.

'Eva, talk to me, damn it!' Markos hands were clenched into fists at his sides. 'Help me to understand what happened between the two of us earlier today.'

She released a heavy sigh. 'Can't we both just accept that we made a mistake—?'

'Is that truly what you believe?' He stood still as a statue and looked at her from between narrowed lids.

Eva nodded abruptly as she stood up to slip the shirt off her shoulders and slide it off her arms before dropping it down onto the barstool. 'It's time that I left.'

'You have nothing else to say?' Markos could only stare at her with frustrated anger.

She looked up at him with eyes of deep, smoky amber. 'I've behaved badly, unprofessionally. Otherwise I don't know what else you want me to say.'

Markos wanted Eva to dismiss the lies Donna Cresswell had told her about him—to assure him that she had come to know him for herself this past week, and that she at least liked what she had come to know of him, that they had spent the day in bed together because of that liking.

The guarded expression in Eva's eyes told him that was never going to happen.

'Nothing,' he said flatly. 'Obviously there is nothing more you can or wish to say to me.'

She nodded abruptly. 'Which is why I am going to collect my bag from the bedroom and leave.'

Just an hour ago Markos had been filled with a feeling of well-being, of contentment in a woman's company and in lovemaking such as he had never experienced before. Only for all of those feelings to have been completely shattered by one telephone call.

He nodded abruptly. 'I will need to accompany you.'

'I'm perfectly capable of seeing myself out, Markos!' she assured him heavily.

His jaw tightened. 'The lift will not work without putting in my security code, and the same applies to the outside door.'

Colour darkened the pallor of her cheeks at the obvious rebuke. 'I'll just go and get my bag.'

Markos was filled with regret as he turned to watch Eva leave the kitchen—her back very straight and proud, her hips swaying slightly, sensuously, as she walked, her legs long and shapely in the high-heeled black sandals—but he knew he was too angry still to attempt to set things right between the two of them.

If such a thing was even possible...

Eva held back the tears for as long as it took her to reach Markos's bedroom, then she couldn't hold back her emotions any longer and instead allowed the tears to cascade down her cheeks with the heat of molten lava.

How could this be ending so badly?

How could she and Markos be parting like virtual strangers after having made love together so tenderly, and then so wildly, only hours ago?

The answer to that, Eva knew, lay firmly at her own door. Because she had too easily accepted Donna's telephone calls and her conversation as a link with her otherwise uncaring family rather than remembering her cousin as how she really was: a shallow social climber who had always had to have everything bigger and better than Eva.

She had been a fool, Eva accepted dully, a blind, stupid fool. There was absolutely no excuse for her initial scathing behaviour towards Markos. No foundation in it either—as she now knew.

Neither did it do any good now to tell herself that she should have looked beyond Donna's claims of Markos's mistreatment, should have seen Markos for the man he truly was—if not from the beginning then at least following his warmth and kindness towards her last night.

And now it was too late.

Yes, Markos was a man who was extremely attractive to women, and it was an attraction he had no doubt taken every advantage of over the years. But, as Eva now knew, he was also a man of principle. A man who had been both protective and caring when she had fallen apart at Jonathan's home the evening before following her introduction to the pregnant Yvette Cabot Grey. The same man who had allowed Eva to cry on his shoulder even though he had mistakenly believed those tears to have been because she still had feelings for her ex-husband. The same man who had brought her back to his apartment, put her in his own bed, undressing her and tucking her beneath the bedcovers.

The womanising Markos Lyonedes that Donna had led Eva to believe in wouldn't have bothered himself doing any of those things, let alone left her to sleep alone in his bed because he had no intention of taking advantage of her in her emotional state.

Eva hadn't just been a fool where Markos was concerned, she had been both blind and stupid too!

A realisation, an admission, which made absolutely no difference to the fact that she was now about to leave Markos's apartment and would in all probability never see him again.

But there was something she needed to say to him before she left...

'I'm sorry.'

Markos was standing in front of one of the huge picture windows in the sitting room, staring sightlessly out at the New York skyline, but he turned now to face Eva, his expression unreadable as he took in the fact that she was still very pale, and her eyes were that deep and troubled amber. As well they might be.

'What are you apologising for?' he returned impatiently.

She shrugged as she came further into the room, her gaze not quite meeting his as instead she stared at the centre of his chest. 'I— It's no excuse, but I—I was obviously misled about your involvement with Donna—or rather your lack of it,' she amended hastily as Markos's expression darkened.

'Yes?'

Her smile was rueful. 'You aren't about to make this easy for me, are you.'

He raised dark brows. 'Can you think of any reason why I should?'

'No,' she accepted heavily, before raising her chin and at last allowing her gaze to meet his. 'I do sincerely apologise for my earlier behaviour towards you. My lack of professionalism. I really should have known better than to believe Donna's lies.' She sighed. 'Or at the very least given you the benefit of the doubt—as you several times requested I might do,' she added.

'Yes, you should,' Markos bit out grimly.

She shifted her shoulders uncomfortably. 'I— And thank you for being so understanding yesterday evening. You really were very kind.'

'Maybe you believe there was an ulterior motive to my kindness and understanding?' Markos came back challengingly. 'After all, I did succeed in getting you into my bed—eventually!' He gave a derisive grimace. 'Which should fit in very nicely with what your cousin, the gossips and the newspapers have told you about me.' His mouth twisted scornfully.

Eva knew she deserved every ounce of that scorn, and that there was no way for her to salvage the situation without revealing how much her feelings towards him had changed. She might now know that Markos *wasn't* the cold and callous bastard in regard to women and relationships that Donna had told her he was, but neither was he a man interested in an emotional relationship.

She nodded abruptly. 'I'll leave you now to enjoy the rest of your day. If you would like to do so, you can keep the designs and the swatches of material. Although another designer would probably prefer to—'

'There is not going to be another designer, Eva,' he cut in firmly.

Her eyes widened in surprise. 'You've decided not to bother after all...?'

'On the contrary,' Markos drawled dryly, 'I have decided to keep the interior designer I already have.'

She blinked, long dark lashes briefly brushing against the pallor of her cheeks. 'I'm not sure I understand...?'

'It's quite simple, Eva.' Markos strode into the middle of the room. 'I have already wasted a considerable amount of my time procuring the services of the elusive but celebrated designer Evangeline Grey.' He eyed her mockingly. 'And, having done so, I have no intention of starting the process all over again.'

Eva eyed him warily even as she chewed distractedly on her bottom lip. 'You still want to engage me to redesign your apartment?'

His eyes glittered deeply emerald. 'I don't just want you to do it, Eva, I *insist* upon it!'

And if that determined glitter in his eyes was any

indication then Eva knew he intended making her life very uncomfortable—even more uncomfortable than it already was—while she did it.

'Markos, you can't seriously want to have me hanging around here for the next few weeks—or months—after we... Well, you just can't,' she protested weakly once she had regained her breath enough to speak at all.

'On the contrary, I believe I would very much enjoy the experience,' he drawled mockingly.

Her heart sank at the implacability of his expression. 'Of watching me squirm with embarrassment every time I have to come here?'

Markos shrugged those broad, uncompromising shoulders. 'If that's what it takes, yes.'

This was a side of him that Eva had never seen before. The arrogantly powerful Markos Lyonedes side of him—Greek, half-owner of the world-renowned company Lyonedes Enterprises, cousin of the equally arrogant and powerful Drakon Lyonedes, and a man accustomed to issuing orders and expecting them to be obeyed. Without question or argument.

Until he had actually made that statement Markos had had no idea he had even decided on that particular course of action. But it did make perfect sense; Eva had already done all the groundwork towards redesigning this room at least, and he had no doubt she would be as successful in her designs for the rest of the apartment.

Besides which, he hadn't decided yet exactly what he was going to do about Evangeline Grey.

Part of him definitely wanted to strangle her for having believed Donna Cresswell's lies about him, just as there was still a part of him that hungered to make love to her. And Markos had absolutely no idea which of those emotions was going to win once he had recovered from the disappointment he was currently feeling.

In the meantime, while he waited for those feelings to settle, it seemed like a good idea to keep Eva exactly where he could see her.

Even if his body *had* already made its decision, now engorged and throbbing in favour of taking Eva back to bed and making love to her until she had no strength with which to leave his bed...

'I will expect you to begin work on this room immediately,' he bit out abruptly. 'With the intention of presenting designs for the other rooms as soon as possible.'

'All of them?' Eva gasped.

'All of them,' Markos confirmed with satisfaction at her obvious dismay.

Leaving Eva in no doubt that Markos intended exacting his pound of flesh for her ever having harboured doubts as to his true nature.

She should never have allowed herself to jump to conclusions where Markos was concerned based only on what Donna had told her, or allowed those conclusions to influence her into behaving so badly, so unprofessionally, towards him at the beginning.

In truth, Eva now felt deeply ashamed of her behaviour. Something which wasn't going to be in the least alleviated during the telephone call she intended making to her duplicitous cousin as soon as she had reached the privacy of her apartment!

For now she just had to concentrate on leaving *this* apartment—leaving Markos—with at least some of her pride intact. 'If you're sure that's what you want...?'

'It is,' he rasped harshly.

'Fine.' Eva nodded briskly as she turned to leave.

'Oh, and, Eva…?'

'Yes?' She turned back warily.

'After, as you have so rightly called it, your lack of professionalism in regard to working for me, I will now expect you to give me your services exclusively for the next few weeks, at least.'

'That's imp—'

'And for you to inform me immediately if you have any further trouble with Cabot Grey,' he continued grimly.

'I don't consider *that* any of your business!' Eva gasped incredulously.

Markos's tread was light and predatory as he strode across the sitting room until he was standing only inches in front of her. 'After today I am *making* it my business.' His voice was dangerously soft. 'Do you understand, Eva?'

Oh, yes, she understood—only too well. And she resented the hell out of Markos's arrogant assumption that the two of them having made love together gave him any right to know anything about her private life.

Except it wasn't just a case of the two of them having made love together, was it? She had no idea what might have happened if Markos hadn't been with her last night when she'd realised Jack's second wife was pregnant—if he hadn't been so supportive of her in front of Jack and then later, here at his apartment.

'If I have any further trouble with Jack I will tell you about it,' she bit out tightly. 'Now can I leave?' she prompted angrily.

'Of course.' Markos smiled his satisfaction—both at Eva's reply and the fact that her fighting spirit had so obviously returned. He enjoyed verbally sparring with her almost as much as he had enjoyed making love with her. Almost…

'How kind of you!' Her eyes flashed deeply gold.

'In future, kindness is my middle name,' he drawled mockingly.

'And I thought it was arrogance,' she came back tartly.

Markos gave a husky chuckle. 'I will very much look forward to seeing you back here promptly at nine o'clock tomorrow morning.'

The fire dissipated from her eyes and she looked at him uncertainly. 'Markos—'

'Nine o'clock tomorrow morning, Eva,' he repeated firmly.

No matter how much Eva might wish it otherwise, Markos knew that things were far from settled between them…

CHAPTER ELEVEN

'SO, WHAT do you think...?' Eva looked at Markos uncertainly as he stood on the threshold of his newly decorated sitting room.

Markos thought that during the past three weeks he had learnt first-hand exactly what hell was!

It wore figure-hugging denims, form-fitting white T-shirts over full and luscious breasts, had long ebony hair, golden eyes, kissable lips, smelled of something lightly floral and sensual—and went under the guise of interior designer Evangeline Grey!

Because that was exactly who Eva had become during these three hellish weeks. Crisp, no-nonsense, utterly professional and bearing absolutely no resemblance to the woman Markos had made love with during that memorable Sunday.

The first week hadn't been too excruciating. Eva had only appeared at his apartment on the Monday and Tuesday, when she came in to take precise measurements for the carpets, curtains and other draperies.

The second week she had been more in evidence—calling in briefly every day in order to supervise her team of decorators, and to present Markos with the designs she had made for the rest of the rooms in his apartment.

And each time she'd arrived Markos had been the one who met her at the main lift before taking her up to his apartment.

By the time the furniture and fittings had arrived in the third week Markos had contacted Security and instructed them to let Eva in to the building any time she arrived, as well as giving her his security code to the private lift going straight up to his apartment.

All in an effort to spare himself the ordeal of so much as *seeing* the coolly remote stranger that Eva had become, let alone actually speaking to her.

And yet…any time Eva was in the building Markos instinctively knew she was up there—in his apartment, in the room just above his office.

He had been both angry and hurt the day he had insisted she would continue to redesign the interior of his apartment—and now he had found *he* was the one being punished, as day after day he was forced to suffer the cold professionalism of her manner towards him.

None of which was helped by the fact that every time he walked into his apartment his senses were bombarded with…well, with the presence of Eva.

He could see her influence now everywhere he looked in this newly furnished and decorated room: the pale terracotta-coloured walls adorned with bold coloured paintings of Greek islands, the carpet the colour of the Aegean Sea in summer, the deep rust colour of the comfortable sofas and chairs adorned with many scatter cushions in colours of blues and greens and yellows, the curtains draped at the huge picture windows in those same rich colours.

Such boldness of colour should have been too much, and yet somehow it not only worked but it also seemed to fill a hole in Markos's soul—a tiny oasis of need which was his love of Greece, a hunger that he hadn't even realised was there until he saw the colours and the warmth of his native country reflected so vividly in this room.

A hunger that Eva had not only seen and recognised in him, but addressed and filled with this warmth of colour...

He turned to her now. 'It's...amazing,' he said huskily.

'In a good way or a bad way?'

Markos gave a rueful smile as he recognised the wariness in Eva's tone. 'A good way, of course.' He stepped further into the room and allowed those warm Aegean colours to seep into his inner being, filling him with the same sense of peace and tranquillity he felt whenever he returned to Greece. Which was nowhere near as often as he would have liked it to be.

Eva heaved a deep sigh of relief as she felt the heavy weight of responsibility lift from her shoulders. She watched Markos's pleasure in his surroundings; as she had imagined, the richness and boldness of the earth tones suited Markos perfectly, bringing that same warm richness to his eyes and his swarthy, chiselled features as he strolled about the room.

She still couldn't believe she had been so stupid as to believe Donna's fantastic series of lies. Although, in her defence, she *had* started to doubt her cousin's version of things shortly after meeting Markos herself.

But she had only doubted Donna's version—she had never even thought that the whole thing had been a complete fabrication from start to finish. Nothing more than a figment of Donna's over-achieving imagination. Something, having spoken bluntly with Donna herself, Eva now knew without a shadow of a doubt to be the real truth.

Not that her cousin had apologised for the lies—in fact Donna appeared to be more angry towards Eva than anything else, for what she now saw as Eva's family disloyalty in befriending Markos herself.

Befriending?

Eva would hardly class the fantastic, earth-shattering lovemaking she and Markos had shared as 'befriending' each other!

God, just remembering the depth and feeling of that lovemaking now was enough to make her nipples tingle and tighten, to make her clench and unclench between her thighs.

She straightened abruptly. 'I'm pleased you're happy with it.'

'That would be an understatement.' Markos turned to look across at her from between narrowed lids. 'Praise where praise is due, Eva: you've done a fantastic job on this room.'

She avoided meeting that piercing gaze. 'Let's hope you're as pleased with the rest of the apartment once it's finished,' she dismissed briskly as she looked around for her shoulder bag.

'Perhaps we should have a glass of champagne to celebrate? Oh, come on, Eva,' he drawled dryly as she turned to him with wide eyes. 'I can't be the first satisfied customer who has wanted to toast the success of your hard work?'

He was the first satisfied customer that Eva had gone to bed with.

The only man, besides Jack, she had *ever* been to bed with...

And Eva now knew beyond a shadow of a doubt that there was absolutely no comparison between the two men. Jack had been a selfish lover, whereas Markos was a generous one. She had been a virgin when she'd married Jack, had had no idea that making love should be the way it had been between her and Markos—a delight for all the senses.

And those memories weren't helping her in the least to keep this meeting on a business footing! 'I really do have to go—'

'Do you have a date this evening?'

'No, of course not,' she answered with irritation.

'Have you heard from Cabot Grey?'

Eva drew her breath in sharply. 'I've spoken to Jack again, yes,' she confirmed guardedly.

Markos looked at her from between narrowed lids, having absolutely no idea what thoughts were going on behind those shuttered gold-coloured eyes. 'I believe I asked you to tell me—'

'If I had any further trouble from Jack. Which I haven't,' she added firmly. 'We spoke. Nothing more.'

'About what?'

She gave a pained frown. 'As I've said before, I don't believe that to be any of your business—'

'That's bull—' He abruptly broke off his angry response, aware that he had been about to voice an unacceptable expletive. His jaw was tight as he continued between gritted teeth, 'As the man who helped you to pick up the pieces after your last conversation with your ex-husband, I happen to think it's very *much* my business!' His eyes glittered darkly.

A blush heightened Eva's cheeks. 'I believe I've already thanked you sufficiently for the…assistance you gave me that weekend.'

'I sincerely hope that was *not* a reference to our lovemaking, Eva,' he bit out coldly.

'Of course not!' she gasped.

'No?'

She gave another pained wince. 'Markos, I've already thanked you several times for your kindness the evening I met Jack again at his father's house. And it's because of that kindness that I refuse to argue with you now—'

'Then what *are* you going to do with me?'

She blinked. 'Sorry?'

'Not half as sorry as I am!' Markos muttered grimly under his breath. He spoke more loudly. 'I asked what are you going to do about me, Eva?'

She gave a puzzled shake of her head. 'I'm sorry, but I still don't understand what you mean…'

No, Markos could see by the blankness of Eva's expression that she really didn't understand—that as far as she was concerned theirs was now a purely business relationship.

Which was exactly what Markos had implied it was going to be three weeks ago. Before he had been forced to live every day in this living hell of wanting Eva, of being driven quietly but surely out of his mind with the knowledge of that desire for her, while she obviously had had absolutely no difficulty in resuming their previous business relationship, shutting out all memory of their hours of intimacy.

Or perhaps she hadn't shut them out at all? Maybe she really had just forgotten them altogether?

It was an idea Markos found totally unacceptable.

He gave a shake of his head. 'Is this what you do, Eva? Is this what your marriage to Cabot Grey did to you? Did you have a couple of dates with Glen too, a night in bed together, and then not only discard him as unimportant but forget about him altogether?'

'Of course not,' she gasped tremulously, her eyes now amber pools of hurt. 'That really isn't fair, Markos. You not only flirted with me outrageously the evening we met, but once you realised who I was you also ensured I had no choice but to come here for our appointment on the Monday evening. If anyone forgot about Glen, discarded him, then it was *you*!'

His mouth twisted derisively. 'Have you seen him again since that evening?'

'No,' she breathed shakily.

'Why not?'

Eva flinched at the coldness in Markos's tone. At the subject of this whole conversation. 'How can you even *ask* me that?'

Markos raised mocking brows. His inner frustrations this past three weeks was making him determined to get some sort of response from Eva. Even if it was a negative one. 'Because if you haven't been seeing me, and you haven't been seeing Glen, then I'm interested to know who it is you're hurrying off to meet this evening. Your ex-husband, perhaps?'

'Don't be ridiculous!' Her face had paled to the colour of delicate white porcelain.

'Is *that* what I'm being?' Markos grated tautly.

'Where Jack is concerned, yes! Markos, you were there—you saw my reaction to seeing Jack again.'

'I saw your reaction to seeing his pregnant wife,' he corrected harshly. 'Which isn't the same thing at all.'

No, it wasn't, Eva acknowledged heavily. Not the same thing at all.

Jack had called her, as his parting comment that evening about 'being in touch' had promised that he would, and the two of them had agreed to meet in a suitably neutral coffee shop. The conversation had been stilted and awkward, but once Eva had convinced Jack that she had absolutely no interest in telling anyone that Yvette's baby couldn't be his the two of them had reached an uneasy truce, with an agreement that they would both stay out of the other's life, and if they met again socially would at least be polite to each other. Nothing more, but nothing less, either.

It wasn't perfect, but it was far better than the anger which had burned so strongly between them before Eva had realised she was allowing her life to be ruined because of her failed marriage.

It was a realisation which had made her determined to put that part of her life behind her and move on to whatever kind of future might be in store for her, rather than the future she had so neatly planned out for herself.

In a perfect world Eva knew that future would have included Markos—the man she had come to realise these past three weeks she was so very much in love with...

Not that bedazzled young love she had felt for Jack, but the love of a mature woman who knew what and who she was, and also knew how and who she loved.

Eva had no idea how or when it had happened. Perhaps when Markos had defended her so gallantly in front of Jack. Or perhaps it had been the gentleness of his care when he'd rescued her from the bathroom and taken her back to his apartment, before undressing her and leaving her to sleep alone in his bed. Or during that wild and glorious lovemaking the following day, the memory of which still caused Eva to tremble just thinking about it.

Or maybe, just maybe, it had happened the first moment she'd set eyes on him at Senator Ashcroft's cocktail party...

It didn't really matter when or how it had happened, only that it had. She was in love with Markos Lyonedes. Completely. Utterly. And he was obviously still as disgusted with her as he had been three weeks ago.

She gave a weary sigh, accepting that perhaps she *did* owe Markos at least some answers to his questions. 'I did meet Jack again after his father's party—'

'You *met* him?' Markos echoed incredulously. 'He's a married man, about to become a father, and the two of you still sneaked away together behind his wife's back—'

'It wasn't like that!' Eva protested painfully.

'No?' The look Markos gave her down the long length of his aristocratic nose spoke of his disgust. 'Then tell me what it *was* like, Eva.'

Eva had absolutely no doubt that this past three weeks—with the two of them skirting around each other, being outwardly polite and inwardly a seething mass of emotions and unanswered questions—had been leading up to this confrontation. A confrontation she had no idea whether or not she was ready for, but she accepted it was coming anyway.

'Did Jack tell Yvette about your meeting?' Markos pressured.

'I have no idea,' she answered honestly. 'He may have done. There's no reason why he shouldn't have.'

Markos gave a disgusted snort. 'I can think of plenty of reasons a man wouldn't tell his heavily pregnant second wife that he was going off to meet his first wife!'

'I said it wasn't like that!' Eva glared at Markos. 'Jack and I had...unresolved issues we needed to talk about—no, damn it, *not* those sort of issues!' she snapped angrily when she saw how the censure in Markos's eyes had deepened. 'There was so much anger between us still when we parted and divorced. I had wanted a baby so much, and Jack— He refused even to consider adoption, and he was totally against the idea of IVF with another man's donated sperm. It caused a huge rift and we drifted apart. He began to have affairs—'

'Just a minute.' Markos's voice was husky as he halted her. 'I thought you told me that you were the one who couldn't have children.'

A frown creased her creamy brow as she slowly shook her head. 'I couldn't have said that because it isn't true.'

No, she *hadn't* exactly said that, Markos realised, slightly dazed.

What Eva had said was that she and Jack had had tests, and that it wasn't possible for them to have a child together. *He* had made the assumption that night, because of Eva's distress, that she was the one incapable of having a child of her own.

Markos frowned darkly. 'But if Cabot Grey is sterile, then how are he and Yvette—?'

'Don't ask.' Eva gave a weary shake of her head. 'As far as the world is concerned—and, more importantly, Jonathan Cabot Grey Senior—the baby Yvette is expecting is Jack's son and heir. And I think it's best for all concerned if it remains that way.'

Markos felt short of breath—as if someone had punched him hard in the chest. Damn it, he hadn't used contraception when the two of them made love because he had believed a pregnancy was impossible! 'So you *are* able to have children?'

'Yes,' she confirmed flatly. 'In fact I— Look, as our conversation has gone this far, I might as well be completely honest with you.'

'That would certainly be a novelty!' He looked at her coldly.

Her eyes flashed deeply golden. 'I have *never* been dishonest with you!'

'Except by omission.'

'Perhaps,' she acknowledged heavily, her gaze no longer quite meeting his. 'The truth is I decided some months ago to have a child of my own by IVF.'

Markos's thoughts were already reeling from one realisation to another, one question to another, and each one was becoming wilder than the last. Eva *could* have a baby, after all. In fact it now appeared she had coolly and calmly decided to do exactly that 'some months ago'…

His gaze sharpened. 'And can it be that you were considering the blue-eyed blond-haired Glen Asher as a possible candidate to be the donor for this IVF?'

The warmth of colour entered the paleness of Eva's cheeks. 'I considered it, yes.'

'And did he agree?' Markos grated harshly, feeling a fury building up inside him the like of which he had never experienced before.

Eva's smile was completely lacking in humour. 'We didn't get far enough in our friendship for me to broach such a sensitive subject as IVF with him.'

Markos gave a disgusted shake of his head. 'Why not just forget the whole idea of IVF and instead just go to bed with him and hope for the desired result? He would certainly have been willing!'

Her throat moved convulsively as she swallowed before speaking. 'After my marriage to Jack I didn't want the trauma of being intimately involved again. Nor did I want the complication of having my child's life ripped apart by estranged parents, and so I thought—I thought a legal contract with a sperm donor, followed by IVF—'

'It seems to me, with all your talk of "I didn't want" and "nor did I want", that you weren't thinking of anything or anyone but yourself, Eva,' Markos cut in coldly.

No, she hadn't, Eva acknowledged numbly. The woman she had been—cool and businesslike, and determined not to become physically involved with any man—had made her decision to have a baby without emotion, without any real thought for the emotional consequences of those actions.

The woman she had been...

Eva knew she was no longer that hurt and disillusioned woman. She had ceased being that woman even before she and Markos had made love together. She had become another woman completely when she'd fallen in love with him...

It was a love which she knew, just from looking at the disgust now on Markos's face when he looked at her, was even more doomed than her marriage to Jack had been.

'Did you seriously think that Glen Asher—that *any* man,' Markos continued disgustedly, 'would just calmly agree to cold-bloodedly, cold-heartedly donate his sperm for you to be impregnated with?'

She moved agitatedly. 'As you've just pointed out, I don't believe I had been thinking straight for some time.'

She didn't particularly care for the way Markos was now looking at her from between narrowed lids, as if she were a specimen under a microscope—a hitherto unknown species he was trying, and not succeeding, to understand. And what little he *did* understand he didn't particularly like.

'You could be pregnant now, Eva.'

'What...?'

His mouth was a thin straight line. 'Three weeks ago I believed, from our previous conversation, that you were incapable of becoming pregnant, rendering precautions unnecessary when we made love together. Did you take any steps yourself to prevent a pregnancy?'

Eva stared at him uncomprehendingly. No, of course she hadn't. There had never been any reason for her to. She had known she couldn't become pregnant during her marriage, and there had been no other man intimately in her life since her divorce, so there had never been any need for the use of any sort of contraception.

Markos had now been intimately in her life—however briefly. Several times.

'Are you pregnant, Eva?' Markos repeated harshly.

Was she? Eva desperately tried to recall when she had last had a period and failed utterly, her mind having gone a complete blank.

Of *course* she wasn't pregnant!

Was she...?

Markos didn't feel in the least encouraged by the way Eva's face had turned a sickly grey colour. As if she were fighting down nausea.

Nausea possibly caused by early pregnancy...

The irony of this situation wasn't lost on Markos. Eva's cousin, and other ambitious women like her, would, he knew, quite happily become pregnant as a way of entrapping a wealthy man into marriage. Typically Eva—contrarily so!—she had decided to become pregnant by totally eliminating any physical intimacy or personal knowledge of the man who had made her so!

Unfortunately for Eva that was never going to happen if it turned out she was now carrying his child.

'Well?' he prompted tersely.

Eva determinedly gathered her scattered thoughts together, knowing this was neither the time nor the place for her to dwell on the chaos of her own thoughts. 'I can't believe you're so full of yourself, Markos, that you actually believe yourself to be so virile a woman would become pregnant from just one day of unprotected sex with you!' she added mockingly.

The coldness in those deep emerald eyes deepened. 'One day during which we indulged in several occasions of unprotected sex,' he corrected harshly.

She gave an unconcerned shrug. 'Well, I'm sorry to

disappoint you, Markos, but I guess you really aren't as potent as you thought you were.'

Was that disappointment he was feeling? Markos wondered scowlingly. Or did he feel disappointment because he had realised, with the flatness of Eva's denial of pregnancy, that their relationship—friendship—whatever—had now to come to an end?

There had been too much said for the two of them to carry on with even their business arrangement as if nothing had happened.

'Damn it!' Markos cursed. 'Why do you have to be so damned complicated?'

She gave a wistful smile. 'Just unlucky for you, I guess.'

Markos thought back to the first time he had seen Eva at Senator Ashcroft's drinks party, to his instant awareness of her, his instant attraction to the voluptuously beautiful woman in the red gown who'd drawn him towards her like a magnet. *Then* the situation had been uncomplicated. *Then* she had just been a lushly beautiful woman in a red gown that he had wanted to make love to.

Markos had never done complicated. A woman either was or was not interested in a brief and meaningless affair. He had never had the time or the inclination for anything more than that.

'Am I allowed to leave now?'

Markos's mouth tightened and he looked up to find himself the focus of beautiful gold-coloured eyes that danced with bittersweet laughter.

'I'm glad one of us finds this situation amusing!'

Eva wasn't in the least amused at the idea of never seeing Markos again, but it was better than crying.

She had already broken down emotionally enough in Markos's company. She certainly didn't intend to let him see her doing it now because she knew, despite everything, that she was in love with him. That would just be too humiliating.

She drew in a deep breath. 'Can I take it that you would now be happier if another interior designer took over refurbishing the rest of your apartment?'

A nerve pulsed in his tightly clenched jaw. 'You can.'

'That's what I thought.' Eva nodded abruptly. 'Well, it's been…interesting meeting you, Markos.' She slung her bag over her shoulder in preparation for leaving.

'Don't forget to send me the bill for the work you've already done,' he reminded her flatly.

'And don't *you* forget to change the security code on your private lift,' she said lightly.

He arched one dark and mocking brow. 'Is there any danger of your ever wanting to come back here?'

'Probably not,' she acknowledged with a tight smile.

'Then why would I bother changing the security code?' He shrugged unconcernedly.

Eva hesitated. 'I'm sure you're not really interested, but I—I've now decided not to go ahead with my plans for IVF.'

A nerve pulsed in his jaw. 'Why not?'

She gave a wistful smile, knowing she couldn't tell Markos the real reason—that, having fallen in love with him, it was impossible for her ever to want anyone else's child but his. 'Maybe I'm no longer that selfish.'

'I was wrong to say that,' Markos spoke huskily. 'After what you went through during your marriage to Cabot Grey it was not selfish to want a child of your own, Eva.'

'Merely ill-advised?' She grimaced.

'Not that either.' He gave a slow shake of his head.

'Then what was it?'

'I have absolutely no idea,' he admitted evenly.

She nodded abruptly. 'Goodbye, Markos.'

'Eva,' he returned tersely.

She wouldn't cry, Eva told herself firmly as she walked over to step inside the waiting lift before turning to look across at Markos where he stood so tall and darkly handsome—and icily distant—across the room.

She would *not* cry.

She had loved and lost, yes, but she had no one to blame for that but herself.

It was a loss Eva had a feeling she was going to have to live with for the rest of her life...

CHAPTER TWELVE

EVA paced restlessly up and down her apartment the following morning, checking her watch constantly as she waited—and waited!—for what might be considered a reasonable time to telephone someone—to telephone Markos!—on a Saturday morning.

Seven a.m.

Seven-fifteen.

Seven-thirty.

Seven forty-five.

And each of those minutes seemed like an hour as the second hand on Eva's watch crawled round more slowly with every second, increasing her tension. Those minutes had been crawling round all night as Eva had felt too restless even to go to bed, let alone try to sleep.

Eight a.m.

Eight fifteen.

Eight-thirty.

Was eight thirty still too early to telephone Markos? Would he still be in—?

Eva's nerves were strung out so tightly that she jumped about two feet in the air as the tune of her mobile ringing broke shrilly into the silence. She took several seconds to settle her jitteriness before picking up the phone, distractedly noting that the caller ID was 'unknown' and hoping whoever it was would get off the line quickly, so that she could put her own call through to Markos. Before she lost her nerve.

'Evangeline Grey,' she answered briskly.

'Eva.'

Just her name. Just that one word. And yet Eva knew without a shadow of a doubt that the person on the other end of the line was Markos.

'How strange, Markos, I was just about to call you…' she told him huskily.

'You were?'

She could hear the surprise in his tone. 'I need to talk to you.'

'You do?'

Eva gave a slightly breathless laugh as Markos also continued to sound less than his usually arrogantly confident self. 'Yes, I do. Is it convenient for me to come over now?'

'Not necessary. I'm already in the car on my way over to see you,' he came back dryly.

Now it was Eva's turn to feel surprised, and her fingers tightened about the mobile, the inside of her mouth having gone suddenly dry.

'You are?'

'I am,' he assured her firmly—*grimly*? 'I should reach your apartment in fifteen minutes or so, traffic allowing.'

She heaved a shakily relieved sigh, longing to see him again, to speak with him. 'Markos—'

'I would rather we talked face to face, Eva,' he cut in determinedly.

'Okay.' It was what she wanted too. 'I'll tell Security

to expect you.' She moistened her lips. 'Drive carefully,' she added huskily.

'Depend on it.' Markos abruptly ended the call.

Eva switched off her mobile before replacing it carefully back on the coffee table, hardly daring to believe that Markos wanted to speak to her—that he was actually on his way to her apartment right now.

She had spent hours the previous night, pacing from room to room in her apartment as she tried to decide what to do for the best. Talk to Markos. Don't talk to him. And in the end it had all come back to the realisation that she *had* to talk to him.

Did the fact that Markos seemed to have decided the same thing, in regard to her, make what she had to say to him easier or harder?

No doubt in fifteen minutes or so Eva would have the answer to that question. And several more.

'I brought coffee...' Markos held up a cardboard tray holding two take-away coffees when Eva opened her apartment door to him fifteen minutes later. 'The "hot" young man who works in the coffee shop across the road on weekends assured me this is how you take your coffee,' he added dryly.

Eva felt warmth in her cheeks as she remembered that deliberately provocative conversation. On her part at least.

'You told him it was for me...?'

Markos arched mocking brows. 'I only had to mention that you lived in this particular apartment building and he knew exactly who you were, and how you take your coffee. So much for him not noticing you, hmm?' he added teasingly as Eva tacitly invited him into her apartment by opening the door wider and stepping aside.

Her apartment seemed much smaller once Markos was inside, Eva noted—his very presence, in faded denims and a casual black shirt unbuttoned at the throat, with the sleeves turned up to just below his elbows, seemed to dominate even the air she breathed in so shallowly as she entered the sitting room behind him.

'This is beautiful.' Markos placed the cardboard tray down on the coffee table as he looked about the comfort of Eva's sitting room. The décor was in autumn colours—reds, golds, oranges, and all shades in between—and a perfect foil for her dark-haired golden-eyed beauty. 'It suits you.'

Eva's face was a little pale this morning, but otherwise she looked as arrestingly beautiful as usual, in fitted black denims and a pale lemon T-shirt.

'Here.' Markos picked up the coffee he had brought for her and held it out to her. 'You look as if you need it,' he added.

Her hand shook slightly as she took the insulated cup from him. 'And then we'll talk?' She smiled warily.

'And then we'll talk,' Markos confirmed, frowning as he once again noted the fragility of Eva's appearance.

He had spent a restless evening and a sleepless night after Eva had left his apartment the evening before, as he'd tried to accept that they were never going to see each other again. He had spent hours going over and over everything they had said during that last conversation, ultimately coming to the conclusion that none of it was of the least consequence when all he wanted was to see Eva again. To be with her. Once Markos had accepted that truth, everything else had become unimportant.

Convincing Eva to feel the same way about him might take a little longer!

'Markos…?' Eva had no idea what thoughts were currently going through Markos's head—when had she *ever* known what this enigmatic man was really thinking?—but whatever they were, they were causing him to frown darkly.

He shook off that darkness as he straightened. 'You said you wanted to speak to me this morning…?'

She moistened her lips before speaking. 'I believe we admitted we wanted to speak to each other?'

He gave a derisive smile. 'I'm really not in the mood to play games today, Eva.'

'Me either,' she assured him.

This situation, the conversation they needed to have, was too important for that.

'Which one of us should go first?'

Markos was tired—not only from his lack of sleep the night before, but by the way the two of them seemed to be skirting so warily around each other this morning.

'Will you marry me, Eva?'

'*What?*' she managed to burst out, eyes wide and disbelieving, her cheeks paling even more before colouring with a deep flush.

Not the most encouraging reaction to his first marriage proposal—the only marriage proposal Markos intended ever making. If Eva didn't accept him, then he couldn't see himself ever wanting to be with anyone else.

'I asked if you would become my wife,' he replied. 'Don't turn it down without due consideration,' he added quickly, when Eva seemed to be searching for the right words in answer to his proposal. No doubt a refusal that she hoped would cause the least embarrassment for both of them.

'Are you serious?' she finally managed to ask.

He nodded tersely. 'Think about it, Eva. I'm very wealthy. Socially acceptable—'

'I've already been married to someone with those particular attributes,' she reminded him huskily. 'It was a disaster!'

'I have no reason to believe I'm infertile,' Markos continued firmly. 'Although I'm willing to have the necessary tests to prove it, if that is what it takes to convince you to marry me.' He grimaced. 'Once we are married you can have as many babies as you want. One a year if you want to— Eva…?' he prompted sharply as she sat down abruptly in one of the armchairs and buried her face in her hands. 'Eva!' He went down on his haunches beside her chair. 'Do not cry, my Eva,' he pleaded. 'I hate it when you cry.'

Eva didn't doubt that for a moment. She could hear the distress in Markos's voice, and the way his accent became more pronounced whenever he was disturbed or upset.

But what he had just said was so unexpected, so totally beyond the realms of what she had expected him to say, that she couldn't quite take it in.

'I'm not crying, Markos.' She gave a firm shake of her head and took her hands from in front of her face to look up at him, crouching down only inches in front of her, his expression anxious. 'I was laughing.'

'Laughing?' he repeated incredulously as he surged abruptly to his feet. 'I propose marriage and you *laugh*!'

He scowled darkly. 'Is the idea of marrying me so amusing, then?'

Eva sobered completely when she saw Markos's hurt reflected in those deep green eyes. 'No, of course it isn't. I just— It was— I didn't expect—'

'For me to propose to you?' he guessed. 'If it is any consolation, it was the last thing I expected of myself when I made this move to New York just a matter of weeks ago!'

Yes, Eva could imagine it was. She doubted that Markos had seen himself married to anyone, in his near future.

'Why?' she prompted bluntly.

His brows rose. 'Why am I surprised? Or why did I propose to you?'

'The latter,' Eva replied dryly.

He shrugged broad shoulders. 'Why does any man propose marriage to a woman?' he came back defensively.

It was a defensive attitude that Eva knew was wholly merited when as far as Markos was concerned she had laughed at his proposal. 'Markos, I wasn't laughing at you just now, but at the irony of this situation,' she told him huskily. 'Did you mean what you said just now?'

'When I proposed—?'

'No, not that,' Eva cut in firmly.

'That if you married me we could have a dozen children together, if that is what you want? You really *are* about to cry now, Eva!' He groaned as he saw the tears well up in her eyes. 'I promise not to mention marriage to you again if this hysteria of emotions is the effect it has on you.'

'Markos.'

Just the husky softness of his name was enough to silence him as Eva rose determinedly to her feet, her cheeks looking hot and flushed, her eyes glowing brightly.

'Markos, I couldn't marry anyone who didn't love me in the way I'm in love with them.'

His breath caught in his throat. 'You—'

'In the way I'm in love with *you*…'

Markos became very still, his eyes a deep and glowing emerald as he stared at her incredulously. 'You *love* me…?'

'So very much,' she breathed determinedly.

Markos blinked. 'And after you left me yesterday I realised, at the thought of not seeing you again, how very much in love with *you* I am—which is why I—'

'Will you marry me?'

He gave a dazed shake of his head. 'I do not understand. You seemed amused just now by my own marriage proposal, and now you are asking—'

'Will you wait here a moment?' she asked excitedly, before turning to leave.

'Where are you going?' Markos called after her incredulously.

'Eva, you cannot tell me you love me, allow me to tell you I love you, ask me to marry you, and then just leave the room—'

She turned. 'I have something I want to show you.'

'Eva, now is *not* the time for me to look at more of your designs for my apartment!' he told her exasperatedly, and he crossed the room in long determined strides, before taking a firm hold of the tops of her arms as he looked down at her intently. 'I love you, Eva. I am insane with love for you. I can think of nothing else, see nothing else, but *you*!'

'I love you in exactly the same way, Markos,' she assured him huskily, reaching up tenderly to cup the side of his face with her hand as she looked at him with that love glowing in her eyes. 'I've known how I feel about you for some weeks now—'

'How many weeks?'

Her lashes lowered at his continued incredulity. 'Almost from the beginning, I think...'

'From the beginning?' Markos's fingers tightened about her arms even as the love he felt for this beautiful, wonderful woman welled up strongly inside him. 'The night we met at Senator Ashcroft's drinks party?'

'Well, perhaps not quite then.' She looked up, her eyes alive with amusement. 'Admittedly Donna's lies didn't help the situation, but I was still feeling more than a little jaundiced about the whole idea of love and marriage then. So it came as something of a surprise to me when I found myself attracted to you anyway,' she acknowledged ruefully. 'When I continued to fall for you a little bit more each time we met.' She gazed steadily into his eyes. 'I believe I fell all the way in love with you after we went to Jonathan's party and you were so protective and caring of me.'

'Before or after we made love?' he teased gruffly.

'Oh, definitely before,' Eva answered him without hesitation. 'Markos, there has never been anyone else for me. Not before I was married. Or in the three years since. And I don't believe I would have made love with you that day if I hadn't already been in love with you.'

'And now?'

'Now I love you so much that I just want to be with

you all the time,' she admitted softly. 'With or without marriage.'

'And I will settle for nothing less than to be married to you for the rest of our lives,' Markos told her firmly.

'Does that mean you accept my marriage proposal?'

Markos felt the last of his tension leaving him as he grinned down at her. 'On the understanding that you realise after accepting I will then tease you mercilessly for the next fifty years about your having been the one who proposed!'

'I would expect nothing less,' she assured him unconcernedly.

Markos gave a triumphant laugh as he drew her fully into his arms and hugged her tightly against him. 'I love you so very much, Evangeline Grey-soon-to-be-Lyonedes!' he murmured huskily, and at last he claimed her mouth with his own.

It was a long, long time later before Eva remembered she had something else she wanted to tell Markos, to show him. The intensity and wonder of their love-making had wiped everything else from her mind but Markos and the joy of being in his arms.

She looked at him almost shyly as he lay back against the pillows in her bed, holding her cradled tenderly against him in the aftermath of that lovemaking.

'Markos, I have an early wedding present I would like to give you.'

He looked down at her indulgently, all the strain and tension now erased from his wonderfully handsome face. 'I have no need of anything else but the love you feel for me, my darling Eva, and the love I feel for you, and the long and happy life we are going to have together,' he assured her emphatically.

Eva sat up beside him to kiss him lingeringly on the lips before straightening. 'I'm hoping that you'll love the gift I'm about to give you just as much.'

Markos reached out to grasp one of her hands in his as she would have risen from the bed. 'Believe me when I tell you I could never love anything or anyone as much as I love you, my Eva.'

Her eyes glowed deeply golden with the love she felt for him. 'Wait and see…'

Markos lay back against the pillows, feeling his desire returning as he watched Eva get up and leave the bedroom, knowing that he would always feel this way about her.

It had been an agonisingly long and sleepness night after he and Eva had parted so badly the evening before. A long and restless night during which Markos had realised that in just a few short weeks Eva had not only taken possession of his heart but become the centre of his world, that he loved her, would always love her, more than life itself.

To be here with her now and know that she loved him in exactly the same way was joy beyond imagining.

'Here.'

Markos looked up uncomprehendingly as Eva sat down beside him on the bed, holding out what looked like a thermometer. 'I do not understand—'

'It's blue, Markos!' She glowed at him, looking heartbreakingly beautiful with her cheeks flushed and her eyes fever-bright.

He gave a puzzled shake of his head. 'What—?'

'We're pregnant, Markos!' She smiled widely, joyously. 'I hadn't even considered the possibility until you mentioned it last night. But once I did I stopped off at a pharmacy on the way home and bought one of these instant pregnancy kits. It's positive, Markos. We're *pregnant*!' she said again excitedly. 'I think I was in shock last night, once I'd found out, and by the time I recovered I thought it was too late to call you. And then the hours seemed to go by so slowly until I felt it was late enough to call you this morning—but then you called me instead, and— Markos…?' The flow of words came to a halting stop as she realised he hadn't yet said a word in response to her announcement.

Markos was in shock. He felt as if his heart had stopped beating, that no air could enter his lungs. His whole world had tilted on its axis before tilting back again, leaving himself, Eva and the baby—*their* baby!—having miraculously taken up residence in her gloriously beautiful body. Not only did he have Eva's love, but the two of them were going to have a baby together.

The important word being *together*…

'You're going to be a father, Markos,' Eva told him excitedly, still hardly able to believe the wonder of it all herself.

All those years of trying to have a baby, of longing for a baby, and when it had finally happened she hadn't had a clue until Markos had put forward the possibility of it yesterday.

Her initial shock the evening before had quickly been followed by a feeling of absolute awe. She was pregnant at last. Nestled safe inside her was the baby of the man Eva loved so much she ached with the emotion.

'That's why I was going to call you this morning. I

couldn't wait to share the wonderful news with you.'
Her excitement wavered slightly as she looked down
at Markos uncertainly. 'Markos, please say something,
my darling…'

He sat up to take her gently in his arms. 'Thank
you, my Eva,' he murmured gruffly into the silkiness
of her hair.

'You're pleased about the baby?'

Markos pulled back slightly when he heard the uncertainty in Eva's voice, his hands moving up to cradle
each side of her face. 'I am ecstatic about the baby,' he
assured her firmly.

The way in which Eva had told him the news—the
way in which she had said, 'We're pregnant, Markos!'—
not *I'm* pregnant, but *we're* pregnant—and that he was
going to be a father—dear Lord, the wonder of such
a thing! It told Markos more than anything else ever
could have done that those plans Eva had once had to
have a baby on her own, without the complication of a
man in either her bed or the life of her baby, no longer
existed. She had wanted to share their baby with him
from the moment she knew of its existence.

'I love you, Eva. I will always love you!' His arms
tightened about her with a possessiveness he hadn't
known he was capable of feeling until this moment of
holding Eva and their baby in his arms.

Eva was his.

As Markos was hers.

And the baby she carried was and always would be
theirs to share, and love, and nurture…

Together.

* * * * *

AN OFFER SHE
CAN'T REFUSE

EMMA DARCY

Initially a French/English teacher, **Emma Darcy** changed careers to computer programming before the happy demands of marriage and motherhood. Very much a people person, and always interested in relationships, she finds the world of romance fiction a thrilling one and the challenge of creating her own cast of characters very addictive.

CHAPTER ONE

'It's like a great big sail, Mama,' Theo said in awe, staring up at the most famous building in Dubai—Burj Al Arab, the only seven-star hotel in the world.

Tina Savalas smiled at her beautiful five-year-old son. 'Yes, it's meant to look like that.'

Built on a man-made island surrounded by the sea, the huge white glittering structure had all the glorious elegance of a sail billowed by the wind. Tina was looking forward to seeing as much of its interior as she could. Her sister, Cassandra, had declared it absolutely fabulous, a must-see on their two-day stopover before flying on to Athens.

Actually staying in the hotel was way too expensive—thousands of dollars a night—which was fine for the super-rich to whom the cost was totally irrelevant. People like Theo's father. No doubt *he* had occupied one of the luxury suites with butler on his way back to Greece from Australia, having put his *charming episode* with her behind him.

Tina shut down on the bitter thought. Being left pregnant by Ari Zavros was her own stupid fault. She'd been a completely blind naive fool to have believed he was as much in love with her as she was with him. Sheer fantasy land. Besides, how could she regret having Theo? He was the most adorable little boy, and from time to time, knowing Ari was missing out on his son gave her considerable secret satisfaction.

Their taxi stopped at the checkpoint gates which prevented anyone but paying guests from proceeding to the hotel. Her mother produced the necessary paperwork, showing confirmation that they had booked for the early afternoon tea session. Even that was costing them one hundred and seventy dollars each, but they had decided it was a once-in-a-lifetime experience they should indulge in.

The security man waved them on and the taxi drove slowly over the bridge which led to the hotel entrance, allowing them time to take in the whole amazing setting.

'Look, Mama, a camel!' Theo cried, delighted at recognising the animal standing on a side lawn.

'Yes, but not a real one, Theo. It's a statue.'

'Can I sit on it?'

'We'll ask if you can, but later, when we're leaving.'

'And take a photo of me on it so I can show my friends,' he pressed eagerly.

'I'm sure we'll have plenty of great photos to show from this trip,' Tina assured him.

They alighted from the taxi and were welcomed into the grand lobby of the hotel which was so incredibly opulent, photographs couldn't possibly capture all of its utter magnificence. They simply stood and stared upwards at the huge gold columns supporting the first few tiers of inner balconies of too many floors to count, the rows of their scalloped ceilings graduating from midnight-blue to aqua and green and gold at the top with lots of little spotlights embedded in them, twinkling like stars.

When they finally lowered their heads, right in front of them and dividing two sets of escalators, was a wonderful cascade of dancing fountains, each level repeating the same range of colours in the tower of ceilings. The escalators were flanked by side-walls which were gigantic aquariums where hosts of gorgeous tropical fish darted and glided around the underwater rocks and foliage.

'Oh, look at the fish, Mama!' Theo cried, instantly entranced by them.

'This truly is amazing,' Tina's mother murmured in awe. 'Your father always liked the architecture of the old world. He thought nothing could beat the palaces and the cathedrals that were built in the past, but this is absolutely splendid in its own way. I wish he was here to see it.'

He had died a year ago and her mother still wore black in mourning. Tina missed him, too. Despite his disappointment in her—getting pregnant to a man who was not interested in partnering her for life—he had given her the support she'd needed and been a marvellous grandfather to Theo, proud that she'd named her son after him.

It was a terrible shame that he hadn't lived long enough to see Cassandra married. Her older sister had done everything right; made a success of her modelling career without the slightest taint of scandal in her private life, fell in love with a Greek photographer—the *right* nationality—who wanted their wedding to take place on Santorini, the most romantic Greek island of all. He would have been bursting with pride, walking Cassandra down the aisle next week, his *good* girl.

But at least the *bad* girl had given him the pleasure of having a little boy in the family. Having only two daughters and no son had been another disappointment to her father. Tina told herself she had made up for her *mistake* with Theo. And she'd been on hand to take over the management of his restaurant, doing everything *his* way when he'd become too ill to do it all himself. He'd called her a *good girl* then.

Yet while Tina thought she had redeemed herself in her father's eyes, she didn't feel good inside. Not since Ari Zavros had taken all that she was and walked away from her as though she was nothing. The sense of being totally crushed had never gone away. Theo held her together. He made life worth living. And there were things to enjoy, like this hotel with all its splendours.

There was another glorious fountain at the top of the escalator. They were escorted down a corridor to the elevator which would whiz them up to the SkyView Bar on the twenty-seventh floor. They walked over a large circle of mosaic tiles, a blazing sun at its centre, over a carpet shaped like a fish in red and gold. Her mother pointed out vases of tightly clustered red roses, dozens of them in each perfect pompom-like arrangement. The

doors of the elevator were patterned in blue and gold—
everything unbelievably rich.

On arriving in the shimmering gold lobby of the bar,
they were welcomed again and escorted into the dining
area where the decor was a stunning blue and green,
the ceiling designed like waves with white crests. They
were seated in comfortable armchairs at a table by a
window which gave a fantastic view of the city of Dubai
and the man-made island of Palm Jumeirah where the
very wealthy owned mansions with sand and sea front-
age.

A whole world away from her life in every sense,
Tina thought, but she was having a little taste of it today,
smiling at the waiter who handed them a menu listing
dozens of varieties of tea from which they could choose,
as many different ones as they liked to try throughout
the afternoon. He poured them glasses of champagne to
go with their first course which was a mix of fresh ber-
ries with cream. Tina didn't know how she was going
to get through all the marvellous food listed—probably
not—but she was determined on enjoying all she could.

Her mother was smiling.

Theo was wide-eyed at the view.

This was a good day.

Ari Zavros was bored. It had been a mistake to invite Felicity Fullbright on this trip to Dubai with him,
though it had certainly proved he couldn't bear to have
her as a full-time partner. She had a habit of notching
up experiences as though she had a bucket list that had

to be filled. Like having to do afternoon tea at the Burj Al Arab hotel.

'I've done afternoon tea at The Ritz and The Dorchester in London, at the Waldorf Astoria in New York, and at The Empress on Vancouver Island. I can't miss out on this one, Ari,' she had insisted. 'The sheikhs are mostly educated in England, aren't they? They probably do it better than the English.'

No relaxing in between his business talks on the Palm Jumeirah development. They had to visit the indoor ski slope, Atlantis underwater, and of course the gold souks where she had clearly expected him to buy her whatever she fancied. She was not content with just his company and he was sick to death of hers.

The only bright side of Felicity Fullbright was she did shut up in bed where she used her mouth in many pleasurable ways. Which had swayed him into asking her to accompany him on this trip. However, the hope that she might be compatible with him on other grounds was now comprehensively smashed. The good did not balance out the bad and he'd be glad to be rid of her tomorrow.

Once they flew into Athens he would pack her off back to London. No way was he going to invite her to his cousin's wedding on Santorini. His father could rant and rave as much as he liked about its being time for Ari to shed his bachelor life. Marriage to the Fullbright heiress was not going to happen.

There had to be someone somewhere he could tolerate as his wife. He just had to keep looking and assessing whether a marriage would work well enough. His father was right. It *was* time to start his own family. He did want children, always enjoying the time he spent with his nephews. However, finding the right woman to partner him in parenthood was not proving easy.

Being head over heels in love like his cousin, George, was not a requirement. In fact, having been scorched by totally mindless passion in his youth, Ari had never wanted to feel so *possessed* by a woman again. He had a cast-iron shield up against being sucked into any blindly driven emotional involvement. A relationship either satisfied him on enough levels to be happily viable or it didn't—a matter of completely rational judgement.

His *dissatisfaction* with Felicity was growing by the minute. Right now she was testing his patience, taking millions of photographs of the inside of the hotel. It wasn't enough to simply look and enjoy, share the visual pleasure of it with him. Using the camera to the nth degree was more important, taking pictures that she would sift through endlessly and discard most of them. Another habit he hated. He liked to live in the moment.

Finally, *finally,* they got in the elevator and within minutes were being led to their window table in the SkyView Bar. But did Felicity sit down and enjoy the view? No, the situation wasn't perfect for her.

'Ari, I don't like this table,' she whispered, grasping his arm to stop him from sitting down.

'What's wrong with it?' he asked tersely, barely containing his exasperation with her constant self-centred demands.

She nodded and rolled her eyes, indicating the next

table along. 'I don't want to be next to a child. He'll probably play up and spoil our time here.'

Ari looked at the small family group that Felicity didn't like. A young boy—five or six years old—stood at the window, staring down at the wave-shaped Jumeirah Beach Hotel. Seated beside the child on one side was a very handsome woman—marvellous facial bones like Sophia Loren's—dark wavy hair unashamedly going grey, probably the boy's grandmother. On the other side with her back turned to him was another woman, black hair cropped short in a modern style, undoubtedly younger, a slimmer figure, and almost certainly the boy's mother.

'He won't spoil the food or the tea, Felicity, and if you haven't noticed, all the other tables are taken.'

They'd been late arriving, even later because of feeding her camera in the lobby. Having to wait for Felicity to be satisfied with whatever she wanted was testing his temper to an almost intolerable level.

She placed a pleading hand on his arm, her big blue eyes promising a reward if he indulged her. 'But I'm sure if you ask, something better could be arranged.'

'I won't put other people out,' he said, giving her a hard, quelling look. 'Just sit down, Felicity. Enjoy being here.'

She pouted, sighed, flicked her long blonde hair over her shoulder in annoyance, and finally sat.

The waiter poured them champagne, handed them menus, chatted briefly about what was on offer, then quickly left them before Felicity could kick up another fuss which would put him in a difficult position.

'Why do they have all those chairs on the beach set out in rows, Yiayia?'

The boy's voice was high and clear and carried, bringing an instant grimace to Felicity's pouty mouth. Ari recognised the accent as Australian, yet the boy had used the Greek word for grandmother, arousing his curiosity.

'The beach belongs to the hotel, Theo, and the chairs are set out for the guests so they will be comfortable,' the older woman answered, her English thick with a Greek accent.

'They don't do that at Bondi,' the boy remarked.

'No. That's because Bondi is a public beach for anyone to use and set up however they like on the sand.'

The boy turned to her, frowning at the explanation. 'Do you mean I couldn't go to that beach down there, Yiayia?'

He was a fine-looking boy, very pleasing features and fairish hair. Oddly enough he reminded Ari of himself as a child.

'Not unless you were staying in the hotel, Theo,' his grandmother replied.

'Then I think Bondi is better,' the boy said conclusively, turning back to the view.

An egalitarian Australian even at this tender age, Ari thought, remembering his own experiences of the people's attitudes in that country.

Felicity huffed and whined, 'We're going to have to listen to his prattle all afternoon. I don't know why people bring children to places like this. They should be left with nannies.'

'Don't you like children, Felicity?' Ari enquired, hoping she would say no, which would comprehensively wipe out any argument his father might give him over his rejection of this marital candidate.

'In their place,' she snapped back at him.

Out of sight, out of mind, was what she meant.

'I think family is important,' he drawled. 'And I have no objection to any family spending time together, any-where.'

Which shut her up, temporarily.

This was going to be a *long* afternoon.

Tina felt the nape of her neck prickling at the sound of the man's voice coming from the table next to theirs. The deep mellifluous tone was an electric reminder of another voice that had seduced her into believing all the sweet things it had said to her, believing they had meant she was more special than any other woman in the world.

It couldn't be Ari, could it?

She was torn by the temptation to look.

Which was utterly, utterly stupid, letting thoughts of him take over her mind when she should be enjoying this wonderfully decadent afternoon tea.

Ari Zavros was out of her life. Well and truly out of it. Six years ago he'd made the parting from her abso-lutely decisive, no coming back to Australia, no inter-est in some future contact. She had been relegated to *a fond memory,* and she certainly didn't want *the fond memory* revived here and now, if by some rotten coin-cidence it was Ari sitting behind her.

It wouldn't be him, anyway.

The odds against it were astronomical.

All the same, it was better not to look, better to keep her back turned to the man behind her. If it was Ari, if he caught her looking and recognised her…it was a stomach-curdling thought. No way was she prepared for a face-to-face meeting with him, especially not with her mother and Theo looking on, becoming involved.

This couldn't happen.

It wouldn't happen.

Her imagination was making mountains out of no more than a tone of voice. Ridiculous! The man was with a woman. She'd heard the plummy English voice complaining about Theo's presence—a really petty complaint because Theo was always well-behaved. She shouldn't waste any attention on them. Her mind fiercely dictated ignoring the couple and concentrating on the pleasure of being here.

She leaned forward, picked up her cup and sipped the wonderfully fragrant *Jasmin Pearls*. They had already eaten a marvellous slice of Beef Wellington served warm with a beetroot puree. On their table now was a stand shaped like the Burj, its four tiers presenting a yummy selection of food on colourful glass plates.

At the top were small sandwiches made with different types of bread—egg, smoked salmon, cream cheese with sun-dried tomatoes, cucumber and cream cheese. Other tiers offered seafood vol-au-vents with prawns, choux pastry chicken with seeded mustard, a beef sandwich, and basil, tomato and bocconcini cheese on squid ink bread. It was impossible to eat everything. Predictably,

Theo zeroed in on the chicken, her mother anything with cheese, and the seafood she loved was all hers.

A waiter came around with a tray offering replenishments but they shook their heads, knowing there was so much more to taste—fruit cake, scones with and without raisins and an assortment of spreads; strawberry and rose petal jam, clotted cream, a strawberry mousse and tangy passionfruit.

Tina refused to let the reminder of Ari Zavros ruin her appetite. There wasn't much conversation going on at the table behind her anyway. Mostly it was the woman talking, carrying on in a snobby way, comparing this afternoon tea to others she'd had in famous hotels. Only the occasional murmur of reply came from the man.

'I'm so glad we stopped in Dubai,' her mother remarked, gazing at the view. 'There's so much amazing, creative architecture in this city. That hotel shaped like a wave just below us, the stunning buildings we passed on the way here. And to think it's all happened in the space of what…thirty years?'

'Something like that,' Tina murmured.

'It shows what can be done in these modern times.'

'With the money to do it,' Tina dryly reminded her.

'Well, at least they have the money. They're not bankrupting the country like the aristocrats did in Europe for their grand palaces in the old days. And all this has to be a drawcard for tourists, bringing money into the country.'

'True.' Tina smiled. 'I'm glad we came here, too. It certainly is amazing.'

Her mother leaned forward and whispered, 'Seated at the next table is an incredibly handsome man. I think he must be a movie star. Take a look, Tina, and see if you recognise him.'

Her stomach instantly cramped. Ari Zavros was an incredibly handsome man. Her mother nodded encouragingly, expecting her to glance around. Hadn't she already decided it couldn't—wouldn't—be him? One quick look would clear this silly fear. *Just do it. Get it over with.*

One quick look…

The shock of seeing the man she'd never expected to see again hit her so hard she barely found wits enough to give her mother a reply.

'I've never seen him in a movie.'

And thank God the turning of her head towards him hadn't caught his attention!

Ari!—still a beautiful lion of a man with his thick mane of wavy honey-brown hair streaked through with golden strands, silky smooth olive skin, his strongly masculine face softened by a beautifully sculptured full-lipped mouth, and made compelling by thickly lashed amber eyes—eyes that Theo had inherited, and thank God her mother hadn't noticed that likeness!

'Well, he must be *someone,*' her mother said in bemusement. 'One of the beautiful people.'

'Don't keep staring at him, Mama,' Tina hissed, everything within her recoiling from any connection with him.

Her mother was totally unabashed. 'I'm just returning the curiosity. He keeps looking at us.'

Why??? screamed through Tina's mind.

Panicky thoughts followed.

Had the Australian accent reminded him of the three months he'd spent there?

He could not have identified her, not from a back view. Her hair had been long and curly when he'd known her.

Did he see a similarity to himself in Theo?

But surely he wouldn't be making a blood connection to himself personally, unless he was in the habit of leaving love-children around the world.

Tina pulled herself up on that dark thought. He had used condoms with her. It was unlikely he would think his safe sex had ever been unsafe. Whatever had drawn his interest…it presented a very real problem to her.

Since he and his companion had arrived late at this afternoon tea, it was almost inevitable that she and Theo and her mother would leave before them and they would have to pass his table on their way out. If he looked straight at her, face-to-face…

He might not remember her. It had been six years ago. She looked different with her hair short. And he'd surely had many women pass through his life in the meantime. But if he did recognise her and stopped her from making a quick escape, forcing a re-acquaintance, introductions…her mind reeled away from all the painful complications that might follow.

She did not want Ari Zavros directly touching her life again. That decision had been made before her pregnancy had to be revealed to her parents. It would have been unbearable to have him questioning an unwelcome paternity or sharing responsibility for Theo on some dutiful basis—constantly in and out of her life, always making her feel bad for having loved him so blindly.

It had been a wretched business, standing firm

against her father's questioning, refusing to track down a man who didn't want her any more, insisting that her child would be better off without any interference from him. Whether that decision had been right or wrong she had never regretted it.

Even recently when Theo had asked why he didn't have a father like his kindergarten friends, she had felt no guilt at telling him that some children only had mothers and that was the way it was for them. She was convinced that Ari could only be a horribly disruptive influence in their lives if, given the chance, he decided to be in them at all.

She didn't want to give him the chance.

It had taken so much determination and hard work to establish the life she and Theo now had, it was imperative to hold onto the status quo. This terrible trick of fate—putting Ari and herself in the same place at the same time with Theo and her mother present—could mess up their lives so badly.

A confrontation *had* to be avoided.

Tina pushed back the sickening waves of panic and fiercely told herself this shouldn't be too difficult. Ari had company. Surely it would be unreasonable of him to leave his tete-a-tete with one woman to re-connect with another. Besides, he might not recognise her anyway. If he did, if he tried to engage her in some awful memory-lane chat, she had to ensure that her mother had already taken herself and Theo out of this possible scenario.

She could manage that.

She had to.

CHAPTER TWO

THE rest of afternoon tea took on a nightmarish quality for Tina. It was difficult to focus on the delicacies they were served, even more difficult to appreciate the marvellous range of tastes. Her mind was in a hopelessly scattered state. She felt like Alice in Wonderland at the mad hatter's tea party, with the red queen about to pounce and cut off her head.

Her mother demolished the fig tart and green-tea macaroon. Theo gobbled up the white chocolate cake. She forced herself to eat a caramel slice. They were then presented with another plate of wicked temptations: a strawberry dipped in white chocolate and decorated with a gold leaf, a meringue lemon tart, a passionfruit ball with an oozing liquid centre...more, more, more, and she had to pretend to enjoy it all while her stomach was in knots over Ari's presence behind her.

She smiled at Theo. She smiled at her mother. Her face ached with the effort to keep smiling. She silently cursed Ari Zavros for spoiling what should have been a special experience. The fear that he could spoil a lot more kept jogging through her mind. Finally her mother called enough and suggested they return to the grand lobby and take another leisurely look at everything before leaving.

'Yes, I want to see the fish again, Yiayia,' Theo agreed enthusiastically. 'And sit on the camel.'

Tina knew this was the moment when she had to take control. Every nerve in her body twanged at the vital importance of it. She had already planned what to say. It had to come out naturally, sound sensible. She forced her voice to deliver what was needed.

'I think a toilet visit first might be a good idea. Will you take Theo, Mama? I want to get a few photographs from different windows up here. I'll meet you at the elevator.'

'Of course I'll take him. Come, Theo.'

She stood up and took his hand and they went off happily together. Mission accomplished, Tina thought on a huge wave of relief. Now, if she could get past Ari without him taking any notice of her she was home free. If the worst happened and he chose to intercept her departure, she could deal with the situation on her own.

Having slung her travel bag over her shoulder, she picked up her camera, stood at the window, clicked off a few shots of the view, then, with her heart hammering, she turned, meaning to walk as quickly as she could past the danger table.

Ari Zavros was looking straight at her. She saw the jolt of recognition in his face, felt a jolt of shock run right through her, rooting her feet to the floor, leaving her standing like a mesmerised rabbit caught in headlights.

'Christina...' He spoke her name in a tone of pleasurable surprise, rising from his chair, obviously intent on renewing his *fond memory* of her.

No chance of escape from it. Her feet weren't receiving any messages from her brain which was totally jammed with all the misery this man had given her.

He excused himself from his companion who turned in her chair to give Tina a miffed look—long, silky, blonde hair, big blue eyes, peaches and cream complexion, definitely one of the beautiful people. Another *fond memory* for him, or something more serious this time?

It didn't matter. The only thing that mattered was getting this totally unwelcome encounter over and done with. Ari was approaching her, hands outstretched in charming appeal, his mouth tilting in a wry little smile.

'You've cut your beautiful hair,' he said as though that was a wicked shame.

Never mind the shame he'd left her in.

Her tongue leapt into life. 'I like it better short,' she said tersely, hating the reminder of how he'd enjoyed playing with the long curly tresses, winding it around his fingers, stroking it, kissing it, smelling it.

'What are you doing in Dubai?' he asked, his amber eyes twinkling with interest.

'Having a look at it. Why are you here?' she returned.

He shrugged. 'Business.'

'Mixed with pleasure,' she said dryly, with a nod at the blonde. 'Please...don't let me keep you from her, Ari. After all this time, what is there to say?'

'Only that it feels good to see you again. Even with

your cropped hair,' he replied with one of his megawatt smiles which had once melted her knees.

They stiffened in sheer rebellion. How dared he flirt with her when he was obviously connected to another woman? How dared he flirt with her at all when he'd used her up and left her behind him?

And she hated him saying it felt good to see her again when it made her feel so bad. He had no idea of what he'd done to her and she hated him for that, too. She wanted to smack that smile off his face, wanted to smack him down for having the arrogance to even approach her again with his smarmy charm, but the more dignified course, the *safer* course was simply to dismiss him.

'I'm a different person now to the one you knew,' she said oddly. 'If you'll excuse me, I'm with my mother who'll be waiting for me to catch up with her.'

Her feet obeyed the command to side-step, get moving To her intense frustration, Ari shot out a hand, clutching her arm, halting a swift escape from him. She glared at him, resentment burning deep from the touch of his fingers on her skin, from the power he still had to affect her physically. He was so close she could smell the cologne he used. It made her head swim with memories she didn't want to have.

The amber eyes quizzed hers, as though he didn't understand her cutting him off so abruptly. He wanted to know more. Never mind what she wanted.

'Your mother. And the boy...' he said slowly, obviously considering her family group and what it might mean.'You're married now? He is your son?'

Tina seethed. That, of course, would be so nice and neat, dismissing the intimacy they had shared as nothing important in her life, just as it hadn't been important to him.

She should say *yes*, have done with it. Let him think she was married and there was no possible place for him in her life. He would shut the door on his *charming episode* with her and let her go. She would be free of him forever.

Do it, do it! her mind screamed.

But her heart was being ripped apart by a violent tumult of emotions.

Another voice in her head was yelling *smack him with the truth!*

This man was Theo's father. She could not bring herself to palm his fatherhood off on anyone else. *He* ought to be faced with it. A savage recklessness streaked through her, obliterating any caring over what might happen next.

'I'm not married,' she slung at him. 'And yes, Theo is my son.'

He frowned.

Single motherhood did not sit so well with him. She was free but not free, tied to a child.

No ties for Ari Zavros.

That thought enraged Tina further. She fired bitter truth straight at him.

'He's also your son.'

It stunned him.

Totally stunned him.

No seductive smile.

No twinkly interest.

Blank shock.

With a sense of fiercely primitive satisfaction, Tina got her feet moving and strode past him, heading for the elevator where she hoped her mother and Theo would be waiting for her. She didn't think Ari would follow her. Not only had she cut his feet out from under him, but he was with another woman and it was highly unlikely that he'd want to face her with the complication of an illegitimate son.

Though a fast getaway from this hotel was definitely needed. No loitering in the lobby. She'd tell her mother she didn't feel well—too much rich food. It was true enough anyway. Her stomach was churning and she felt like throwing up.

She shouldn't have told Ari he was Theo's father. She hadn't counted on how much he could still get to her—his eyes, his touch, the whole insidious charisma of his close presence. Hopefully telling his wouldn't make any difference. For a start, he wouldn't want to believe her. Men like him usually denied paternity claims. Not that she would ever make any official claim on him. All the same, it had been stupid of her to throw the truth in his face and give herself this panic attack, stupid and reckless to have opened a door for him into her life again when she wanted him out, out, out!

Please, God, let him not follow up on it.

Let him shrug it off as a put-down line.

Let him just go on with his life and leave her alone to go on with hers.

That boy...his son? *His* son?

Ari snapped out of the wave of shock rolling through

his mind, swung on his heel, and stared after the woman who had just declared herself the mother of his child. Christina Savalas wasn't waiting around to capitalise on her claim. Having delivered her bombshell she was fast making an exit from any fall-out.

Was it true?

He quickly calculated precisely *when* he had been in Australia. It was six years ago. The boy's age would approximately fit that time-frame. He needed to know the actual birth date to be sure if it was possible. That could be checked. The name was Theo. Theo Savalas. Who looked very like himself as a child!

A chill ran down Ari's spine. If Theo was his, it meant he had left Christina pregnant, abandoned a pregnant woman, left her to bring up his child alone. But how could that happen when he was always careful to sheath himself against such a consequence? Not once had he ever failed to use protection. Had there been a slip-up with her, one that he didn't remember?

He did remember she'd been an innocent. Unexpectedly and delightfully so. He hadn't felt guilty about taking her virginity. Desire had been mutual and he'd given her pleasure—a good start to her sexual life, which he'd reasoned would become quite active as time went by. Any man would see her as desirable and it was only natural that she would be attracted to some of them.

But if he had left her pregnant... That would have messed up her career, messed up her life—reason enough for those extremely expressive dark eyes of hers to shoot black bolts of hatred and contempt at him with her punishing exit line.

Impossible to ignore what she'd said. He had to check it out. If the boy was his son… Why hadn't Christina told him about his existence before this? Why go it alone all these years? Why hit him with it now? There was a hell of a lot of questions to be considered.

'Ari…'

His teeth automatically gritted. He hated that whiny tone in Felicity's voice.

'What are you standing there for? She's gone.'

Gone but not forgotten.

'I was remembering my time in Australia, which was where I'd met Christina,' he said, forcing himself to return to his chair and be reasonably civil to the woman he had invited to be his companion.

'What were you doing in Australia?'

'Checking out the wine industry there. Seeing if any improvements could be made to the Santorini operation.'

'Was this Christina connected to the wine industry?'

The tone had changed to a snipe.

He shrugged. 'Not really. She was part of an advertising drive for the Jacob's Creek label.'

One eyebrow arched in knowing mockery. 'A model.'

'She was then.'

'And you had fun with her.'

He grimaced at her dig, which he found extremely distasteful in the circumstances. 'Ancient history, Felicity. I was simply surprised to see her here in Dubai.'

'Well, she's loaded down with a child now,' she said with snide satisfaction. 'No fun at all.'

'I can't imagine it is much fun, being a single mother,' he said, barely containing a wave of anger at Felicity's opinion.

'Oh, I don't know. Quite a few movie stars have chosen that route and they seem to revel in it.'

Ari wanted this conversation finished. He heaved a sigh, then mockingly drawled, 'What do I know? I'm a man.'

Felicity laughed, leaned over and stroked his thigh. 'And a gorgeous one, darling. Which is why I don't like you straying, even for a minute.'

The urge to stray to Christina Savalas had been instant.

He'd had his surfeit of self-centred women like Felicity Fullbright and the flash of memory—a sweet, charming time—had compelled him out of his seat. But it wasn't the same Christina he'd known. How could it be, given the passage of years? A different person, she'd said. He would need to get to know her again if she was the mother of his child.

He would track her down in the very near future. Obviously she was on a tourist trip with her mother and would be on the move for a few weeks. Best to wait until she was back on home ground. In the meantime, he had to sever any further involvement with Felicity, attend his cousin's wedding, then free himself up to pursue the big question.

Was Theo Savalas his son?

If the answer was a definitive yes, changes to his life had to be made.

And Christina Savalas would have to come to some accommodation with him, whether she liked it or not.

A father had rights to his child, and Ari had no qualms about enforcing them.

Family was family.

CHAPTER THREE

TINA felt continually tense for the rest of their short stay in Dubai, knowing Ari Zavros was in the same city. Although she didn't think he would pursue the paternity issue, and a second accidental encounter with him was unlikely, she only felt safe on the red tour bus in between its stops at the various points of interest; the gold souks, the spice markets, the shopping centres. It was a huge relief to board their flight to Athens on the third day, not having had any further contact with him.

They were met at the airport by Uncle Dimitri, her father's older brother. After a brief stop to check in at their hotel, he took them on to his restaurant which was sited just below the Acropolis and where all their Greek relatives had gathered to welcome them home. It wasn't home to Tina or Theo, both of whom had been born in Australia, but it was interesting to meet her mother's and father's families and it was a very festive get-together.

Her mother revelled in the company and Theo was a hit—*such a beautiful grandchild*—but Tina couldn't help feeling like an outsider. The women tended to talk about her in the third person, as though she wasn't there at all.

'We must find a husband for your daughter, Helen.'

'Why did she cut her hair? Men like long hair.'

'She is obviously a good mother. That is important.'

'And if she is used to helping in a restaurant...'

Not helping, *managing,* Tina silently corrected, observing how Uncle Dimitri was managing his. He was constantly on watch, signalling waiters to wherever service was required. All the patrons were treated to a plate of sliced watermelon at the end of their meals—on the house—a nice touch for long hot evenings. People left happy, which meant return visits and good word-of-mouth. It was something she could copy at home.

Most of the tables were out on the sidewalk, under trees or umbrellas. Herbs were grown in pots, their aromas adding to the pleasant ambience. The food was relatively simple, the salads very good. She particularly liked the olive oil, honey and balsamic vinegar dressing—a combination she would use in future. It was easy to relax and have a taste of Athens.

There'd been a message from Cassandra at the hotel, saying she and her fiancé would join them at the restaurant, and Tina kept looking for their arrival, eager to meet up with her sister again. Cass had brought George home to Sydney with her six months ago, but had been working a heavy international schedule ever since. They had just flown in from London and were spending one night in Athens before moving on to the island of Patmos where George's family lived.

'Here they come!' her mother cried, seeing them first.

Tina looked.

And froze in horror.

There was her beautiful sister, her face aglow with happy excitement, looking every inch the supermodel she had become.

Hugging her to his side was George Carasso, grinning with pride in his bride-to-be.

Next to him strolled Ari Zavros.

Her mother turned to her. 'Tina, isn't that the man we saw...'

She heard the words but couldn't answer. Bad enough to find herself confronted by him again. It was much, much worse with him knowing about Theo!

People were on their feet, greeting, welcoming, hugging and kissing. Ari was introduced as George's cousin who was to be his best man at the wedding. *His best man!* And she was Cass's only bridesmaid! The nightmare she had made for herself was getting more torturous by the second and there was no end to it any time soon. It was going to be impossible to enjoy her sister's wedding. She would have to suffer through being Ari's partner at the ceremony and the reception.

If she hadn't opened her mouth in Dubai and let her secret out, she might have managed to skate over their past involvement. There was little hope of that now. No hope at all, given the look Ari Zavros had just turned her way, a dangerously simmering challenge in the riveting amber eyes.

'And this is your sister?' he prompted Cass, who immediately obliged with the formal introduction.

'Yes. Tina! Oh, it's so good to see you again!' she bubbled, dodging around the table to give her a hug. 'George and I are staying in Ari's apartment tonight and when we told him we were meeting up with you, he insisted on coming with us so you won't be strangers to each other at the wedding.'

Strangers!

He hadn't let the cat out of the bag.

Tina fiercely hoped it suited him not to.

Cass swooped on Theo, lifting him up in her arms and turning to show him off to Ari. 'And this is my nephew, Theo, who is going to be our page boy.'

Ari smiled at him. 'Your Aunty Cassandra told me it's your birthday this week.'

He'd been checking, Tina thought grimly.

Theo held up his hand with fingers and thumb spread. 'Five,' he announced proudly.

'It's my birthday this month, too,' Ari said. 'That makes us both Leos.'

'No. I'm Theo, not Leo.'

Everyone laughed at the correction.

'He didn't mean to get your name wrong, darling,' Cass explained. 'We're all born under star signs and the star sign for your birthday is Leo. Which means a lion. And you have amber eyes, just like a lion.'

Theo pointed to Ari. 'He's got the same colour eyes as me.'

Tina held her breath. Her heart was drumming in her ears. Her mind was screaming *please, please, please don't claim parentage now.* It was the wrong place, the wrong time, the wrong everything!

'There you are, then,' Ari said with an air of indulgence, taking Theo's outstretched hand and giving it a light shake. 'Both of us are lions and I'm very glad to meet you.' He turned to Tina. 'And your mother.'

Relief reduced her to jelly inside. He wasn't pushing his fatherhood yet. Maybe he never would. She should be saying *hello,* but she was so choked up with nervous tension it was impossible to get her voice to work.

'Tina?' He gave her a slightly quizzical smile as he offered his hand to her. 'Short for Christina?'

'Yes.' It was a husky whisper, all she could manage.

Then she was forced by the occasion to let his strong fingers close around hers. The jolting sensation of electric warmth was a searing reminder of the sexual chemistry that had seduced her in the past. It instantly stirred a fierce rebellion in her mind. No way was she going to let it get to her again, making her weak and foolish. If there was to be a fight over custody of Theo, she couldn't let Ari Zavros have any personal power over her. She wriggled her hand out of his as fast as she could.

Seating was quickly re-arranged so that Cass and George could sit beside her mother. Uncle Dimitri produced an extra chair for Ari at the end of the table, right next to her and Theo. It was impossible for Tina to protest this proximity, given they would be partners at the wedding and apparently Ari had already stated his intention to *make her acquaintance.*

The situation demanded polite conversation. Any

failure to follow that course would raise questions about her behaviour. As much as Tina hated having to do it, she adopted the pretence of being strangers, forcing herself to speak to George's *best* man with an air of natural enquiry.

'When did you meet my sister?'

It was a good question. She needed information and needed it fast to help her deal with Ari in the most sensible way. If it was possible to avoid a showdown with him over Theo, grasping that possibility was paramount.

'Only this evening,' he answered with a wry little smile. 'I knew of her, of course, because of her engagement to George, but within the family she was always referred to as simply Cassandra since she is famously known by that name in the supermodel world. I'd never actually heard her surname. I chanced to see it written on her luggage when she set it down in the apartment. Very opportune, given the circumstances.'

The fact that he'd immediately seized the opportunity for a face-to-face meeting with her gave no support to the wishful thought of avoiding an ultimate showdown.

'So you proceeded to draw her out about her family,' Tina said flatly, feeling as though a trap was closing around her.

'Very enlightening,' he drawled, his eyes mocking the secrecy which was no longer a secret to him.

Fear squeezed her heart. Sheer self-defence demanded she ignore his enlightenment. 'You live in Athens?'

'Not really. The apartment is for convenience. Anyone in the family can use it, which is why George felt free to bring Cassandra there for tonight. More private for her than a hotel.'

'Very considerate of him,' she dryly remarked. 'Where do you normally live then?'

All she'd previously known about him was he belonged to a wealthy Greek family with an involvement in the wine industry. During the time they'd spent together, Ari had been more interested in everything Australian than talking about himself.

He shrugged. 'Various business interests require quite a bit of travelling but my family home is on Santorini.'

'We're going to Santorini,' Theo piped up, looked at Ari as though he was fascinated by the man.

Ari smiled at him. 'Yes, I know. Perhaps we could do something special together on your birthday.'

Tina's stomach contracted. He was intent on moving in on her, getting closer to their son.

'Like what?' Theo asked eagerly.

'Let's wait and see what we might like to do, Theo,' Tina cut in firmly, inwardly panicking at spending any more time than she absolutely had to with Ari Zavros. She didn't know if it was curiosity driving him or he was dabbling with the idea of claiming Theo as his flesh and blood. She turned hard, quelling eyes to him. 'You said *family home*. Does that mean you're married with children?'

He shook his head and made an ironic grimace. 'Much to my father's vexation, I am still single. It's his home I was referring to.'

'Not exactly single, Ari,' she tersely reminded him.

He knew she'd seen him with a woman in Dubai. She didn't have to spell that out. If he thought he could start playing fast and loose with her again, cheating on the beautiful blonde, he was on an ego trip she would take great satisfaction in smashing.

'I assure you I am, Christina,' he replied without the blink of an eyelid.

Her teeth gnashed over the lilted use of her full name—a reminder of intimate moments that were long gone. She raked his steady gaze with blistering scepticism. The amber eyes burned straight back at her, denying the slightest shift in what he had just declared.

'Another *charming episode* over?' she sliced at him.

He frowned, probably having forgotten how he had described his relationship with her. Whether he recollected it or not, he shot her a look that was loaded with determined purpose. 'Not so charming. In fact, it convinced me I should free myself up to look for something else.'

His gaze moved to Theo, softening as he said, 'Perhaps I should become a father.'

Tina's spine crawled with apprehension. This was the last thing she wanted. The very last! Somehow she had to fight him, convince him that fatherhood would not suit him at all.

'I don't have a father,' Theo gravely informed him. 'I had a grandfather but he got sick and went to heaven.'

'I'm sorry to hear that,' Ari said sympathetically.

'I think people should be aware there's a very real and lasting responsibility about becoming a parent,'

Tina quickly stated, hoping to ward off any impulsive act that would end up badly.

'I agree with you,' Ari said blandly.

'Fly-by-night people shouldn't even consider it,' she persisted, desperately determined on pricking his conscience.

'What are fly-by-night people, Mama?' Theo asked curiously.

Ari leaned forward to answer him. 'They're people who come and go without staying around long enough to really be an important part of your life. They don't stick by you like your mother does. And your grandmother. And your friends. Do you have some friends, Theo?'

'I have lots of friends,' Theo boasted.

'Then I think you must be a happy boy.'

'Very happy,' Tina cut in, giving Ari a look that clearly telegraphed *without you*.

'Then you must be a very special mother, Christina,' he said in his soft, seductive voice. 'It could not have been easy for you, bringing him up alone.'

She bridled at the compliment. 'I wasn't alone. My parents supported me.'

'Family,' he murmured, nodding approvingly. 'So important. One should never turn one's back on family.'

The glittering challenge in his eyes spurred her into leaning over to privately mutter, 'You turned your back first, Ari.'

'I never have to any blood relative I knew about,' he shot back, leaning towards her and keeping his voice low enough for Theo not to hear his words. 'We can do this the easy way or the hard way, Christina.'

'Do what?'

'Fighting over him is not in our son's best interests.'

'Then don't fight. Let him be.'

'You expect me to ignore his existence?'

'Why not? You've ignored mine.'

'A mistake. Which I will correct.'

'Some mistakes can never be corrected.'

'We shall see.'

The fight was on!

No avoiding it.

The rush of blood to her head as she'd tried to argue him out of it drained away, leaving her dizzy and devastated by his resolute counter to everything she'd said.

He straightened up and smiled at Theo who was tucking into a slice of watermelon. 'Good?' he asked.

Theo nodded, his mouth too full to speak but his eyes twinkling a smile back at Ari. Tina seethed over his charming manner to her son. He'd been so very charming to her once. It meant *nothing!* But it was impossible to explain that to a five-year-old boy.

Ari turned his attention back to her. 'Cassandra told me you now manage a restaurant at Bondi Beach.'

'Yes. It was my father's. He trained me to take over when…when he could no longer do it himself.' Another bad time in her life but she had coped. The restaurant was still thriving.

'That surely means working long hours. It must be difficult, being a mother, too.'

She glared at him, fiercely resenting the suggestion

she might be neglecting her son. 'We live in an apartment above the restaurant. Theo attends a pre-school, which he loves, during the day. He can be with me or my mother at all other times. And the beach is his playground, which he also loves. As you remarked, he is a happy boy.'

And he doesn't need you. For anything.

'Mama and I build great sandcastles,' Theo informed him.

'There are lots of beaches on the Greek islands,' Ari said.

'Can anyone go on them?' Theo asked.

'There are public beaches which are for everyone.'

'Do they have chairs in rows like we saw in Dubai?'

'The private beaches do.'

'I don't like that.'

'There's one below where I live on Santorini that doesn't have chairs. You could build great sand-castles there.'

'Would you help me?'

Ari laughed, delighted he had won Theo over.

'I don't think we'll have time for that,' Tina said quickly.

'Nonsense!' Ari grinned triumphantly at her. 'Cassandra told me you're spending five days on Santorini, and Theo's birthday is two days before the wedding. It would be my pleasure to give Theo a wonderful time—a trip on the cable-car, a ride on a donkey...'

'A donkey!' Theo cried excitedly.

'...a boat-ride to the volcanic island...'

'A boat-ride!' Theo's eyes were as big as saucers.

'...and a trip to a beach where we can build the biggest sandcastle ever!'

'Can we, Mama? Can we?'

His voice was so high-pitched with excitement, it drew her mother's attention. 'Can you what, Theo?' she asked indulgently.

'Ride a donkey and go on a boat, Yiayia. For my birthday!'

'I said I would take him,' Ari swiftly slid in. 'Give him a birthday on Santorini he will always remember.'

'How kind of you!' Her mother beamed at him—the man gorgeous enough to be a movie star, giving his time to make her grandson's stay on Santorini so pleasurable!

The trap was shut. No way out. With both her mother and Theo onside with Ari, Tina knew she would just have to grit her teeth and go along with him. Being a spoilsport would necessitate explanations she didn't want to give. Not at this point. He might force her to make them in the very near future but she would keep it a private issue between them as long as she could.

Cass didn't deserve to have her wedding overshadowed by a situation that should never have arisen. With that one crazy urge to slap Ari with the truth in Dubai... but the damage was done and somehow Tina had to contain it. At least until after the wedding.

With the whole family's attention drawn to them, she forced herself to smile at Ari. 'Yes, very kind.'

'Cassandra mentioned you'll be staying at the El Greco resort,' he said, arrogantly confident of her agreement to the plan. 'I'll contact you there, make arrangements.'

'Fine! Thank you.'

With that settled, conversation picked up around the table again and Theo plied Ari with questions about Santorini, which were answered with obvious good humour.

Tina didn't have to say anything. She sat in brooding silence, hating Ari Zavros for his facile charm, hating herself for being such a stupid blabbermouth, gearing herself up to tolerate what had to be tolerated and savagely vowing that Ari would not get everything his own way.

Eventually Cass and George excused themselves from the party, saying they needed to catch up on some sleep. To Tina's huge relief, Ari stood up to take his leave, as well. She rose from her chair as he offered his hand which she had to be civil enough to take in front of company.

He actually had the gall to enclose her hand with both of his with a show of enthusiastic pleasure. 'Thank you for trusting me with Theo's birthday, Christina.'

'Oh, I'm sure I can trust you to give the best of yourself, Ari,' she answered sweetly, before softly adding with a touch of acid mockery, 'For a limited time.'

Which told him straight out how very little she trusted him.

He might have won Theo over—for a day—but he'd won nothing from her.

'We shall see,' he repeated with that same arrogant confidence.

General goodnights were exchanged and finally he was gone.

But he'd left his presence behind with her mother raving on about him and Theo equally delighted with the nice man.

No relief from the trap.

Tina had the wretched feeling there never would be.

CHAPTER FOUR

MAXIMUS Zavros sat under the vine-covered pergola at one end of the vast patio which overlooked the Aegean Sea. It was where he habitually had breakfast and where he expected his son to join him whenever Ari was home. Today was no exception. However he was taking no pleasure in his surroundings and none in his son, which was obvious from the dark glower of disapproval he directed at Ari the moment he emerged from the house.

'So, you come home without a woman to marry again!' He folded the newspaper he'd been reading and smacked it down on the table in exasperation. 'Your cousin, George, is two years younger than you. He does not have your engaging looks. He does not have your wealth. Yet he can win himself a wife who will grace the rest of his life.' He threw out a gesture of frustration. 'What is the problem with you?'

'Maybe I missed a boat I should have taken,' Ari tossed at his father as he pulled out a chair and sat down, facing him across the table.

'What is that supposed to mean?'

Ari poured himself a glass of orange juice. This was

going to be a long conversation and his throat was already dry. He took a long sip, then answered, 'It means I've met the woman I must marry but I let her go six years ago and somehow I have to win her again. Which is going to prove difficult because she's very hostile to me.'

'Hostile? Why hostile? You were taught to have more finesse than to leave any woman hostile. And why *must* you marry her? To saddle yourself with a sourpuss will not generate a happy life. I credited you with more good sense than that, Ari.'

'I left her pregnant. Unknowingly, I assure you. She gave birth to a son who is now five years old.'

'A son! A grandson!' The tirade was instantly diverted. His father ruminated over this totally unanticipated piece of news for several minutes before speaking again. 'You're sure he is yours?'

'No doubt. The boy not only has a strong resemblance to me but the birth date places the conception during the time I was with Christina.'

'Who is this Christina? Is it possible she could have been with another man?'

Ari shook his head. 'I can't even entertain that as a possibility. We were too intimately involved at the time. And she was a virgin, Papa. I met her when I was in Australia. She was at the start of a promising modelling career…young, beautiful, utterly captivating. When I concluded my business there I said goodbye to her. I had no plans for marriage at that point in my life and I thought her too young to be considering it, either. I thought her life was just starting to open up for her.'

'Australia...' His father frowned. 'How did you meet again? You haven't been back there.'

'George's wife-to-be, Cassandra...when they stayed overnight in the apartment at Athens, I discovered that she was Christina's sister. Christina is to be brides-maid at the wedding and her son, Theo—*my* son—is to be page boy. They were already in Athens en route to Santorini and I went to a family party to meet them.'

'Is it known to the family that you are the father?'

'No. They were obviously in ignorance of my in-volvement. But I cannot ignore it, Papa. Christina wants me to. She is appalled to find herself caught up in a sit-uation with me again.'

'She wants to keep the boy to herself.'

'Yes.'

'So... her mind-set against you has to be changed.'

It was a relief that his father had made a straight leap to this conclusion, although it had been fairly predict-able he would arrive at it, given the pull of a grandson.

'I intend to make a start on that tomorrow. It's Theo's fifth birthday and I managed to manipulate an agree-ment for the two of them to spend it with me.'

'She was not a willing party?'

'I made it unreasonable for her to refuse. The fact that she doesn't want to reveal to her family that I'm Theo's father gives me a lever into her life. At least until after the wedding. I suspect she doesn't want to take any focus off her sister at this time.'

'Caring for her family... I like that. Will she make you a good wife, Ari?'

He made an ironic grimace. 'At least she likes children which cannot be said for Felicity Fullbright. I still find Christina very attractive. What can I say, Papa? I've made my bed and I shall lie in it. When you meet the boy you'll know why.'

'When do they arrive on Santorini?'

'Today.'

'Staying where?'

'The El Greco resort.'

'I shall call the management personally. All expenses for their stay will be paid by me. Fresh fruit and flowers in their rooms. A selection of our best Santorini wines. Everything compliments of the Zavros family. They need to be acquainted with our wealth and power. It tends to bend people's minds in a positive manner.'

Ari kept his own counsel on this point. His father could be right. Generosity might have a benign influence. However, he was well enough acquainted with the Australian character to know they had a habit of cutting down tall poppies. However high people rose on their various totem poles, it did not make them better than anyone else. Apart from which, Christina had already demonstrated a strong independence. He doubted she could be bought.

'The mother might be favourably impressed,' he commented. 'Her name is Helen and she is a widow. It might help if you and Mama pay her some kind attention at the wedding.'

His father nodded. 'Naturally we will do so. As a grandparent she should be sympathetic to those who wish to be. I will make my feelings on the subject known.'

'She is Greek. So was her husband. The two daughters were born and brought up in Australia, but she
would be familiar with the old ways…arranged mar-
riages between families. If she understands it could be
best for Christina and Theo to have the support and security our family can give them…'

'Leave it to me. I shall win over the mother. You win
over the daughter and your son. It is intolerable that we
be left out of the boy's life.'

That was the crux of it, Ari thought.

Whatever had to be done he would do to be a proper
father to his son.

Ten hours was a long ferry ride from Athens to
Santorini. Theo was fascinated by the wake of the boat
so Tina spent most of the time on the outer rear deck
with him while her mother relaxed inside with a book.
They passed many islands, most of them looking quite
barren and unattractive, and to Tina's mind, not the
least bit alluring like the tropical islands back home.
It was disappointing. She had expected more magic.
However, these islands were obviously not the main
tourist drawcards like Mykonos, Paros, Naxos, and most
especially Santorini.

When the ferry finally entered the harbour of their
destination, she easily understood the stunning attraction of the landscape created from the volcanic eruption that had devastated ancient civilisations. The water
in what had been the crater was a gorgeous blue, the
semicircle of high cliffs was dramatic, and perched on

top of them the classic white Greek island townships glistened in the late afternoon sunshine.

She wished Ari Zavros did not live on this island. She had looked forward to enjoying it, wanted to enjoy it, and decided she would do so in spite of him. If he had any decency at all, he would let the paternity issue drop, realizing he didn't fit into the life she'd made for herself and Theo, and they were not about to fit into his with his obvious bent for a continual stream of *charming episodes*.

Transport was waiting for them at the ferry terminal. Theo was agog with how the mini-bus would negotiate the amazing zig-zag road which would take them from the bottom of the cliff to the top. As it turned out, the trip was not really hair-raising and the view from the bus-window was beautiful.

The El Greco resort faced the other side of the island, built in terraces down the hillside with rooms built around the swimming pools on each terrace. The buildings were all painted blue and white and the gardens looked very tropical with masses of colourful bougainvillea and hibiscus trees. The reception area was cool and spacious, elegantly furnished and with a view of the sea at the far end. A very attractive place, Tina thought. A place to relax. Except relaxation switched instantly to tension when they started to check in at the reception desk.

'Ah, Mrs Savalas, just a minute please!' the receptionist said quickly, beaming a rather unctuous smile at them. 'I must inform the manager of your arrival.' He ducked away to call through a doorway, 'The Savalas party has arrived.'

A suited man emerged from a back office, beaming a similar smile at them as he approached the desk.

'Is there a problem with our booking?' her mother asked anxiously.

'Not at all, Mrs Savalas. We have put you in rooms on the first terrace which is most convenient to the restaurant and the pool snack-bar. If there is anything that would make you more comfortable, you have only to ask and it will be done.'

'Well, that's very hospitable,' her mother said with an air of relief.

'I have had instructions from Mr Zavros to make you most welcome, Mrs Savalas. I understand you are here for a family wedding.'

'Yes, but...' She threw a puzzled look at Tina whose fists had instinctively clenched at the name that spelled danger all over this situation. 'It's very kind of Ari Zavros to...'

'No, no, it is Maximus Zavros who has given the orders,' the manager corrected her. 'It is his nephew marrying your daughter. Family is family and you are not to pay for anything during your stay at El Greco. All is to be charged to him, so put away your credit card, Mrs Savalas. You will not need it here.'

Her mother shook her head in stunned disbelief. 'I haven't even met this Maximus Zavros.'

It did not concern the manager one bit. 'No doubt you will at the wedding, Mrs Savalas.'

'I'm not sure I should accept this…this arrangement.'

'Oh, but you must!' The manager looked horrified at the thought of refusal. 'Mr Zavros is a very wealthy, powerful man. He owns much of the real estate on Santorini. He would be offended if you did not accept his hospitality and I would be at fault if I did not persuade you to do so. Please, Mrs Savalas… I beg you to enjoy. It is what he wishes.'

'Well…' Her mother looked confused and undecided until a helpful thought struck. She shot Tina a determined look. 'We can talk to Ari about this tomorrow.'

Tina nodded, struggling with the death of any hope that Ari might disappear from her life again. She couldn't believe this was simply a case of a rich powerful Greek extending hospitality. The words—*family is family*—had been like a punch in the stomach. She couldn't dismiss the sickening suspicion that Ari had blabbed to his father. It was the only thing that made sense of this extraordinary move.

'Let me show you to your rooms. A porter will bring your luggage.' The manager bustled out from behind the reception desk. 'I want to assure myself that all is as it should be for you.'

Their adjoining rooms were charming, each one with a walled outside area containing a table and chairs for enjoying the ambience of the resort. Complimentary platters of fresh fruit and a selection of wines were provided. The gorgeous floral arrangements were obvious extras, too. Her mother was delighted with everything. Tina viewed it all with jaundiced eyes and Theo was only interested in how soon he could get into the children's swimming pool.

Their luggage arrived. Tina left her mother in the room Cassandra would share with her the night before the wedding and took Theo into theirs. Within a few minutes she had found their swimsuits in her big suitcase, and feeling driven to get out of the Zavros-permeated room, she and Theo quickly changed their clothes and headed for the water.

She sat on the edge of the shallow pool while Theo dashed in and splashed around, full of happy laughter. Her mind was dark with a terrible sense of foreboding and it was difficult to force an occasional smile at her son. Ari's son. Maximus Zavros's grandson.

Did they intend to make an official claim on him?

People like them probably didn't care how much they disrupted others' lives. If something was desired, for whatever reason, they went after it. And got it. Like the rooms in this resort. Almost anything could be manipulated with wealth.

She couldn't help feeling afraid of the future. She was on this island—their island—for the next five days and it would be impossible to avoid meeting Ari's family at the wedding. Ironically, throwing his fatherhood in his face in Dubai was no longer such a hideous mistake. He would have figured it out at the wedding. There would have been no escape from his knowing. She'd been on a collision course with Ari Zavros from the moment Cassandra had agreed to marry his cousin.

The big question was…how to deal with him?

Should she tell her mother the truth now?

Her head ached from all the possible outcomes of revealing her secret before she absolutely had to. Better to wait, she decided, at least until after she'd spent tomorrow with Ari. Then she would have a better idea of what he intended where Theo was concerned and what she could or couldn't do about it.

Tomorrow... Theo's fifth birthday.

His first with his father.

Tina knew she was going to hate every minute of it.

CHAPTER FIVE

TINA and Theo were about to accompany her mother to breakfast in the nearby restaurant when a call from Ari came through to her room. She quickly pressed her mother to go ahead with Theo while she talked to *the nice man* about plans for the day. As soon as they were out of earshot she flew into attack mode, determined on knowing what she had to handle.

'You've told your father about Theo, haven't you?' she cried accusingly.

'Yes, I have,' he answered calmly. 'He had the right to know, just as I had the right to know. Which you denied me for the past five years, Christina.'

'You made it clear that you were finished with me, Ari.'

'You could have found me. My family is not unknown. A simple search on the Internet...'

'Oh, sure! I can just imagine how much you would have welcomed a cast-off woman running after you. Any contact from me via computer and you would have pressed the delete button.'

'Not if you'd told me you were pregnant.'

'Would you have believed me?' she challenged.

His hesitation gave her instant justification for keeping him in ignorance.

'I thought I had taken care of contraception, Christina,' he said, trying to justify himself. 'I would certainly have checked. However, we now have a different situation—a connection that demands continuation. It's best that you start getting used to that concept because I won't be cut out of my son's life any longer.'

The edge of hard ruthlessness in his tone told her without a doubt that he was intent on making a legal claim. A down to the wire fight over Theo was inevitable. What she needed to do now was buy time. Quelling the threatening rise of panic, she tried bargaining with him.

'You said in Athens we could do this the easy way or the hard way, Ari.'

'Yes. I meant it. Is there something you'd like to suggest?'

'You messed up my life once and I guess nothing is going to stop you from messing it up again. But please...don't make a mess of my sister's day in the sun as a bride. That would be absolutely rotten and selfish, which is typical of your behaviour, but... I'll make it easy for you to get to know your son over the next few days if you hold back on telling everyone else you're his father until after the wedding.'

The silence that followed her offer was nerve-wracking. Tina gritted her teeth and laid out *the hard way*. 'I'll fight you on every front if you don't agree, Ari.'

'When was I ever rotten or selfish to you in our relationship?' he demanded curtly, sounding as though his self-image was badly dented.

'You made me believe what wasn't true... for your own ends,' she stated bitingly. 'And may God damn you to hell if you do that to Theo.'

'Enough! I agree to your deal. I shall meet you at the resort in one hour. We will spend the day happily together for our son's pleasure.'

He cut the connection before Tina could say another word. Her hand was shaking as she returned the telephone receiver to its cradle. At least Cass's wedding wouldn't be spoiled, she told herself. As for the rest... the only thing she could do was deal with one day at a time.

It took Ari the full hour to get his head around Christina's offensive reading of his character. Anger and resentment kept boiling through him. He wasn't used to being so riled by any situation with a woman. It was because of Theo, he reasoned. It was only natural that his emotions were engaged where his son was concerned.

As for Christina, her hostility towards him was totally unreasonable. He remembered romancing her beautifully, showering her with gifts, saying all the sweet words that women liked to hear, wining and dining her, not stinting on anything that could give her pleasure. No one could have been a better first lover for her.

Was it his fault that the contraception he'd used had somehow failed to protect her from falling pregnant?

He had never, *never* intended to mess up her life. He would have dealt honourably with the situation had he known about it. She could have been living in luxury all these years, enjoying being part of a family unit instead of struggling along with single parenthood.

That was her decision, not his. She hadn't allowed him a decision. If there was any condemnation of character to be handed out on all of this, it should be placed at her door. It was *selfish* and *rotten* of her to have denied him the joys of fatherhood.

Yet…there was nothing selfish about not wanting anything to spoil her sister's wedding.

And he could not recall her ever making some selfish demand on him during the time they'd spent together. Not like Felicity Fullbright. Very, very different to Felicity Fullbright. A delight to be with in every sense.

Gradually he calmed down enough to give consideration to her most condemning words… *You made me believe what wasn't true…for your own ends.*

What had he made her believe?

The answer was glaringly simple when he thought about it. She'd been very young, inexperienced, and quite possibly she'd interpreted his whole seduction routine as genuine love for her. Which meant she'd been deeply hurt when he'd left her. So hurt, she probably couldn't bear to tell him about her pregnancy, couldn't bear to be faced with his presence again.

And she thought he might hurt Theo in the same way—apparently loving him, then leaving him.

He had to change her perception of him, make her

understand he would never abandon his child. He had to show her that Theo would be welcomed into his family and genuinely loved. As for winning her over to being his wife...trying to charm her into marrying him wasn't likely to work. Those blazing dark eyes of hers would shoot down every move he made in that direction. So what would work?

She had just offered him a deal.

Why not offer her one?

Make it a deal too attractive to refuse.

Ari worked on that idea as he drove to the El Greco resort.

'He looks just like a Greek God,' her mother remarked admiringly as Ari Zavros strode across the terrace to where they were still sitting in the open-air section of the restaurant, enjoying a last cup of coffee after breakfast.

Tina's stomach instantly cramped. She had thought that once—the golden Greek with his sun-streaked hair and sparkling amber eyes and skin that shone like bronze. And, of course, it was still true. The white shorts and sports shirt he wore this morning made him look even more striking, showing off his athletic physique, the masculine strength in his arms and legs, the broad manly chest. The man was totally charismatic.

This time, however, Tina wasn't about to melt at his feet. 'Bearing gifts, as well,' she said ironically, eyeing the package he was carrying under his arm.

'For me?' Theo cried excitedly.

Ari heard him, beaming a wide grin at his son as he

arrived at their table and presented him with the large package. 'Yes, for you. Happy birthday, Theo.'

'Can I open it?' Theo asked, eagerly eyeing the wrapping paper.

'You should thank Ari first,' Tina prompted.

'Thank you very much,' he obeyed enthusiastically.

Ari laughed. 'Go right ahead. Something for you to build when you have nothing else to do.'

It was a Lego train station, much to Theo's delight.

'He loves Lego,' her mother remarked, finding even more favour with the Greek God.

'I thought he would,' Ari answered. 'My nephews do. Their rooms are full of it.'

'Talking of family,' her mother quickly slid in. 'Your father has apparently insisted on paying for all our accommodation here and...'

'It is his pleasure to do so, Mrs Savalas,' Ari broke in with a smile to wipe out her concern. 'If you were staying on Patmos, George's family would see to it. Here, on Santorini, my father is your host and he has asked me to extend an invitation to all of you for dinner tonight at our family home. Then we will not be strangers at the wedding.'

Her mother instantly melted. 'Oh! How kind!'

Tina glared at Ari. Had he lied about keeping the deal? And what of his parents? Had he warned them not to reveal their relationship to Theo? He was pursuing his own agenda and she wasn't at all sure he would respect hers. Far from melting at his *kindness,* every nerve in her body stiffened with battle tension.

Ari kept smiling. 'I've told my mother it's your birthday, Theo. She's planning a special cake with five candles for you to blow out and make a wish. You've got all day to think about what to wish for.'

All day to worm his way into Theo's heart with his facile charm, Tina thought grimly. She knew only too well he could be *Mr Wonderful* for a while. It was the long haul that worried her—how *constant* Ari would be as a father.

'Are you coming with us today, Mrs Savalas?' he asked, apparently happy to have her mother's company, as well, probably wanting the opportunity to get her even more onside with him.

'No, no. It sounds too busy for me. I shall stroll into the township in my own time, take a look at the church where the wedding is to be held, do a little shopping, visit the museum.' She smiled at Tina, her eyes full of encouraging speculation. 'Much better for you young people to go off together.'

Tina barely stopped herself from rolling her own eyes at what was obviously some romantic delusion. Gorgeous man—unmarried daughter—Greek island in the sun.

'I shall look forward to the family dinner tonight,' her mother added, giving whole-hearted approval to Ari's plans for the whole day.

Tina smothered a groan.

No escape.

She had agreed to letting him into their lives in return for his silence until after the wedding, but if he or his parents let the cat out of the bag tonight, she would bite their heads off for putting their self-interest ahead of everything else.

After a brief return to their room to put the Lego gift on Theo's bed, refresh themselves, and collect hats and swimming costumes, they re-met Ari and set off for the five-minute walk into the main township of Fira. Tina deliberately placed Theo between them. He held her hand, and unknowingly, his father's. She wondered how she was going to explain this truth to him—another nail in her heart.

'Are your parents aware of our deal?' she asked Ari over Theo's head.

'They will be in good time,' he assured her.

She had to believe him…until his assurance proved false, like the words he had spoken to her in the past. Would he play fair with her this time? She could only hope so. This wasn't about him. Or her. It was about the life of their child.

The view from the path into town was spectacular, overlooking the fantastic sea-filled crater with its towering cliffs. Two splendid white cruise ships stood in the middle of the glittering blue harbour and Theo pointed to them excitedly.

'Are we going to ride in one of those boats?'

'No, they're far too big to move close to land,' Ari answered. 'See the smaller boats going out to them? They're to take the people off and bring them to the island. We'll be riding in a motor-launch that can take us wherever we want to go. You can even steer it for a while if you like.'

Theo was agog. 'Can I? Can I really?'

Ari laughed. 'You can sit on my lap and be the captain. I'll show you what to do.'

'Did you hear that, Mama? I'll be captain of the boat.'

'Your boat, Ari?' Tina asked, anxiously wondering what other goodies he had up his sleeve, ready to roll out for Theo's pleasure.

'A family boat. It will be waiting for us at the town wharf.'

His family. His very wealthy family. How could she stop the seduction of her son by these people? He was a total innocent, as she had been before meeting Ari. He was bound to be deeply impressed by them and the outcome might be a terrible tug-of-war for his love.

Tina suffered major heartburn as they strolled on into town. It was so easy for Ari to win Theo over. It had been easy for him to win her over. He had everything going for him. Even now, knowing how treacherous it was, she still had to fight the pull of his attraction. After him, no other man had interested her, not once in the years since he had left her behind. While he, no doubt, had had his pick of any number of beautiful women who had sparked his interest. Like the blonde in Dubai and probably dozens of others.

It was all terribly wrong. He had been the only man in her life and she'd meant nothing to him. She only meant something to him now because she was the mother of his child and he had to deal with her.

On the road up to the beautiful white church dominating the hillside, a statue of a donkey stood outside a tourist shop displaying many stands of postcards. The donkey was painted pink and it had a slot for letters in its mid-section. Over the slot was painted a red heart with the words POST OF LOVE printed on it.

'I didn't get to sit on the camel, Mama. Can I sit on this donkey?' Theo pleaded.

'You'll be sitting on a real donkey soon. Won't that be better?' Tina cajoled, mentally shying from anything connected with *love*.

Theo shook his head. 'It won't be pink. I'd like a photo of me on this one.'

'Then we must do it for the birthday boy,' Ari said, hoisting Theo up on the donkey and standing beside him to ensure he sat on it safely.

They both grinned at her, so much a picture of father and son it tore at Tina's heart as she viewed it through the camera and took the requested shot.

'Now if you'll stand by Theo, I'll take one of the two of you together,' Ari quickly suggested.

'Yes! Come on, Mama!' Theo backed him up.

She handed Ari her camera and swapped places with him.

'Smile!' he commanded.

She put a smile on her face. As soon as he'd used her camera he whipped a mobile phone out of his shirt pocket and clicked off another shot of them. To show his parents, Tina instantly thought. *This is the woman who is Theo's mother and this is your grandson*. It would probably answer some fleeting curiosity about her, but they would zero straight in on Theo, seeing Ari in him—a Zavros, not a Savalas.

'You have a beautiful smile, Christina,' Ari said

warmly as he returned her camera and lifted Theo off the donkey.

'Stop it!' she muttered, glaring a hostile rejection at him. She couldn't bear him buttering her up when he probably had some killing blow in mind to gain custody of his son.

He returned a puzzled frown. 'Stop what?'

Theo was distracted by a basket of soft toys set out beside the postcard stands, giving her space enough to warn Ari off the totally unwelcome sweet-talking.

'I don't want any more of your compliments.'

His gesture denied any harm in them. 'I was only speaking the truth.'

'They remind me of what a fool I was with you. I won't be fooled again, Ari.'

He grimaced. 'I'm sorry you read more into our previous relationship than was meant, Christina.'

'Oh! What exactly did you mean when you said I was special?' she sliced back at him, her eyes flashing outright scepticism.

He gave her a look that sent a wave of heat through her, right down to her toes. 'You were special. Very special. I just wasn't ready to take on a long-term relationship at the time. But I am now. I want to marry you, Christina.'

Her heart stopped. She stared at him in total shock. No way had she expected this. It was Theo, her stunned mind started to reason. Ari thought it was the best way—the easiest way—to get Theo. Who *she* was, and what *she* wanted was irrelevant.

'Forget it!' she said tersely. 'I'm not about to change my life for your convenience.'

'I could make it convenient for you, too,' he quickly countered.

Her eyes mocked his assertion. 'How do you figure that?'

'A life of ease. No fighting over Theo. We bring him up together. You'll have ample opportunity to do whatever you want within reason.'

'Marriage to you is no guarantee of that. You can dangle as many carrots as you like in front of me, Ari. I'm not biting.'

'What if I give you a guarantee? I'll have a prenuptial agreement drawn up that would assure you and Theo of financial security for the rest of your lives.' His mouth took on an ironic twist. 'Think of it as fair payment for the pain I've given you.'

'I'm perfectly capable of supporting Theo.'

'Not to the extent of giving him every advantage that wealth can provide.'

'Money isn't everything. Besides, I don't want to be your wife. That would simply be asking for more pain.'

He frowned. 'I remember the pleasure we both took in making love. It can be that way again, Christina.'

She flushed at the reminder of how slavishly she had adored him. 'You think a seductive honeymoon makes a marriage, Ari? Taking me as your wife is just a cynical exercise in legality. It gives you full access to our son. Once you have that, I won't matter to you. You'll meet other women who will be happy to provide you with a *special* experience. Can you honestly say you'll pass that up?'

'If I have you willing to share my bed, and the family I hope we'll have together, I shall be a faithful husband like my father,' he said with every appearance of sincerity.

'How can I believe that?' she cried, sure that his sincerity couldn't be genuine.

'Tonight you will meet my parents. Their marriage was arranged but they made it work. It was bonded in family and they are completely devoted to each other. I see no reason why we cannot achieve that same happiness, given enough goodwill between us. Goodwill for the sake of our son, Christina.'

'Except I don't trust you,' she flashed back at him. 'I have no reason to trust you.'

'Then we can have it written into the prenuptial agreement that should you file for divorce because of my proven infidelity, you will get full custody of our children, as well as a financial settlement that will cover every possible need.'

Tina was stunned again. 'You'd go that far?'

'Yes. That is the deal I'm offering you, Christina.' As Theo moved back to claim their attention, Ari shot her one last purposeful look and muttered, 'Think about it!'

CHAPTER SIX

ARI was deeply vexed with himself. Christina *had* pushed him too far. He should have stuck to the financial deal and not let her mocking mistrust goad him into offering full custody if he didn't remain faithful to their marriage. It was impossible to backtrack on it now. If she remained cold and hard towards him, he'd just condemned himself to a bed he certainly wouldn't want to lie in for long.

The will to win was in his blood but usually his mind warned him when the price to be paid was becoming unacceptable. Why hadn't he weighed it up this time? It was as though he was mesmerised by the fierce challenge emanating from her, the dark blaze of energy fighting him with all her might, making him want to win regardless of the cost.

The stakes were high. He wanted his son full-time, living in his home, not on the other side of the world with visits parcelled out by a family law-court. But something very strong in him wanted to win Christina over, too. Maybe it was instinct telling him she could make him the kind of wife he'd be happy to live with—

better than any of the other women he knew. She'd proved herself a good mother—a deeply caring mother. As for the sharing his bed part, surely it wouldn't prove too difficult to establish some workable accord there.

She'd been putty in his hands once, a beautiful rose-bud of a girl whose petals he had gradually unfurled, bringing her to full glorious bloom. She was made of much stronger stuff now. The power of her passion excited him. It was negative passion towards him at the moment, but if he could turn it around, push it into a positive flow...

She did have a beautiful smile. He wanted to make it light up for him. And he wanted to see her magnificent dark eyes sparkling with pleasure—pleasure in him. The marriage bed need not be cold. If he could press the right buttons...he had to or he'd just proposed the worst deal of his life.

He took stock of this different Christina as they wandered through the alleys of shops leading up to the summit of the town. The short hair did suit her, giving more emphasis to her striking cheekbones and her lovely long neck. Her full-lipped mouth was very sexy—bee-stung lips like Angelina Jolie's, though not quite as pronounced. She wasn't quite as tall as her sister, nor as slim. She was, in fact, very sweetly curved, her breasts fuller than when she was younger, her waist not as tiny—probably because of childbirth—but still provocatively feminine in the flow to her neatly rounded hips.

Today she was wearing a pretty lemon and white striped top that was cut into clever angles that spelled designer wear—possibly a gift from Cassandra. She'd teamed it with white Capri pants and she certainly had the legs to wear them with distinction—legs that Ari wanted wound around him in urgent need. She could make him a fine wife, one he would be proud to own, one he wouldn't stray from if she let herself respond to him.

He would make it happen.

One way or another he had to make it happen.

Marriage! Never in her wildest imagination had Tina thought it might be a possibility with Ari Zavros, not since he'd left Australia, putting a decisive end to any such romantic notion. But this wasn't romance. It was a coldly calculated deal to get what he wanted and he probably thought he could fool her on the fidelity front.

How on earth could she believe he wouldn't stray in the future? Even as they strolled along the alleys filled with fascinating shops women stared at him, gobbling him up with their eyes. When she stopped to buy a pretty scarf, the saleswoman kept looking at him, barely glancing at Tina as she paid for it.

The man was a sex magnet. Despite how he'd left her flat, she wasn't immune to the vibrations, either, which made it doubly dangerous to get involved with him on any intimate level. He'd only hurt her again. To marry him would be masochistic madness. But it was probably best to pretend to be thinking about *his* deal until after Cass's wedding to ensure he kept *her* deal.

Then the truth could come out without it being such a distracting bombshell and visitation rights could be discussed. She wouldn't deny him time with his son since he seemed so intent on embracing fatherhood, but he would have to come to Australia for it. Greece was not Theo's home and she wasn't about to let that be changed.

They reached the summit of the town where a cable-car ran down to the old port. Alternatively one could take a donkey-ride along a zig-zag path from top to bottom. Tina would have much preferred to take the cable-car. Ari, however, was bent on making good his promise to Theo, and she made no protest as he selected three donkeys for them to ride—the smallest one for their son, the biggest one for himself and an average-sized one for her.

Theo was beside himself with excitement as Ari lifted him onto the one chosen for him. Tina quickly refused any need for his help, using a stool to mount her donkey. She didn't want to feel Ari's hands on her, nor have him so close that he would have a disturbing physical effect on her. She'd been unsettled enough by his ridiculous offer of marriage.

He grinned at her as he mounted his own donkey, probably arrogantly confident of getting his own way, just as he was getting his own way about Theo's birthday. She gave him a *beautiful* smile back, letting him think whatever he liked, knowing in her heart she would do what *she* considered best for her child, and being a miserable mother in a miserable marriage was definitely not best.

'I'll ride beside Theo,' he said. 'If you keep your

donkey walking behind his, I'll be able to control both of them.'

'Are they likely to get out of control?' she asked apprehensively.

'They're fed at the bottom and some of them have a tendency to bolt when they near the end of the path.'

'Oh, great!'

He flashed another confident grin. 'Don't worry. I'll take care of you both. That's a promise, Christina.'

His eyes telegraphed it was meant for the future, too.

He could work overtime on his deal, making it as attractive as he could, but she wasn't having any of it, Tina thought grimly. However, she did have to concede he kept their donkeys at a controlled pace when others started to rush past them. And he cheerfully answered Theo's constant questions with all the patience of an indulgent father.

Her son was laughing with delight and giving Ari an impulsive hug as he was lifted off the donkey. For Tina, it was a relief to get her feet back on solid ground. She'd been far too tense to enjoy her ride.

'We'll take the cable-car back up when we return,' Ari said soothingly, aware of her unease.

She nodded, muttering, 'That would be good.'

'Which boat is ours?' Theo asked, eagerly looking forward to the next treat.

Ari pointed. 'This one coming into the wharf now.'

'Looks like you already have a captain,' Tina remarked.

'Oh, Jason will be happy to turn the wheel over to Theo while he's preparing lunch for us. It will be an easy day for him. When the boat is not in family use, he takes out charters, up to eight people at a time. Today he only has three to look after.'

The good-humoured reply left her nothing to say. Besides, she was sure everything on board would run perfectly for Theo's pleasure. Ari would not fail in his mission to have his son thinking the *nice* man was absolutely wonderful. He'd been wonderful to her for three whole months without one slip for any doubt about him to enter her head.

The white motor launch was in pristine condition. A blue and white striped canopy shaded the rear deck which had bench seats softened by blue and white striped cushions. Tina was invited to sit down and relax while Jason got the boat under way again and Ari took Theo to fetch drinks and give him a tour of the galley.

She sat and tried to concentrate on enjoying the marvellous view, let the day flow past without drawing attention to herself. Tonight's family dinner would test her nerves to the limit, but at least her mother would be there, helping to keep normal conversation rolling along. And despite the stress this meeting with Ari's parents would inevitably cause, Tina told herself she did need to see the Zavros home environment, check that it would be a good place for Theo to be if visits to Santorini had to be arranged.

She smiled as she heard Theo say, 'I'm not allowed to have Coca-Cola. Mama says it's not good for me. I can have water or milk or fruit-juice.'

Welcome to the world of parenting, Ari. It isn't all fun and games. Making healthy choices for your child

is an important part of it. Would he bother to take that
kind of care or would he hire a nanny to do the real
business of parenting?

Tina mentally ticked that off as an item to be discussed before agreeing to visits.

'Okay, what would you like?' he asked, not questioning her drinks ruling.

'Orange juice.'

'And what does your Mama like?'

'Water. She drinks lots of water.'

'No wine?'

Not since you put intoxicating bubbles in my brain.

'No. It's water or coffee or tea for Mama,' Theo said
decisively.

'Well, after our hot walk, I guess iced water would
be the best choice.'

'Yes,' Theo agreed.

He carried out jugs of orange juice and iced water,
setting them on the fixed table which served the bench
seats. Theo brought a stack of plastic glasses, carefully separating them out as Ari returned to the galley,
emerging again with a platter containing a selection of
cheeses and crackers, nuts, olives and grapes.

'There we are! Help yourselves,' he invited, though
he did pour out the drinks for them—water for him, too.

'I love olives,' Theo declared, quickly biting into one.

'Ah! A true Greek,' Ari said proudly.

Tina instantly bridled. 'Theo is an Australian.'

'But Yia Yia is Greek, Mama,' Theo piped up.

'Definitely some Greek blood there,' Ari declared,

a glittering blast from his golden eyes defying Tina's claim.

'True,' she agreed, deciding the point that needed to be made could be driven home when Theo was not present. Australia was their home country. Theo was an Australian citizen. And the family court in Australia would come down on Tina's side. At least she had that in her favour.

Ari chatted away to their son who positively basked in his father's attention. He explained about the volcano as they sailed towards what was left of it, telling the story of what had happened in the far distant past, how the volcano had erupted and destroyed everything. Theo lapped it up, fascinated by the huge disaster, and eager to walk up to the crater when they disembarked there.

Then it was on to the islet of Palea Kameni for a swim in the hot springs—another new exciting experience for Theo. Tina didn't really want to change into her bikini, being far too physically conscious of Ari looking at her to feel comfortable in it, but she liked the idea of letting Theo go alone with him even less. He was *her son* and she was afraid of giving Ari free rein with him without her supervision.

Unfortunately Ari in a brief black swimming costume reduced her comfort zone to nil. His almost naked perfectly proportioned male body brought memories of their previous intimacy flooding back. She'd loved being with him in bed; loved touching him, feeling him, looking at him, loved the intense pleasure he'd given her in so many ways. It had been the best time of her life. It hurt, even now, that it had only been *a charming episode* for him. It hurt even more that she couldn't control the treacherous desire to have him again.

She could if she married him. She probably could anyhow. He'd lusted after her before without marriage in mind. But having sex with him again wouldn't feel the same. She wouldn't be able to give herself to him whole-heartedly, knowing she wasn't the love of his life. There would be too many shadows in any bed they shared.

It was easier to push the memories aside when they were back on the boat and properly dressed again. Ari in clothes was not quite so mesmerising. He and Theo took over the wheel, playing at being captain together, steering the boat towards the village of Oia on the far point of Santorini while Jason was busy in the galley.

They had a delicious lunch of freshly cooked fish and salad. After all the activity and with his stomach full, Theo curled up on the bench seat, his head on Tina's lap and went to sleep. Jason was instructed to keep the boat cruising around until the boy woke. If there was still time to visit Oia, he could then take them into the small port.

'We don't want him too tired to enjoy his birthday party tonight,' Ari remarked to Tina.

'No. I think we should head home when he wakes. We've done all you promised him, Ari. He should have some quiet time, building the Lego train station before more excitement tonight,' Tina said, needing some quiet time for herself, as well. It was stressful being constantly in the company of the man who was intent on breaking into her life again.

'Okay.' He gave her an admiring look. 'You've done a good job with him, Christina. He's a delightful child.'

She gritted her teeth, determined not to be seduced by his compliments, deliberately moving her gaze to the black cliffs ahead of them. 'I think it's important to instill good principles in a child as early as possible,' she said, a sudden wave of resentment towards him making her add, 'I don't want him to grow up like you.'

His silence tore at her nerves but she refused to look at him.

Eventually he asked, 'What particular fault of mine are you referring to?'

'Thinking women are your toys to be picked up and played with as you please,' she answered, wishing he could be honest about himself and honest to her. 'I want Theo to give consideration to how he touches others' lives. I hope when he connects with people he will always leave them feeling good.'

Another long silence.

Out of the corner of her eye she saw Ari lean forward, resting his forearms on his thighs. 'If you had not fallen pregnant, Christina,' he said softly, 'wouldn't I have left you with good memories of our relationship?'

'You left me shattered, Ari,' she answered bluntly. 'My parents had brought me up to be a good girl believing that sex should only be part of a loving relationship. I truly believed that with you and it wasn't so. Then when I realised I was pregnant, it made everything so much worse. I had to bear their disappointment in me, as well as knowing I'd simply been your sex toy for a while.'

In some ways it was a relief to blurt out the truth to him, though whether it meant anything to him or not was unknowable. Maybe it might make him treat her with more respect. She was not a pawn to be moved around at his will. She was a person who had to be dealt with as a person who had the right to determine her own life and this time she would do it according to her principles.

Ari shook his head. He was in a hard place here. He wasn't used to feeling guilty about his actions or the decisions he'd made. It was not a feeling he liked. Christina had just given a perspective on their previous relationship that he'd never considered and quite clearly it had to be considered if he was to turn this situation around.

She was staring into space—a space that only she occupied, shutting him out. Yet her hand was idly stroking the hair of their sleeping son. He was the connection between them—the only connection Ari could count on right now. He was no longer sure he could reach her sexually, though he would still give it a damned good try. In the meantime he had to start redeeming himself in her eyes or she would never allow herself to be vulnerable to the physical attraction which he knew was not completely dead.

He'd felt her gaze on him at the hot springs, saw it quickly flick away whenever he looked at her. She kept shoring up defences against him by reliving how he'd wronged her in the past. Would she ever let that go or would he be paying for his sins against her far into the future?

'I'm sorry,' he said quietly. 'It was wrong of me to take you. I think it was your innocence that made you so entrancing, so different, so special, and the way you looked at me then... I found it irresistible, Christina. If it means anything to you, there hasn't been a woman since whose company has given me more pleasure.'

As he spoke the words which were designed to be persuasive, there was a slight kick in Ari's mind—a jolting realization that he was actually stating the truth. When he'd moved on, he'd mentally set her aside—too young, not the right time for a serious relationship—but the moment he'd recognised her in Dubai, he'd wanted to experience the sweetness of her all over again, especially when he'd just been suffering the sour taste of Felicity Fullbright.

Christina shook her head. She didn't believe him.

'It's true,' he insisted.

She turned to look at him, dark intense eyes scouring his for insincerity. He held her testing gaze, everything within him tuned to convincing her they could make another start, forge a new understanding between them.

'You didn't come back to me, Ari,' she stated simply. 'You forgot me.'

'No. I put you away from me for reasons that I thought were valid at the time but I didn't forget you, Christina. The moment I recognised you in Dubai, the urge to pick up with you again was instant. And that was before you told me about Theo.'

She frowned, hopefully realising the impulse had been there before she had spoken of their son. 'You were with another woman,' she muttered as though that urge was tarnished, too.

'I was already wishing that I wasn't before I saw you. Please…at least believe this of me. It's true.'

For the first time he saw a hint of uncertainty in her eyes. She lowered her long thick lashes, hiding her thoughts. 'Tell me what your valid reasons were.'

'To my mind, we both still had a lot to achieve on our own without ties holding us back from making choices we would have made by ourselves. You'd barely started your modelling career, Christina, and it was obvious you had the promise of making it big on the international scene. As your sister has done.'

Her mouth twisted into a wry grimace as she looked down at their sleeping son. 'If you didn't forget me, Ari, did you ever wonder why I never broke into the international scene?'

'I did expect you to. I thought you had chosen to stay in Australia. Some people don't like leaving everything that is familiar to them.'

'I wasn't worth coming back to,' she murmured, heaving a sigh that made him feel she had just shed whatever progress he had made with her.

'I was caught up dealing with family business these past six years, Christina,' he swiftly argued. 'It's only now…meeting you again and being faced with my own son that my priorities are undergoing an abrupt change.'

'Give it time, Ari,' she said dryly. 'They might change again.'

'No. I won't be taking my marriage proposal off the table. I want you to consider it very seriously.'

She slid him a measuring look that promised nothing. 'I'll think about it. Don't ask any more of me now.' She nodded down at Theo. 'I'm tired, too. Please ask Jason to head back to Fira.'

'As you wish,' he said, rising from the bench seat to do her bidding.

Trying to push her further would not accomplish any more than he had already accomplished today. She didn't trust him yet but at least she was listening to him. Tonight would give him the chance to show her the family environment he wanted to move her and Theo into. He had to make it as attractive as he could.

CHAPTER SEVEN

WHILE Theo was occupied fitting the pieces of the Lego train station together, Tina tried to imagine what her life might have been like if she hadn't fallen pregnant. Would she have picked herself up from the deeply wounding disillusionment of her love for Ari and channelled all her energy into forging a successful modelling career?

Almost certainly.

She had been very young—only eighteen at the time—and having been rejected by him she would have wanted to *show* him she really was special—so special he would regret not holding onto her.

Cassandra would have helped her to get a foot in on the international scene. Given the chance, she would have tried to make it to the top, delivering whatever was required to keep herself in demand and in the public eye; fashion shows, magazine covers, celebrity turn-outs that would give her even more publicity. Ambition would have been all fired up to make Ari have second thoughts about his decision, make him want to meet her again.

When and if he did she would have played it very cool. No melting on the spot. She would have made him chase her, earn her, and she wouldn't have given in to him until he'd declared himself helplessly in love with her and couldn't live without her. He would have had to propose marriage.

Which he'd done today.

Except the circumstances were very different to what might have been if Theo had never been conceived. That completely changed the plot, making the marriage proposal worth nothing to her.

Though Ari's face had lit up with pleasure at seeing her in Dubai.

But that was only a *fond memory* rekindled.

She wasn't the same naive, stars-in-her-eyes girl and never would be again, so it was impossible for him to recapture the pleasure he'd had in her company in the past. Surely he had to realise that. Empty words, meaning nothing.

She shouldn't let herself be affected by anything he said. Or by his mega sex appeal which was an unsettling distraction, pulling her into wanting to believe he was sincere when he was probably intent on conducting a softening-up process so she would bend to his will. It was important to keep her head straight tonight. He had rights where Theo was concerned. He had none over her.

It was still very hot outside their room when it came time to dress for the birthday party. Her mother, of course, was wearing black—a smart tunic and skirt with an array of gold jewellery to make it look festive.

Tina chose a red and white sundress for herself, teaming it with white sandals and dangly earrings made of little white shells.

She put Theo in navy shorts, navy sandals, and a navy and white top with red stripes across the chest. He insisted on having the big red birthday badge with the smiley face and the number 5 pinned onto it. Ari had bought it for him this morning on their stroll around the shops and Theo wore it proudly.

'See!' he cried, pointing to his badge when Ari came to pick them up.

Ari laughed, lifted him up high, whirled him around, then held him against his shoulder, grinning at him as he said, 'It's a grand thing to be five, Theo.'

There was little doubt in Tina's mind that Theo would love to have Ari as his Papa. Her heart sank at the thought of how much would have to change when the truth had to be admitted. Ari's parents already knew. She could only hope they would handle this meeting with care and discretion.

To her immense relief, Ari seated her mother beside him on the drive to his home on the other end of the island. It was near the Santo winery, he said. Which reminded Tina that he had come to Australia on a tour of the wine industry there. As they passed terraces of grapevines, it was fascinating to see the vines spread across the ground instead of trained to stand in upright rows. To protect the grapes from the strong winds, Ari explained to her mother who happily chatted to him the whole way.

Eventually they arrived at the Zavros home. The

semicircular driveway was dominated by a fountain with three mermaids as its centrepiece, which instantly fascinated Theo. The home itself appeared to be three Mediterranean-style villas linked by colonnades. Naturally it was white, like most of the buildings on Santorini. Ari led them to the central building which was larger than the other two. It all shrieked of great wealth. Intimidating wealth to Tina.

'We're dining on the terrace,' he informed them, shepherding them along a high spacious hallway that clearly bisected this villa.

The floor was magnificently tiled in a pattern of waves and seashells. They emerged onto a huge terrace overlooking the sea. In front of them was a sparkling blue swimming pool. To the left was a long vine-covered pergola and Tina's heart instantly kicked into a faster beat as she saw what had to be Ari's parents, seated at a table underneath it.

They rose from their chairs to extend a welcome to their guests. Tension whipped along Tina's nerves as both of them looked at Theo first. However their attention on him didn't last too long. They greeted her mother very graciously and waited for her to introduce her daughter and grandson.

Maximus Zavros was an older version of Ari in looks. His wife, Sophie, was still quite a striking woman with a lovely head of soft wavy hair, warm brown eyes and a slightly plump, very curvaceous figure. Although they smiled at her as she was introduced, Tina was acutely conscious of their scrutiny—sizing her up as the mother of their grandson. It was a relief when they finally turned their gaze to Theo again.

'And this is the birthday boy,' Sophie Zavros said indulgently.

'Five!' Theo said proudly, pointing to his badge. Then he gave Ari's father a curious look. 'Your name is Maximus?'

'Yes, it is. If it is easier for you, tonight you can call me Max,' he invited, smiling benevolently.

'Oh, no! I *like* Maximus,' Theo said with a broad smile back. 'Mama took me to a movie about a girl with very long hair. What was her name, Mama?'

'Rapunzel,' Tina supplied, barely stopping herself from rolling her eyes at what was bound to come next.

'Rapunzel,' he repeated. 'But the best part of the movie was the horse. His name was Maximus and he was a great horse!'

'I'm glad he was a great horse,' Ari's father said, amused by the connection.

'He was so good at everything!' Theo assured him. 'And he saved them in the end, didn't he, Mama?'

'Yes, he did.'

Ari's father crouched down to Theo's eye level. 'I think I must get hold of this movie. Maybe you and I could watch it together sometime. Would you like to see it again?'

Theo nodded happily.

'Well, I'm not a horse but I can give you a ride over to the table.'

He swept his grandson up in his arms and trotted him to the table, making Theo bubble with laughter. It star-

tled Tina that such a powerful man would be so playful. Her mother and Sophie were laughing, too—any
awkwardness at meeting strangers completely broken.
She glanced at Ari who was also looking on in amusement.

He quickly moved closer to her, murmuring, 'Relax,
Christina. We just want to make this a special night for
Theo.'

'Have you told them of your plan to marry me?' she
asked quickly, wanting to know if she was being sized
up as a possible daughter-in-law.

'Yes, but there will be no pressure for you to agree
tonight. This is a different beginning for us, Christina,
with our families involved, because it is about family
this time.'

His eyes burned serious conviction into hers.

It rattled her deep-seated prejudice against believing anything he said. She sucked in a deep breath and
tried to let her inner angst go. This *was* a different scenario between them with their families involved. She
decided to judge the night on its merits, see how she
felt about it afterwards. To begin with she told herself
to be glad that Ari's parents were the kind of people
Theo could take to because there was no avoiding the
fact they would feature in his future.

Maximus Zavros had seated Theo in the chair on
the left of his own at the head of the table. Sophie ushered Tina's mother to the chair next to Theo's and to
the right of her own chair at the foot of the table. Ari
guided Tina to the chair opposite Theo's, putting her
next to his father before sitting beside her.

As soon as they were all seated a man-servant appeared, bringing two platters of hors d'oeuvres. Another followed, bringing jugs of iced water and orange juice.

Ari's father turned to her, pleasantly asking, 'Can I persuade you to try one of our local wines?'

She shook her head. 'No, thank you. I prefer water.'

He looked at her mother. 'Helen?'

'I'm happy to try whatever you suggest, Maximus. I've tasted two of the wines that were sent to my room and they were quite splendid.'

'Ah, I'm glad they pleased your palate.' He signalled to the servant to pour the chosen wine into glasses while he himself filled Tina's glass with water and Theo's with orange juice. He beamed a smile at his grandson. 'Ari tells me you can swim like a fish.'

'I love swimming,' was his enthusiastic reply.

'Did your Mama teach you?'

Theo looked at Tina, unsure of the answer. 'Did you, Mama?'

'No. I took you to tadpole classes when you were only nine months old. You've always loved being in water and you learnt to swim very young.' She turned to Maximus. 'It's important for any child to be able to swim in Australia. There are so many backyard pools and every year there are cases of young children drowning. Also, we live near Bondi Beach, so I particularly wanted Theo to be safe in the water.'

'Very sensible,' Maximus approved, nodding to the pool beyond the pergola. 'There will be no danger for him here, either.'

That was just the start of many subtle and not so

subtle points made to her throughout the evening, by both of Ari's parents. They were clearly intent on welcoming their grandson into their life, assuring her he would be well taken care of and greatly loved. And not once was there any hint of criticism of her for keeping them in ignorance of him until now.

She fielded a few testing questions from Maximus about her own life, but for the most part Ari's parents set out to charm and Tina noticed her mother having a lovely time with Sophie, discussing the forthcoming wedding and marriage in general.

After the hors d'oeuvres, they were served souvlaki and salad which Theo had informed Ari on the boat was his favourite meal. Then came the birthday cake and Ari reminded Theo to make a wish as he blew out the candles—all five of them in one big burst. Everyone clapped and cheered at his success.

The cake was cut and slices of it were served around the table. It was a rich, many layered chocolate cake, moist and delicious, and Theo gobbled his piece up, the first to finish.

'Will I get my wish?' he asked Ari.

'I hope so, Theo. Although if you were wishing for a horse like Maximus, that might be asking for too much.'

'Is wishing for a Papa too much?'

Tina's hands clenched in her lap. Her lungs seized up. The silence around the table felt loaded with emotional dynamite.

'No, that's not asking for too much,' Ari answered decisively.

Her mother leaned over and pulled Theo onto her

lap, giving him a cuddle. 'You miss your Papou, don't you, darling?' She gave Sophie a rueful smile. 'My husband died a year ago. He adored Theo. We didn't have sons, you see, and having a grandson was like a beautiful gift.'

'Yes. A very beautiful gift,' Sophie repeated huskily, her gaze lingering on Theo for a moment before shooting a look of heart-tugging appeal at Tina.

'I think with Ari giving him such a wonderful time today...' her mother rattled on.

'Ari is very good with children,' Sophie broke in. 'His nephews love being with him. He will make a wonderful father.'

Ostensibly she was speaking to her mother but Tina knew the words were for her. Maybe they were true. He might very well be a wonderful father, but being a wonderful husband was something else.

'Maximus and I very much want to see him settled down with his own family,' Sophie carried on.

'Mama, don't push,' Ari gently chided.

She heaved a sigh which drew Tina's mother into a string of sympathetic comments about young people taking their time about getting married these days.

Tina sat in frozen silence until Ari's father leaned towards her and asked, 'Who is managing your family restaurant while you are away, Christina?'

She had to swallow hard to moisten her throat before answering, 'The head chef and the head waiter.'

'You trust them to do it well?'

'Yes. My father set it up before he died that both men

get a percentage of the profits. It's in their best interests to keep it running successfully.'

'Ah! A man of foresight, your father,' he said with satisfaction.

Tina *knew* he was thinking the restaurant could keep running successfully without her. 'It needs an overall manager and my father entrusted me with that job,' she said with defiant pride.

'Which is a measure of his respect for your abilities, Christina. But as a Greek father myself, I know it was not what he wanted for you.'

His amber eyes burned that certain knowledge into her heart. There was no denying it. Her father had not been against his daughters having a career of their choice but he had believed a woman was only truly fulfilled with the love of a good husband and the love of their children.

It hurt, being reminded of her failure to live up to his expectations of her, but the big word in her father's beliefs was love, and Ari did not love her. She faced his father with her own burning determination. 'I have the right to choose what I do with my life. My father respected that, as well.'

'I don't think the choice is so unequivocal when you are a mother, Christina,' he shot back at her. 'The rights of your child have to be considered.'

'Papa...' Ari said in a low warning voice.

'She must understand this, Ari,' was the quick riposte.

'I do,' Tina told him flatly. 'And I am considering them.' She lowered her voice so as not to be overheard at the other end of the table as she fiercely added, 'I hope you do, too, because I *am* Theo's mother and I always will be.'

She would not allow them to take over her son. She would concede visits but knew she would hate every minute Theo was away from her. Not all their wealth and caring would make any difference to the hole that would leave in her life until he returned to her. Tears pricked her eyes. Her head was swimming with all the difficulties that lay ahead.

'Please, forgive me my trespasses,' Ari's father said gruffly. 'You're a fine mother, Christina. And that will always be respected by our family. The boy is a credit to you. How can I put it? I want very much to enjoy more of him.'

A warm hand slid over one of her clenched fists and gently squeezed. 'It's all right, Christina,' Ari murmured, 'You're amongst friends, not enemies.'

She stared down at his hand, biting her lips as she tried to fight back the tears. He'd offered his hand in marriage, which was the easiest way out of the custody issue, but how could she take it when she felt so vulnerable to what he could do to her—twisting up her life all over again?

She swallowed hard to ease the choking sensation in her throat and without looking at either man, said, 'I want to go back to the resort now, Ari. It's been a long day.'

'Of course.' Another gentle squeeze of her hand. 'It's been good of you to let us spend this time together.'

'Yes. A wonderful evening,' his father chimed in. 'Thank you, Christina.'

She nodded, not wanting to be drawn into another stressful conversation. She felt painfully pressured as it was. Her gaze lifted to check Theo who was now nodding off on her mother's lap.

Ari rose from his chair. 'Helen, Mama… Christina is tired and it looks like Theo is ready for bed, as well. It's time to call it a night. I'll carry him out to the car, Helen.'

Ari's parents accompanied them out to the car, walking beside her mother who thanked them profusely for their hospitality. All three expressed pleasure in meeting up again at the wedding. Both Maximus and Sophie dropped goodnight kisses on Theo's forehead before Ari passed him over to Tina in the back seat. She thanked them for the birthday party and the car door was finally closed on it, relieving some of the tension in her chest.

Theo slept all the way back to the resort and the conversation between Ari and her mother in the front seats was conducted in low murmurs. Tina sat in silence, hugging her child, feeling intensely possessive of him and already grieving over how much she would have to part from him.

Having arrived at El Greco, Ari once again lifted Theo into his arms and insisted on carrying him to their accommodation. Tina did not protest, knowing that to her mother this was the natural thing for a man to do. The problem came when she unlocked her door and instead of passing Theo to her, Ari carried him straight into her room.

'Which bed?' he asked.

She dashed past him to turn back the covers on Theo's bed and Ari gently laid him down and tucked him in, dropping a kiss on his forehead before straightening up and smiling down at his sleeping son, making Tina's heart contract at the memory of Theo's wish for a Papa. He had one. And very soon he had to know it.

Ari turned to her and she instantly felt a flood of electricity tingling through her entire body. He was too close to her, dangerously close, exuding the sexual magnetism that she should be immune to but wasn't. Being in a bedroom with Ari Zavros, virtually alone with him, was a bad place to be. She quickly backed off, hurrying to the door, waving for him to leave.

He followed but paused beside her, causing inner havoc again. He raised a hand to touch her cheek and she flinched away from the contact. 'Just go, Ari,' she said harshly. 'You've had your day.'

He frowned at her unfriendliness. 'I only wanted to thank you, Christina.'

She forced her voice to a reasonable tone. 'Okay, but you can do that without touching me.'

'Is my touch so repellent to you?'

Panic tore through her at how vulnerable she might be to it. She stared hard at him, desperate not to show him any weakness. 'Don't push it, Ari. I've had enough, today.'

He nodded. 'I'll call you in the morning.'

'No! Tomorrow is *my* family day,' she said firmly. 'Cassandra will be joining us and so will all our relatives from the mainland. We'll meet again at the wedding.'

For one nerve-wracking moment she thought he would challenge her decision. It surprised her when he smiled and said, 'Then I'll look forward to the wedding. Goodnight, Christina.'

'Goodnight,' she repeated automatically, watching him in a daze of confusion as he walked away from her.

He hadn't done anything *wrong* all day. For the most part, he'd been perfectly charming. And she still *wanted* him, despite the grief he'd given her. There had never been any other man who made her feel what he did. But he probably made every woman feel the same way. It meant nothing. It would be foolish to let it cloud her judgement.

When Theo was told that Ari was his Papa, he would want them to be all together, living happily ever after.

But that was a fairy-tale and this story didn't have the right ingredients. The prince did not love the princess, so how could there be a happy ever after?

Tina fiercely told herself she must not lose sight of that, no matter what!

CHAPTER EIGHT

ARI stood beside George in the church, impatient for the marriage service to be over, his mind working through what had to be accomplished with Christina. Theo was not a problem. His son had grinned broadly at him as he had carried the cushion with the wedding rings up the aisle. He would want his Papa. But Christina had only smiled at George, keeping her gaze averted from him.

She looked absolutely stunning in a dark red satin gown. Desire had kicked in so hard and fast Ari had struggled to control the instinctive physical response to instantly wanting her in his bed again. 'She is magnificent, is she not?' George had murmured, meaning his bride, and she was, but Cassandra stirred nothing in him.

There were many beautiful women in the world. Ari had connected to quite a few of them, but none had twisted his heart as it was being twisted right now. He had to have Christina again. Perhaps she touched something deep in him because she was the mother of his child. Or perhaps it was because he had taken her innocence and she made him feel very strongly about righting the wrong he had done her. The reasons didn't matter. Somehow he had to persuade her to be his wife.

His parents certainly approved of the marriage and not only because of Theo.

'She's lovely, Ari, and I could be good friends with Helen,' his mother had remarked.

His father had been more decisive in his opinion. 'Beautiful, intelligent, and with a fighting spirit I admire. She's a good match for you, Ari. Don't let her get away from you. The two of you should have many interesting children together.'

Easier said than done, Ari thought grimly.

She didn't want him to touch her.

Today, she didn't want to look at him.

Was she frightened of the attraction she still felt with him, frightened of giving in to it? She would *have* to look at him at the wedding reception *and* suffer his touch during the bridal waltz. Not just a touch, either. Full body contact. He would make the waltz one of the most intimate dances she'd ever had, force the sexual chemistry between them to the surface so she couldn't hide from it, couldn't ignore it, couldn't deny it.

She was not going to get away from him.

Tina listened to the marriage service as she stood beside her sister. These same words could be spoken to her soon if she said *yes* to Ari's proposal. Would he take the vows seriously, or were they just mumbo-jumbo to him—the means to an end?

He *had* offered the fidelity clause in a prenuptial agreement. She would get full custody of Theo and any other children they might have together if he faltered on that front. Could she be happy with him if he kept faith with his marriage deal?

It was a risk she probably shouldn't be considering. Cass's wedding was getting to her, stirring up feelings that could land her in a terrible mess. Plus all the marriage talk amongst her Greek relatives yesterday had kept Ari's offer pounding through her mind—no relief at all from the connection with him.

Her mother had raved on about how kind he'd been—taking Tina and Theo out for the day, the birthday party at his parents' home—which had reminded the relatives of how attentive he'd been to Tina at the family party in Athens. Comments on how eligible he was followed, with speculative looks that clearly said Helen's daughter might have a chance with him. Being a single mother was...*so unfortunate.*

Little did they know that Theo was the drawcard, not her. They would all be watching her with Ari today—watching, hoping, encouraging. She would have to look at him soon, take his arm as they followed Cass and George out of the church, be seated next to him at the wedding reception, dance with him. The whole thing was a nightmare with no escape, and it would be worse when the truth was told.

Her mother would want her to marry Ari.

Her relatives would think her mad if she didn't.

Only Cass might take her side, asking what *she* wanted, but Cass wouldn't be there. She and George would be off on their honeymoon. Besides, what Tina *wanted* was impossible—utterly impossible to go back to the time when she had loved Ari with all her heart and believed he loved her. How could she ever believe that now?

She felt a sharp stab of envy as George promised to love Cass for the rest of his life. There was no doubting the fervour in his voice, no doubting Cass, either, as she promised her love in return. A huge welling of emotion brought tears to Tina's eyes as the two of them were declared husband and wife. She wished them all the happiness in the world. This was how it should be between a man and a woman, starting out on a life together.

She was still blinking away the wetness in her eyes when she had to link up with Ari for the walk out of the church. He wound her arm around his and hugged her close, instantly causing an eruption of agitation inside Tina.

'Why do women always weep at weddings?' he murmured, obviously wanting her to focus on him.

She didn't. She swept her gaze around the gathered guests, swallowed hard to unblock her voice and answered, 'Because change is scary and you hope with all your heart that everything will work out right.'

'What is right in your mind, Christina?' he persisted.

Christina...he invariably used her full name because it was what she had called herself for the modelling career that had been cut short after he had left her pregnant. During the months they'd spent together she'd loved how that name had rolled off his tongue in a caressing tone. She wished he wouldn't keep using the same tone now, that he'd call her Tina like everyone else. Then she wouldn't be constantly reminded of the girl she had been and how much she had once loved him.

She wasn't that girl any more.

She'd moved on.

Except Ari could still twist her heart and shoot treacherous excitement through her veins.

It was wrong for him to have that power. *Wrong!* And the pain of her disillusionment with him lent a vehement conviction to her voice as she answered him. 'It's right if they keep loving each other for the rest of their lives, no matter what happens along the way.' She looked at him then, meeting the quizzical amber eyes with as much hard directness as she could muster. 'We don't have that basis for marriage, do we?'

'I don't believe that love is the glue that keeps a marriage together,' he shot back at her. 'It's a madness that's blind to any sensible judgement and it quickly burns out when people's expectations of it aren't met. Absolute commitment is what I'm offering you, Christina. You can trust that more than love.'

His cynical view of love was deeply offensive to her, yet she felt the strength of his will encompassing her, battering at her resistance to what he wanted. 'I'd rather have what Cass and George have than what you're offering,' she muttered, resenting the implication that her sister's happiness with her marriage wouldn't last.

'I understand that change must be scary to you, Christina,' he murmured in her ear. 'I promise you I'll do all I can to make the transition easy for both you and Theo.'

The transition! He expected her to give up her life in Australia—all she'd known, all she'd worked for—to be with him. It wouldn't work the other way around. She knew that wouldn't even be considered. She was supposed to see marriage to him as more desirable than anything else, and she would have seen it that way once, *if he'd loved her.*

That was the sticking point.

Tina couldn't push herself past it.

The hurt that he didn't wouldn't go away.

Outside the church they had to pose for photographs. Tina pasted a smile on her face. Her facial muscles ached from keeping it there. Ari lifted Theo up to perch against his shoulder for some shots and everywhere she looked people seemed to be smiling and nodding benevolently at the grouping of the three of them—not as bridesmaid, best man and page boy, but as wife, husband and son. Ari's parents stood next to her mother and Uncle Dimitri. They would all be allied against her if she decided to reject the marriage proposal.

She ached all over from the tension inside her. At least the drive to the reception spared her any active pressure from Ari. Theo rode in their car, sitting between them on the back seat, chatting happily to the man he would soon know as his father. Tina was grateful not have to say anything but she was acutely aware of Theo's pleasure in Ari and Ari's pleasure in his son. How could she explain to a five-year-old boy why they couldn't all be together with the Papa he had wished for?

They arrived at the Santo winery. Its reception centre was perched on top of a cliff overlooking the sea. To the side of the dining section was a large open area shaded by pergolas and normally used for wine-tasting. Guests gathered here while the bridal party posed for more photographs. Waiters offered drinks and canapés. A festive mood was very quickly in full swing.

Tina thought she might escape from Ari's side for a while after the photographer was satisfied but that proved impossible. He led her straight over to George's family who were all in high spirits, delighted to meet their new daughter-in-law's sister and press invitations to be their guest on Patmos at any time.

Then he insisted on introducing her to his sisters and their husbands—beautiful women, handsome men, bright beautiful people who welcomed Tina into their group, making friendly chat about the wedding. Their children, Ari's nephews, all four of them around Theo's age, quickly drew him off with them to play boy games. Which left Tina very much the centre of attention and as pleasant as the conversation was, she knew they were measuring her up as wife material for Ari.

After a reasonable interval she excused herself, saying she should check if Cass needed her for anything.

It didn't provide much of an escape.

'I'll come with you,' Ari instantly said. 'George might require something from me.'

As soon as they were out of earshot, Tina muttered, 'You told them, didn't you?'

'Not the children. Theo won't hear it from them. Keeping it from your family until after the wedding will be respected, Christina. I simply wanted my sisters to understand where you are with me.'

'I'm not anywhere with you,' she snapped defensively, giving him a reproachful glare.

He held her gaze with a blaze of resolute purpose. 'You're my intended wife and I told them so.'

'Why are you rushing into this?' she cried in exasperation. 'We can make reasonable arrangements about sharing Theo. Other people do it all the time. You don't have to *marry* me!'

'I *want* to marry you.'

'Only because of Theo and that's not right, Ari.'

'You're wrong. I want you, too, Christina.'

She shook her head in anguished denial, instantly shying away from letting herself believe him. Cass and George were chatting to a group of their modelling-world friends and Tina gestured to the gorgeous women amongst them. 'Look at what you could have. I'm not in their class. And I bet they'd lap up your attention.'

'You're in a class of your own and I don't want their attention. I want yours.'

'Today you do, but what about the rest of your future, Ari?'

'I'll make my future with you if you'll give it a chance.'

Again she shook her head. There was no point in arguing with him. He had his mind set on a course of action and nothing she said was going to shift him from it.

'It's worth a chance, isn't it, Christina?' he pressed. 'We were both happy when we were intimately involved. It can be that way again. You can't really want to be separated from Theo during the time he spends with me if you insist he has to bounce between us.'

She would hate it.

But she was also hating the way Cass's girlfriends were gobbling Ari up with their eyes, watching him approach the bride and groom. Not that she could blame them for doing it. He was even more of a sex magnet today, dressed in a formal dinner suit which enhanced his perfect male physique, highlighting how stunningly handsome he was. *A Greek God.* Tina had no doubt they were thinking that. And envying her for having him at her side.

Could she stand a lifetime of that with Ari?

Would he always *stay* at her side?

She felt sick from all the churning inside her. Any distraction from it was intensely welcome. Hopefully Cass would provide it for a while. She and Ari joined the celebrity group and were quickly introduced around. One of George's friends, another photographer, took the opportunity to give Tina his business card.

'Come to me and I'll turn you into a model as famous as your sister. No disrespect to you, Cass, but this girl has quite a unique look that I'd love to capture.'

Cass laughed and turned a beaming smile to Tina. 'I've always said you don't have to be a homebody.'

'But I like being a homebody.' She tried to hand the card back, embarrassed by the spotlight being turned on her. 'Thank you, but no.'

'Keep it,' he insisted. 'I mean it. I would love to work

with that wonderful long neck and those marvellous cheekbones. Your short hair sets them off to perfection.'

'No, please, I don't want it. I have nowhere to put your card anyway.'

'I'll keep it for you. You might have second thoughts,' Ari said, taking the card and sliding it into his breast pocket. He smiled around at the group. 'No disrespect to any of you lovely ladies, but I also think Christina is unique. And very special.'

Which was virtually a public declaration of his interest in her, putting off the interest that any of the lovely ladies might want to show in him.

Tina's *marvellous cheekbones* were instantly illuminated by heat.

Cass leaned over to whisper in her ear. 'Mama is right. Ari is very taken by you. Give him a chance, Tina. He's rather special, too.'

A chance!

Even Cass was on Ari's side.

Tina felt the whole world was conspiring to make her take the step she was frightened of taking.

'I think I need some cool air,' she muttered.

Ari heard her. He took her arm. 'Please excuse us, everyone. We're off to catch the sea breeze for a breather.'

He drew her over to the stone wall along the cliff edge. Tina didn't protest the move. It was useless. She was trapped into being Ari's companion at this wedding and he was not about to release her.

'Why did you take that card?' she demanded crossly.

'Because it was my fault that you didn't continue the modelling career you might have had. It's not too late to try again, Christina. You actually have a more individual beauty now. If you'd like to pursue that path you'd have my full support.'

She frowned at him. 'I'm a mother, Ari. That comes first. And isn't it what you want from me, to be the mother of your children?'

'Yes, but there are models who are also mothers. It can be done, Christina.' He lifted his hand and gently stroked her hot cheek, his eyes burning with what seemed like absolute sincerity. 'I destroyed two of your dreams. At least I can give one of them back to you. Maybe the other…with enough time together. '

She choked up.

It was all too much.

Her mind was in a total jumble. She wanted to believe him, yet he couldn't give her back what he had taken. Whatever they had in the future would be different. And was he just saying these things to win her over? She'd trusted him with her heart and soul once and here she was being vulnerable to his seduction again. How could she believe him? Or trust him? She desperately needed to clear her head.

She stepped back from the tingling touch on her cheek and forced herself to speak. 'I'd like a glass of water, Ari.'

He held her gaze for several moments, his eyes searching for what he wanted to see in hers—a softening towards him, cracks in her resistance. Tina silently pleaded for him to go, give her some space, some relief from the constant pressure to give in and take what he was offering.

Finally he nodded. 'I'll fetch you one.'

She stared out to sea, gulping in fresh air, needing a blast of oxygen to cool her mind of its feverish thoughts.

It didn't really work.

Despite her past experience with Ari Zavros, or maybe because of it, one mind-bending thought kept pounding away at her, undermining her resistance to the course he was pressing her to take.

Give it a chance.

Give it a chance.

Give it a chance.

CHAPTER NINE

The bridal waltz...

Tina took a deep breath and rose to her feet as Ari held back her chair. He'd been the perfect gentleman all evening. The speech he'd made preceding his toast to the bride and groom had contained all the right touches, charming the guests into smiling and feeling really good about this marriage. An excellent Best Man.

Maybe he was the best man for her, given that she'd not felt attracted to anyone else in the past six years. If she never connected with some other man... did she want to live the rest of her life totally barren of the sexual pleasure she had known with Ari?

Give it a chance...

As he steered her towards the dance floor, the warmth of his hand on the pit of her back spread a flow of heat to her lower body. The band played 'Moon River,' a slow jazz waltz that Cass and George obviously revelled in, executing it with great panache; gliding, twirling, dipping, making it look both romantic and very, very sexy.

Little quivers started running down Tina's legs as

she and Ari waited for their cue to join in. It had been so long since he had held her close. Would she feel the same wild surge of excitement when she connected to his strong masculinity? It was impossible to quell the electric buzz of anticipation when their cue came and he swept her onto the dance floor, yet she stiffened when he drew her against him, instinctively fighting his power to affect her so *physically.*

'Relax, Christina,' he murmured. 'Let your body respond to the rhythm of the music. I know it can.'

Of course, he knew. There was very little he didn't know about her body and how it responded. And she had to find out what it might be like with him now, didn't she? *If she was to give it a chance.*

She forced herself to relax and go with the flow of the dance. He held her very close; her breasts pressed to his chest, her stomach in fluttering contact with his groin area, her thighs brushing his with every move he made. Her heart was pounding much faster than the beat of the music. Her female hormones were stirred into a lustful frenzy. She was in the arms of a Greek God who was hers for the taking and the temptation to take whatever she could of him was roaring through her.

Ari made the most of Christina's surrender to the dance, hoping the sexual chemistry sizzling through him was being transmitted through every sensual contact point. She felt good in his arms. She was the right height for him, tall enough for their bodies to fit in a very satisfying way as he moved her around the dance floor. The sway of her hips, the fullness of her breasts impacting with their lush femininity, the scent of her skin and hair…everything about her was firing up his desire to have her surrender to him.

The waltz ended. She didn't exactly push out of his embrace but eased herself back enough to put a little distance between them. Her cheeks were flushed and she kept her eyes lowered, their thick black lashes hiding any vulnerable feelings. He was sure she had been physically affected by the intimacy of the dance but whether that was enough to sway her his way he didn't know.

The Master of Ceremonies invited all the guests to dance to the next song which had been especially requested by the bride. Ari instantly understood its significance when the band started playing the tune. He and Christina had heard Stevie Wonder's version of it on the car radio on one of their trips together.

'*You are the sunshine of my life,*' he said, recalling how he had applied the words to her. 'It's your father's favourite song.'

'Yes,' she said huskily. 'Cass misses him, too. He would have been very proud of her today.' Her lashes lifted and she gave him a wry little smile. 'I'm surprised you remembered.'

'Special songs can be very evocative. You *were* the sunshine of my life while we were together, Christina.'

The smile twisted into a grimace. 'There's been a long night since then, Ari. Though I'm sure you found plenty of sunshine elsewhere.'

'Not of the same quality.'

Her gaze slid away from his. 'We have to dance,' she muttered.

She allowed him to hold her close again without any initial resistance. It was *some* progress, he thought, though he savagely wished she wouldn't keep harping on the other women who'd been in his life. The past was the past—impossible to change it. If she'd just set her sights on the future, that was the progress he needed.

He bent his head closer to hers and murmured, 'What you and I can have *now* is what matters, Christina.'

She didn't answer.

Hopefully she was thinking about it.

Tina fiercely wished she could forget everything else but *now,* pretend she was meeting Ari for the first time, feeling all that he made her feel, her whole body brilliantly alive to exciting sensations. She wouldn't care about the other women if this was her first experience with him. She'd be blissfully thinking that he was the man who could make her life complete.

Maybe he would if she set the pain he'd given her aside. He'd said he wanted to give her back the dreams he'd destroyed. Yet it was a terribly risky step, trusting his word. If he didn't keep it, she would hate herself for being a fool, hate him for his deceit, and end up a totally embittered woman.

But she could make him pay for it.

He would lose Theo and any other children they might have if he broke his promise of fidelity. She wouldn't have to worry over the custody issue. All rights would be hers. In which case, it was worth taking the chance, wasn't it?

Her father's favourite song came to an end. She saw Cass go over to her mother who had danced with Uncle Dimitri and give her a hug and a kiss. It caused a painful drag on Tina's heart. She knew her father would have wanted her to marry Ari. It might have made him proud of her if she did.

She looked up at the man who was her son's father, and the seductive amber eyes instantly locked onto hers, simmering with the promise of all the pleasure they'd once had together. Her heart quivered over the decision she had made but it *was* made and she wasn't going to fret over it any longer.

'Let's go where we can talk privately,' she said firmly.

He nodded, quickly obliging her by steering her off the dance floor, then taking her arm and walking her out to the large open patio where they'd been before the reception dinner.

'Would you like to sit down?' he asked, waving to the wooden tables under the pergola.

'Yes.' Her legs were feeling wobbly. Besides, sitting across from him at a table would be more comfortable for laying out the deal she would accept.

They sat. Ari spread his hands in an open gesture, inviting her confidence. 'What do you want to say, Christina?'

Her hands were tightly clenched in her lap. This was it—the moment when her life would begin to take a totally different direction. A wave of trepidation man-

gled her vocal chords. She looked hard at him, forcing
her imagination to see him as a caring and committed
father and husband. If she could believe it, maybe the
marriage would work out right. She desperately wanted
it to.

The first step was to say the words.

Say them.

Just do it and have done with the whole nerve-
wracking dilemma.

'I… I…'

'Yes?' Ari encouraged, leaning forward, giving her
his concentrated attention.

A surge of panic had made her hesitate. Her mind was
screaming *wait! Don't commit yet!* But what would she
be waiting for? The situation wasn't going to change.
This man was Theo's father and she had loved him with
all her heart once. If he was serious about forging a good
relationship with her, shouldn't she give it a chance?

'I'll marry you,' she blurted out, sealing the decision.

His face broke into a happy grin. His eyes sparkled
with pleasure. Or was it triumph, having won what he
wanted? 'That's great, Christina!' he enthused. 'I'm
glad you've decided it's the best course because it is.'

He was *so* positive it instantly raised doubts in Tina's
mind. Was she a fool for giving in? She had to put a
high value on the marriage so he would treat her as he
should.

'Give me your hand,' he pressed, reaching across the
table to take it.

She shook her head, keeping both hands tightly in
her lap. 'I haven't finished what I want to say.'

He frowned at her reluctance to meet his offered hand. He spread his fingers in open appeal. 'Tell me what you need from me.'

'I need you to sign the prenuptial agreement you offered me,' she threw back at him, determined that those terms be kept. It was her safeguard against being used to give Ari a stronger paternal position than he had now.

He drew back, his mouth twisting into an ironic grimace. A sharp wariness wiped the sparkle from his eyes. Tina's stomach cramped with tension. If he retracted the offer, she could not go ahead with the marriage, regardless of any pressure from any source. It was risking too much. He might walk away from her again and take Theo with him.

She waited for his reply.

Waited…and waited…her nerves stretching tighter with every second that passed.

Ari's mind was swiftly sifting through Christina's possible motivations. She didn't trust his word. He understood where she was coming from on that score. What concerned him most was if she had a vengeful nature.

The prenuptial agreement he'd offered gave her everything if he didn't remain a faithful husband. What if she planned to be such a cold, shrewish wife, he would be driven to find some pleasure in other company? If she was secretly determined not to be responsive to him, he'd be condemning himself to a hellish marriage. He needed more than her public compliance to a couple of dances to feel secure about winning her over in bed.

Out here alone together, she wouldn't even give him her hand.

What was in her mind?

What was in her heart?

A totally selfish revenge on him…or hope that they could make a happy future together?

He was risking a lot.

He decided she had to meet him halfway before he tied a knot which could not be undone.

'I am prepared to sign it, Christina,' he said, his eyes burning a very direct challenge at her as he added, 'If you're prepared to spend one night with me before I do.'

She stared at him, startled by the provision he was laying down. 'Why? You'll have all the nights you want with me after we're married.'

'I want to be sure that I will want them. I won't sign away my right to my son to a woman who'll turn her back on me. I need you to show me that won't happen, Christina. Right now your attitude towards me is hardly encouraging. You won't even give me your hand.'

Heat surged up her neck and scorched her cheeks. Her eyes glittered a challenge right back at him. 'I think it's a good idea for us to spend a night together before either of us commit ourselves to anything. Maybe you're not as good a lover as you used to be, Ari.'

Relief swept through him at her ready acceptance of a sex-test. He smiled. 'And maybe you'll warm to me once I prove that I am.'

Again her lashes swept down, veiling her feelings. She heaved a sigh, probably relieving tension. 'We're scheduled to leave Santorini the day after tomorrow,' she muttered.

'That can easily be changed.'

She shook her head. 'I'll spend tomorrow night with you.' Her lashes lifted and there was resolute fire in her eyes. 'That can be the decider for both of us.'

She would bolt if he didn't satisfy her. Ari was confident that he could if she was willing to let it happen.

'Agreed,' he said. 'However, our other deal ends tonight, Christina. Tomorrow you tell your mother and Theo that I am his father. Whatever happens between us, this has to be openly acknowledged.'

She nodded. 'I'll do it in the morning.'

'Make sure your mother understands the circumstances, that I was not told you had my child until we met in Dubai. I would have come back to you had I known, Christina.'

She made a wry grimace. 'Since I've decided I might marry you, naturally I'll put you in as good a light as possible to my mother.'

'It's the truth,' he rammed home as hard as he could, wanting her to believe at least that much of him.

'And my truth is you left me and I didn't want you back,' she shot out, her eyes glittering with angry pride. 'Don't you start harassing me, Ari. I'll do what I have to do to smooth the path to a workable future.'

His father's words about Christina were instantly replayed in his mind...*beautiful, intelligent, and with a fighting spirit I admire.* If she shared his own strong desire for everything to turn out well, there was no need to concern himself about her presentation of the past to her mother.

'I'd like to be there when you tell Theo I'm his father,' he said softly, needing to remove the anger he'd unwittingly triggered. 'I've missed so much—not being there when he was born, his first words, his first step, learning to swim, his first day at kindergarten. I want to see the expression in his eyes when he realises I am the Papa he wished for. Will you give me that, Christina?'

Her eyes went blank, probably focussing inward on the memories she hadn't shared with him. He willed her to be more generous now. Yet when she did speak, her whole expression was one of deep anxiety.

'I hope you really mean to be a good father to him, Ari. Please don't lead him on and then drop him, pursuing other interests.'

He knew she felt he had done that to her.

It had been wrong of him, letting temptation overrule good sense. She had been too young, too impressionable. Theo was much more so and she was frightened for him. Her fear evoked a powerful surge of emotion in him. He wanted to say he'd look after them both for the rest of his life. He hated seeing the fretful doubts in her eyes. But laying them to rest would take time.

'Give me your hand, Christina,' he gently commanded, his eyes pleading for her acquiescence.

Very slowly she lifted it from her lap and held it out to him.

He enclosed it with his. 'I promise you I'll do everything I can to win Theo's love and keep it,' he said fervently. 'He's my son.'

Tears welled into her eyes. She nodded, unable to speak. He stroked her palm with his thumb, wanting to give comfort and reassurance, wishing he could sweep her into his embrace but cautious about rushing her where she might not be ready to go.

'If it's okay with you, I'll come to the El Greco resort tomorrow afternoon. We can spend some time with Theo before having our night together,' he quietly suggested.

She nodded again, sucked in a deep breath and blurted out, 'I'm sorry. It was mean of me…leaving you out of Theo's life.'

'You had your reasons,' he murmured sympathetically. 'It's how we take it from here that will count most to Theo.'

'Yes,' she agreed huskily, taking another deep breath before adding, 'He usually takes a nap after lunch. If you come at four o'clock, we'll tell him then.'

'Thank you.'

She gave him a wobbly smile. 'If that's everything settled, we should go back to the wedding reception. We'll be missed. It is Cass's night and I want to be there for her.'

'And I for George.'

Their first deal was still in place. He had to wait until tomorrow before taking what he wanted with Christina, yet her hand was still in his and as he rose from the table, the temptation to draw her up from her seat and straight into his embrace was irresistible. She didn't try to break free but her free hand fluttered in agitation against his chest and there was a heart-piercing vulnerability in the eyes that met his.

He hated her fear. It made him feel even more wrong about what he'd taken from her in the past. He pressed a soft kiss on her forehead and murmured, 'I'll make it right, Christina. For you and for Theo.'

He gave her what he hoped was a reassuring smile as he released her, only retaining her hand, keeping that physical link for the walk back to the wedding reception, wanting her to feel secure with him.

Tonight belonged to Cassandra and George.

Tomorrow was his.

He could wait.

CHAPTER TEN

TINA waited until after their Greek relatives departed for the mainland so she could have a private chat to her mother about her connection to Ari. Everyone had still been revelling in Cass's wedding—such a wonderful family celebration. Amongst the happy comments were a few arch remarks about Ari's interest in her.

'He didn't have eyes for anyone else.'

'Never left your side all evening.'

'Such a charming man!'

'And so handsome!'

Tina had shrugged off the curiosity, discouraging it by refocussing the conversation on her sister's life. However, she saw the same curiosity in her mother's eyes, and when they were finally alone together, relaxing on the lounges by the swimming pool, watching Theo practice diving into it, she didn't have to think about how to lead into revealing the truth. Her mother did it for her.

'Are you seeing Ari again today, Tina?'

'Yes. And there's something I have to tell you, Mama.' She took a deep breath to calm her jumpy nerves and started at the beginning. 'Ari Zavros and I were not meeting for the first time in Athens. Six years ago he was in Australia on a three-month tour of the wineries in our country. I met him on a modelling assignment and fell in love with him.'

Her mother instantly leapt to the truth, understanding of Ari's behaviour towards them flashing straight into her eyes. 'He's Theo's father.'

'Yes. I didn't expect to ever see him again. It was a shock when he was presented to us as George's best man. I asked him to wait until after the wedding before revealing that my son was also his because it would have been a major distraction from Cass and that wasn't fair, but today we have to deal with it, Mama.'

'Oh, my dear!' Her mother swung her legs off the lounge to face her directly with a look of anxious concern. 'These past few days must have been very difficult for you.'

Tina had to fight back tears. She hadn't expected such a rush of sympathy from her mother. Shock and perhaps criticism for her silence, worry over the situation, fretting over the choices to be made… she'd geared herself to cope with all this but not the caring for her feelings and the quick understanding of the distress she had been hiding.

'I thought…he was gone from my life, Mama,' she choked out. 'But he's not and he never will be again. He's made that very clear.'

'Yes…very clear,' her mother repeated, nodding as she recollected how Ari had inserted himself and his family into their time on Santorini. 'I don't think that's going to change, Tina. He's definitely intent on making a claim on his son.'

'And he has the wealth and power to back it up. There's no point in trying to resist his claim, Mama. I have to give way.'

'Has he said how he wants to deal with the situation?'

Tina's mouth instantly twisted into an ironic grimace. 'He wants me to marry him.'

'Ah!'

There was no real shock in that *Ah!*—more a realisation of the bigger claim being made—one that would completely change her daughter's life, as well as her grandson's.

After a few moments' thought, her mother asked, 'His family knows all this?'

'He told them after our meeting in Athens. He had no doubt that Theo was his child. His age…his eyes…'

'Yes…now I see.' Her mother nodded a few times. 'They have been extending a welcome to join their family because of Theo.'

'He is the main attraction,' Tina said dryly.

'But they have been very gracious to us, as well, Tina. Which shows they are prepared to accept you as Ari's wife. How do you feel about it?'

She shook her head. 'I don't know. He said he would have come back to me had I told him he'd left me pregnant. I didn't tell him because he didn't love me. I was only a…a charming episode…that he could walk away from.'

'But you loved him.'

'Yes. Totally.'

'And now?'

'I doubt there will ever be anyone else for me, Mama, but it's Theo he wants. I can't fool myself that I'm suddenly the woman he loves above all others.'

'Perhaps you are more special to him now because you are the mother of his child. It's a very Greek way of thinking, Tina. And sometimes love grows from sharing the most precious things to both of you.'

Tina choked up, remembering Ari listing how much he had missed of Theo because she had denied him knowledge of his son.

Her mother heaved a sigh. 'It's not for me to say what you should do, my darling. What do you think is best for you?'

'Oh, probably to marry him,' Tina said in a rush, relieved in a way to finally have it out in the open. 'I think he will be a good father. He's asked me to wait until he comes here this afternoon for us to tell Theo together that he does have a Papa. And after that—well, Ari and I need some time alone to...to see how we feel about each other, Mama. He wants to take me somewhere. Will you look after Theo, have him in your room tonight?'

'Oh, dear!' Her mother shook her head in dismay at realising what the all-night arrangement most probably meant. 'There's so much to take in. I wish your father was here.'

'Don't worry, Mama. I have to make a decision and I think this is the best way to do it.'

'Well, of course I will look after Theo, but...do be careful, Tina,' she said anxiously. 'If you decide not to marry Ari…I remember how you were when you were pregnant with Theo.'

'That won't happen again, Mama,' Tina assured her. It didn't matter this time if Ari used a contraceptive or not. She knew she was in a safe period of her cycle. She reached across and took her mother's hand. 'Thank you taking all this so well. I hate being a problem to you.'

'Not a problem, dear. Just… I do so want you to have a happy life and I wish with all my heart that everything turns out well with Ari.'

The fairy-tale happy ending.

Maybe if she could believe in it enough, it might happen. She'd have a better idea of how the future would run after tonight. Right now she couldn't trust Ari's word that he would remain a faithful husband. Even if they did find sexual pleasure with each other, that was no guarantee he would always be satisfied with her. She might begin to believe they really could forge a good marriage together after he signed the prenuptial agreement.

If he did.

Ari spent an extremely vexatious morning with his lawyer who was dead against signing away paternal rights under any circumstances. A financial settlement was fine in the case of divorce but giving up one's children was utter madness, especially since Ari was marrying to have his son.

'I'm not here for your advice,' Ari had finally said. 'Just draw up the agreement I've spelled out to you. It's an issue of showing good faith and I *will* show it.'

'Show it by all means,' his lawyer shot back at it him, 'but don't sign it.'

He hadn't…yet.

He'd done many deals in his life but none as risky as the one he'd proposed to Christina. The money didn't worry him. He would never begrudge financial support for her and their children. But if the response he needed from her was not forthcoming tonight, marrying her might be too much of a gamble.

His head told him this.

Yet his heart was already set on having Christina Savalas as his wife.

She touched him in ways no other woman had. He had been her first lover, almost certainly her only one, which made her his in a very primal sense. Plus the fact she had carried his child made her uniquely special. Besides, his wealth was not a big attraction to her or she would have gone after a slice of it to support their son rather than taking complete responsibility for him. She was only concerned about the kind of person he was. Looks, money…none of that counted. If he didn't measure up as a man she wanted in her life, he'd be out of it.

He'd never been challenged like this. Who he was on the surface of it had always been enough. Christina was hitting him at deeper levels and he felt totally driven to prove he did measure up—driven to remove all fear from her eyes. Winning her over had somehow become more important than anything else in his life.

The compelling tug of having Theo was a big part of it, but she was part of Theo, too. Ari couldn't separate them in his mind. Didn't want to separate them. The three of them made a family. *His* family. He had to make it so by any means possible because he couldn't tolerate the idea of Christina taking their son back to Australia and shutting him out of their lives as much as she legally could.

He lunched with his parents who were eager for another visit with their grandson. 'Tomorrow,' Ari promised them. 'I'll bring Christina and Theo and Helen back here tomorrow to sort out what is to be done.'

He had to stop them leaving Santorini on schedule. Even if Christina rejected his offer of marriage, she had to see reason about discussing future arrangements for their son. If she accepted his proposal, they would have a wedding to plan. More than a wedding. There would be many decisions to be made on setting up a life together—tying up ends in Australia, where best to make their home.

Ari was tense with determination as he drove to the El Greco resort. He told himself the meeting with Theo was relatively uncomplicated. There was no need to be uptight about his son's response. He had wished for a Papa. Revealing who that Papa was would certainly be a pleasure. What happened afterwards with Christina was the critical time. He fiercely hoped that was going to be a pleasure, too. If it wasn't... He instantly clicked his mind off any negative train of thought. This had to work.

Tina and her mother and Theo were sitting at one of the snack bar tables having afternoon tea when Ari arrived. He came striding down the ramp to the pool patio, a hard purposeful expression on his face, and headed straight towards where their rooms were located.

'We're here!' Tina called out, rising from her chair to catch his attention, her heartbeat instantly accelerating at what his arrival meant for both her and Theo.

His head jerked around and his expression immediately lightened on seeing them. Theo jumped off his chair and ran to meet him. Ari scooped him up in his arms and perched him against his shoulder, smiling broadly at his son's eagerness to welcome him.

'I finished the train station. You must come and see it, Ari,' Theo prattled happily.

'As soon as I say hello to your mother and grandmother,' he promised.

He shot a sharp look of enquiry at Tina as he approached their table. She nodded, assuring him her mother had been told. He smiled at both of them but the smile didn't quite reach his eyes. It made Tina wonder how tense he was over the situation. Marriage was a big step and it might not be the best course for them to take. Was he having second thoughts about his proposal?

He addressed her mother directly, speaking in a quiet tone that carried an impressive intensity of purpose. 'Helen, I want you to know I will look after your daughter with much more care than I did in the past. Please trust me on that.'

'Tina and Theo are very precious to me, Ari,' her mother answered. 'I hope your caring will be as deep as mine.'

He nodded and turned his gaze to Tina. 'Theo wants me to see his train station.'

'I'll take you to our room. He did a great job putting all the Lego together.' She smiled at her son. 'It was very tricky, wasn't it, darling?'

'Very tricky,' he echoed, then grinned triumphantly at Ari. 'But I did it!'

'I knew you were a clever boy,' he warmly approved.

'Will you wait here, Mama?' Tina asked.

'Yes, dear. Go on now.'

Theo was full of questions about Ari's nephews whom he'd spent most of his time with at the wedding reception. Tina didn't have to say anything on their walk to her room. She was acutely conscious of the easy bond Ari had already established with their son and felt fairly sure there would be no trauma attached to revealing the truth. If she made it like a fairy-tale to Theo, he might accept it unquestioningly. On the other hand, there could be a host of questions both of them would have to answer.

Her chest ached with tension as she opened the door to her room and stood aside for Ari to carry Theo inside. He paused a moment, giving her a burning look of command as he said, '*I'll* tell him.'

She felt an instant wave of resentment at his arbitrary taking over from her, yet it did relieve her of the responsibility of explaining the situation to Theo. *Let him get it right for their son,* she thought, closing the door behind them, then parking herself on the chair at the writing desk while Ari duly admired the Lego train station.

'Does your Mama tell you bed-time stories, Theo?' he asked, sitting down on the bed beside the fully constructed station.

'Yes. She points to the words in the book and I can read some of them now,' he answered proudly.

'I think you must be very quick at learning things. If I tell you a story, I wonder if you could guess the ending,' Ari said with a teasing smile.

'Tell me! Tell me!'Theo cried eagerly, sitting cross-legged on the floor in front of Ari, his little body bent forward attentively.

Ari bent forwards, too, his forearms resting on his knees, his gaze locked on the amber eyes shining up at him. 'Once upon a time a prince from a faraway country travelled to a land on the other side of the world.'

Tina was totally stunned that Ari had chosen to use a fairy story to convey the truth, yet how much of the truth would he tell? The tension inside her screwed up several notches.

'There he met a beautiful princess and she was like no one else he'd ever met. He wanted to be with her all the time and she wanted to be with him so they were together while he was in her country. But eventually he had to leave to carry out business for his kingdom back home. It hurt the princess very much when he said goodbye to her and when she found out that she was going to have a baby she decided not to send any message to the prince about it. She didn't want him to come back, then leave her again because it would hurt too much. So she kept the baby a secret from him.'

'Was the baby a boy or a girl?' Theo asked.

'It was a boy. And he was very much loved by her family. This made the princess think he didn't need a Papa because he already had enough people to love him. She didn't know that the boy secretly wished for a Papa.'

'Like me,' Theo popped in. 'But I didn't wish for one until I went to school. It was because my friends there have fathers.'

'It is only natural for you to want one,' Ari assured him.

'Does the boy in the story get his?'

'Let me tell you how it happened. After a few years the sister of the princess was to marry a man who came from the same country as the prince, so her family had to travel halfway around the world to attend the wedding. The princess didn't know that this man was a cousin of the prince and she would meet him again. It was a shock to her when she did, and when the prince saw her son, he knew the boy was his son, too. They had the same eyes.'

'Like you and me,' Theo said, instantly grasping the point.

'Yes. Exactly like that. But the princess asked the prince to keep her secret until after her sister's wedding because she didn't want to take people's attention away from the bride. The prince understood this but he wanted to spend as much time as he could with his son. And he also wanted the princess to know that being a father meant a lot to him. It made him very sad that he had missed out on so much of his son's life and he wanted to be there for him in the future.'

'Can I guess now?' Theo asked.

Ari nodded.

Theo cocked his head to the side, not quite sure he had it right, but wanting to know. 'Are you my Papa, Ari?'

'Yes, Theo. I am,' he answered simply.

Tina held her breath until she saw a happy grin break out on Theo's face. The same grin spread across Ari's. Neither of them looked at her. This was their moment—five years in the waiting—and she couldn't resent being excluded from it. It was her fault they had been kept apart all this time. Ari had been fair in his story-telling and she now had to be fair to the bond she had denied both of them.

'I'm glad you're my Papa,' Theo said fervently, rising to his feet. 'After my birthday party I dreamed that you were.'

Ari lifted him onto his knee, hugging him close. 'We'll always celebrate your birthday together,' he promised huskily.

'But I don't want you to hurt Mama again.'

Tears pricked Tina's eyes, her heart swelling at the love and loyalty in Theo's plea to his father.

'I am trying very hard not to,' Ari said seriously. 'I kept her secret until today, and now your Mama and I are going to work out how best we can be together for the rest of our lives. Will you be happy to be with your grandmother while we do that?'

'Does Yiayia know you're my Papa?'

'Yes. Your Mama told her this morning. And now that you know, too, you can talk about it to your grandmother. Tomorrow, if it's okay with your Mama, I'll take you to visit your other grandparents whom you met at your birthday party.'

Theo's eyes rounded in wonderment. 'Is Maximus my Papou?'

'Yes, and he very much wants to see you again. So does my mother. You will have a much bigger family. The boys you played with at the wedding are your cousins.'

'Will they be there tomorrow?'

'Yes.' Ari rose to his feet, hoisting Theo up in his arms. 'Let's go back to your grandmother because your Mama and I need to have some time to talk about all this.'

The face Theo turned to Tina was full of excitement. 'Is it okay with you, Mama?' he asked eagerly.

'Yes,' she said, not yet ready to commit to a mass family involvement until after her night with Ari, but smiling at her son to remove any worry from his mind.

It was enough for Theo.

He was content to be left with her mother, happy to share the news that his birthday wish had come true and ask a million questions about what might happen next. He waved goodbye to Tina and Ari without a qualm.

All the qualms were in Tina's stomach.

She was about to face a new beginning with Ari Zavros or an end to the idea of marrying him.

CHAPTER ELEVEN

ARI took her hand as they walked up the ramp to the courtyard in front of the reception building. The physical link flooded her mind with thoughts of the intimacy to come. For him it was probably just another night of sex—the performance of an act that had been commonplace in his life, varied only by the different women he'd taken to bed with him.

For her…a little shiver ran down her spine…it had been so long, and she wasn't dazzled by him this time.

Could she really shut off her disillusionment with the love she'd believed he'd shared and take pleasure in what he could give her? He'd said he'd try very hard not to hurt her. There was no need to be frightened of him, but she was frightened of the feelings he might evoke in her. This was not a time to be weak or confused. There was too much at stake to blindly follow instincts that had led her astray in the past.

Though she had to concede that Ari had been very good with Theo. He'd also saved her from the dilemma of how to explain the truth to their son. At least that was done with, and done well, which was only fair to acknowledge.

'I liked your fairy story,' she said, slanting him an appreciative little smile.

He flashed a hopeful smile back. 'We have yet to give it a happy ending.'

'To dream the impossible dream...' tripped straight off her tongue.

'Not impossible, Christina. Open your mind to it.'

They reached his car and he opened the passenger door for her. She paused, looking directly at him before stepping in. 'I don't know *your* mind, Ari. That's the problem.'

Intensity of purpose glittered in his amber eyes as he answered, 'Then I hope you'll know it better by tomorrow morning.'

'I hope I do, too.' She gestured to the car. 'Where are you taking me?'

'To Oia, the northern village of Santorini, the best place for watching the sunset. I've arranged for a suite in a boutique hotel which will give us the perfect view. I thought you would like it.'

'That's...very romantic.'

'With you I want to be romantic,' he replied, his whole expression softening with a look of rueful tenderness that twisted her heart.

She tore her gaze from his and quickly settled herself in the passenger seat, silently and furiously chastising herself for the craven wish to be romanced out of all her mistrust of his fairy-tale happy ending. He was going to make it all too easy to surrender to his charm and there was a huge vulnerable part of her that wanted to believe she was special to him this time and there would be no turning away from her ever again.

But it was his child he really wanted. She was the package deal. And she had no idea how long the package would stay attractive to him. Even if Ari romanced her beautifully tonight, she had to keep her head on straight and insist on the prenuptial agreement he'd offered. It was her insurance against making another big mistake with him.

He chatted to her about the various features of the island they passed on their way to Oia, intent on establishing a companionable mood. Tina did her best to relax and respond in an interested fashion. She remembered how interested he had been in Australia, always asking her questions about it whenever they were driving somewhere together.

'Where would you want us to live if I marry you, Ari?' she asked, needing to know what he had in mind.

He hesitated, then bluntly answered, 'Australia is too far away from my family's business interests, Christina. We could base ourselves anywhere in Europe. Athens if you would like to be near your relatives. Perhaps Helen would like to return there. She would see more of Cassandra and George in the future if she did, and put her closer to us, as well.'

It meant completely uprooting herself. And Theo. Though Ari had made a good point about her mother. So much change…she would end up leading an international life like Cass. Her sister had acclimatised herself to it. Loved it. Perhaps she would learn to love it, too.

'It's also a matter of choosing what might be best for our children's education,' Ari added, shooting her a quick smile.

Our children... It was a very seductive phrase. She adored having Theo. She'd love to have a little girl, as well. If she didn't marry Ari, it was highly unlikely that she would have any more children. But if she had them with Ari, she didn't want to lose them to him.

'Are you okay with that, Christina?' he asked, frowning at her silence.

'I'm opening my mind to it,' she tossed at him.

He laughed, delighted that it wasn't a negative answer.

They had to leave the car on the outskirts of the village and continue on foot through the narrow alleys to the hotel. Both of them had brought light backpacks with essentials for an overnight stay. It only took a minute to load them onto their shoulders and Ari once again took possession of Tina's hand for the walk into the village. It felt more comfortable now, especially as they navigated past the steady stream of tourists that thronged the alleys lined with fascinating shops.

Again she was acutely aware of women looking Ari over but the handhold meant he belonged to her, and she firmly reminded herself that not even Cass's beautiful model friends had turned his head last night. If she could just feel more confident that he could be content with only having her, the female attention he invariably drew might not worry her so much. It hadn't worried her in the past. She had been totally confident that he was hers. Until he wasn't hers any more.

But marriage was different to a *charming episode*.

A wedding ring on Ari's finger would make him legally hers.

Very publicly hers.

That should give her some sense of security with him.

In fact, being the wife of Ari Zavros would empower her quite a bit on many levels.

If she could make herself hard-headed enough to set aside any possible hurt from him in the future and simply go through with the marriage, dealing with each day as it came, her life could become far more colourful than she would ever manage on her own. Besides which if it ended in divorce, the financial settlement would give her the means to do whatever she chose. Wanting Ari to love her…well, that was probably wishing for the moon, but who knew? Even that might come to pass if her mother was right about sharing what was precious to both of them.

All the buildings in Oia were crammed up against each other, using every available bit of space. The entrance to the hotel opened straight onto an alley with pot-plants on either side of the door its only adornment. It was certainly boutique size. The man at the reception desk greeted Ari enthusiastically and escorted them to a suite on what proved to be the top level of three built down the hillside facing the sea. The bathroom, bedroom and balcony were all small but perfectly adequate and the view from the balcony was spectacular.

'Sunset is at eight o'clock,' their escort informed them before departing.

Almost three hours before then, Tina thought, dumping her backpack on a chair and gravitating straight to the balcony, suddenly too nervous to face Ari in the bedroom. A spiral staircase ran down the side of the hotel, linked by landings to each balcony, giving guests easy access to the small swimming pool which took up half the courtyard that extended from the hotel's lowest level. A few people were lounging on deck chairs beside it. She stared down at them, wondering where they had come from and what had brought them here. Probably nothing as complicated as her own situation.

Behind her she heard the pop of a champagne cork. A few moments later Ari was at her side carrying two glasses fizzing with the bubbly wine.

'You used to drink this with me. Will you try it again, Christina? It might relax you,' he said kindly.

She heaved a sigh to ease the tightness in her chest and took the glass he offered. 'Thank you. It's been six years since I was in an intimate situation with a man,' she said with a rueful smile. 'This might take the edge off.'

'I guess having Theo made it difficult for you to form relationships,' he remarked sympathetically.

Not Theo. You. But telling him so would let him know she was stuck on him and it was better that he didn't know. She didn't want him taking anything for granted where she was concerned.

'Don't worry that I'll make you pregnant tonight. I'll be very careful,' he assured her.

She shook her head. 'You won't anyway. This is a safe week for me.'

'Ah!' He grinned, the amber eyes twinkling with pleasure. 'Then we may be totally carefree which will be much better.' He clinked her glass with his. 'To a night of re-discovery, Christina.'

She took a quick sip of the champagne, hoping to settle the flock of butterflies in her stomach. Ari's arm slid around her waist, his hand resting warmly on the curve of her hip, bringing his body closer to hers, stirring memories of how well they had fitted together in the past and triggering the desire to re-discover every sweet nuance of her sexuality.

'I don't want to wait until tonight,' she said decisively, setting her glass down on the top of the balcony wall and turning to face him, a wave of reckless belligerence seizing her and pouring into urgent words. 'Let's just do it, Ari. I don't want to be romanced or seduced or…or treated to any other lover routine you've got. This is a need to know thing, isn't it?'

He set his glass down next to hers and scooped her hard against him, his freed hand lifting to her chin, tilting it up, his eyes blazing a heart-kicking challenge right at her. 'A great many needs to be answered on both sides and I don't want to wait, either.'

His mouth came down on hers so hard she jerked her head back, afraid of what she had just invited. He'd been a tender lover to her, never rough. Panic kicked into her heart. What did she know of him now? If he had no real feeling for her…

'Damn!' he muttered, his chest heaving as he sucked in breath, a glint of anguish in the eyes that bored into hers. 'I *will* control myself. Let me start again, Christina.'

He didn't wait for a reply. His lips brushed lightly over hers, back and forth, back and forth, making them tingle to the point where she welcomed the running of his tongue-tip over them. *Yes,* she thought dizzily, the stiffness melting from her body, panic washed away by a soothing flood of warmth. She lifted her arms and wound them around his neck as she gave herself up to a kiss that was more familiar to her, a loving kind of kiss.

She didn't mind opening her mouth to the gentle probe of his tongue, liking the intimate sensation of tangling her own with it, the slow gathering of excitement. It was easy to close her eyes and forget the years of nothing, remembering only the girl she had been in this man's arms, experiencing sexual pleasure for the first time.

His hand slid down over her bottom, pressing her closer to him, and the hardness of his erection filled her mind with giddy elation. He couldn't fake that. He really did want her. She was still desirable to him so it was okay to desire him, too. And she did, quite fiercely, given the confidence that this wasn't just a cynical seduction to weaken her stance against him.

A wild ripple of exultation shot through her when his kissing took on a more passionate intensity, his tongue driving deep, challenging her to meet its thrust, revel in the explosion of need behind it. Her hands slid into his hair, fingers digging in hard to hold his head to hers,

the desire to take possession of him and keep him forever running rampant through her mind.

He couldn't walk away from this.

Not ever again.

She wouldn't let him.

He wrenched his head from her tight grasp, lifting it
back from her mouth enough to gasp, 'Must move from
here. Come.'

He scooped her off the balcony and into the bedroom,
striding for the bed with her firmly tucked to his side.
Tina's heart was pounding with both fear and excitement. This was the moment to undress. She would see
him again fully naked. But he would see her, too. How
did she measure up against the other women who'd been
in his life... the blonde in Dubai whose breasts had been
more voluptuous?

But he *was* aroused, so maybe the *idea* of her made
physical factors irrelevant. And although she was carrying more flesh than when he had been with her before,
her body was still okay—no looseness from having the
baby. It was silly to fret over it. He wanted sex with her.
He was up and ready for it and it was going to happen.

He stopped close to the bed and swung her to face
him, his hands curling around her shoulders, his eyes
sweeping hers for any hint of last-minute rejection. She
stared back steadily, determined not to baulk at this
point.

'You move me as no other woman ever has,
Christina,' he murmured, and planted a soft warm kiss
on her forehead.

Her heart contracted at those words. Whether they

were true or not, the wish to believe them was too strong to fight. She closed her eyes wanting to privately hug the strong impression of sincerity in his, and he gently kissed her eyelids, sealing the positive flow of feeling he had evoked.

She felt his thumbs hook under the straps of the green sundress she'd worn and slowly slide them down her upper arms. He kissed her bared shoulders as he unzipped the back of her bodice. Tina kept her eyes shut, fiercely focussing on her other senses, loving the soft brush of his lips against her skin and the gentle caress of his fingers along her spine as it, too, was bared. She breathed in the slightly spicy scent of his cologne. It was the same as when they were together before. He hadn't changed it. And the thrill of his touch was the same, too.

Her dress slithered down to the floor. The style of it hadn't required a bra so now her breasts were naked. Her only remaining garment was her green bikini pants, but he didn't set about removing this last piece of clothing. His hands cupped her breasts, stroking them with a kind of reverence that she found emotionally confusing until he asked, 'Did you breast-feed Theo, Christina?'

He was thinking of his son. He was not looking at her as a woman but as the mother of his child.

'Yes,' she answered huskily, telling herself it was okay for him to see her in this light. It made her different to the other women who'd been in his life. More special. Her body had carried his child, had nurtured his child.

'He must have been a very happy baby,' he murmured, and his mouth enclosed one of her nipples, his tongue swirling around it before he sucked on it.

Tina gasped at the arc of piercing pleasure that hit her stomach and shot past it to the apex of her thighs. Her hands flew up and grasped his shoulders, fingers digging into his muscles, needing something strong to hold onto as quivers ran through her entire body. He moved his mouth to her other breast, increasing the sweet turbulence inside her. For her it had been a physical pleasure breast-feeding Theo but it hadn't generated this acute level of sexual excitement. Tina was so wound up in it, she didn't know if it was a relief or a disappointment when he lifted his head away.

Almost immediately he was whipping down her bikini pants and her feet automatically stepped out of them. Any concern about how she looked to him had completely disappeared. He scooped her into such a crushing embrace she could feel his heart thumping against his chest-wall and then he was kissing her again; hard, hungry kisses that sparked an overwhelming hunger for him. She wanted this man. She'd never stopped wanting him.

He lifted her off her feet and laid her on the bed. The sudden loss of contact with him instantly opened her eyes. He was discarding his clothes with such haste Tina was in no doubt of his eagerness to join her, and it was thrilling to watch his nakedness emerge. He was a truly beautiful man with a perfect male body. His olive skin gleamed over well-defined muscles. His smooth hairless chest was sculpted for touching, for gliding hands over it. He had the lean hips and powerful thighs of a top athlete. And there was certainly no doubt about his desire for her, his magnificent manhood flagrantly erect.

Yet when he came to her he ignored any urgency for instant sexual satisfaction. He lay beside her, one arm sliding under her shoulders to draw her into full body contact with him, his free hand stroking long, lovely caresses as his mouth claimed hers again, more in a slow seductive tasting than greedy passion. It gave her the freedom to touch him, to revel in feeling his strong masculinity against her softer femininity, the whole wonderfully sensual intimacy of flesh against flesh.

His hand dipped into the crevice between her thighs, his fingers moving gently, back and forth, intent on building excitement until she felt the exquisite urgency he had always made her feel in the past. Tina lifted her leg over his, giving him easier access to her, refusing to let any inhibitions deny her the pleasure she remembered. He changed the nature of his kissing, his tongue thrusting and withdrawing, mimicking the rhythm of what was to come, accelerating the need to have him there.

But still he didn't hurry. He moved down the bed, trailing kisses to the hollow of her throat, then sucking briefly on her breasts, heightening their sensitivity before sliding his mouth to her stomach, running his tongue around her navel.

'Was it a difficult labour with Theo, Christina?' he asked in a deeply caring tone.

She'd been so focussed on feeling, it took a concentrated effort to find her voice. 'Some…some hard hours,' she answered, savagely wishing he wasn't thinking of their son. Yet that was why he was here, with her, doing what he was doing, and she wouldn't be having this if she hadn't had his child.

'I should have been there,' he murmured, pressing his mouth to her stomach as though yearning for that lost time. 'I would have been there. And I will be for the rest of our children,' he said more fiercely before lifting himself further down to kiss her where his son had emerged from her womb.

I'm not going to think of why, Tina decided with wild determination. *I want this. I want him inside me again.*

The tension building in her body obliterated any further thought. Need was screaming through every nerve. It reached the point where she jack-knifed up to pluck at his shoulders, crying out, 'Enough! Enough!' She couldn't bear another second of waiting for him.

To her intense relief he responded instantly, surging up to fit himself between her legs which were already lifting to curl around his hips in a compulsive urging for the action she frantically craved. Her inner muscles were convulsing as he finally entered her and just one deep plunge drove her to an explosive climax, the exquisite torture peaking then melting into wave after wave of ecstatic pleasure as Ari continued the wonderfully intimate stroking.

It was incredibly satisfying, feeling him filling her again and again. Her body writhed exultantly around him. Her hands dragged up and down his back, urging on the rhythm of mutual possession. The sheer elation of it was so marvellously sweet nothing else existed for Tina, not the why or the where or the how.

When Ari cried out at his own climax, it sounded like a triumphant trumpet of joy to her ears. *She* had brought him to this. He shared the same heights of sensation he had led her to. And she revelled in that sense of intense togetherness as all his mighty strength collapsed on her and she hugged him with all her strength. He rolled onto his side, clutching her tightly against him, holding onto the deep connection, clearly wanting it to last as long as possible.

He didn't speak for quite a long time and Tina didn't want to break the silence. She lay with her head tucked under his chin, listening to his pulse-rate slowing to a normal beat. It was the first time today she actually felt totally relaxed. The sex-test was over. He had certainly satisfied her as a lover and if he was satisfied that she wouldn't turn her back on him, maybe they could move towards a commitment to each other.

It might even have a chance of sticking.

If she kept on having his children.

Was that the key to having him come to love her?

If only she could be sure he would in the end...truly love her for herself...and never want any other woman.

Marrying Ari was a terrible gamble.

But having had him again, she didn't want to let him go.

CHAPTER TWELVE

Ari felt happy. Usually after sex he felt satisfied, content, relaxed. Happiness was something more and it made him wonder if it was a temporary thing or whether having Christina would always give him this exultant sense of joy. Maybe it was simply a case of having risen to the challenge and won the response he wanted from her.

It had been damnably difficult to rein himself in to begin with. Having been forced to exercise control on the physical front for the past few days and suddenly being presented with the green light to go ahead, all the bottled-up desire he'd felt had blown his mind. And almost blown his chance with her.

But she wasn't pulling away from him now. He wished she still had long hair. He remembered how much he'd enjoyed running his fingers through it when she'd lain with him like this in the past. Though it didn't really matter. It was so good just having her content to stay where she was—no barriers between them. No *physical* barriers. He hoped the mental resistance she'd had to him had been stripped away, too.

He knew he'd given her intense sexual pleasure. Was it enough to sway her into marrying him? She had to be considering what Theo wanted in his life, too, and there was no doubt he wanted his father. What more could be done to clinch a future together?

He probably should be talking to her, finding out what was in her mind, yet he was reluctant to break the intimate silence. They had all night, plenty of time for talking. It was great being able to revel in the certainty that she would not be cold to him in the marriage bed.

She stirred, lifting her head. 'I need to go to the bathroom, Ari.'

He released her and she instantly rolled away and onto her feet on the other side of the bed, only giving him a back view of her as she walked swiftly to the bathroom, no glimpse of the expression on her face. However, he couldn't help smiling at the lovely curve of her spine, the perkiness of her sexy bottom and the perfect shape of her long legs.

There was nothing unattractive about Christina Savalas. No one would be surprised at his choice of wife. Not that he cared about what anyone else thought but it would make it easier for Christina to be readily accepted as his partner in life. Women could be quite bitchy if they perceived any other woman as not measuring up to what they expected. Felicity Fulbright had sniped about quite a few while in his company.

Of course he would be on guard to protect Christina from any nastiness but there were always female get-togethers when he wouldn't be present. On the other hand, the fighting spirit his father admired in her was undoubtedly a force to be reckoned with in any kind of critical situation. She would have no qualms about setting people straight as she saw it. She'd done it to him repeatedly in the past few days.

All in all, Ari was quite looking forward to a future with Christina now that the sexual question was answered. However, his satisfaction took a slight knock when she re-emerged from the bathroom, wearing a white cotton kimono which covered her from neck to ankle. It signalled that she wasn't about to jump back into bed with him.

'I found this hanging on a peg behind the bathroom door,' she said, putting a firm knot in the tie-belt and not quite meeting his gaze as she added, 'There's another one for you if you want to wear it after your shower. Easier than re-dressing for sitting on the balcony to watch the sunset.'

And easier for undressing afterwards, Ari thought, accepting her plan of action without argument. It was obvious that she had already showered—no invitation for him to join her—so she was putting an end to their intimacy for a while, which raised questions about how eager she was to continue it. An intriguing combination—hot in bed, cool out of it—another challenge that he had to come to grips with.

She wasn't won yet.

'Have a look at the menu on the desk while I shower,' he said invitingly. 'See what you'd like for dinner. We can order it in.'

It stopped her stroll towards the balcony. She paused at the desk to pick up the menu and began to study it, not even glancing at him as he rose from the bed and moved towards the bathroom. Was she embarrassed by her body's response to his love-making? Was she always going to close up on him afterwards? How much was she truly willing to share with him?

Ari mused over these questions while taking a shower. In every one of his relationships with women there had always been mutual desire and mutual liking, at least at the beginning. It had certainly been so with Christina six years ago. In fact, looking back, that had been the only relationship he'd been reluctant to end. Nothing had soured it. Christina had not deceived him in any way, nor done anything to turn him off. The timing had been wrong, nothing else.

He was still sure his reasons for limiting it to his time in Australia were valid, yet his decision then kept coming between them now and he was no longer sure that good sex was the answer to reaching the kind of relationship he wanted with his wife.

Though it still made the marriage viable.

The mutual desire was right.

He just had to work on getting the mutual liking right again.

Having picked up their clothes from the floor and hung them over a chair, Tina took the menu out to the balcony and sat down at the small table for two. She was hungry, having only had a very light lunch, too full of nervous tension to enjoy food. Now that she felt less uptight about spending the night with Ari, a sunset dinner was very appealing.

She studied the list of dishes with interest, thinking this was the first meal she would spend alone with Ari since meeting him again. It was an opportunity to extend her knowledge of his lifestyle, which was an important preparation for being his wife. There was more to marriage than good sex and she wasn't about to let Ari think that was all he had to give her.

Though it was a very powerful drawcard, completely meddling with Tina's common sense when he strolled out to the balcony. His white kimono barely reached his knees and left a deep V of gleaming olive-skinned chest, causing her to catch her breath. He was so overwhelmingly male and so vitally handsome, all her female hormones were zinging as though caught in an electrical storm. Chemistry still humming from the sex they'd just shared, Tina told herself, but the desire for more of it could not be denied.

'Found what you'd like?' he asked, gesturing towards the menu.

'Yes.' She rattled off a starter, a main dish, and sweets, as well.

He grinned approval at her. 'I've worked up an appetite, too. Give me the menu and I'll call in an order now.' He nodded at the lowering sun. 'It will be pleasant to dine as we watch the sunset.'

Both the sky and the sea were already changing colour. Ari tucked the menu under his arm, picked up the half-empty champagne glasses from the balcony wall and returned to the bedroom to make the call. Tina watched the shimmering waves with their shifting shades of light, trying to calm herself enough to conduct a normal conversation without being continually distracted by lustful thoughts.

Ari brought back two clean wine glasses and an ice-bucket containing a bottle of light white wine which he said would go well with their starters. Tina decided she might as well give up her alcohol ban. Wine was part and parcel of Ari's life and it was more appropriate for his wife to partake of some of it.

He was standing by the balcony wall, opening the bottle of wine when he was hailed from below.

'Ari… Ari… It is you, isn't it?'

Tina's nerves instantly twanged. It was a female voice with a very British accent, like that of the woman who'd been with him in Dubai.

He looked down, his shoulders stiffening as he recognised the person. He raised a hand in acknowledgement but made no vocal reply, quickly turning back to the task of filling their glasses. His mouth had thinned into a line of vexation. His eyes were hooded.

Clearly this was an unwelcome intrusion and Tina felt impelled to ask, 'Who is it?' Facing other women who'd been in his life would have to be done sooner or later and it was probably better that she had a taste of it now, know whether or not she could deal with it.

He grimaced. 'Stephanie Gilchrist. A London socialite.'

'Not a fond memory?' she queried archly, pretending it wasn't important.

His eyes blazed annoyance. 'An acquaintance. No more. I see she's here with her current playmate, Hans

Vogel, a German model who's always strutting his stuff. I had no idea they were booked into this hotel.'

Just two people he didn't want to mix with tonight, Tina thought with considerable relief. She didn't really want to be faced with a woman who had shared his bed, not when the intimacies they had just shared were so fresh in her mind, not when her body was still reacting to them. This new beginning would not feel so good. Later on, when she felt more confident about being Ari's partner—when he made her feel more confident—it might not matter at all.

'Ari!' Stephanie called more demandingly.

'Damned nuisance!' he muttered savagely as he swung around to deal with the problem.

Having regained his attention, Stephanie bluntly asked, 'What are you doing here? I thought you had a home on Santorini. I'm sure Felicity told me…'

'This hotel has a better view of the sunset,' Ari swiftly cut in. 'Why don't you and Hans just lie back on your lounges and enjoy it?'

He waved his hand dismissively but Stephanie apparently had some personal axe to grind with him. 'I'm coming up,' she announced belligerently.

Ari cursed under his breath. He turned sharply to Tina, his brow creased with concern, the amber eyes glittering with intense urgency. 'I'm sorry. I can't stop her. The spiral staircase is open to all guests. I will get rid of her as fast as I can.'

Tina shrugged. 'I can be polite to one of your acquaintances for a few minutes,' she said, eyeing him warily, wondering if he had lied to her about the less than intimate connection to this woman.

Ari swiftly rattled out information. 'She's a close friend of Felicity Fullbright. Felicity was the woman you saw me with in Dubai. Since Stephanie is here, I don't know if she's been told I've ended the relationship with her friend. Anything she says… it's irrelevant to us, Christina. Don't let it worry you.'

It worried him.

Here's where I learn if I'm a fool to even consider marrying him, Tina thought, putting a steel guard around her vulnerability to this man.

Her heart started a painful pounding. 'How long were you with Felicity, Ari?' she asked, needing to know more.

'Six weeks. It was enough to decide she didn't suit me,' he answered tersely.

'You haven't been with me for a week yet,' she pointed out just as tersely.

The clip-clop of sandals was getting closer.

Ari frowned, shaking his head at her assertion. 'It's different with you, Christina.'

Because of Theo. But if they married, he would have to live with her, too, and how long would that suit him? They had had a harmonious relationship for three months but still he'd left her. It hadn't been enough to keep him at her side.

Stephanie's arrival on the staircase landing adjacent to their balcony put a halt to any further private conversation. She was a very curvy blonde with a mass of long, crinkly hair, and wearing a minute blue bikini that left little to the imagination. Her very light, almost aquamarine eyes instantly targeted Tina.

'Well, well, off with the old and on with the new,' she drawled. Her gaze shifted to Ari. 'That must be a quick-change record even for you. I ran into Felicity at Heathrow just a few days ago. She was flying in from Athens and Hans and I were on our way here. She said you'd split but she sure didn't know you had a replacement lined up.'

No waiting for an introduction.

No courtesy at all.

Tina sat tight, watching Ari handle the situation.

'You're assuming too much, Stephanie,' he said blandly, gesturing towards Tina. 'This is Christina Savalas whom I met in Australia quite a few years ago. She happens to be Cassandra's sister who married my cousin, George, yesterday. The wedding gave us the opportunity to catch up again, which has been amazingly good.' He smiled at Tina. 'Wouldn't you say?'

'Amazing,' she echoed, following his lead and smiling back at him.

Stephanie arched her eyebrows. 'Australia? Are you heading back there now that the wedding is over?'

Tina shrugged. 'I shall have to go sometime.'

'Not in any hurry since you've snagged Ari again,' came the mocking comment.

The woman's sheer rudeness goaded Tina into a very cold retort. 'I'm not into snagging men. In fact...'

'I'm the one doing all the running,' Ari cut in. 'And having found out what you wanted to know, why don't you run along back to Hans, Stephanie? You're not exactly endearing yourself to a woman I care about.'

'Really care?' She gave Ari a derisive sneer. 'It's not just a dose of the charm you used to bowl over Felicity? You didn't care about her one bit, did you?'

'Not after she displayed a dislike for children, no,' he answered bitingly.

'Oh!' With her spite somewhat deflated, she turned to Tina for a last jeer. 'Well, I've just done you a favour. You'd better show a liking for children or he'll throw you over as fast as he caught up with you. Good luck!'

With a toss of her hair she flounced off their balcony.

Tina stared out to sea as Stephanie's sandals clattered down the spiral staircase. She wondered if it was good luck or bad that had brought her back into Ari's life. Whatever…luck had little to do with making a marriage work. At least, a liking for children was one thing they definitely shared. Ari wouldn't be throwing her over on that issue. But Stephanie had implied he had a quick turnover of women in his life, which meant he wasn't in the habit of holding onto a relationship. What if she didn't *suit* him after a while?

'You hardly know me, Ari,' she said, suddenly frightened that her suitability might be very limited.

'I know enough to want you as my wife,' he whipped out, an emphatic intensity in his voice. 'And not only because you've given me a son. There's nothing I don't like about you, Christina.'

She sliced him a wary look. 'What do you actively *like?*'

He sat down at the table, pushing one of the glasses

of wine over to her, obviously playing for time to think. 'Take a sip. It doesn't have a sour taste like Stephanie,' he assured her.

She picked up the glass and sipped, eyeing him over its rim.

The expression on his face softened, the amber eyes telegraphing appreciation. 'I like how much you care for your family. I like the way you consider others. I like your good manners. I think you have courage and grit and intelligence—all qualities that I like. They make up the kind of character that I want in a partner.'

He wasn't talking love. He was ticking off boxes. She could tick off the same boxes about him. A matchmaking agency would probably place them as a likely couple, especially since there was no lack of sexual chemistry between them. But there was one big factor missing.

Tina heaved a sigh as she remembered how Cass and George had acted towards each other yesterday. It hurt that she would never have that wonderful emotional security with Ari. What if she married him and he was bowled over by some other woman further down the track? It could happen. She had to be prepared for it, safeguard herself against it, be practical about what she could expect from him and what she couldn't.

'Tell me about your life, Ari,' she said, needing to feel more informed about what a future with him would entail. 'What are the business interests that take you travelling? I only know of your connection to the wine industry.'

He visibly relaxed, happy to have the Stephanie can of worms closed.

Tina listened carefully to the list of property investments the Zavros family had made in many countries as far apart as Spain and Dubai where Ari had so recently been checking up on an estate development. Mostly they were connected to the tourist industry—resorts and theme parks and specialty shops. They had also tapped into the food industry with olives, cheeses and wine.

'You're in charge of all this?' she enquired.

He shook his head. 'My father runs the ship. I report and advise. The decisions are ultimately his. Most of the family is involved in one capacity or another.'

It was big business—far more complex than managing a restaurant. Tina continued to question him about it over dinner which was as tasty as it had promised to be. The sunset was gorgeous, spreading a rosy hue over all the white buildings on the hillside that faced it. For real lovers this had to be a very romantic place, Tina thought, but she couldn't feel it with Ari. As charming as he was, as good a lover as he was, no way could she bring herself to believe she was the light of his life.

Her own experience prompted her to ask, 'Have you ever been in love, Ari? So in love that person mattered more than anything else? Wildly, passionately, out of your mind...*in love?*'

As she'd been with him.

He frowned, obviously not liking the question. His jaw tightened as he swung his gaze away from hers, staring out to sea. She saw the corner of his mouth turn down into a grimace. He had experienced it, she thought, but not with her. A lead weight settled on her heart. He might very well experience it again with someone else.

CHAPTER THIRTEEN

IN LOVE...

Ari hated that memory. It was the one and only time he'd completely lost his head over a woman. He'd been her fool, slavishly besotted with her while she had only been amusing herself with him.

He wished Christina hadn't asked the question. Yet if he wasn't honest with her she would probably sense it and that would be a black mark against him in her mind. Besides, he was a different person to the boy he was then. He just didn't like dragging up that long-buried piece of the past and laying it out but he had to now. He'd left Christina too long without a reply.

He turned to her, the cynicism he'd learnt from that experience burning in his eyes and drawling through his voice. 'Wildly, passionately in love...yes, that happened to me when I was eighteen. She was very beautiful, exotically glamorous, and incredibly erotic. I would have done anything for her and did do everything she asked.'

'How long did it last?'

'A month.'

Christina raised her eyebrows. 'What made you fall out of love?'

'Being faced with reality.'

'Something you didn't like?'

'I hadn't understood what I was to her. I knew she was years older than me. It didn't matter. Nothing mattered but being with her. I thought she felt the same about me. It was so intense. But she was simply enjoying the intensity, revelling in her power to make me do whatever she wanted.'

'How did you come to realise that?'

'Because I was her Greek toy-boy, a last fling before she married her much more mature American millionaire. *It's been fun,* she said as she kissed me goodbye. *Fun...*'

He snarled the word and immediately cursed himself for letting it get to him after all these years.

'You were badly hurt,' Christina murmured sympathetically.

He shrugged. 'I'm not likely to fall in love again, if that's what you're worried about, Christina. Being someone's fool does not appeal to me.'

'You think your head will always rule your heart?'

'It has since I was eighteen.'

Except with her and Theo. His heart was very much engaged with his son and according to his lawyer, he'd completely lost his head in proposing the prenuptial agreement to induce Christina to marry him, ensuring that Theo would be a constant in his life. But he did feel the fidelity clause was not so much of a risk now. And he did like and admire Christina. He would make

the marriage work. They would have more children...
a family...

'I was eighteen when I fell in love with you.'

The quietly spoken words jolted Ari out of his confident mood and sent an instant chill down his spine. Her dark eyes were flat, expressionless, steadily watching whether he understood the parallel of what had been done to him—not only the hurt, the rejection of any lasting value in the love offered, but also the shadow it cast over any deep trust in a relationship. Giving oneself completely to another was not on. He'd never done it again.

Was this how Christina felt about him? Had he just ruined every bit of progress he'd made with her, bringing the past back instead of focussing her mind on the future they could have? Was this why he couldn't reach what he wanted to reach in her? He had to fix this. It was intolerable that she cast him in the same mould as the woman who'd taken him for a ride.

Before he could find the words to defend himself she spoke again, cocking her head to one side, her eyes alert to weighing up his reply. 'Did you think it was *fun* at the time?'

'Not like that!' he denied vehemently. He leaned towards her, gesturing an appeal for fairness. 'There was no one else in my life, Christina. I wasn't having a fling with you, cheating on a woman I intended to marry. The thought of having a little fun with you never crossed my mind. That was not part of it, I swear. I was enchanted by you.'

'For a while.' Her mouth twisted with irony. 'I can

imagine an older woman being enchanted by you when you were eighteen, Ari. You would have been absolutely beautiful. But her head ruled her heart, just as yours did with me. Too young...wasn't that how you explained leaving me behind?'

'You're not too young now.' The urgent need to stop this treacherous trawling through the past pushed Ari to his feet. He took Christina's hands, pulling her out of her chair and into his embrace, speaking with a violence of feeling that exploded off his tongue. 'I wanted you beyond any common sense then. And God knows I've lost any common sense since I've met you again. I want you so much it's been burning me up from the moment I saw you in Dubai. So forget everything else, Christina. Forget everything but this.'

He forgot about being gentle with her. The fierce emotion welling up in him demanded that he obliterate any bad thoughts from her mind and fill it with the same all-consuming desire he felt. He kissed her hard, storming her mouth with intense passion. A wild exultation ran through him as she responded with her own fierce drive to take what he was doing and give it right back.

No hesitation.

No holding back.

Frenzied kisses.

Frenzied touching.

Mutual desire riding high, her body pressed yearningly to his, making him even more on fire for her. Primitive instincts kicked in. He needed, wanted, had to have total possession of this woman. He swept her off her feet, crushed her to his chest as he strode to the bed. Even as he laid her down she was pushing her kimono apart, opening her legs wide for him, not wanting to wait, eagerly inviting instant intimacy.

He tore his own robe off, hating the thought of it getting in the way. Then he was with her, swiftly positioning himself. She was slick and hot, exciting him even further with her readiness. Her legs locked around him, heels digging into his buttocks, urging him on. He pushed in hard and fast and barely stopped himself from climaxing at the very first thrust, just like a teenage boy experiencing the ultimate sex fit.

He sucked in a quick breath, savagely telling himself to maintain control. He tried to set up a slow, voluptuous rhythm with his hips but she wouldn't have it, her body rocking his to go faster, faster. He felt her flesh clenching and unclenching around his and her throat emitted an incredibly sexy groan.

His head was spinning, excitement at an intense level. Her fingers dug into the nape of his neck. Her back arched from the bed. He felt the first spasm of her coming and was unable to hold off his own release any longer. He cried out as it burst from him in violent shudders, and the flood of heat from both of them was so ecstatically satisfying he was totally dazed by the depth of feeling.

He'd collapsed on top of her. She held him in a tightly possessive hug. Was she feeling the same? He had to know. Had to know if all the bad stuff from the past had been wiped out of her mind. He levered himself up on his elbows to see her face. Her eyes were closed, her head thrown back, her lips slightly apart, sucking in air and slowly releasing it.

'Look at me, Christina,' he gruffly commanded.

Her long lashes flicked up. Her eyes were dilated, out of focus. A thrill of triumph ran riot through Ari's mind. She was still feeling him inside her, revelling in the sheer depth of sensation. It gave him a surge of confidence that she wouldn't walk away from this—what they could have together. The glazed look slowly cleared. Her tongue slid out and licked her lips. He was tempted to flick his own tongue over them, but that would start them kissing again and this moment would be swallowed up and he wouldn't know what it meant to her.

'This is now, Christina,' he said with passionate fervour. 'The past is gone. This is now and you're feeling good with me. Tell me that you are.'

'Yes.' The word hissed out on a long sigh. She half-smiled as she added, 'I'm feeling good.'

He nodded. 'So am I. And I truly believe we can always make each other feel good if the will is there to do it.' He lifted a hand to stroke the soft black bangs of hair away from her forehead, his eyes boring into hers to enforce direct mental contact with her. 'We can be great partners in every sense there is, starting now, Christina. We look ahead, not back. Okay?'

There was no instant response but her eyes didn't disengage from his. Their focus sharpened and he had the feeling she was trying to search his soul. He had nothing to hide, yet he was acutely conscious of tension building inside him as he waited for her answer.

He'd hurt her in the past and she'd nursed that hurt for years. It had erupted in his face tonight and he was asking her to let it go, leave it behind them. It was a big ask. He recalled the look of heart-piercing vulnerability he'd seen after they'd made the sex-deal last night. But he'd just proved she had nothing to fear from an intimate connection with him. She'd conceded he'd made her feel good.

He willed her to grasp what could be grasped and take it into the future with them. It was best for their son, best for their lives, too. Surely she could see that.

'Have you had the prenuptial agreement you offered me drawn up, Ari?'

It wasn't what he wanted to hear from her. It meant that it didn't matter what he said or did, she still had a basic mistrust of how he would deal with her in the future. He could pleasure her all night but that verbal kick in the gut told him it would make no difference.

'Yes. It's in my backpack,' he said flatly.

'Have you signed it?'

'Not yet.'

'Will you do so in the morning if…if you're still feeling good with me?'

'Yes,' he said unequivocally, though hating the fact it was still necessary in her mind.

She hadn't faked her response to him. There was nothing fake about Christina Savalas and it was clear that she needed a guarantee that if there was anything fake about him, she would not lose her son by marrying him.

She reached up and gently stroked his cheek. 'I'm

sorry I can't feel more secure with you, Ari. I promise you to do my best to be a partner to you in every sense. If I fail and you end up finding someone else who suits you better, I won't deny you a fair share of Theo. I just need protection against your taking him from me.'

'I'd never do that,' he protested vehemently. 'You're his mother. He loves you.'

She heaved a deep sigh as though that claim meant little in the bigger scheme of things. 'It's impossible to know how things will turn out along the track,' she said in a fatalistic tone. 'As sincere as your commitment might be to me now, as sincere as mine is to you, it's in our minds, Ari, not our hearts, and you might not think so now, but hearts can over-rule minds. I know. It's why I never told you about Theo when I should have. My heart wouldn't let me.'

There was sadness in her eyes—the sadness of be-trayed innocence—and Ari knew he'd done that to her. Determination welled up in him to replace it with joy—joy in him and the children they would have together.

'Our marriage will be fine, Christina,' he promised her. 'I don't mind signing the prenuptial agreement. I want you to feel secure, not frightened of anything. And given more time, I hope you'll come to trust me, know-ing without a doubt that I mean you well and want you to be happy with me.'

It brought a smile back to her face. 'That would be good, Ari.' Her hand slid up and curled around his head. 'I could do with some more of feeling good.'

He laughed and kissed her.

The night was still young. They proceeded to a more

languorous love-making for a while, pleasuring each other with kisses and caresses. It delighted Ari that Christina had no inhibitions about her sexuality and no hesitation in exploring his. He hoped it would always be like this, no holding back on anything.

The commitment was made now.

Ari felt right about it—more right than he'd ever felt about anything else in his life. And he'd make it right for Christina, too. It would take more than a night to do it. It might take quite a long while. But he was now assured of all the time he would need to wipe out her doubts and win her trust. When that day came—he smiled to himself—all of life would be good.

CHAPTER FOURTEEN

TINA was determined not to regret marrying Ari Zavros but to view her time with him—regardless of what happened in the end—as an experience worth having. In any event, she would not lose Theo or any other children they might have. The signed prenuptial agreement was in her keeping.

Everyone was happy that a wedding would soon take place. The Zavros family seemed particularly pleased to welcome her into their clan and Theo was over the moon at belonging to so many more people. Plans were quickly made. Her mother had no hesitation in deciding that Athens would be the best place for her to live— much closer to her daughters—and Maximus immediately offered to find the best property for her while they dealt with winding up their lives in Australia.

Ari accompanied them back to Sydney. He organised the sale of the restaurant to the head chef and the head waiter. Tina suspected he financed the deal. Everything in their apartment was packed up by professionals— also organised by Ari—and stored in a container which would be shipped to Athens. He was a whirlwind of activity, determined on moving them out with the least amount of stress. Her mother thought he was wonderful.

Tina couldn't fault him, either. He was attentive to their needs, carried out their wishes, and to Tina's surprise, even purchased an extremely expensive three-bedroom apartment overlooking Bondi Beach.

'To Theo it's the best beach in the world,' he explained. 'He might get homesick for it. You, too, Christina. We can always take time out to come back here for a while.'

His caring for their son was so evident, so constant, it continually bolstered her decision to marry him. Theo adored him. Her reservations about his constancy where she was concerned remained in her mind but were slowly being whittled away in her heart. He was so good to her, showing consideration for whatever she wanted in every respect.

Within a month they were back on Santorini. Her mother was to be a guest in the Zavros villa until her furniture arrived for her new apartment in Athens. Maximus, of course, had found the perfect place for her. She quickly became fast friends with Ari's mother who had been organising the wedding in their absence. It was almost the end of the tourist season when most places closed down on the island. They only had a week to finalise arrangements—a week before Tina's life began as Ari's wife.

Cass had been informed of the situation via email and was delighted that everything seemed to be working out well. She insisted on buying Tina's wedding dress and kept sending photographs of glorious gowns until Tina chose one. She let Cass select her own bridesmaid dress. George was to be best man—a reversal of their previous roles.

The same church was to be used for the marriage service and the same reception centre. Both places had also been chosen for the weddings of Ari's sisters. Apparently it was customary for the Zavros family and Tina didn't raise any objection although privately she would have preferred not to be following in her sister's footsteps, being reminded of the real love Cass and George had declared for each other.

She didn't feel like a bride. She looked like one on the day. And despite the lateness of the season, the sun was shining. It made her wonder if Ari had arranged that, too, everything right for the Golden Greek. It was a weird feeling, walking down the aisle to him—more like a dream than reality. Everything had happened so fast. But her feet didn't falter and she gave him her hand at the end of the walk, accepting there was no turning back from this moment.

Her ears were acutely tuned to the tone of Ari's voice as he spoke his marriage vows. It was clear and firm, as though he meant them very seriously. Which Tina found comforting. She had to swallow hard to get her own voice working at all, and the words came out in jerky fashion which she couldn't control. But they were said. It was done. They were declared man and wife.

To Tina, the reception was a blur of happy faces congratulating her and Ari and wishing them well. Everyone from both families was there, along with Ari's close business connections and friends. Tina couldn't remember all their names. She just kept smiling, as a bride should. Ari carried off the evening with great panache and he carried her along with him—his wife.

He took her to Odessa for a honeymoon. It was a beautiful city, called The Pearl of The Black Sea, and for the first time since her future with Ari had been decided, Tina could really relax and enjoy herself. There was nothing that had to be done. Theo was undoubtedly having a great time with his doting grandparents. She was free of all responsibility. And Ari was intent on filling their days—and nights—with pleasure.

The weather was still hot and they lazed away mornings on the beach, had lunch in coffee shops or restaurants beside lovely parks, browsed around the shops that featured crafts of the region—marvellous cashmere shawls, beautifully embroidered blouses, and very different costume jewellery.

They went to a ballet performance at the incredibly opulent opera house—totally different architecture and interior decoration to the amazing hotel in Dubai but just as mind-boggling in its richness.

When she commented on this to Ari he laughed and said, 'Europe is full of such marvels, Christina, and I shall enjoy showing them to you. When we go to Paris, I'll take you to Versailles. You'll be totally stunned by it.'

He was as good as his word. In the first six months of their marriage, she accompanied him on many trips around Europe—Spain, Italy, England, France, Germany. All of them were related to business but Ari made time to play tourist with her. He was the perfect companion, so knowledgeable about everything and apparently happy to spend his free time with her.

There were business dinners they had to attend, and parties they were invited to which invariably made Tina nervous, but Ari never strayed from her side whenever they were socialising. He bought her beautiful clothes so that she always felt confident of her appearance on these occasions and he constantly told her she was beautiful, which eased her anxiety about other women.

They had decided on Athens as their home base. Tina wanted to be close to her mother and it was easier for Theo to be enrolled in the same private English-speaking school as his cousins. He accompanied them on trips which didn't interfere with his schooling but at other times he was happy to stay with family while they were away.

However, when Tina fell pregnant, as happy as she was about having a baby, the morning sickness in the first trimester was so bad she couldn't face travelling anywhere and she couldn't help fretting when Ari had to leave her behind to attend to business. Each time he returned she searched for signs that he was growing tired of her, finding her less attractive, but he always seemed pleased to be home again and eager to take her to bed.

She expected his desire for her to wane as her body lost its shape but it didn't. He displayed a continual fascination with every aspect of her pregnancy, reading up on what should be happening with the child growing inside her, lovingly caressing her lump, even talking to

it in a besotted manner and grinning with delight whenever he felt a ripple of movement. He always smiled
when he saw her naked, his eyes gloating over her as
though she presented an incredibly beautiful image to
him, pregnant with his child.

Tina reasoned that obviously having children meant
a lot to Ari. He had married her because of Theo and
being the mother of his children did make her uniquely
special to him. If he never fell in love with anyone else,
maybe their marriage would become very solid and lasting. She fiercely hoped so because she couldn't guard
against the love that she hadn't wanted to feel with him.

It sat in her heart, heavy with the need to keep it hidden. Pride wouldn't let her express it. Sometimes she
let herself imagine that he loved her, but he never said
it. Their marriage was based on family. That had to be
enough.

She was eight months pregnant and looking forward
to the birth of the baby when fate took a hand in ending
her happy anticipation. She'd been shopping with her
mother, buying a few extra decorations for the newly
furnished nursery at home; a gorgeous mobile of butterflies to hang over the cot, a music box with a carou-
sel on top, a kaleidoscope to sit on the windowsill.

They planned to finish off their outing with a visit
to a hairdressing salon which was located a few blocks
away from the department store where they had purchased these items. Tina felt too tired and cumbersome
to walk that far, so they took a taxi for the short trip. It
was crossing an intersection when a truck hurtled across
the road from the hilly street on their right, clearly out

of control, its driver blaring the horn of the truck in warning, his face contorted in anguish at being unable to avoid an accident.

It was the last thing Tina saw—his face. And the last thing she thought was *the baby!* Her arms clutched the mound of the life inside her. It was the last thing she did before the impact robbed her of consciousness.

Ari had never felt so useless in his life. There was nothing he could do to fix this. He had to leave it up to the doctors—their knowledge, their skill. He was so distressed he could barely think. He sat in the hospital waiting room and *waited.*

Theo was taken care of. His parents had flown over from Santorini to collect him from school and take him back home with them. He was to be told that Mama and Papa had been called away on another trip. There was no point in upsetting him with traumatic news. When the truth had to be told—whatever it turned out to be— Ari would do it. He would be there for his son.

His sisters had wanted to rush to the hospital, giving their caring support but he'd told them not to. He didn't want their comforting gestures. He was beyond comfort. Besides, it would be a distraction from willing Christina to get through this. She had to. He couldn't bear the thought of life without her.

Cassandra was flying in from Rome to be with her mother. He didn't have to worry about Helen—just bruises, a broken arm, and concussion. Her relatives were sitting with her and she would be allowed out of hospital tomorrow. She was frantically worried about

Christina. They all were, but he didn't want to listen to any weeping and wailing. He needed to be alone with this until the doctors came back to him.

Head injuries, smashed clavicle, broken ribs, collapsed lung, ripped heart, and damage to the uterus, but the baby's heart was still beating when they'd brought Christina into the emergency ward. A drug-induced coma was apparently the best state for her to be in while undergoing treatment for her injuries and it had been deemed advisable to perform a Caesarian section. It wasn't how Christina had wanted the baby delivered but he'd been told there was no choice in these circumstances.

Their second child...

A brother or sister for Theo...

They'd been so looking forward to its birth, sharing it together. Now it felt like some abstract event...in the hands of the doctors. No mutual joy in it. A baby without a mother unless Christina survived this.

She had to, not only for their children, but for him.

She was his woman, the heart of his life, and his heart would be ripped out if she died. Just thinking about it put one hell of a pain in his chest.

One of the doctors he'd spoken to entered the waiting room, accompanied by a nurse. Ari rose to his feet, his hands instinctively clenching although there was nothing to fight except the fear gripping his stomach.

'Ah, Mr Zavros. The Caesarian went well. You're the father of a healthy baby girl.'

The announcement hit the surface of his mind but didn't engage it. 'And Christina?' he pressed.

'Your wife will be in the operating theatre for some hours yet. The baby has been taken to an intensive care ward and placed in a humidicrib. We thought…'

'Why?' Ari cut in, fear for the life of their child welling up to join his fear for Christina. 'You said she was healthy.'

'Purely a precautionary measure, Mr Zavros. She is very small, a month premature. It is best that she be monitored for a while.'

'Yes…yes…' he muttered distractedly, his mind jagging back to Christina. 'The injuries to my wife…it *is* possible that she can recover from them?'

'One cannot predict with certainty but there is a good chance, yes. The surgeons are confident of success. If there are no complications…' He shrugged. 'Your wife is young and healthy. That is in her favour.'

Please, God, let there be no complications, Ari fiercely prayed.

'If you would like to see your daughter now…?'

His daughter. Their daughter. Seeing her without Christina at his side. It felt wrong. There was a terrible hollowness in his heart. It should have been filled with excitement. And that was wrong, too. Their baby girl should be welcomed into this world, at least by her father.

'Yes… please…' he replied gruffly.

He was escorted to the maternity ward and led to where his daughter lay in a humidicrib attached to monitoring wires. She looked so little, helpless, and again Ari was assaulted by a wretched sense of powerlessness. Right now he couldn't take care of Christina or their child. He had to leave them both in the hands of others.

A smile tugged at his lips as he stared down at the shock of black hair framing the tiny face. Christina's hair. Her lips were perfectly formed, too, just like her mother's.

'Would you like to touch her?' the nurse beside him asked.

'Yes.'

She lifted the lid of the humidicrib. He reached out and gently stroked the super-soft skin of a tiny hand. It startled and delighted him when it curled tightly around one of his fingers. Her eyes opened—dark chocolate eyes—and seemed to lock onto his.

'I'm your Papa,' he told her.

Her little chest lifted and a sigh whispered from her lips as though the bond she needed was in place. She closed her eyes. The grip on his finger slowly eased.

'Be at peace, little one. I'm here for you,' Ari murmured.

But she would need her mother, too.

He needed Christina, though he wasn't sure how much that would mean to her. She had accepted him as her husband. He saw the love she openly showered on their son, but whatever was in her heart for him had always been closely guarded.

So he willed her to live for their children.

That was the stronger pull on her.

Her son and her daughter.

CHAPTER FIFTEEN

Six weeks… They'd been the longest six weeks of Ari's life. The doctors had explained it was best that Christina remain in a coma until the swelling of her brain had gone down and her injuries had healed. They had also warned him she would initially feel lost and confused when they brought her out of it and would need constant reassurance of where she was, why, and what had happened to her.

Most probably any dreams she may have had during this time would be more real to her than reality and it would require patient understanding from him to deal with her responses to the situation. Ari didn't care how much patient understanding he had to give as long as Christina came back to him. Yet as mentally prepared as he was to deal with anything, it hit him hard when she woke and stared at him without any sign of recognition.

Tears welled into her eyes.

He squeezed her hand gently and quickly said, 'It's okay, Christina. Everything's okay.'

'I lost the baby.'

'No, you didn't,' he vehemently assured her. 'We have a beautiful little baby girl. She's healthy and happy and Theo adores her. We've named her Maria—your favourite name for a girl—and she looks very like you.'

The tears didn't stop. They trickled down her cheeks.

Ari told her about the accident and the need for a Caesarian birth and how their daughter was thriving now. She kept staring at him but he didn't think she was registering anything he said. The look of heart-breaking sadness didn't leave her face. After a while she closed her eyes and slid back into sleep.

He took Theo and Maria with him on his next visit, determined to set Christina's mind at rest.

Again she woke and murmured the mournful words, 'I lost the baby.'

'No, you didn't,' he assured her. 'Look, here she is.'

He laid Maria in her arms and she stared at the baby wonderingly as he explained again about the accident and their daughter's birth. Then Theo, super-excited at having his mother finally awake from her long sleep, chattered non-stop, telling her everything about his new sister. She smiled at him and was actually smiling at the baby as her eyes closed. Ari hoped her sleep would be less fretful now.

Yet from day to day she seemed to forget what had been said and he would have to remind her. He started to worry that she might never fully recover from her head injuries. The doctors explained that it could take a while for the drugs to wash out of her system. Until she completely emerged from her dream-state, it was impossible to gauge if there was some negative side-effect that would have to be treated.

Mostly he just sat by her side and prayed for her to be whole again.

It felt like a miracle when one day she woke up and looked at him with instant recognition. 'Ari,' she said in a pleased tone.

His heart kicked with excitement, then dropped like a stone when her expression changed to the darkly grieving one that had accompanied her other awakenings. But her words were slightly different.

'I'm sorry. I lost the baby.'

'No!'

Encouraged by the certainty that she was actually talking to him this time, he explained the situation again. There was an alertness in her eyes that hadn't been there before. He was sure she was listening, taking in all the information he gave, sifting through it, understanding. A smile started to tug at her mouth.

'A daughter,' she said in a tone of pleasure. 'How lovely!'

Elation soared through him. 'She's beautiful. Just like you, Christina,' he said, smiling back.

A frown of concern puckered her brow. 'And Theo? I've been here…how long?'

'Two months. Theo is fine. Missing his Mama but happily distracted by having a baby sister. I'll bring both of them in for you to see as soon as I can.'

'Maria…' She smiled again, a look of blissful relief on her face. 'Oh, I'm so glad I didn't lose her, Ari.'

'And I'm so glad I didn't lose you,' he said fervently.

Her eyes focussed sharply on him for several moments before her gaze slid away to where her fingers started plucking at the bed-sheet. 'I guess that would have been...inconvenient for you.'

Inconvenient!

Shock rattled Ari's mind. It took him several moments to realise she had no idea how much she meant to him. He'd never told her. He reached out and enclosed the plucking fingers with his, holding them still.

'Look at me, Christina,' he quietly commanded.

She did so, but not with open windows to her soul. Her guard was up, as it had been from the day she had agreed to marry him. He had never worn it down. He should have felt grateful for this return to normality, but the need to break through it was too strong for patience in laying out what was very real to him—had been real for a long time although he hadn't recognised it until faced with losing her from his life.

'Do you remember asking me about falling in love and I told you about the American woman I'd met when I was eighteen?' he asked.

She slowly nodded.

'It was nothing but blind infatuation, Christina,' he said vehemently, his eyes burning into hers to make her believe he spoke the truth. 'I didn't love her. I didn't know her enough to love the person she was. Being with you this past year...I've learnt what it is to really love a woman. I love you.'

Her eyes widened but still they searched his warily.

'If you'd died from this accident, it would have left a hole in my life that no one else could ever fill. It wouldn't have been an inconvenience. Christina. It would have been…' He shook his head, unable to express the terrible emptiness that had loomed while he'd waited for the miracle of her return to him. 'I love you,' he repeated helplessly. 'And please, please, don't ever leave me again.'

'Leave you?' she echoed incredulously. 'I've always been afraid of you leaving me.'

'Never! Never! And after this, let me tell you, I'm going to be nervous about letting you out of my sight.'

She gave him a rueful little smile. 'That's how I felt… nervous when you were away from me. Women always look at you, Ari.'

'They don't make me feel what I do for you, Christina. You're my woman, the best in the world. Believe me.'

Tina wanted to. Somehow it was too much…waking up from the dreadful nightmare of loss and being handed a lovely dream. She lifted her free hand to rub her forehead, get her mind absolutely clear.

'My hair! It's gone!'

'It's growing back,' Ari instantly assured her. 'They had to shave it for the operation.'

Tears spurted into her eyes as she gingerly felt the ultra-short mat of hair covering her scalp. Ari had liked it long so she had let it grow after their wedding. She remembered taking the taxi to the hairdressing salon…

'My mother!'

'She's fine. Minor injuries. She was only in hospital for one day. Everything's fine, Christina. Nothing for you to worry about.'

'Who is looking after the children?'

'The housekeeper, the nanny for Maria, your mother, my mother, my sisters, your aunts…our home is like a railway station for relatives wanting to help.'

The sudden rush of fear receded, replaced by a weird feeling of jealousy that a nanny was replacing her for Maria. 'I need to go home, Ari,' she pleaded.

'As soon as the doctors permit it,' he promised.

'I need to see my children.'

He squeezed her hand. 'You rest quietly now and I'll go and get them, bring them here for you to see. Okay?'

'Yes.'

He rose from the chair beside her bed and gently kissed her forehead. 'Your hair doesn't matter, Christina,' he murmured. 'Only you getting well again matters.'

The deep caring in his voice washed through her, soothing the tumult of emotions that had erupted. Everything was all right. Ari always made perfect arrangements. And he'd said he loved her.

She didn't rest quietly. No sooner had Ari gone than doctors came, asking questions, taking her blood pressure, checking tubes and wires, removing some of them. She had questions for them, too. By the time they left she knew precisely what she had been through and how devoted her husband had been, visiting her every day, doing his best to console her whenever she'd shared her nightmare with him.

The doctors had no doubt that Ari loved her.

Tina started to believe it.

Theo came running into the hospital room, his face

lighting up with joy at seeing her awake and smiling for him. 'Mama! Mama! Can I hug you?'

She laughed and made room on the bed for him to climb up beside her. 'I want to hug you, too.' Her beautiful little son. Hers and Ari's. It was wonderful to cuddle him again.

'And here is my sister,' he declared proudly as Ari carried their baby into the room, grinning delightedly at the two of them together.

Theo quickly shuffled aside to let Ari lay the baby in her arms. Tina felt a huge welling of love as her gaze roved over her daughter, taking in the amazing perfection of her.

'Maria's got more hair than you, Mama,' Theo said, and she could laugh about it, no longer caring about the loss of her long, glossy locks.

'She has your mother's hair, and her eyes and her mouth,' Ari said, as though he was totally besotted by the likeness to her.

Tina couldn't help smiling at him. He smiled back and the words simply spilled out of the fullness of her heart. 'I love you, too, Ari.'

His eyes glowed a warm gold. He leaned over and kissed her on the mouth. 'I will thank God forever that you've come back to us, Christina,' he murmured against her lips, leaving them warm and tingling, making her feel brilliantly alive.

A new life, she thought. Not only for the baby in her arms, but for her and Ari and Theo, too.

A family bonded in love.

It was what her father had wanted for her.

No more disappointment.

She had it all.

It was summer on Santorini again and both families had gathered in force to attend Maria's christening. The same church, the same reception centre, but for Tina, this was a much happier occasion than her wedding. Although Ari's family had welcomed her into it before, she really felt a part of it now, and she also felt much closer to her own family, no longer having the sense of being an outsider who had broken the rules.

It was a truly joyous celebration of life and love. The sun shone. There were no shadows between her and Ari. She saw desire for her simmering in his eyes all day and her own desire for him was zinging through her blood. No sooner was the party over and the children finally asleep in their part of the Zavros villa, than they headed off to their own bedroom, eager to make love. But before they did, there was one thing Tina wanted to do.

She'd put the prenuptial agreement in the top drawer of the bedside table and she went straight to it, took it out and handed it to Ari. 'I want you to tear this up.'

He frowned. 'I don't mind you having it, Christina. I want you to feel secure.'

'No. It's wrong. It's part of a bad time that's gone, Ari. If you were asking me to marry you now, I wouldn't insist on a prenuptial agreement. I trust you. I believe what we have is forever. It is, isn't it?'

He smiled. 'Yes, it is.'

He tore it up.

She smiled and opened her arms to him, opened her

heart to him. 'I love you. I love our family. We're going to have a brilliant life together, aren't we?'

He laughed, lifted her off her feet, twirled her around and dumped her on the bed, falling on top of her, although levering his weight up on his elbows as he grinned down at her. 'Brilliant and beautiful and bountiful, because I have you, my love.'

She reached up and touched his cheek, her eyes shining with all he made her feel.

'And I have you.'

* * * * *

PRETENDER TO
THE THRONE

MAISEY YATES

To my readers. This book exists because you asked for it. And I'm so very glad you did!

USA Today bestselling author **Maisey Yates** lives in rural Oregon with her three children and her husband, whose chiselled jaw and arresting features continue to make her swoon. She feels the epic trek she takes several times a day from her office to her coffee maker is a true example of her pioneer spirit. Visit her online at her website www.maiseyyates.com.

CHAPTER ONE

"Either die or abdicate. I'm not particular about which one you choose, but you'd better make a decision, and quickly."

Alexander Drakos, heir to the throne of Kyonos, dissolute rake and frequent gambler, took a drag on his cigarette before putting it out in the ashtray and dropping his cards onto the velvet-covered table.

"I'm a little busy right now, Stavros," he said into his phone.

"Doing what? Throwing away your fortune and drinking yourself into a stupor?"

"Don't be an idiot. I don't drink when I gamble. I don't lose, either." He eyed the men sitting around the table and pushed a pile of chips into the pot.

"A shame. If you did, then maybe you would have had to come home a long time ago."

"Yeah, well, you haven't seemed to need me."

It was time for the cards to go down, and those who hadn't folded earlier on in the round put their hands face up.

Xander laughed and revealed his royal flush before leaning in and sweeping the chips into his stack. "I'm cashing out," he said, standing and putting his chips into a velvet bag. "Enjoy your evening." He took his black suit jacket off the back of the chair and slung it over his shoulder.

He passed a casino employee and dropped the bag into

the man's hands. "I know how much is in there. Cash me out. Five percent for you, no more."

He stopped at the bar. "Scotch. Neat."

"I thought you didn't drink while you gambled," his brother said.

"I'm not gambling anymore." The bartender pushed the glass his way and Xander knocked it back before continuing out of the building and onto one of Monaco's crowded streets.

Strange. The alcohol barely burned anymore. It didn't make him feel good, either. Stupid alcohol.

"Where are you?"

"Monaco. Yesterday I was in France. I think that was yesterday. It all sort of blurs together, you know?"

"You make me feel old, Xander, and I am your younger brother."

"You sound old, Stavros."

"Yes, well, I didn't have the luxury of running out on my responsibilities. That was your course of action and that meant someone had to stay behind and be a grown-up."

He remembered well what had happened the day he'd taken that luxury. Running out on his responsibilities, as Stavros called it.

You killed her. This is your fault. You've stolen something from this country, from me. You can never replace it. I will never forgive you.

Damn.

Now that that memory had surfaced another shot or four would be required.

"I'm sure the people will build a statue in your honor someday and it will all be worth it," Xander said.

"I didn't call to engage in small talk with you. I would rather strangle myself with my own necktie."

Xander stopped walking, ignoring the woman who ran

into him thanks to his sudden action. "What did you call about then?"

"Dad had a stroke. It's very likely he's dying. And you are the next in line for the throne. Unless you abdicate, and I mean really, finally, abdicate. Or you know, chain a concrete ball to your neck and hurl yourself into the sea, I won't mourn you."

"I would think you'd be happy for me to abdicate," Xander said, ignoring the tightness in his chest. He hated death. Hated its suddenness. Its lack of discrimination.

If death had any courtesy at all, it would have come for him a long time ago. Hell, he'd been baiting it for years.

Instead, it went after the lovely and needed. The ones who actually made a difference to the world rather than those who left nothing but brimstone and scorch marks in their wake.

"I have no desire to be king, but make no mistake, I will. The issue, of course, lies in the production of heirs. As happy as Jessica and I are with our children, they are not eligible to take the throne. Adoption is good enough for us, but not sufficient per the laws of Kyonos."

"That leaves…Eva."

"Yes," Stavros said. "It does. And if you hadn't heard, she is pregnant."

"And how does she feel? About her child being the heir?"

"She hates it. She and Mak don't even live in Kyonos and they'd have to uproot their lives so their child could be raised in the palace, so he or she could learn their duty. It would change everything. It was never meant to be this way for her and you know it."

Xander closed his eyes and pictured his wild, dark-haired sister. Yes, she would hate it. Because she'd always hated royal protocol. As he had.

He'd taken her mother from her. Could he rob her of the rest of her dreams, too?

"Whatever you decide, Xander, decide quickly. I would ask that you do so in two days' time," Stavros continued, "but if you want my opinion…"

"I don't." He hung the phone up and stuffed it into his pocket.

Then he walked toward the dock. And he wondered where he might find a concrete ball.

Layna Xenakos dismounted and patted her horse on the neck. Layna was sweaty and sticky, and the simple, long-sleeved shift she was wearing didn't do very much to diffuse the heat.

But she was smiling. Riding always did that for her. Up here, the view of the sea was intoxicating, the sharp, salty ocean breeze tangling with the fresh mountain air, a stark and bright combination she'd never experienced anywhere else.

It was one of the many things she liked about living at the convent. It was secluded. Separate. And here, at least, lack of vanity was a virtue. A virtue Layna didn't have to strive for. Vanity, in her case, would be laughable.

She pulled her head scarf out of her bag and wound her hair up, putting everything back in place. The only thing she could possibly feel any vanity about—her hair— safely covered again.

"Come on, Phineas," she said to the horse, leading the animal up to the stables and taking care of his tack and hooves before putting him in his stall and walking back out into the sunlight.

Technically, that had probably been a poor use of meditation time, but then, she rarely felt more connected to God, or to nature, than when she was riding. So, she imagined that had to count for something.

She walked toward the main building of the convent. Dinner would be served soon and she was hungry, since her afternoon's contemplation had been conducted on horseback.

She paused and looked over the garden wall, noticing tomatoes that were ready to be picked, and diverted herself, continuing on into the garden, humming something tunelessly as she went.

"Excuse me."

She froze when a man's voice pierced the relative silence. They interacted with men in the village often enough, but it was unusual for a man to come to the convent.

For a second, right before she turned, she experienced a brief moment of anxiety. Would he look at her like she was a monster? Would his face contort with horror? But before she turned fully, the fear had abated. God didn't care about her lack of outer beauty, and neither did she.

And moments like this were only a reminder that she did have to worry about vanity having a foothold. That it was an impediment to the service of others.

That, in a nutshell, was why she was a novice and not a sister, even after ten years at the convent.

"Can I help you?" The sun was shining on her face, and she knew he could see her fully. All of her scars. The rough, damaged skin that had stolen her beauty. Beauty that had once been her most prized feature.

The sun also kept her from seeing him in detail. Which spared her from whatever his expression might be, whatever reaction he might be having to her wounds. He was tall, and he was wearing a suit. An expensive suit. Not a man from the village. A man who looked like he'd stepped out of the life she'd once lived.

A man who reminded her of string quartets, glittering ballrooms and a prince who would have been her husband. If only things had been different.

If only life hadn't crumbled around her feet.

"Possibly, Sister. Although, I'm doubting I'm in the right place."

"There isn't another convent on Kyonos, so it's unlikely."

"I find it strange I'm at a convent at all." He looked up, the sun backlighting him, obscuring his features. "At least, I find it strange I haven't been hit by a lightning bolt."

"That isn't really how God works."

He shrugged. "I'll have to take your word for it. God and I haven't spoken in years."

"It's never too late," she said. Because it seemed like the right thing to say. Something the abbess would say.

"Well, as it happens, I'm not looking for God. I'm looking for a woman."

"Nothing but Sisters here, I'm afraid," she said.

"Well, I'm led to believe that she is that, too. I'm looking for Layna Xenakos."

She froze, her heart seizing. "She doesn't go by that name anymore." And that was true, the sisters called her Magdalena. A reminder that she was changed, and that she lived for others now and not herself.

And then he started walking toward her, a vision from a dream, or a nightmare. The epitome of everything she'd spent the past fifteen years running from.

Xander Drakos. Heir to the throne of Kyonos. Legendary playboy. And the man she'd been promised to marry.

Quite literally the last man on earth she wanted to see.

"Why not?" he asked.

He didn't recognize her. And why would he? She'd been a girl last time they'd seen each other. She'd been eighteen. And she'd been beautiful.

"Maybe because she doesn't want people to find her," she said, bending down to pick tomatoes off the vine, trying to ignore him, trying to ignore her heart, which was pounding so hard she was certain he could hear it.

"She's not hard to find. Simple inquiries led me here."

"What do you want?" she asked. "What do you want with her?"

Xander looked at the petite woman, standing in the middle of the garden. She had mud on the hem of her long, simple dress, mud on the cuffs of her sleeves, too. Her hair was covered by a scarf, the color given away only by her eyebrows, which were finely arched and dark.

One side of her face showed smooth, golden skin, high cheekbones and a full mouth that turned up slightly at the corners. But that was only one half of her face. That was where her beauty ended. Because the other side, from her neck, across her cheeks and over the bridge of her nose, was marred. Rough and twisted, her lips nearly frozen on that side, too encumbered by scar tissue to form a smile. Not that she was smiling at him. Even if she were, though, he imagined that grimace was permanent, at least on that part of her face.

This was the sort of woman he expected to find up here. Not a giggling, glittery socialite like Layna. She'd practically been a girl when they'd been engaged—only eighteen, on her way to womanhood. And beautiful beyond belief. Golden eyes and skin, and honey-colored hair that had likely been lightened via a bottle. But whether or not it was natural hadn't mattered. It had been beautiful— shining waves of spun gold mingled with deep chocolate browns.

He'd known even then that she would make a perfect queen. What was more important was that she'd been loved by the people. And she came with wonderful connections, since her father had been one of the wealthiest government officials in Kyonos, much of his success derived from manufacturing companies based out of the country.

As far as he could tell since his return two days ago, the Xenakos family was no longer on the island. Except for Layna. And he needed to find her.

He needed her. She was the anchor to his past. His surest ally. For the press, for the people. They had loved her, they would love her again.

They would not, he feared, feel the same way about him.

"We have some old business to discuss."

"The women who live here don't want to discuss old business," she said, her voice trembling. "Women come here for a new start. And old…old anything is not welcome." She turned away from him, and started to walk into the main building. She was going to walk away from him without answering his questions.

No one walked away from him.

He started toward the garden, and blocked her path. She raised her face to him, her expression defiant, and his heart dropped into his stomach.

He hadn't realized. Of course he hadn't. But now that he could see her eyes, those unusual eyes, fringed with dark lashes, he knew exactly who she was.

She was Layna Xenakos, but without her beauty. Without the laughing eyes. Without the dimple in her right cheek. No, now there were only scars.

Not very much shocked him. He'd seen too much. Done too much. He and the ugly side of life were well-acquainted. And he knew well that life's little surprises were always waiting to come and knock you in the teeth.

But even with that, this wasn't anything he'd expected. Nothing he could have anticipated.

From the time he'd left Kyonos, he'd very purposefully avoided news regarding his home country. Only recently, when his sister had married her bodyguard and when Stavros had married his matchmaker, had he read articles concerning his homeland, or the royal family.

Because he hadn't been able to stop himself. Not then. But every time he opened the window on that part of his past, it was like scrubbing an open wound.

And it took a lot to wipe his mind and emotions free of it all again. A lot of drinking. A lot of women. Things that made him feel like a different man than the one he'd once thought he was, than the one he was trained to be. Things that created happiness. Before they created a gigantic headache.

One thing he'd never thought to look for had been the fate of the woman he'd left behind. But obviously, something had happened.

"Layna," he said.

"No one calls me that," she said, her tone hard, her expression flat.

"I did."

"You do not now, your highness. You don't have that right. Do you even have the right to a title?"

That burned. Deeper than he'd imagined it could. Because she was edging close to a pain he'd rather forget.

"I do," he growled. "And I will continue to." His decision was made. Whether or not it made sense to anyone, including himself, his decision was made. He had come back, and he would stay. Though, no one knew it yet.

He'd felt compelled to come and see the state of things first. And then...and then he'd felt compelled to find Layna. Because if there was one thing he knew, it was that he had grown unsuitable to the task of ruling. And if he knew anything else, it was that no one was more suited to be queen than Layna.

He had thought it unlikely she would still be unmarried. He hadn't counted on her being both unmarried and at a convent, but he supposed it wasn't any less likely than what he'd been doing with his time for the past fifteen years.

No, he took that back. It was unlikely. Everything about this was unlikely. Layna Xenakos, the toast of Kyonosian society, renowned beauty and bubbly hostess, shut away in a convent, wearing a drab dress. With scars that made her mostly unrecognizable.

"I should like you to go," she said, walking toward him with purpose. He could tell she meant to go right on past him.

He stepped in front of her, blocking her way. She froze, those eyes, so familiar, like a shot straight out of the past, locked with his. "I would like for you to unhand me as well, then leave."

"So unhospitable, Sister, and to your future ruler."

"Hospitality is one thing, allowing a man to touch me as though he owns me is another thing entirely." She stepped away from him, her expression fierce. "You might rule the country, you might own the land, but you do *not* own me, or anyone else here."

"You belong to God now then, is that it?"

"Less worrisome than belonging to you."

"You did once."

She shook her head. "I never did."

"You wore my ring."

"But we hadn't taken vows yet. And you left."

"I let you keep the ring," he said, looking down at her hands and noticing they were bare.

"An engagement ring isn't very useful when there is no

fiancé attached to it. And anyway, I've changed. My life has changed. I suppose you thought you could come back here and pick up where we left off."

He had. And why not? It would be the story of the decade. The heir's return and his reunion with the woman the nation had always been so fond of. Except, for some reason, a very large part of him had assumed she'd simply been here in Kyonos, frozen in time, waiting for his return.

A large part of him had assumed that all of Kyonos had done so. But he had been mistaken.

There were casinos now. An electric strip by the beach. His brother Stavros's doing. The old town had been renewed. No longer simply a quarter where old men sat and played chess, it was now a place for hipsters and artists to hang out and "be inspired" by the beach and the architecture.

His sister was not the same. Not a dark-haired, mischievous girl, but a woman now. Married and expecting a child. His brother had become a man, instead of a rail-thin teenage boy.

His father was old. And dying. His father…

And Layna Xenakos had joined a convent.

"I will be straight with you," he said. "I am not the favored son of the Drakos family."

She nodded once but remained silent, so he continued.

"But I have decided that I will rule. For the next generation even more than for this one."

"What do you mean?" she asked.

"Stavros's children cannot inherit. And that would leave my sister's child. The changes it would require…it was never her cross to bear. I have done a great many selfish things in my life, Layna, and I intend to keep doing many of them. But what I cannot do, when it comes down to it, is condemn my brother to a life he never wanted. Or give to my sister's child a responsibility it was never meant to take on." He had ruined things for his siblings already. Their childhoods had passed by while he was gone. Children who'd had no mother.

Especially Eva. She'd been so young then. It was unfair. He couldn't continue to hurt her. He *wouldn't*.

"You speak of the crown as though it's a poison cup," she said, her words muted.

"It is in many ways. But it is mine. And I have spent too many years trying to pass it off to others." Yes, his. As far as anyone knew, it was his. It was the expectation. What he had trained for until he was twenty-one.

The truth, was another matter. But it didn't change Stavros's reality. It didn't change Eva's.

It didn't change what had to be done.

"A conscience, Xander?" she asked, using his first name, the sound sending a shiver through him. A ripple of memory.

"I'm not so certain I'd go that far. Maybe a bit of forgotten honor bred into me. Thanks to all that royal blood," he said, his tone dripping sarcasm. "Imagine my disappointment when I realized I hadn't replaced it all with alcohol."

"A disappointment for many," she said. She sounded more like her old self now. He'd officially destroyed her serenity. Perhaps a lightning bolt would be in the offing after all.

"I'm sure. But I had thought there might be a way of softening the blow."

"And that is?"

"You," he said. "I'm going to need you, Layna."

CHAPTER TWO

LAYNA FELT LIKE the world had just inverted beneath her feet, and only the wooden gate was keeping her from folding. "Excuse me?"

"I need you."

"I can't imagine why you think that, but trust me, you don't."

"The people love you. They don't love me, Layna."

"The people love me?" she spat, anger rising in her, anger she always thought was dealt with. Until something came up and reminded her that it wasn't. Something small and insignificant, like catching sight of herself in the mirror. Or burning her finger when she was cooking. In this instance, it wasn't a small something. It was the ghost of fiancés past, talking about the people. The people who had loved her.

She'd made her peace with some of the people of Kyonos. She served them, after all, but she didn't feel the way she once had about them—confident that she had a country filled with adoring fans.

Quite the opposite.

"Yes," he said, his voice certain still, as though he hadn't heard the warning in her tone.

"The people," she said, "behaved more like animals after you left. Everything fell apart, but I assume you know that."

"I didn't watch the news after I left. A tiny island like Kyonos is fairly easy to ignore when you aren't on it. And when you're drunk headlines look a little blurry."

"So you don't know, then? You don't know that everything…everything went to hell? That companies pulled up stakes, stocks went down to nothing, thousands of people lost their jobs?"

"All because I left?"

"Surely you knew some of this."

"Some of it," he said, his voice clipped. "But there's a lot you can avoid when you're only sober for a couple hours a day."

"I wouldn't know."

"I imagine vice isn't so much your thing."

"No."

"So the economy collapsed and I'm to blame? That's the sum of it?"

She shrugged. "You. The death of the queen. The king's depression. It was an unhappy combination, and no one was confident in the state of things. People were angry."

She looked at him and she tried to find a place of serenity. Of strength. What happened to her wasn't a secret. It was in newspapers, online. It was widespread news. It was just hard to say out loud.

But you aren't going to show him that you care. You aren't going to be weak. It doesn't matter. Vanity. All is vanity.

"There were riots in the streets. In front of the homes of government officials, who were blamed for the economic crisis. There were different kinds of attacks made. Several attempts at…acid attacks. We were leaving our home when a man pushed up to the front and tried to throw a cup of acid onto my father. He stumbled, though, and the man missed. I was hit instead. I don't think I need to tell you where," she said, attempting to smile. Smiling could be difficult enough at the best of times since half of her mouth had trouble obeying that command, but when she didn't feel like smiling it was completely impossible.

But telling the story was easier when she imagined it was another girl. When she remembered what happened without remembering the pain.

She searched his face. She seemed to have succeeded in shocking him, which was something she hadn't imagined would be possible.

"So, I think it's fair to say maybe the people don't love me as much as you think they do." She pushed past him now, determined to put an end to this. To this strange bit of torment from the past.

He grabbed hold of her, his hand on her arm sending a rush of heat through her. She breathed in sharply, his scent hitting her, like a punch in the chest.

Her head was swimming. With glittering palaces and silk dresses. Dancing in a sparkling ballroom in a man's warm embrace. A trip to the garden where his lips almost touched hers. Her full, beautiful lips, unencumbered by scar tissue. It would have been her first kiss. And right then she wanted to weep for the loss of it because now there would never be one.

Not on those lips. They were gone forever.

Not even on the lips she had now. Because she had vowed to never know that pleasure of life. To forego it in favor of serving others, and release her hold on her own needs. Not that it should matter. No man would ever want to kiss her anyway.

But Xander was…he was too much. He was here, right when she didn't want him, and not fifteen years ago when she'd needed him.

Right now, she didn't need him. She needed distance.

The more Xander filled up her vision, the more faded everything else seemed to become. Xander was a look into a life that she didn't have anymore. Couldn't have. Didn't want.

She just needed him gone. So that she could start to forget again.

"I suppose you should go now," she said. "Now that you know how it is. If you're looking for a ticket to salvation, Xander, I'm not it."

"I'm not interested in salvation," he said. "But I do want to do the right thing. Novel, isn't it?"

"Well, I can't help you. Perhaps it's best you found your way back to the village."

"I'm staying here tonight."

"What?" she asked, shock lancing her.

"I spoke to the abbess, and explained the situation. I don't want the public knowing I'm here yet, not until I'm ready. And I intend to bring you with me."

"I see. And nothing of what I said matters?"

He shook his head, his jaw tight. "No."

"The fact that I'm not me anymore doesn't matter?"

He studied her face, the cold assessment saying more than any insult could. Before the attack, men…Xander… had never looked at her with ice in their eyes. There had always been heat.

"I'll let you know in the morning."

He turned and walked away from her, into the main building. She waited out in the yard, cursing silently and not caring that it was a sin as she stood there, hoping he was putting enough distance between them that she wouldn't run into him again.

She would speak to the abbess tonight and in the morning, hopefully Xander would leave. And he would go back to being a memory she tried not to have.

* * *

It was early the next morning when Mother Maria-Francesca called her into her office.

"You should go with him."

"I can't," Layna said, stepping back. "I don't want to go back to that life. I want to be here."

"He only wants you to help him get established. And as you want to serve, I think it would be good for you to serve in this way."

"Alone. With a man."

"If I have to concern myself with how you would behave alone with a man then perhaps this isn't your calling."

It wasn't spoken in anger or in condemnation, just as a simple, quiet fact that settled in the room and made Layna feel hideously exposed. As though her motives—motives she'd often feared were less than wholly pure—were laid out before the woman she considered her spiritual superior in every way.

All that ugly fear and insecurity. Her vanity. Her anger. And old desires that never seemed to fully die. Just sitting there for anyone to see.

"It isn't that," Layna said. "I mean, I'm not afraid of falling into temptation." And even less worried about Xander falling into temptation with her. "It's just that appearances…"

"Are what men look at, my dear. But God sees the heart. So what does it matter what people might think? Of the arrangement, or of you?"

Such a simple perspective. And one of the main reasons she felt so at home here. But that didn't mean her ease and tranquility transferred to every place she went.

"I suppose it doesn't matter." And what she wanted certainly wouldn't come into play. She could hardly throw herself on the ground and say she didn't want to. Of course she didn't. True sacrifice was hard. Serving others could be hard. Neither were excuses she would accept.

"This is an opportunity to do the sort of good that most of us never get the chance to do. You have the ear of a king, in heaven and now on earth. You must use this chance."

"I'll...think about it. Pray...about it." Layna blinked back tears as she walked out of the room. By the time she'd hit the hall, she was running. Out the door and to the stables.

She couldn't breathe. She couldn't think. She needed to ride.

And she did. Until the wind stung her eyes. Until she couldn't tell if it was the burn from the air that made tears stream down her face, or the deep well of emotion that had been opened up inside of her. Threatening to pull her in and drown her.

She rode up to the top of the hill, the highest point that was easily accessible, and looked down at the waves, crashing below, against the rocks. That was how she felt. Like the waves were beating her against stone. Breaking her down.

Like life was asking too much of her. When she'd already given everything she had.

She leaned forward and buried her face in Phineas's neck. Maria-Francesca was right. It hurt to admit it. Even in her own mind, it hurt to admit it. She'd never taken her vows. And so much of that was down to herself.

Was down to that piece of her that missed the ballrooms. That longed for a husband. For children. For the life she'd left behind.

If she stayed here, she would be safe. But she would be stuck. She would never take her vows. Because it wasn't her calling. And she'd been too afraid to admit it for so long because she didn't know where else to go.

You can go with him.

Not for him. For her. For closure. So that the ache she felt when she thought of Xander, and warm nights in a palace garden, would finally fade.

As it was, he'd been gone from her life with no warning. A wound that had cut swift and deep. An abandonment that had become all the more painful after her attack.

It was safe here at the convent. But it was stagnant. And she saw now, for the first time, that it shielded her, instead of healing her.

She could do this. She would do it. And when it was over...maybe something inside of her would be changed. Maybe she would find the transformation she ached for.

Maybe then...maybe then she would come back here and find more than a hiding place. Maybe then, she would be changed enough to take the final step. To take her vows.

Maybe if she finished this, she could finally find her place.

All of her belongings fit into one suitcase. When you didn't need hair products, makeup, or anything beyond bare essentials to wear, life was pretty simple. And portable, it turned out.

She shifted, standing in the doorway, looking at Xander, who had his focus on the view of the sea. "I suppose you have an ostentatious car ready to whisk us back to civilization?"

Xander turned and smiled, his eyes assessing. She didn't like that. Didn't like how hard he looked at her. She preferred very much to be invisible.

"Naturally," he said. "It's essentially an eight-cylinder phallus."

"Compensation for your shortcomings?"

The words escaped her lips before she even processed

them. They were a stranger's words. A stranger's voice. One from the past.

So weird. Being with him resurrected more than just memories, it seemed to bring out old tendencies. In her life at the convent, sarcasm and smart replies were not well-received. But when she'd been one of the many socialites buzzing around Xander, wanting to catch his attention, when she'd moved in such a sparkling and sometimes cutthroat circle, it had been the best way to communicate.

They had all been like that. Pretending to be so bored by their surroundings, showing their cool with cutting remarks and brittle laughter. It struck her then that Xander had changed, too. He hadn't joined a convent, but he lacked the air of the smug aristocrat he used to carry himself with.

He still had that lazy smile, that wicked mouth. But beneath the glitter in his eyes, she sensed something deeper now. Something dark. Something that made her stomach clench and her heart pound.

"I apologize," she said. "That was neither gracious nor appropriate. I'm ready to go."

He shrugged and took her suitcase from her, starting to walk across the expanse of green. She followed him, over the hill and to the lot where a red sports car was parked.

"I'm a cliché," he said. "The playboy prince. It would be embarrassing if it weren't so much fun."

"There's more to life than fun."

"But fun is a part of it," he countered.

"Certainly."

He deposited her suitcase in the trunk of the car. "I think you might have forgotten the fun part," he said.

"You have that covered for the both of us, I think." She moved her hand in a wide sweep, like she was presenting the car on a game show.

He smiled. "You have no idea."

For some reason that smile, that statement, made her stomach tight. "I imagine I don't."

"Why don't you get in the car and we can continue this while we head back down to Thysius?"

She hadn't been to the capitol in a couple of years, and just the thought of it filled her with dread. "What exactly are we doing?"

"Get in the car."

Fear wrapped its fingers around her throat, the desire to turn and run almost overwhelming. But she didn't. "Not yet. Where are we staying? What are we going to do?"

"The palace," he said. "You're familiar with it."

"Yes." Much too familiar. There was a time when it would have been her home. When she would have been the queen. Memories that seemed like they belonged in another life were crowding in, trying to remind her of all the things she'd tried so hard to let go of.

"The press will think it's all sensational." He opened his door and got inside and she stood outside, looking at her warped reflection in the slightly rounded window.

"That's what I'm afraid of." She pulled the car door open and got inside, closing it behind her.

The leather interior smelled new. And an awful lot like money. Such a strange contrast to the old stone walls of the convent. When he turned the key and the engine roared to life she couldn't help but think it was a very strange contrast. The pristine newness. The noise. So different than the ancient quiet she'd lived in for so long.

"This is the story that I need. You and me, collaborating on bringing the country into a new era."

"Why do I feel a bit like you just told me together we will rule the galaxy as father and son...."

"Are you saying I'm asking you to join the Dark Side?"

"I feel like it."

"Seems a strange reference for a nun."

"I'm not a nun, actually. Not yet. I'm a novice." And she had been for a near record amount of time. Speaking of movies, her life was becoming a bit *"How do you solve a problem like Maria."*

"And I do watch movies," she said. "There isn't a lot that happens up here, and we aren't all serious all the time."

He pulled out of the parking area and onto the road. And she wasn't "here" anymore, either. She was leaving. Heading into the world. Away from the convent, away from the village. Into the city. Toward people. And the press.

Panic clawed at her, a desperate beast trying to escape. But she held it in. Did she pray for serenity or was this part of her test? To do what she didn't want, for it to be hard. To have to persevere.

Suddenly, she just felt angry. She hadn't asked for any of this. Not for Xander to come back, not to have to be in the public eye again.

She hadn't asked to be attacked. To have her life stolen from her. And hadn't she taken it and turned it into something worthy? Why was she having to do this now?

Fear was doing its best to take her over completely. And its best was far too good for her taste. The farther she got from her home, the closer they drew to the capitol city, the more it grew.

She was shaking. A tremor that seemed to start from the inside and built outward until her teeth were chattering. She tightened her hands into fists, trying to will it to stop. But she didn't have the strength.

They took so much. He took so much. Don't let them have anything else.

That voice. That strong, quiet voice inside of her made the shaking stop. Because it was right. Too much of her pain belonged to Xander, to the people of Kyonos, and she wouldn't give them one bit more.

She would help. Help restore the nation, get it all back on track, get Xander into a good position. But she wouldn't give of herself. Her actions, her presence, yes. But nothing of her.

"It isn't just you," he said, his voice rough.

"What?"

"You aren't the only one who will be judged."

He was so in tune with her train of thought that she was almost afraid she'd voiced her fears out loud. "Maybe not. But I'm the only one of us who didn't earn the judgment."

It was true, even if it was unkind. So, okay, maybe she wasn't holding back all of herself from Xander. She was letting him have some of her anger.

He laughed and the car engine roared louder, the cypress trees outside the window turning into an indistinct blur of green as he accelerated. "Very true. I did earn mine. And I had a hell of a lot of fun doing it."

CHAPTER THREE

XANDER FELT LIKE he sometimes did after a night of heavy drinking. His head hurt. His stomach was unsettled. And memories pushed at the edges of his mind, threatening to crowd into the forefront.

Yes, it was just like the aftermath of being drunk. Or being hungover was a bit like coming home.

He paused the car at the gate. Stavros didn't know he was coming. It had been a phone call he hadn't been certain he could make. Stavros might bring up the option of hurling himself into the sea again and he might end up taking him up on it. Instead of returning to this.

He picked his phone up and dialed Stavros's number.

"Are you at the palace?" Xander asked when he heard an answer on the other end.

"I am not." Stavros's response was measured.

"Where are you then?"

"Vacation. My wife wanted to go to Greece and my children are enjoying a slight change of pace. Palace life is quite boring to them, I fear."

"I do remember the drudgery," he said, looking up at the turrets, bright white against a sun-bleached sky.

And he was walking back into it. Back into the past. Suddenly, he couldn't breathe.

He wanted to run again in that moment. Because he

could remember what had pushed him to it now, all too easily.

Blood. Death. Blame.

So much easier to run. To wrap himself in life's pleasures and ignore the pain.

"I can't imagine anything ever felt like drudgery to you. You never took it seriously enough."

"Maybe not then. But I'm here now. Oh, yes, I've decided to come back and assume the throne, I don't believe I mentioned that."

There was a long pause. He looked across the car at Layna, who was sitting there looking straight ahead, as though she was pretending she couldn't hear.

"I'm glad," Stavros said, at last, and Xander believed him. "But if this is a game to you, then I suggest you take your ass back to wherever you came from. It's been my life's work to bring Kyonos back from the brink, and I'll not have you destroy it."

"Don't worry, Stavros, I've only ever been interested in destroying myself."

"And yet, somehow, you seem to destroy others in the process."

Xander looked at Layna and felt an uncomfortable pang in his gut. "Not this time," he said. "Now, call and have them admit me, please."

"You'll find your quarters just as you left them."

He laughed. "I hope there's still porn under the mattress."

There was. Though it was hideously dated and nowhere near as scandalous as he'd imagined it to be when he was a young man only just starting down the path of debauchery.

The head of palace hospitality had ushered Layna to her room, and his father's advisor had walked him to his own quarters. The man, as old as the king, was blustering, shocked and trying to get answers from Xander who was, unfortunately for him, not in the mood to answer questions.

Instead he shut the man out, shut the door and looked around. That was when he found the magazines, just as he left them. They used to thrill him. He remembered it well. Now they just left him with this vague feeling of the stale familiar.

But then, life in general didn't thrill him much at this point. He'd seen too much. Done too much. He was less a carefree playboy than he was a jaded one. It was hard to show shock or emotion when one barely felt it anymore.

The glittering mystery had worn off life. Torn away the day his mother died. Forcing him to look at every ugly thing hidden behind the facade. And so he'd walked further into that part of life. The underbelly. Into all the things people wanted to revel in, but could never bring themselves to discard their morals—or their image—in order to do so.

But he'd done it. Morals didn't mean a thing to him. Neither did his image.

It was too hard to go on living in a beautiful farce when you knew that was all it was. So he never bothered. He was honest about what he wanted. He took what he wanted. As did those around him. Whether it was gambling, drugs or sex, it was done with a transparency, an unapologetic middle finger at life.

He'd found a strange relief in it. In being around all that sin in the open. Because it was the secrets, the pretense of civility, he couldn't handle.

And now he was back in the palace. Center stage for the show. Back in chains. Pretending to be someone he was never born to be.

He threw the magazines down onto the bed and looked

around. He'd expected a few more ghosts. Or something. But he felt the same as he had before returning home.

Shame and regret were his second skin. They existed with him, over him. And so he'd spent his life reveling in the most shameful things imaginable. He would feel it either way. At least if he sought it out, it was his choice. Not something forced upon him by life.

Like standing beneath water that was too hot. Until you were scalded to the point where you didn't feel it anymore.

In truth, it had worked to a degree.

But only to a degree.

He pushed his hands through his hair and turned toward where his suitcases had been put. He would need ties, he supposed. He didn't wear ties. One of the things he'd cast off when he'd left Kyonos.

For now, he just had his suits and shirts he wore open-collared, but it would have to do. Just the thought of ties made it feel hard to breathe. Or maybe it was the palace in general.

Her pulled open the door to his room and stalked down the corridor, not sure where he was going. He grabbed the passing housekeeper. "Where is Layna?"

"Oh!" She looked completely shocked. "Your Highness…"

"Xander," he said. He had no patience for station and title. "Which room is she in?"

"Ms. Xenakos is in the east wing, in the Cream Suite."

"Great." He started in that direction. Because there was nothing else to do. There was no one else in the palace he wanted to talk to.

He wasn't certain why that was. He should seek out his father's major domo. He should go and see his father, who was in the hospital. He should call his sister.

He didn't do any of those things. He just walked through

the expansive corridors, past openmouthed palace staff, and toward the Cream Suite. He got lost. Twice. It was an embarrassment, but he just kept going until he got his bearings again.

Then he pushed open the heavy wooden doors without knocking, and saw Layna, sitting on the edge of the bed. Her face snapped up, and again, he was shocked by her appearance.

It hit him like a slug to the gut. She had been so beautiful. So many beautiful things had been destroyed in that time. Either by his actions, or his very birth. The fault was bred into him, in many ways.

"What are you doing?"

"I'm here to speak to you. And to…escort you to dinner."

It had been a long time since he'd escorted a woman to dinner. Usually he had sex with them, then they ordered room service and ate it naked. Although, on a good night, he kicked the woman out quickly, then ate room service by himself.

She blinked. "Escort me to dinner? Where?"

"Here will do. The staff has been alerted to my presence, and I have no doubt they're eager to welcome me back with my favorite food," he said, his tone dry. "Or at the very least they won't let me starve."

"I don't suppose the heir is of much use to anyone if he's starved to death. I also don't suppose he's much use to anyone if he's absent and drunk."

"No, it doesn't seem that I've done any good during my time away," he said, his voice tight. "But I'm not sure what I could have done here, either. I was not the king then. I am not now. I'm simply in line."

"But you left us," she said, a note in her voice, so sad, so fierce, he felt it in his bones.

"I left you," he said.

"Yes."

"Did I break your heart, Layna?"

She shook her head slowly. "Not in the way you mean. I didn't love you, Xander. I was infatuated, surely, but we didn't truly know each other. You were very handsome, and I can't deny being drawn to you. I'm a bit of a magpie for shiny things, you know."

"I was shiny?"

"Yes. The shiniest prize out there."

"Not sure how I feel about that."

"You'll live." She looked down. "I loved the idea of being queen. I was raised for it, after all."

"Yes, you were." He didn't have to say that he hadn't been in love with her. That much had been obvious by his actions. When he'd left Kyonos he'd hardly spared a thought for what it would mean to Layna. He hadn't been able to spare a thought for anything but his own pain.

"But I thought I would find someone else. Maybe Stavros."

"You wanted to marry Stavros?"

She shrugged. "I would have. But then… Then the attack happened and I didn't especially want to see anyone much less marry anyone."

"So you joined a convent? Seems extreme."

"No. I spent years struggling with depression, actually, but thank you for your rather blithe commentary on my pain."

That shocked him into silence, which was a rare and difficult thing. He didn't shock easily. Or, as a rule, at all.

"When did you join?"

"Ten years ago. I was tired of muddling through. And I saw a chance to make myself useful. I couldn't fit back into the life I had been in, so it was time to make a new one."

"And you've been happy?"

"Content."

"Not happy?"

"Happiness is a temporary thing, Xander. Fleeting. An emotion like any other. I would rather exist in contentment."

He laughed. "Funny. I don't think I've been happy. Not content, either. I like to chase intense bursts of euphoria."

"And have you managed to catch them?" she asked, her voice tight.

"Yeah," he said, shoving his hands in his pockets and leaning against the doorjamb, "I have. But let me tell you, the highs might be high...the comedowns are a bitch."

"I wouldn't know. I strive for a more simple and useful existence."

"Do you want to dress for dinner?"

She looked down at the simple, shapeless dress she was wearing. It was blue and flowered, the sweater she had over it navy and button-down, hanging open and concealing her curves entirely, whatever those curves might look like. "What's wrong with this?"

"Really?"

"I'm not exactly given to materialism these days, and unless you were dead set on looking at my figure," she said dryly, as though it were the most ridiculous thing on the planet, "I fail to see why you should be disappointed. I'm clean, my clothing is serviceable. I don't know what more you could possibly need from me. If I am to be an accessory in your attempt at being seen by your people as palatable, then I'm sure my more conservative style could be to your advantage."

"I don't think that was what people liked about you."

"Perhaps not, but it can't be helped," she said, her voice tart.

She bowed her head, brown hair falling forward. "You used to sparkle," he said, not sure where the words came from, or why he'd voiced them.

She looked up at him, fire burning in her golden eyes. "And I used to be beautiful. Things change."

He pushed away from the door, and images from the past fifteen years—the casinos, the women—rolled through his mind. "Yes, they do. I'll see you at dinner."

He turned and walked out of the room, back down the corridor. And he got lost again on the way back to his room.

This damned palace was never going to feel like home. But he'd been a lot of places in the past fifteen years and none of them felt like home, either.

He was starting to believe it was a place that simply didn't exist for him.

CHAPTER FOUR

HE'D MADE HER feel self-conscious about her dress. More than that, his words had sliced through her like a knife, hitting her square in a heart she'd assumed would be invulnerable to such things.

I used to be beautiful. Things change.

Yes, they certainly did.

She was realistic about the situation with her face. Fifteen years of living with it, and there was no other option. It had been hard. She'd been a woman defined by her looks, by her position in the public eye, and in one moment, it had all changed.

She was still a woman defined by her looks. But people didn't like what they saw.

The press called her disfigured. The former beauty. The walking dead.

Going out into the town had meant a chance she'd get her photo taken, and that meant a chance she'd appear in the news the next day.

It had driven her deeper into her own darkness. Into isolation. It had been hell. And she'd had to escape.

Finding a way to a new life had been the hardest thing she'd ever done. Her family hadn't known what to do with her, they hadn't known how to help her. Their existence had been shaken, too. Their promised position as in-laws to the royal family vanished.

In the end, they'd all moved to Greece. Her mother, father and sisters. But Layna had stayed. And what she'd weathered should have made her immune to things like Xander's comments.

She was thirty-three. She wasn't a child. She knew now that life wasn't defined by dresses, balls and beauty. She did know it. So curse Xander for making her feel insecure. For making her feel like she should make an effort to look pretty when she met him for dinner.

Those things, they didn't matter. She had changed, and at the end of the day, she liked herself better now. At least now she didn't think the only way to live was by shopping the day away before going to a ball and pretending to be bored by all of it.

In some ways, she had more freedom now. If something made her feel joy, she had no problem showing it. Her face made it impossible for her to blend in, impossible for people to do anything but judge her. So why worry about trying to seem cool and unaffected? There was no reason at all.

"I'm glad you could make it."

Layna paused at the entrance to the grand dining room. Another unholy mash-up between her life then and now. The expansive banquet table held no one but Xander. In the past, there would have been fifty dignitaries in attendance. And Layna would have worn her best dress. Xander would have worn a tie. They would have sat beside each other.

He was wearing a black suit jacket and a crisp white shirt open at the collar, revealing a wedge of golden skin and a dark dusting of hair.

She tried to remember if he'd had chest hair during their engagement. He certainly hadn't been as broad or muscular. He'd been lean. Soft-faced and handsome.

His face was more angular now, his jaw more pronounced thanks to the black stubble there. And his eyes, those eyes were so much sharper.

He was a man now.

"I'm not late," she said, walking slowly into the room. She wasn't sure if she should walk up to where he was, at the head of the table, and sit near him or not.

"No, but I was still wondering if you would bother to join me."

"I said I would. So I did."

"You aren't a soft girl, are you, Layna?"

"Have I ever been, Xander?"

A half smile curved his lips and it sent a strange, tightening sensation through her stomach. "No. Now that you mention it, you never were. Though you used to look like you might be."

"All that blond hair dye and the pink gowns. I suspect it was deceiving."

"Maybe to some. I remember, though, standing out on the balcony with you while you looked at the other guests."

So did she. Making snide observations about how Lady So-and-so had worn that gown to a previous event, and how Madame Blah-blah-blah's hair looked like a bird had chosen to nest in it.

Yes, she'd had opinions on everyone's looks. Specifically their shortcomings. The irony of that still burned.

"Yes, well, I was young. I had a lot of growing up to do. And I've had a lot of years to do it."

"And have you?" He leaned back in his chair, an arm rested on the table, an insolent expression on his face.

"Of course."

"See, I thought you might be playing hide-and-seek."

She stiffened and walked toward his end of the table and sat down, leaving an empty place between them. "What about you?"

"That's certainly what I'm doing. But I've been found, and I am now 'it,' as they say. Means I have to face all this."

"You sound about as thrilled as a man facing the gallows."

Several servants entered with food on trays, laid out in front of them grandly, their glasses filled with wine.

"Are you permitted?" he asked.

She nodded. "Yes. So long as it's not to excess. And anyway, I haven't taken my vows yet, remember?"

He nodded slowly. "I do. That is significant."

"It is." The servants uncovered the platters and began to dish portions of rice, quail and vegetables onto her plate. She was surprised by how hungry she was. She hadn't eaten all day and she hadn't felt it. Because she'd been too filled up with nerves to do much of anything but worry.

"Why haven't you?"

Her face heated. "I haven't been permitted to take them yet."

"So it isn't your choice?"

She shook her head. "No. I'm committed." She hesitated to say the words because they felt false somehow. Especially after her revelation just before she left the convent. That part of her still wanted something from this life. From this palace. From Xander. She pushed her doubts away. "I was miserable before I went to the convent. I had no idea what to do with myself, no idea what I was supposed to... do with my life. Everything changed for me after."

"After I left," he said.

The servants cleared the room and they were left alone in the vast dining area. Layna looked out the windows, into the darkness, trying to find a point to focus on, something to anchor her to earth. Something to make her feel like the world hadn't changed entirely in the past twelve hours.

It was night out. There were still stars. She was still breathing.

"After you left," she said. "And then after the attack."

"I didn't think of you when I left," he said.

She laughed, and she surprised herself with her own bitterness. She'd done nothing but think about him. Worry for him. Pine for him. She'd lied a bit when she'd said he hadn't broken her heart. As much as she didn't believe she'd truly been in love with him, she'd cared.

Her heart and her future had been bound up in him. He'd been the man she'd imagined going to bed with at night. The man she'd thought she would have children with. The man who would make her a queen.

And then he'd gone, and taken with him her dreams. Her purpose.

Followed closely by the attack that took so many other things…gaining traction again had been nearly impossible.

"I didn't imagine you had."

"It was easier not to. But now I want to know."

"It was your father who told me you'd gone," she said. "And he asked that I return the ring."

"Did he?" Xander asked, his voice soft, deadly sounding.

"Yes. It was part of the Drakos family crown jewels, I could hardly keep it."

"Well, I'm sure it was badly missed in that dusty cabinet they keep it all in," he said, his tone dry.

"Are you really offended on my behalf?" she said, her throat tightening, anger pouring through her, hot and fast. "A bit hypocritical since you were the one who left."

"My leaving had nothing to do with you."

"No, as you said, you never thought of me again."

"I did. I thought of you after. It's true that when I ran, I only thought of me, and I am sorry for that. But later, I thought of you. I couldn't have been a husband to you, not under those circumstances."

She took a bite of the rice and the rich flavor knocked out some of her anger. She did not eat food like this at the convent. Even considering the unfortunate nature of the conversation, the food was amazing. As was the wine.

She let silence fall between them while she enjoyed her meal. She made a mistake when she looked up, and her eyes caught his. And she couldn't look away. Everything in her went taut, her breath pausing, her heart slamming forward. All she could do was stare at him.

He was so familiar. A face she tried never to remember. That perfect golden skin, the dark brown eyes fringed with thick black lashes. Lips that promised heaven when he smiled, and made a woman imagine he could take her to a beautiful sort of hell with a kiss.

All of that was so familiar.

But the lines around his mouth were harder now. Marks by his eyes showed the ghosts of his smiles.

He had been beautiful at twenty-one. At thirty-six he was no less stunning.

Time had not been quite so kind to her. And anyway, she had absolutely no business looking at him like she was. No business memorizing the new lines on his face. It was like she'd been in a coma, and she was slowly waking up. Slowly seeing new things. Or, remembering old things. She didn't like it. She was starting to remember why she'd worked so hard to forget.

"I wasn't meant to be your wife," she said, looking back at her food.

"You don't think?"

"Clearly not. I found a new calling. The place I'm supposed to be."

"You think you're better off hiding in the mountains than you are as the queen of Kyonos?"

She'd always thought she would be a good queen. But with a girl's insight. She'd loved the idea of the status and power. That everyone else was so jealous of her for having caught Xander's eye, or, more honestly, the eye of his parents.

Now she understood it had been her father's merit more than her own that had earned her the consideration. At the time it hadn't mattered. She'd only thought how beautiful she would look wearing the crown.

But now, ironically, that the position was no longer on the table, she saw all the good she could do. All that needed to be done to fix her country.

Prince Stavros had done an admirable job with it, more than admirable, but there were still things to be done on a humanitarian level, and as someone who had done nothing but serve for the past ten years she was well familiar with what tasks needed to be tackled head-on.

Nice that she knew all that. Now that there was nothing she could do about it. That would be for the woman who married Xander. And that woman would not be her.

A twinge of anger hit her in the chest, burned like a pinprick and spread outward. This had been her future. And she was sitting in it now, not a part of it.

She looked back up and saw him watching her, and it hit her then. What she'd lost. They would have been married for nearly fifteen years by now. There would have been children. She wouldn't be scarred.

It did no good to dwell on the past. It did no good to turn over what-ifs. But it was so hard when your biggest what-if was sitting across from you eating dinner, like he might have done if you'd married him way back then.

Yes, it was a whole lot harder not to what-if in that situation. Easier when cloistered in a convent, away from any part of the life she'd once lived. Impossible here and now.

"I wasn't meant to be queen," she said, her tone strong, a sharp contrast to what she actually felt.

"Perhaps I wasn't meant to leave." His words burned through her. Because he had left. It didn't matter what should have happened, only what had.

"Why bother turning it over, Xander? It's what happened. You did leave. And things have changed. We didn't freeze in time here while you were gone like I'm sure you imagined we did. We went on. Things have happened, things that can't be undone. I would have been…a silly and selfish princess back then anyway. And now…now it just couldn't be."

"It's hard not to turn it over here, though, isn't it?"

She put her palms flat on the table, her heart pounding, blood rushing through her ears. "Why did you come back? Really. I mean…what changed? You left, and no one ever thought you would be back, but here you are now, and you're dragging me into it, so I want to know why."

He shook his head, didn't say anything. He only stared out the windows into the darkness outside.

"Answer me, Xander," she said. "I have a right to know why you've crashed back into my life."

"Because there was nothing out there," he said. "No answers. It fixed nothing. If Stavros wanted the throne, if it didn't throw Eva's future into disarray, I would never have come back. But I don't do any good by being gone. I'm not sure I'll do much good being back. I'm not sure I'm even capable of doing good. I think that where I'm concerned, all of the bad might run too deep." When he said it like that, she believed he might be right. "But I came back, because if I didn't it would stay broken. And now that I'm here, it might all remain that way, but at least it's my broken mess and not theirs."

"You love them, don't you?"

"I don't love easily," he said, his voice rough. "But I would die for them."

"That's something."

"A sliver of humanity?"

"Yes," she said, taking a deep breath. "What am I doing here, Xander? You've given me a reason. The press. But I have to tell you, I'm not sure I believe it."

"It's part of it," he said.

"I need all of it."

"Do you want an honest answer?"

"If you know how to give one."

"I don't lie, Layna, it's the one sin I don't indulge in. Do you know why?"

She put her fork down. "I'm on the edge of my seat."

"Because people lie to protect themselves. To make people like them. To hide what they've done because they're ashamed. I have no shame, and I don't care if people like me. My sins are public property."

"Then give me an honest answer."

"I thought I might marry you," he said, his tone conversational, light. As though he'd mentioned that it was a clear night and the food was lovely, and not that he'd been considering asking her to be his wife.

"You did?" she asked, her lips numb, her entire body numb suddenly, from fingertips on down.

A wife. *Xander's* wife.

It was impossible. And she didn't want it anyway. Her life was in the convent, it was serving people and living simply. It was shunning the frivolous things in the world. Denying passions and finding contentment in the small things. In the things that were worthy.

It was this palace. This man. They washed those old memories in brilliant colors, where for years they'd always been faded.

And now she could see again, so clearly, how lovely it had all been. She could taste the excitement of it. That secret ache bloomed, flourished, let her dream. Let her see the glitter, the sparkle and what might be for one beautiful moment.

But it only lasted for a moment. Until a root of bitter anger rose up and choked out the bloom.

"Obviously," he continued, "that can't happen now."

She felt the sting of his words like a slap. "Obviously not. What would people think if you took me as a wife?"

"I only meant because you've chosen to forego marriage by joining a convent. Had I found you anywhere else I would have stuck to my original plan and proposed on the spot."

She bit down hard and tried not to say what she was thinking. Tried. And failed. "I would have told you to go to hell. On the spot," she said.

"You haven't changed as much as I initially thought."

She stood up. "That's where you're wrong. Everything's changed. I've changed, my whole life has changed."

He stood and started to walk toward her, dark eyes pinned to hers. "No, Layna, see I don't think you've changed as much as you think you have. When I look at you, I can so easily see the girl you were. You were blond then."

"Because I used to dye it."

"I suspected. But it did suit you."

"It's pointless vanity," she said, waving her hand.

"How is it pointless if you enjoy it? It can still be vanity, but it doesn't mean it's pointless."

"Yes it does. But make your point and be done."

He took another step toward her and her heart climbed up into her throat and lodged itself there. "You had fire. Beneath that airhead, mean-girl surface, you had more to you than anyone guessed. You were a little flame ready to become a wild fire."

She shook her head. "It doesn't matter. I've changed now and…"

"No. You're still doing it. You're still hiding who you are beneath something else. Beneath a shield. The flame is still there, you just want to hide it. Up in the mountains."

"It's not my fire I'm hiding. It's my face. And if you want to pretend it doesn't matter then I'm going to tell you right now, Xander, no matter what you said before, you are a liar." Rage rattled through her, fueled her, spurred her on.

It hit her, as the force of it threatened to consume her, that of all the emotions she'd felt since her attack, she'd never been angry. Sad. Depressed. Lonely. She'd hit rock-bottom with those. Then she'd found a sort of steady tranquility in her existence at the convent.

But she'd never been angry.

Just now she was so furious she thought she might break apart with it. "Look at me," she said, "really look. Can you imagine me on newspapers and magazines? The face for our country? Can you imagine me trying to go to parties as if nothing had happened? Trying to continue on as if I was the same Layna as before? That's why I went to the convent. Because there it didn't matter if my face was different. There it's practically a virtue and here…here it's just not. I'm ugly, Xander, and whether or not I accept myself there will always be people who want to point it out. I've never seen a reason for putting myself through it."

He shoved his hands into his pockets, his eyes hard. "It will be commented on. I won't lie about that. But do you think people will resent your scars or my abandonment more?"

"Don't tell me you're honestly still considering me as queen material."

"I was very interested by the fact that you haven't yet taken your vows."

"My intent remains the same, whether or not I've taken final vows."

He reached out, took a piece of her hair between his thumb and forefinger. She froze. She hadn't been touched by a man in longer than she could remember. Male doctors were the last ones, she was certain. And then she hadn't registered the touch in any significant way.

But Xander had never been easy to ignore. Now, with his hand on her hair, just her hair, a flood of memories assaulted her. The catalog of moments when Xander had touched her in the past opened, forcing her to remember.

His hand over hers, or low on her back. An arm around her waist. His warm palm on her cheek as his lips nearly brushed hers.

If they had married then, they would have kissed thousands of times by now. But as it was, they had never kissed once.

"But nothing is final," he said.

He lowered his hand, releasing her hair, and sanity flooded in a wave. She stepped back, blinking, that fresh and newfound anger coming to her rescue.

"Yes, Xander, everything is final. I have made my decision, like you made yours. I'll help you in any way I can, but don't insult me by pretending, even for a second, that you would consider making me your wife. Don't consider that I might allow it."

She turned and walked out of the room and when she hit the halls she suddenly realized that she was gasping for breath. She put a hand on her chest and blinked hard, fighting tears, fighting panic.

Xander was reaching into places inside of her no one had touched in so long, she'd forgotten they were there. Longings and regrets she'd buried beneath a mountain of all that lovely contentment she'd learned to cultivate from the sisters at the convent.

Xander made her restless. This palace made her remember. It made her want things....

She shook her head. No. She wouldn't let this happen. She wouldn't be shaken. She would help him. If only to help her country, her people.

But she wouldn't forget who she'd become. Who Xander's actions had forced her to become.

CHAPTER FIVE

XANDER UNBUTTONED HIS shirt and threw it onto the bed. He hadn't intended to bring up the marriage proposal like that. Hell, he hadn't meant to bring it up at all. She was a nun. Well, close enough to being one, anyway.

And then there were the scars. He couldn't pretend they didn't matter. She was right on that score. He needed a wife that would help improve his image in the public, and before he'd seen her, he'd imagined that she could do that. That their reunion would be seen as a true romance in the eyes of the media.

But how would they respond to a scarred princess? A princess who had been scarred during the turmoil caused by his leaving? A constant reminder of dark times for all of them. It had to be considered.

As for him, it didn't much matter. He would marry someone, he had to. But just because he had to marry didn't mean he had to be monogamous. He would be honest on that score with whomever he married, of course. But marriage was a necessity because he had to produce heirs, and preferably sooner rather than later. At thirty-six he was hardly getting any younger, and added to that, the people needed assurance that he could provide what was needed.

His plans were officially screwed.

Tomorrow, he was taking Layna to Kyonos's largest

hospital, where he would make his first public appearance. And where he would be giving a sizable donation of his personal fortune, and making his intentions of ruling Kyonos known.

Because nothing eased the way like throwing charitable donations around. At least, he hoped it would ease the way.

The people loved Stavros. They wouldn't accept the change lightly. Come to think of it, he was sure it was why his brother remained out of the country, even knowing Xander was back. The bastard.

He nearly laughed out loud. No, Stavros wasn't the bastard here. He never had been. The bastard had always been him.

But it was too late to worry about that now. His decision was made.

He thought of Layna, of his need for a wife. Some of his decisions were made, but not all of them.

He would have to figure that part out as quickly as possible. Of course, in order to have it all figured out, he needed to know what he was dealing with.

He turned to his desk, to his laptop, sitting there, open. He typed in his name on the search engine and hit enter.

It had hit. The servants must have called. Someone had said something, because there were headlines already.

The Disgraced Heir's Return. He clicked the link and skimmed the article. It was filled with bile and innuendo. About all he'd done with his life since he'd been gone.

Prince Alexander Drakos, abandoned Kyonos like a rat when it was a sinking ship, saved, of course by Prince Stavros. All while Xander partied in Monaco, wasting his family fortune, sleeping with countless women while indulging in alcohol and illegal substances.

One source from an exclusive casino was quoted.

"One night, he was so drunk he could hardly stand straight. He put his arms around two women to brace himself and they helped him back to his room. I didn't see them leave until the next morning."

And this is the man who presumes to come back and be king of our great nation.

Xander closed the laptop, heat streaking up the back of his neck. He couldn't remember the night being referenced in the article, but he couldn't say it was a lie.

It wasn't going to be like he'd thought. It was going to be worse. And all he could do was go forward with the plan.

There was no other option.

"I assumed asking you to put on something more appropriate for the occasion would make you look at me like I'd grown a second head."

Layna was at the breakfast table, wearing an insipid pale pink shift and a sweater that was the color of a dirty rose. She looked up, her gaze serene. But it didn't cover the fire beneath. He'd spoken the truth to her last night. The fire was still there, fire she'd always been so desperate to hide. "I have no idea what you're talking about. My dress is the picture of appropriate."

"For a nunnery."

She arched a brow. "Funny that."

"You're not in the convent anymore, Dorothy."

"I don't suppose if I tapped my heels together three times I might find my way back."

"Unlikely. I doubt nuns are allowed to possess magic shoes."

"Novice."

"Either way," he said, crossing the room and planting his hands on the back of one of the dining chairs, "I am wearing a tie. And I don't think you understand just what a concession that is, so all things considered, perhaps you would allow me to get you a more appropriate dress for what I am certain will end up being a press conference."

Her expression went blank at the mention of the press. "What's the point? I'm not speaking in your press conference. I'm there to be your…what am I exactly—some homely, saintly representation of your good intentions? Or am I just supposed to stand close so that the lightning bolt you were concerned about earlier doesn't hit you?"

"I thought God didn't work that way."

She lifted a shoulder. "I said that before I'd spent this much time with you."

"I won't lie to you, you are here to give me a bit more of a savory appearance. And also because I think it lends nice closure to our story. If you can forgive me…"

"Oh, I see. Another layer to my usefulness." She stood, color slowly blooming in her cheeks as her voice rose. "You thought that if I would forgive you the country would follow suit. That if you came back and the woman you were engaged to before you left opened her arms to you, your people would do the same." And then she did something wholly unexpected. She started laughing.

Not just a giggle, but a laugh that seemed to take over her whole body. She put her hand on the back of the chair in front of her and doubled over, laughing so hard he thought she might choke.

"Oh, poor Xander," she gasped. "You came back to find your queen, your key to your redemption and you found a scarred woman who'd given herself to the church. Your plans just aren't going well, are they?"

He wouldn't even mention the unflattering news pieces going around about him.

"You could say that," he said, his words clipped. He did not find the situation as funny as she did. But then, in his mind, none of this was terribly funny. It was all his worst nightmare as far as he was concerned.

He was back here, in the suffocating atmosphere of the palace, trying to pretend like he fit when he didn't. Trying to pretend the scars the past had left on him didn't hurt when they did. Trying to act like this was a future he was entitled to when he knew full well it wasn't.

But he was the only one who did know that. The only one who was still alive who knew it, anyway.

"Sorry I'm making it difficult for you to use me," she said, wiping her eyes. "I'm sure that must really mess things up."

"I thought you lived for the service of others."

"The poor and downtrodden, not entitled royal princes who don't know you can't find responsibility, honor or purpose in the bottom of a gin bottle."

He laughed, bitterness in the sound. "No, I know you can't, but that's not what I was looking for."

"What were you looking for?" she asked.

"I wasn't looking for anything. I was trying to lose something. Now are you ready to go or not?"

"I'm ready," she said, her eyes far too assessing for his liking.

"Fine then, let's go. And do your best to look saintly. If you can cultivate a halo on our way there I would really appreciate it."

Layna held her breath until she thought she would pass out. The press was already waiting at the hospital when they pulled up, so clearly someone on staff had leaked the news. It would be huge, of course it would. The heir to the throne back on Kyonos.

The implications were huge.

And all she could think about was that they would be taking her picture. That people would look at her.

Xander made her revert to a stupid, silly girl who cared about insubstantial things. It was annoying beyond belief.

Just focus on all the good you can do with the kind of budget he has.

Yes, that was the key. She would direct him to the needs she knew existed. It would benefit Kyonos and it would benefit him. Everyone came out a winner. Having her picture in the paper was a small price to pay for doing that kind of good.

It really was. It didn't matter what they said. It didn't matter what they thought. Her body was just the place her soul lived, and the only beauty she had to be concerned with was the kind that was inside.

She repeated that, over and over again, but still when the car came to a stop and Xander got out, her hands started to shake.

They were taking pictures already. Xander's return would be the biggest news since his abandoning the island and it would be on every news station, in every paper.

He opened the limo door and before she could fully process her movements, she got out and was assaulted by a barrage of flashes and shouts. He took her arm and she kept her face tilted down as they walked into the hospital.

He released his hold on her when they were near the doors, then stood in front of her, the gesture oddly protective as he turned, addressing the press. "I will speak to you when we are done here. For now, my priority is to see how the most vulnerable of my country are getting on.

I have brought with me an ambassador, one who knows the struggles of all of you. Please treat her with respect."

He turned back to the doors, his hand on her arm again as he led her into the hospital.

The hospital administrator was waiting for them and after making introductions it was clear Xander was waiting for her to lead things. "Is the hospital large enough to accommodate all of the patients that you need to see?" she asked.

"Prince Stavros has done an amazing job of building up our research center," the woman said. Her manner was reserved. Almost cold. She was trying to be friendly, especially since Xander was there to give money, but there was a brittleness there she wasn't hiding well. "As a result we're well-equipped in many areas, but yes, things are starting to feel understaffed, and the children's ward especially is very small. People travel here seeking treatment."

"A wonderful thing," Xander said, for the first time, his confidence sounding blunted. He knew when to tone himself down, which was a surprise to Layna, and a credit to him.

"Yes," Layna said. "What about emergency medical services?"

They finished the tour of the hospital, which included a trip through the cafeteria. Layna nearly laughed at Xander, trying to deal with a hospital version of a gyro. He was clearly not impressed.

"She was not thrilled to have me here, was she?" Xander asked as he took another bite of food.

"Not as much as one might have hoped," Layna said.

"Well, I imagined that's what I'll be contending with across the board. Stavros is well-liked. And I am not." He looked down at his meal. "I do have an idea of where we might increase the funding," he said, his voice low, only for Layna.

"Better idea, Xander, why don't you put some money aside to send the hospital cooks through a culinary course? Then they have transferable skills."

He paused, a half smile curving his lips. "This is why I brought you."

"I do have my uses," she said. "Even if I can't be made a queen."

He stared at her, for far too long in her opinion. It made her face hot, made her aware of her face. Annoying man.

"Are you ready to leave?" he asked. The hospital administrator had gone back to her office and they were standing in the lobby, staff and patients passing through. Some trying not to stare, some staring openly as they tried to decipher if the larger-than-life man standing there was a Drakos. If he was the long lost heir.

"Yes. As ready as I can be. I appreciated what you said to everyone before we came in. Hopefully they'll find it in them to be human. To both of us."

"Aren't you looking forward to the press ripping into me? They already have, you know."

She paused, waiting to feel some kind of relish at the thought, but she just didn't. "I actually don't want that. A surprise, I know. But I'm tired of this country feeling torn. I'm tired of grieving our losses. Tired of the unrest. Stavros has done an incredible job rebuilding, unifying, and the people love him. But there is a sense that everything isn't settled. That the royal family itself isn't healed. With the king so sick... Xander, I would rather you be accepted with open arms. And then I would like for you to take the people's trust and use it well, not abuse it. That's what I would like."

"And you want to go back up to your mountain then?"

"It's my years on the mountain that are helping you now. You have to admit, this wasn't your area of expertise."

"I've been a patient in hospital emergency rooms," he said, looking around them, "but I've been short on philanthropy in them."

"You have?" She was honestly shocked by that.

He laughed. "I've done no shortage of dumb-ass things in my time away, Layna. Just trust me on that. Too much speed in cars, too much drink, too much…everything." He paused. "Another advantage, I suppose to your being committed elsewhere. If you aren't my queen, you don't have to deal with my past."

"Is it so bad?"

He nodded slowly. "And there's a lot of it. Ready?"

She knew he was talking about facing the press. "Yes."

He walked out of the hospital and she followed slowly, dread filling her, her brain fuzzy, the world titled slightly.

"As has already been reported, in less than flattering words," he said, his voice loud, the microphones unnecessary, "I have returned, and I intend to take my place as heir to the throne. Of course, while my father is unwell, that doesn't mean it will happen now, or even in the next year, but I am here, and I'm here to stay. Layna Xenakos has graciously agreed to partner with me as I get familiarized with my home again. She's been living in service to this country, and she is the best choice, in my opinion, to show me where the greatest needs lie. If Layna can forgive me my choices, and welcome me back, I hope that her forgiveness is the start of my earning forgiveness from everyone. Though, I know that is a lot to ask. We all want what is best for the country. If you can't trust me, at least, for now perhaps, we can stand united in that."

The air roared with questions as the press crushed in on them both. Xander took her hand and pulled her through the crowd. She tried to keep her head down, tried to keep them from being able to snap shots of the worst of her damaged face. Tried to let all of the questions blend into an indistinct blur so that she didn't hear any of them.

But she heard words. *Attack. Scars. Beauty. Ugly.*

She'd never spoken to the press after her attack, and neither had her family. There were so many unanswered questions for them. Between her and Xander the press had the most salacious bits of the past, right there before them, and they were rabid now.

"In the car," Xander said, opening the door. She obeyed and slid inside. He followed, slamming the door behind them. "Back to the palace," he said before putting the divider up between them and the driver.

He let out a rough breath and put his head back on the seat. "Well, that went a bit better than anticipated."

"Did it?" she asked.

"They let me make a statement before mobbing us."

"Okay, yeah, there's that."

"It was better than they can be."

She looked at him. "How have you managed to avoid the press all these years?"

"Easy, actually. I don't go to places where they hang out. There will be no place to avoid them in Kyonos, but in the rest of Europe? In the States? No one cares. I made brief splashes in tabloids for the first couple of years. 'Dishonorable Heir Gambles Away His Fortune,' et cetera. But then people lost interest."

"I suppose it was the same for me. After the attack it was news. But they weren't allowed in the hospital to interview me. Then I was in too much pain to even consider talking to anyone. For a long time. I had a lot of surgeries." She didn't even like to say how many. "After that I didn't go anywhere. My parents moved to Greece where, you're right, no one cares about the drama that happened here, and I stayed on in their house with their servants for a while."

"Why didn't you leave?"

She frowned. "I...I was too tired." It was a terrible thing to admit. Even to remember. The depression had controlled her, not just emotionally, but physically. Breathing had often seemed too big of a trial. To move to Greece? It would have been unthinkable.

Those years were a haze, where she kept herself cradled by the gentle hands of painkillers that helped her sleep, helped her ignore the pain from her most recent surgery, and helped her live her days with blunted senses.

She preferred never to remember them. She'd come too far since then, and that place had been too dark. Although, there were times when it was important to remember it. It reminded her just how bright the sun was. How much better things were now.

Even sitting in the limo with Xander, with the press all but chasing the limo, it was better than that place. Because above all else, she had control now. She could leave if she chose. Could get up and walk away from Xander, from whatever she wanted to.

She had the power now. The energy and strength inside of herself to do it. She would never be stuck again.

"And has it been better here? Are you happy with your decision to stay?"

"It was terrible here, at first. That first five years...it was hell. The recovery was awful, Xander, I won't lie. It wouldn't have mattered where I was, not really. But when I got...well, when I got the worst, and I knew I had to figure out how to get better, it was right to change things as radically as I could. And that's why the convent was best for me. It's impossible to worry too much about your own drama when you have to confront what's happening with others."

"How did you connect with them?" he asked.

She looked down at her hands and smiled. "Some of the Sisters visited me in the hospital when I was recovering. And after every surgery. They checked on me sometimes. They cared. And they didn't look at me and see my scars. But they did see my pain, and they...cared."

"Your family?"

She sighed. "They didn't realize how bad it was. How bad it had gotten for me. Mainly because I lied to them. I told them I was fine when I wasn't and they wanted to believe I was telling the truth because it was so much easier. I don't blame them at all."

"Do you blame me?"

His words were stark in the silence of the car. Emotionless. He was asking, but he gave no indication that he cared either way.

"Yes," she said, and only realized just when she spoke the words that she meant them. That she did blame him, deep down, for the pain, for the isolation.

If he had stayed, at least she would have had a husband to stand by her. And maybe it would never have happened. Maybe the economy wouldn't have crashed, that she could never know. But she could have had someone.

She wouldn't have lost everything.

He nodded slowly. "I think that's fair. And I can handle having another sin added to the list."

"Do you think so?"

"Confession would take too long at this point, Layna. I'm beyond it. I might as well just accept it for what it is and move on from there."

Her heart thundered, anger burning through her veins. "At least you can move on. Gloss over it, pretend it didn't happen. It's a lot harder to do that when you have to look at the effects of the past in the mirror every day."

"Then how about I wake up to the effects of the past every morning?"

"What?" she asked, her stomach hollowing out.

"I've changed my mind about changing my mind." He put his legs out straight in front of him, his eyes fixed ahead. "After thinking about it, I believe the best idea is for you to marry me."

CHAPTER SIX

SHE HAD BEEN silent the rest of the ride back the palace. He supposed that it was probably a no, but he wasn't going to let her get away with not giving an answer. In his mind, it just meant he had to change hers.

"I'm tired," she said, once they reached the entryway of the palace. "I'm going to my room."

"I shall accompany you."

"No, you shall not," she said, starting to walk away from him, down an empty corridor, away from where the servants were bustling around.

"Then we will speak here."

"No, we won't."

He went to stand in front of her and she stopped and backed up quickly, her back making contact with the wall. "Yes," he said, advancing on her. "We will."

He studied her face, really studied it, for the first time since that day at the convent. It was a shame what had been done to her beauty. She'd been uncommon. He could remember her clearly. Those full pink lips, smooth skin, perfectly arched brows. Oh, he had wanted her badly. He could still remember that.

Being twenty-one and wanting his fiancée with a ferocity that he could scarcely understand. He'd been no virgin, even then, but she'd made him feel like one. And his father had made it clear Xander wasn't allowed to touch her, at least not until closer to the wedding. Something about re-spect and honor. About preserving the people's vision of their future queen.

So he had obeyed.

But they never would have made it that long. The chem-istry had been too potent.

He'd nearly kissed her once. He remembered because it had happened the day before his mother's death. The day before the revelation about who he really was.

After that, he hadn't seen her.

He lifted his hand and put his fingertips on her scar-roughened cheek, drawing them down her neck. He could imagine the attack clearly, how it had made these particu-lar scars. A hard hit to her cheek, spray over her nose, eye and forehead, down one side of her neck.

The other side of her face was virtually untouched, but it made her scars all the more shocking. It gave them con-trast. A living, breathing before-and-after shot.

"Can you feel that?" he asked.

She nodded slowly. "Some. Where the grafts are."

"Some of this is a graft?"

"Yes. Not…nothing more than was necessary because I couldn't bear for them to add more scars to my body and… it would never have looked normal anyway. As it is, it's kind of Frankenstein's monster."

"You're hardly a monster," he said.

"Flattery won't get you your way," she said, her tone guarded, hard.

He dropped his hand back to his side. "I don't need flat-tery. You must see that this is going to be a challenge. We were going to marry, we *wanted* to marry."

"A lifetime ago. A face ago."

"Your face doesn't matter to me."

She laughed, a bitter sound. "For God's sake, Xander, don't lie. It insults us both."

"It doesn't matter. I won't be coy with you, Layna. I have to take a wife someday and when I do it will be because she specifically brings a benefit to my position and to Kyonos as a country. At the moment I think you're the most beneficial wife for me. My personal feelings for you as an individual, or for your looks, have no bearing on anything. I doubt I should be faithful to any woman I marry, so I don't see how wild attraction is an issue, either."

She jerked back as though he'd slapped her. "You're asking me to marry you, knowing you don't truly want me, and admitting to me that you will sleep with other women?"

"I'm being honest with you. It's how I would treat any marriage to any woman."

"And why is it you won't be faithful?"

"Does it matter if you aren't truly vying for the position?"

"Pretend I'm considering it," she said, "indulge my curiosities."

He shrugged, a vague sense of shame washing over him as he looked at the woman he would have promised his life to years ago and spoke of planned faithlessness. As he realized that, had he married her as a beauty queen, he would have been unfaithful to her even then.

He'd been young. In lust, not in love. The center of his own universe. Certain of his absolute entitlement.

The moment he'd gotten hard for another woman he would have had her without a thought, no matter the vows he'd made to Layna, because that was the manner of man he'd been. Now...he had no practice in restraint. In turning away from the various and sundry pleasures of the flesh. He'd spent their years apart bathing in them because if he couldn't get clean, then he would at least cover his transgressions in new layers of sin and hope that people never looked deeper. Hoped that he never had to look deeper.

"I have no practice at being with one woman," he said. "I can't imagine a lifetime with the same person in my bed, and I have low expectations of myself in that regard."

"Especially if your wife is ugly," she said.

"It doesn't matter. It's how things are, it's how I am."

"I thought you were changing."

He shook his head, taking a deep breath. "I came back because it was right, not because I have any burning conviction about the rightness of it. I can't condemn Stavros and Eva to a life they don't want when I was the one who was raised for it from the cradle. And it's one thing to walk away and ignore responsibilities when actually having to rule the country is years in the future. But with the way things are now…with the way Stavros's marriage turned out and the fact that the heir will be up to Eva without me. The fact that my father could die at any moment and a decision had to be made, that changed things. But it didn't change me. The one thing I can give for sure is honesty, so I'm giving that. Or would you rather have lies?"

"I rather wish I would have known you, really known you, back when we were engaged. I don't think I would have been so eager to say yes."

"Back then you had other options, too, but now you only have two—the convent, or standing at my side, ruling a country."

Black fire lit up in her eyes, the kind of anger he'd never seen on her face before, not in the time since he'd walked back into her life, and not in the life before. "You're so quick to remind me of how low I've fallen, but let me take a moment to show you a mirror. Your face might be as beautiful as it ever was, Xander, but you are nothing more than a dead limb on the Drakos family tree. Stavros made something with this country after you destroyed it, Evangelina was brave enough to fight for something she wanted, she didn't just run away. And what have you done?"

"Nothing," he said, his voice rough, his heart beating, bloody and ragged. "I have done nothing, and I would seek to change that. I am *trying* to change that. I made mistakes, Layna, and I will not deny it. I was a hurt, frightened child when I left, and then I became jaded. Now I have no heart left to wound and about a thousand things to atone for. So I am here, and I am trying. I am offering you this, the chance to rule with me. To make a difference. To give you children. Or you can go back to your convent and hide—because you're too afraid to face criticism—and make a small ripple in a giant pond with your good deeds when you could be changing the world. You can accuse me of anything you like, and you're probably right. But if you turn me down, you're turning down a chance to make a real difference."

She snorted, her lip curled. "You say that like marrying you, sharing your bed, is an incidental I shouldn't have to worry my head about so long as I can do my duty."

"Lie back and think of Kyonos," he bit out. He didn't know why he was pushing this so hard. He should let her go. He shouldn't be standing in the hall of his palace all but begging her to marry him. And yet he was.

Because he'd decided that Layna Xenakos would be his wife and now he couldn't fathom it being anyone else. No one would make a better queen. No one would help his image, or his country, in a deeper way than she would.

And he wanted her. That was the end of the reasoning really. When he wanted something, he got it.

"You're disgusting."

"And yet you're still here." He put one hand on the wall behind her and leaned in. "Would it be so bad?"

"You realize that I was prepared to swear off sex for life, that if I take my vows it means no men ever. Do you honestly think you're going to entice me with your looks?"

"Your altruism, then. And the chance to rise above where you fell. The chance to show all of Kyonos that, in the end, you have triumphed. Or, keep hiding."

Layna struggled to catch her breath. Rage, sadness and a deep, dark need all pulled at her. Xander, near enough to touch, smelling like rain and sin and man, was enough to make her pulse go into hyperdrive.

She lied when she said sex wasn't the way to tempt her. She was a woman who was prepared to take vows in part because she believed no man would ever want her, and, he was right, because it was easier to hide than to be out in the world experiencing rejection.

She liked men. And had things not changed the way they had, she never would have chosen a life that meant no men. No marriage. No children.

Children. A chance to make a difference.

She looked at Xander, at his strikingly handsome features. He was as perfect as he'd ever been, and the idea of him stuck with her…it was laughable.

And why are you like this? Because of him. Because he left. Because he left the country to rot in its own hell. And he never once thought of you. You needed him and he was gone.

Yes. It had been his decision to leave. To steal the future she'd always dreamed of for herself. Why couldn't she have it back? But if she was going to take him, the decisions wouldn't be his alone. Not again. He'd had enough control for too long.

He would sacrifice, too. She would not be a martyr.

She would have something for herself. And why not? Why ache for a man's touch when she could have it? Why long for the glitter of the palace in deep, secret parts of herself when it could be hers? Why wish that she could have a baby when it could be her reality?

"You can have me," she said, her voice hard, "on one condition."

"What is that?"

"I am the only woman you'll ever have in your bed again."

"I told you already…"

"Yes, and I already told you I wouldn't marry you, but that didn't stop you from building your case and asking again. You don't get to name all the terms, Xander. I am giving up my future at the convent and as much as you belittle it, I did find something there. Peace. With myself. With God and with those around me. You're asking me to leave that, and I'm consenting. To put myself out there before the world and expose myself to ridicule. And I won't do it for free. I won't make all the concessions. From this moment on, you will have no other woman. And you won't have me until vows are made. As I know well given the current state of my life, nothing is final until vows are spoken."

"And if I am unfaithful? If I agree now, but transgress later?"

"I will shame you in the media, your children will know you for the faithless man you are and I will ensure I sign a document that means I get your worldly assets. That's expensive sex, Xander, she would have to be well worth it."

A slow smile curved his lips. "You are quite ruthless under those plain clothes, aren't you?"

"Life has a way of making us that way, doesn't it?"

"I suppose it does."

"You've managed to live through all of this with very little in the way of consequences. Well, consider me your punishment." She turned and walked away from him, shaking with rage and sadness, with the tears that were building inside of her, a hard knot of pressure in her chest that she could hardly breathe past.

She'd just agreed to marry Xander Drakos, to become queen of Kyonos. To share the bed of a man who didn't truly want to be with her. She would never be able to go back to the convent. To the women she considered her friends. Her family.

But she was resolved. She'd made the right decision.

She was taking back a piece of the life that she lost. The life she should have had. It wouldn't be everything, not for either of them. But if felt like her right. She would be queen. A goal she'd fixed herself on at sixteen, from the first moment she'd seen Xander in person at a ball. She would bear the heirs to the throne, children for her to love. The children she'd given up hope of having.

And she would force Xander to face the consequences of his actions, every morning when he woke, and every night when he went to bed.

And she would try to ignore the crawling humiliation that thought made her feel. Tried and failed. As she walked into her bedroom and closed the door, she dissolved into misery, and gave in to her tears.

"I won't be coming back," she said into the phone. It had been hours since she'd accepted Xander's proposal. And now she'd realized she had to call Mother Maria-Francesca and confess.

"I thought you might not."

"You did?"

"He's the reason you were running all this time," she

said, her tone calm, steady. "And he's the reason I never advised you to move ahead with your vows.

"He is?"

"You are dedicated, and I have never doubted your faith, so please don't take me wrong, but I always felt you were driven by your inner demons, and not your convictions. It was good that you had us, to give you the shelter that you needed. But this is a calling that requires your whole life. And it requires a drive that goes beyond fear of the world outside."

She nodded slowly. "I know."

Deep down, Layna had always known it was true. Because she had ached for other things. She used convent life to hide from her desires, desires she felt could never be met. So that she didn't have to see gorgeous men, and mothers with babies, clothes there was no point in her wearing, hairstyles that would make no difference because she would never be pretty again.

She was having some of what she wanted. She felt…in some ways she felt more in control than she had in years. This wasn't about Xander, or his hold on her. It was about claiming the life she desired.

But if she had known this was what she really wanted, she never would have imposed on the Sisters.

"I didn't mean to use anyone," she said, her voice choked.

"You gave back more than you ever took, Magdalena."

Layna smiled at the use of the name. "Thank you. I'm not sure that's true, but thank you. I hope…to continue on giving in my new position I…I suppose I'm going to be a princess. And queen one day."

"I'm glad to hear it."

"I won't forget what you taught me. I'm going to use this. I'm going to do good with my position." Something she wouldn't have cared about if she'd married Xander as a girl of eighteen. She would have just used it to increase her shopping budget.

"That's nice to hear. But you're allowed to want things. You're allowed to have dreams."

"I've tried hard not to have them," she said, wiping away a tear she hadn't realized had escaped.

"I know you have, Layna. You've tried very hard to keep yourself safe. But if I could give you one last piece of advice, it would be not to let fear decide things for you."

"I won't."

And she wouldn't. Her decision was made, and even though the enormity of it made her tremble, there was no going back now.

CHAPTER SEVEN

"I TRUST YOU slept well."

"Your trust is misplaced."

Xander laughed as Layna made her way into the dining room and sat down at the table. He hadn't seen her since she'd run dramatically from him in the hall last night, but he'd had a feeling hunger would ferret her out of her room eventually. And here she was, in time for brunch.

"That is too bad. You haven't changed your mind, have you?"

Hard eyes met his. "No. Sorry, if you were looking for a reprieve you aren't going to get one from me."

"I don't want one."

"Even though you won't be permitted to slake your lusts elsewhere?"

"I've slaked them pretty well over the past fifteen years. More variety than most, so I can't truly complain." Though the idea of monogamy was foreign. Even so, if he promised her fidelity, he would give it. He would hardly sneak around behind her back all for the sake of sex, when he could have it with her if he wanted.

Not for the first time, he was feeling curious about the body beneath those simple shifts. Quite simply, in terms of her looks, he'd been shocked at first. And every time he looked at her, he was shocked. How she'd changed. The extent of the damage. But it was getting easier to let go of. Easier to just accept that it was part of her now.

And honestly, it made him extra curious about her body and if that made him reprehensible, so be it. She was to be his wife, and he hadn't reconciled the scars yet. They didn't turn him off but he wasn't exactly overcome by attraction.

As if to goad his thoughts his gut kicked as she moved into the room, the sunlight spilling over the smooth side of her face, catching fire behind her hair and revealing a golden halo. He got a glimpse of that blonde he'd been missing, subdued without the aid of dye, but there was some there. There was something about her that pulled him to her, there was no mistaking that.

"You will have to be tested," she said, her tone dry as she took a seat at the table. "I'm not risking catching an STD from you, so I'm sorry if you find that a problem, but you've been around."

"I get tested every six months. I'm promiscuous, but I'm responsibly promiscuous."

"Oxymoron."

"Judge not," he said, looking back down at his food.

"You can judge me all you want in that area of my life. I find myself quite blameless."

He raised a brow and looked back up at her. And found himself unbearably curious. How long had it been since she'd been with a man? Since before the convent? Before the accident?

Had she ever?

A ridiculous thought. She was thirty-three. A woman would have had to have been living in a convent to be a virgin at her age. But then, she had been, so all bets were off.

He found himself unreasonably intrigued by the idea. As if there was any doubt of his debauchery. Being fascinated by her innocence confirmed it.

"I find myself lacking in regret," he said. "Which I suppose isn't the same as blameless."

"That would be a seared conscience," she said. "And I have no desire to hear about your exploits beyond looking at medical records and seeing a negative result on the test."

"You're a savvy little thing for a woman who's spent ten years in a convent."

"I wasn't born in one."

"I suppose not. I propose that we set the wedding for early spring."

"That's very soon. Only a couple of months."

"I know," he said, "but it will create a nice celebratory atmosphere. Also, you've told me I have to remain celibate until our wedding night so I'm not eager to put it off."

Red bloomed in her cheeks, visible even beneath her scars. "I shouldn't have thought you would be overly concerned with that."

"You thought wrong. Now—" he reached in front of him and pulled a black velvet drape from over a tray that contained six rings, all a part of the Drakos family collection "—I have a selection of rings for you to choose from. There is, of course, the one that you had back when we were engaged the first time. It's sized to fit you, assuming that's stayed the same. But I know that women often change their tastes, so I wanted to give you options."

Layna swallowed hard and stared at the jewelry in front of her. She'd come down hoping for some coffee and fruit. Maybe eggs and bacon. She hadn't expected diamonds. It was, in her opinion, a little early in the morning for diamonds.

She couldn't tear her eyes from the pear-shaped diamond, surrounded by citrines, glittering in the midmorning light that was filtering through the window.

It had been hers. She could still remember King Stephanos asking for it. He'd called her in with her father, deeply regretful to have to ask for it back. But it had also belonged to his wife, and since Xander was now gone and the wedding wouldn't be taking place, he simply couldn't bear to have it out of the palace.

Leaving, her hand had felt bare and her heart…

How could he leave her? How could he leave all of them? And why had she never kissed his lips?

Looking at the ring made her remember all of that. She hated those memories. They made her feel too much. They interrupted her contentment. But then, her contentment had been interrupted for a while now. Also Xander's fault.

She reached out, her fingers hovering over that ring. It was the one she wanted. She'd been allowed to choose back then, too, and it had been her favorite. But this wasn't the same moment. She wasn't the same girl. He was not the same man.

"I don't care," she said, putting her hand back at her side. "You can choose it for me."

He arched a brow and picked up a ring with a square cut solitaire and an ornate white gold band. "This one, then," he said. "If you don't care."

"I don't."

He stood from his place at the table and walked to where she sat, standing in front of her and taking her hand in his. Then, with her sitting and him looming above her, he slipped the ring onto her finger. "It fits fine, doesn't it?"

She pulled her hand back and curled her fingers into a fist. "Fine," she said, trying to swallow and failing, her throat too dry to manage it.

She looked down at her hand, at the completely different ring that was now on her finger. This was different. This wasn't just going back in time. Recapturing what might have been. He might have the same name, but he was a different man. Just as she was a different woman.

Time had changed them. Time had changed their circumstances. She was no longer half in love with him, that was for sure.

Neither would she be falling in love with him any time soon.

"I do need to go and see my father sometime soon."

She nodded slowly. "I imagine you do."

"And we shall have to plan a party. To celebrate my return, and to celebrate our engagement. And hope it isn't perceived as tacky since my father is ill."

"Maybe you can talk to Stavros about that?"

"Oh, yes, I could talk to Stavros, though it seems he would rather not talk to me."

"Eva, then?"

"I should talk to both of them."

She frowned. "I'm sure we can find a way to make sure it doesn't look tacky. If we try and portray it as a show of strength for the country. No matter how dark the night, the dawn is coming, and so on."

"See," he said, smiling, "this is why I need you."

Those words did something to her. Made her heart feel like it was unfolding, like it was expanding. Made her feel a little bit of pain, a little bit of pleasure. But it was stupid. It wasn't flattering. He only needed her because he was a gigantic PR nightmare. Such a gigantic PR nightmare that a scarred almost-nun looked good by comparison.

"Well, I'll do what I can to help. Though, it's not for you."

"I'm sure it's not."

"It's for my country."

"Do you owe this country anything?" he asked. "After

the way they treated you, do you really owe them anything?"

"One man with a cup of acid isn't Kyonos, Xander."

"And one man with a cup of acid shouldn't be your whole life, Layna," he said, his voice rough, his eyes suddenly serious.

"To what do I owe the sincerity?"

"I don't like seeing you hurt."

"Then why are you so often the one who hurts me?" she asked, her newly unfurled heart closing tightly again. Like a flower suddenly deprived of sunlight.

"It's a gift I have," he said, looking away from her, out the window. "It's what I seem to do. I hurt people who genuinely don't deserve it." He looked back at her. "I guess that's your warning. You can back out now if you want."

Something in his eyes sent a shock through her. It was a window into his pain. It hadn't been there fifteen years ago, but it was there now, as obvious as if he'd spoken about it out loud. In that brief moment she had the sense that she was standing on the edge of a chasm, looking down into an abyss that had no end.

It frightened her. And it made him impossible to turn away from.

"You couldn't possibly hurt me any more than I've already been hurt." Even as she said it, she had a feeling it was a lie. She hadn't kissed him yet, much less gone to bed with him. She hadn't heard about the wounds he carried deep inside of himself.

He knew it was a lie, too. She could tell by the way his lips curved up, could tell now, that the expression was false. That there was no real humor in it. No real warmth. "Well then, we had better make a formal announcement."

"I suppose we'd better."

"You will need a dress, for the engagement party. I

trust you won't mind if I use a professional shopper to select one for you?"

She blinked. "No."

"Then I shall have your measurements done and that will be taken care of as quickly as possible."

"What about your father?" she asked.

"I should go and visit him alone."

Except she had a feeling that he shouldn't. She wasn't sure why. And moreover, she wasn't sure why she should care. Why his pain should interest her or concern her in any way, and yet over the course of the past few seconds she found that it did.

"I'll go with you. It will help solidify your plans. When you announce your engagement… I think your father felt very bad about what happened to me," she said.

"He did?"

"He was consumed by his own grief."

"Yes," Xander said, "I know."

"But he came to see me once. I…I didn't want to talk to him so I pretended to be asleep, but I knew he came."

"Why didn't you want to talk to him?"

"I was just starting to realize, really realize, that nothing in my life was ever going to be the same. That my face wasn't going back to normal. That…that I had maybe twenty surgeries ahead of me."

"Twenty?" he asked.

"It ended up being twenty-one. Skin grafts and reconstruction. Some of the grafts didn't take and…anyway. I knew that I had all kinds of hell ahead and that everything I knew was behind me. I didn't…it was hard to face people. That way you looked at me at the convent, when you realized it was me…it was ten times worse than that every time someone saw me right after the attack happened. I looked like something from a bad zombie movie. And the press said that. More than once. I hardly looked real at all. And it made my mother cry. It made my father sick. I got tired of seeing the expressions so I would close my eyes when visitors would come. And then it was just easier to keep them that way."

"Then of course you can come," he said, his tone light, as though he was content to skip over the graveness of the subject matter. And that suited her just fine. Being with him had forced her to relive her past more than she was comfortable with. "I'm sure my father will be happy to see you."

"I'm sure he'll be overjoyed to see you."

That smile again. That fake smile. "I wouldn't bet on it. But it will be nice to have you there to take some of the focus off of me."

Xander kept finding reasons to put off visiting his father, although, Layna was hardly going to judge him for avoidance since she was a pro at it.

Not that she could blame him. She imagined he was hardly going to have the fatted calf slaughtered in his oldest son's honor when he learned of Xander's return.

The engagement had been announced. On that he hadn't procrastinated. And the date of the ball had been set.

In spite of the fact that he was being hammered by the press, he was soldiering forward.

Prince Stavros and his wife, Jessica, and Princess Eva and her husband, Mak, were set to attend. Which would make for an interesting evening, Layna was sure. She imagined that things wouldn't be easy between Xander and his brother.

She tried to breathe around the terror that started constricting her throat when she thought about exposing herself to all of those people. All of that scrutiny. And Xander had said a selection of dresses would be here soon.

As if cued by her thoughts, there was a knock at the door. But rather than the woman who had come in to take her measurements earlier in the day, she was greeted by Xander, who had a black garment bag in his hand.

"Where's Patrice?" she asked.

"Downstairs having a coffee. I told her this would be between me and my fiancée." He stepped into the room and closed the door behind him and her heart collided with her breastbone.

"It doesn't sound like she's busy. Perhaps you'd like to trade places with her."

"No," he said.

"You work too hard," she said, no conviction in her voice.

"Now, *agape mou*, you and I both know that's not true." He sat down on her bed, the grin on his face wicked, and she felt her entire body tighten like a spool of wire.

That endearment. He'd called her that during their first engagement, too. *My love.* He hadn't meant it then and she was sure he didn't mean it now.

"So what…I'm supposed to put on a fashion show for you?"

"If you wish."

"Some might call it a freak show."

He stood quickly, the motion fluid, shocking. "Let us get one thing straight here and now," he said. "I will not stand for the press speaking of you in any terms that are not flattering. I will not hear it from you, either."

"Why should you care?" she asked. "It's true enough. I'm more sideshow than beauty pageant and we both know that."

"I damn well do not," he growled, advancing on her. "Is that truly what you think?"

"Can you tell me I'm beautiful?"

The fire in his eyes cooled. "No," he said, his voice hushed now, an extinguished flame. "Can you tell me I'm good?"

"No." She ached now. His denial like salt on a wound, but then, what would it have mattered if he would have said yes? It wouldn't have. It would have been a lie all the same and they both would have known it.

"You are, though," he said. "Good, that is. And isn't that the better thing to be?"

"When a camera is pointed at me I think I would prefer the beauty."

"When trials come, it would be better to be you, trust me. Now—" he handed her the garment bag "—it is time for us to preview your dress."

She held the bag to her chest and walked into the bathroom. She wasn't beautiful, but she was good. Wasn't the sort of woman to drive a man to passion, but she was good. She turned that over in her mind as she put on the dress, too distracted, too numb to pay much attention to it.

The trouble was, with Xander, she didn't feel particularly good. He made her feel edgy. Angry. Hot and unpredictable. With him around she did things like accept marriage proposals and demand he sleep only with her.

Which meant he would be sleeping with her.

Her hands shook as she did up the zipper at the back of the dress. She'd sort of bet on dying a virgin. She wasn't thrilled with it, really, but she hadn't seen another way.

The idea of being with him... She wanted him. No point in denying it. She just wished she was certain he wanted her.

She opened the bathroom door and stepped out into the

bedroom. She caught sight of herself in the reflection of the mirror just behind the bed, behind Xander, and froze for a moment. The dress was…well, it was much more revealing than anything she'd worn in ages. And more sophisticated than the saucy dresses she'd chosen as a teenage girl.

It was black, with a neckline that plunged down to the middle of her chest. "I would need duct tape," she said, looking at her breasts, which were attempting to make an escape. The chiffon fabric skimmed her curves and fell to the floor in a ripple, flowing as she moved. It was nearly demure, understated. If not for that neckline.

She looked to Xander and realized that his focus was also on her breasts, not that she should be terribly surprised. Because he *was* a man. Still, she was surprised because he was a man who was looking at her. And she was even more surprised because far from being offended, it made her feel warm and a little bit excited.

"What do you think?" she asked.

"I like it," he said, his voice rough.

"It's…not anything like what I would normally wear."

"No, and that's a good thing. You aren't wearing one of those flowered monstrosities to our engagement party."

"But…people will look at me."

"Yes," he said, his voice rough. "I imagine they will."

"I don't want them to look at me," she said.

"But they will, *agape*. You're to be the princess, one day their queen. You were a woman they all cared about, a woman they adored, back when you were first engaged to be married to me. Their eyes will be on you no matter what you wear. Better that when they look they see a woman with confidence."

"But I don't think I have any," she said.

He moved to her. "You should."

"Why?"

"Because you are the woman most deserving of the crown. You should hold your head high if only for that reason."

He lifted his hand and reached behind her, taking hold of the pins in her hair and releasing the hair from its bun, letting it fall around her face in soft waves. He had touched her hair before, and it had been an oddly sensual experience. His touch, combined with the intense expression on his face, was taking things somewhere beyond sensual now.

He was making her knees kind of weak. Making it hard to breathe.

But he didn't even think she was beautiful.

"We should practice," he said.

"Practice what?"

"They'll expect us to dance."

"Will they?"

"Yes. See? All eyes on us, no matter what you wear. And we need to put up a good front. Because salacious details about my past keep ending up on the front page."

"What now?" she asked.

"'How Many Lovers for the Dishonorable Heir?'"

"Oh, my."

"Yes, indeed."

"And…how many?" she asked.

"Not answering. And I don't know."

"Oh."

"Yes, well. I'm not exactly proud of my behavior. But I am good at dancing."

"This is all so… Oh." He wrapped his arm around her waist and pulled her against his body. Then he took her hand in his, rough and hot, not an aristocrat's hands. But then, he hadn't been living an aristocrat's life.

"Do you know how to dance still, or is that forbidden

for a novice?" he asked, leading her into the first step of a slow dance to no music.

"I'm out of practice," she said, trying hard not to lose her breath. He was so warm and hard, and she was pressed up against him.

And in that moment she realized just how very much she wanted him. A deep, burning ache that spread from her core and ignited in the rest of her body. Such a strange thing. Lust was one of the little luxuries that had to be put away for the kind of life she'd been trying to lead, but she was all but bathing in it now.

She was so aware of his hand on her waist, his fingers entwined with hers. With each breath he took and how it made his chest rise to meet her breasts, how it made her nipples feel tight. Made her feel desperate for more. More of his touch. More of him.

"So am I," he said.

"You don't seem like it."

"Well, there isn't much in the way of formal ballroom dancing in the casinos I frequent."

"Is that all you've done since you left?"

"Basically. I live in the casinos, literally. I don't own a home. There's never been any point."

"You make money gambling?"

He lifted a shoulder and kept dancing. "I have a gift."

"You're a card counter, aren't you?"

"Not on purpose. But if I happen to be a bit more observant than the average person, is it my fault?"

"You really are a bad man."

He chuckled, slow and deep, the sound rumbling through him, and her, sending shock waves of sensation through her body. "And I don't even work at it. It just comes naturally. How about you?" he asked.

"How about me what?"

"Do you have to work at being good?"

She blinked. "Um…I don't know really. In some ways, no. But then, what I do…I don't do it because it's good. I do it because I don't have anything else to do. Because… maybe because it's easy to be good if you don't want much of anything. I could never have gone to hide out at a casino, for example, because I had no desire to be around anyone. I couldn't go sleep my way through Europe like you because I didn't want anyone to see me, much less sleep with me. And I could hardly go get drunk because you aren't supposed to mix alcohol and pain pills," she said, dryly. "All things considered, I don't know that I get any brownie points for good behavior."

"You haven't seemed particularly saintly since I've seen you, I'll tell you that in all honesty." His fingers moved down on her waist, just an inch or so, but enough to edge into somewhat erotic territory. At least, erotic for a woman who hadn't had a kiss in…ever, and was due. Past due.

"Maybe it's because I…I feel like I'm waking up." It was the strangest thing, but as she spoke the words she knew that was the best way to describe it. It was like she'd been sleeping. All those years after the attack, and then at the convent, it had been like hovering between reality and a dream. There was a cushion there, between her and life, and she had needed it.

Now, though, her eyes were wide open, and everything was clear. Frightening. And amazing.

"I thought women needed to be kissed awake," he said, lowering his head, his mouth a whisper away from hers.

"Sleeping Beauty maybe," she said. "But we both know that I'm not—"

He silenced her with the firm pressure of his lips on hers. She was almost too shocked to register the feeling of the kiss. She felt it deeper than she'd imagined she would.

Felt it in the pit of her stomach just as strongly as she felt it against her lips.

It was brief, and it was very nearly chaste, but it tilted her world on its axis completely. And he had no idea, she was sure of that. Because for him, it was just another kiss. But for her it was the first.

"How was that?" he asked.

"I…" She pulled away from him. "I don't think that had anything to do with dancing."

"It had to do with us, as a couple, making our debut at the engagement party, where we'll be dancing. It was a natural extension."

Yes, a natural extension for him, but not for her.

"Well, there's no need for any of that until after… until…"

"You aren't part of a convent anymore," he said, "you're a woman."

"I've been a woman the entire time, thank you. It didn't change when I went to the convent, it didn't change when I left. It didn't change just because you decided to kiss me. Our marriage is based on necessity, not on passion, so let's not pretend."

"Who said I was pretending?"

"Right, Xander, I'm sure you were overwhelmed by lust when you told me that I wasn't beautiful only twenty minutes ago."

"There is something else," he said, his voice tight, strange. "Something…"

She shook her head. "Just don't lie to me."

"This," he said, looking down, "it doesn't lie. I would put your hand on me but I think that would be a step too far."

"Put my hand on…" Her stomach tightened painfully

and she looked down, her eyes following the line his gaze had. "Oh."

"I thought it might be off-limits."

"Yes," she said, her throat dry. "It is. Definitely in the post-marriage vow zone. Anything below the belt."

"You look much more intrigued than you do offended."

"Do I? That's just the shock talking. Well, not talking, forming my facial expressions for me. I'm terribly shocked."

"I look forward to shocking you a bit more after our marriage vows then."

"Don't make it a joke, please," she said, suddenly feeling like she needed to lie down. Or dissolve into a gigantic puddle of wimpy girl tears. "I know you're experienced and cavalier and having pity sex with an ugly girl is just a witty anecdote waiting to happen for you. But this isn't funny to me. It's my life. And I'm the one who stands to be hurt the most by this. I'm the one..."

"You're the one who called yourself my punishment, Layna. I have said nothing cruel to you on that score. I don't look at you and think that you're ugly—neither do I feel like I'm doing you any great favors by marrying you and sharing your bed. In truth, you may find that you are more unhappy with the demanded fidelity than I am."

"Why is that?"

"Because it will ensure that I'm around more, and you may tire of me quickly. You have this idea that I'm somehow more desirable stock because I'm not scarred. Let me assure you that while I may be physically undamaged, you are not by any stretch getting the better end of this deal. I am selfish, I have spent the majority of the past few years battling demons and addictions, and doing neither very well at all. You may think that what I'm giving you is pity sex, but don't for one moment think that I don't realize what I have on my hands is a pity marriage."

She blinked back tears, his words settling over her like a heavy cloak, making it hard to breathe. "I don't pity you. I don't approve of you. I'm not sure that I like you, but I don't pity you. This is…a marriage of no one's convenience. What we do, we do for our country. And…I do it for children. Because I do want them. And I had thought that wasn't possible for me, so to have the chance…I do want it. Power is something I don't crave anymore, status is almost my enemy because it means I'll be under scrutiny."

"A marriage born of a sense of national duty and disdain then," he said, dryly. "You flatter me."

"I would imagine you've been flattered enough in your life that you don't require much from me."

"I'm sure my ego can weather it."

"I'm not sure mine will survive any of this."

"It will," he said, his tone certain, authoritative. And in that moment, she saw a hint of the king he would be. So strange, because she knew the boy he'd been. Cocky and obnoxious in so many ways, but handsome as sin and just as tempting. She'd barely gotten to know the man he was now, wounded, damaged and self-deprecating. As much as the boy had loved himself, she had a feeling the man hated himself just as much.

But for one second, all of that fell away. And she saw nothing more than confidence. Nothing more than a smooth, unswerving focus.

"This is why I'm marrying you," she said, her voice hushed now. "Because I believe that, no matter where you've been in the past, your future is tied to Kyonos. That with you we will rise or fall, and if we fall it will be because the people can't get past what has been done. You leaving…"

"Me killing the queen," he said.

"You didn't kill her," she said. "You were driving, but it was an accident. It was…"

"People think it, Layna. Just as the man who threw acid on you, trying to get to your father blamed him for his troubles."

"Then this is why," she said, suddenly feeling the need to close the gap between them. To make contact. "This is why I'm marrying you. Because if I can help in any way, if I can heal some of the wounds from that time, I will do it. Because you are the future here, Xander."

He frowned and lifted his other hand, touched her damaged cheek with his thumb. "It is a shame that time won't heal your wounds."

"It is."

"Sometimes I think it won't heal mine, either." He released his hold on her and turned and walked out of her room, leaving her standing there in an evening gown, in the middle of the day, more confused than she'd ever been in her life.

CHAPTER EIGHT

HELL. XANDER HAD forgotten how much he hated these kinds of events.

The engagement celebration was small compared to some of the parties thrown at the Kyonosian palace, due to the short notice and out of respect for the king's health.

Xander's recently noisy conscience pricked him. He should go and see the king. It was a hard thing to do. The last time he'd stood before the old man, his father said in no uncertain terms that he blamed Xander for the queen's death.

And because he hadn't been wrong, Xander had finally done what Stavros, and the man who believed he was Xander's father, had wanted. He left.

Because it had been easier for everyone. And it had been easy, most especially, for him.

He wasn't truly the heir after all.

You can't tell him, Xander. You have to be king. You are my firstborn son and the right should be yours, regardless of the mistakes I've made.

Xander shut out the sound of his mother's pleading voice. He hated reliving that conversation. Mainly because it was the last one they'd ever had. It had changed everything.

He straightened and looked across the room at Layna. She looked…well, she did look beautiful in her way.

She was wearing makeup. He'd brought in a team to help her get ready. He wondered if she'd ever bothered to put makeup on her face, or if it had been too discouraging. There was no hiding the fact that the skin was damaged on one side. It looked…aged with makeup on, rather than just scarred.

But her eyes were highlighted to perfection, and they glowed with golden warmth, her lips painted a deep rose. And that dress. That dress that made his body tighten. That made him want…

He wanted her, and that was the most surprising thing about this arrangement. He hadn't expected to want her. He'd had an endless array of models, mainstream actresses and actresses who did the kinds of movies that rarely had scenes outside the bedroom. Women who were perfectly beautiful, either by birth or with the aid of a surgeon's knife.

He'd hardly thought Layna would present a temptation to him, all things considered.

And yet…when he'd kissed her the other day, she had been a surprise. A burst of flavor on his lips unlike any he'd ever tasted before. And newness, to a man as jaded as himself, was so unexpected it was an aphrodisiac that was almost unmatched.

"Congratulations are in order, I suppose."

Xander turned to face Stavros, and Eva, who was standing next to him, a glowing smile on her face, her hand over her rounded belly. He wanted to embrace them both. But he didn't know if he could. And that was a strange thing.

Who didn't feel they could hug their siblings if they wanted to? Who didn't speak to their siblings for fifteen years?

Eva had gone from a child to a woman in that time. Having a child of her own. Stavros was a man as well, not the teenage boy he'd been.

Theos. He felt old.

And more than a little bit tired.

"For both of you as well," he said, keeping back, his hands clasped behind him.

"I'm surprised she agreed to marry you," Stavros said, his eyes flashing over to Layna, who seemed to be shrinking into the corner under the watchful eyes of their many guests.

"Are you?" he asked. "We had an agreement before I left."

"And things have changed."

"I've noticed," he said.

Eva smiled, shy but with a glimmer of that old sparkle in her eyes. "Xander, I'm glad you're back. I don't want things to be weird between us. So let's skip all of the regret and angry stuff. I'll leave that to you and Stavros, since I doubt he'll let it go as fast as I will. I, for one, have missed you for too long, and I won't waste a second of you being back here with anger."

"I appreciate that, Eva," he said, feeling strangely tight around the chest. "I plan on staying."

Stavros frowned. "I would love to never speak to you again. But you're going to be the king. And my wife tells me that I should be nice because not only are you the future king, you are the uncle to our children, and it would be wrong of me to deprive you or them of that relationship."

"She threatened you, didn't she?" Eva asked, smiling.

"I don't want to sleep on the couch for the rest of my life," Stavros said, his tone dry. "But someday…we'll have to talk more. And someday, perhaps I will not be so angry. But not today."

Xander nodded. "Yes." But he knew they wouldn't talk about everything. Never about everything.

He made the rounds with Stavros and Eva, meeting Stavros's wife, Jessica, and their two children, and Eva's husband, Mak.

He looked back at Layna, who was slinking into the wall now, fading. "Excuse me," he said, "I have to go and ask a woman to dance."

He didn't want to see her do this. Didn't want to watch her try and disappear, and he wasn't even certain why. Why it should matter.

It shouldn't. She would get him the positive press he needed, she was a worthy choice to produce heirs. Nothing beyond that should matter.

But it did.

"Are you trying to turn into another coat of paint?" he asked, when he was near to her.

"What?"

"You look like you're trying to become part of the wall," he said.

"You left me alone and I feel…I feel self-conscious."

"You look…"

She shook her head. "Don't."

"But you do."

"Compared to the way I usually look."

"So I'm not allowed to win?"

She blinked, dark lashes fanning over high cheekbones. "Thank you."

"Of course. Now, you will come and dance with me and stop acting like you wish you could melt into the floor."

She looked stricken. "We're really going to dance?"

"That's why we practiced, darling." He extended his hand and she looked at him like he was offering her forbidden fruit. He felt like he was. Like he was on the verge of bringing her into something he had no right to drag her in to.

But it was too late. She was here. In front of hundreds of people, his ring glittering on her finger, tomorrow's headlines being created right now, in the moment.

He didn't deserve to use her like this. To have her as a buffer between himself and the unflattering headlines about his past behavior. But he didn't see another choice.

Delicate fingers wrapped around his and she allowed him to lead her to the dance floor. He pulled her to him, much more gently than he'd done in her room.

"Relax," he said, his lips near her ear.

He breathed in deep, and her scent teased him. It wasn't false, or floral. It was the wind. The sea. The grass. Skin. It was Kyonos. It made his stomach tighten, opened up a well of longing, a strange sense of need and homesickness that washed over him like a wave.

This desire for her came from somewhere deep. It didn't come from looking at her, or even from touching her, it was her very presence. It seemed to be some part of her, some part deep inside, connecting with something in him.

Perhaps it was shared pain meeting a shared goal. Or maybe it was nothing more complex than a bout of celibacy that had gone on for too many months. Either way, it was beginning to feel too strong to fight. He was wondering if there was a reason to bother, anyway.

She was going to be his wife after all.

Not that she had any idea of what that truly meant. Of who he truly was.

"Everyone is staring, aren't they?" she asked.

"Have you ever worn makeup? Since your attack?"

She frowned. "Once. I tried it once. Not very long after my last surgery. It didn't really help I... But I thought tonight I should wear some because I needed to dress up and…"

"You look lovely. And I do mean that."

"They did a better job covering the damage than I ever managed to do."

"That isn't the only reason."

"Let's not do this mushy, stumbling lying thing now, Xander. You were perfectly honest with me the other day about my looks. So don't go trying to smooth it all over just because I tried."

"You are a stubborn woman," he said. "And I want you."

"I don't understand."

"You don't understand want? Desire? Do you know what it means to want someone?"

"I…yes. But I don't need you to lie to me about it."

"I'm not." he said, tightening his hold on her, bringing her curves flush against his body. And he let her feel what she was doing to him. He let his cock harden against her and he didn't bother to suppress his need, his fantasies. He imagined what it would be like to have her bare softness against him, without this damned tux in the way.

What it would be like to make her let go. To make her break out of the little cell she'd locked herself in. The one that meant there was no passion. No desire. Only boring, staid contentment.

He wanted to make her lose herself while he lost himself in her. Because for some reason he felt sure that she was the only one who could make him feel again. The only one who might make a change in him that could last.

The feeling that came with that thought was fleeting, but so intense it nearly buckled his knees. So intense he nearly dragged her from the dance floor and into the nearest dark alcove to make her his without any thought to vows.

But then it cleared. The fire dying down as suddenly as it had flared up.

No, there was no changing him. Not even she could do it. There was no magic to be found on her lips. But there was pleasure. And he was a man who'd spent years consumed by the desire for pleasure.

That was the simple answer to why he felt so drawn to her. It wasn't in his nature to deny himself anything he wanted.

"I'm sorry, I wasn't able to hold myself back this time. You accused me of lying about wanting you and I thought you should know this time, for yourself, that it's true."

She pushed out of his arms and walked away from him, leaving him there in the middle of the dance floor, shocked and hard as hell.

He followed her, through the crowd of people and out onto the balcony. Her shoulders were shaking and guilt stabbed him, low in the gut.

He'd had a lot of bad feelings since returning home. Guilt and regret. He preferred it when his life boiled down to being drunk and horny, but right now he had felt sober, horny and guilty. Which was a combination he wouldn't wish on anyone.

"What did I do? Did I offend you with my erection? Because you're going to have to get used to it if you honestly want to marry me."

She whirled around to face him. "Oh, please. Stop making this about you when it's clearly about me."

"I think we both think it's all only about us."

"Fine," she said, tears on her cheeks, "but…this is…why do you want me? Why…I don't understand this. Any of it."

"Is that really what upset you?"

"It's just a lot. A lot to take. Everything has changed in the past week. Everything I'm supposed to want."

"Do you want me?"

"Xander…"

He walked over to where she was standing and took her chin between his thumb and forefinger. "Do you want me?"

"That's not what this is about."

"But it's part of marriage."

"So is love. We barely have like."

"I'm not big on love," he said. "Personally, I would rather have want. So if that's all we have, I'm okay with it."

She shook her head. "I can't deal with this just now. Not when everyone is in there and we're on show. I've probably already ruined things by storming out."

"It's okay. I might have been a little bit inappropriate. But I'm out of practice when it comes to civilized behavior."

"You make me…you do make me want things, Xander. Things that I thought I'd let go of. And it scares me. Because in my experience, wanting things is just a long road paved with pain."

"That's emotion you're thinking of. Sex can be a lot more simple. And a lot more fun."

She laughed, a shaky, watery sound. "Well, I wouldn't know."

His gut tightened, blood rushing to his arousal. "I could show you."

"I don't understand this. I don't remember being this tempted by you back when I thought you were a decent human being, so how can I be so drawn to you now?"

"Lust doesn't have to make sense, Layna."

"I guess not," she said, looking at him with a weary expression. "Perhaps that's why the church has such a firm stance on it. It could potentially get someone into a lot of trouble. Particularly since our bodies seem to be indiscriminate."

"Is your body being indiscriminate for me?" he asked. So strange how badly he just wanted her to say it. How much he wanted to her to admit, from her prim little mouth, that she wanted him. That she was picturing sweaty, tangled limbs and screams of pleasure.

Yes, screams. He wanted it loud. And he wanted it dirty. He wanted it with a ferocity that shook him to his core.

With a woman who's most likely a virgin. You truly are a rare breed of ass.

Maybe. Did it matter? He was so past the point of redemption anyway. And she was going to be his wife, surely that made it at least partly okay.

And if not, why should he start caring now?

It was too late for him anyway.

"We should go back inside," she said.

"You didn't answer my question."

"And I'm not going to. Here I've stormed out of the ballroom and I'm supposed to be making you look stable. So I think it's time to go back and show solidarity, don't you?"

He nodded slowly. She really was good at this. He'd all but forgotten the ball happening inside. If she'd let him he probably would have just lifted her dress and taken her here on the balcony with the ocean as the backdrop. And people just inside.

He did a much better job of thinking of his own appetites than he did of thinking of his people.

"Can I do it?" he asked, not sure why the words came out just then.

"Can you do what?"

"This," he said. Too late to take them back now.

"Will I really be a good king? For some reason, you seem very confident in me when it comes to that part of things. You have no respect for me on a personal level, but you seem very sure that I'll rule well, why?"

"Because you don't want it," she said. "Because there's nothing easy about it, and the power itself doesn't seem to appeal to you at all. What better man to rule?"

"Because I *don't* want it?"

"Yes. From that I have to assume that your motives are pure."

"My motives are a lot of things. But I doubt they're pure. I doubt anything in me is."

"Are you ready to go back?" she asked.

He was humbled in that moment, by her strength. By the cost of this to her. It was costing him, but what really? His total waste of a life? His meaningless flings with random women? His chance to continue living in different penthouse suites?

It was costing her every shred of pride she had.

He would not let them take it. She was too strong. Standing there with her focus fixed on the ballroom, determined to go back in even though he knew it was difficult for her.

"Yes, *agape*, let's go and show them what the future of their country looks like."

CHAPTER NINE

SHE HONESTLY HAD no idea what her problem was. Why she'd melted down with Xander, why she'd had to run out of the ballroom.

Well, no, she did know why. It was because she had no idea what she was doing. She didn't know how to handle men. Didn't know how to deal with this desire that was starting to wrap itself around her like a creeping vine.

This wasn't supposed to happen.

She was supposed to be…at the very least she was supposed to feel nothing for him. And at most, she'd been willing to allow herself to be angry.

And she was angry. She was angry at him for leaving her. She was angry at life for making her the way that she was.

But in there somewhere, she wanted him, too, and that was the thing she couldn't quite deal with.

She breathed in the sea air. It was such a relief to be outside. To be on the beach instead of in that ballroom, which, as expansive as it was, had made her feel claustrophobic beyond words.

She'd escaped as soon as she could. Most everyone had gone and she'd made her excuses, as soon as was polite. She was dreading tomorrow's headlines. Dreading the future. So funny, because she hadn't thought of the future at all in a long time.

All of her days had been so alike at the convent. Her future had been so certain. So solid. She'd seen her days stretching out before, a calm and endless sea.

But now she was storm-tossed and she had no idea where she would land.

She sat down, not caring that the ground was wet, not caring that there would be sand on her gorgeous black dress. She would hardly be able to wear it again anyway. That was something she remembered from her socialite days. Never wear the same thousand-euro dress twice. Such a sharp contrast to her other life, where she wore the same threadbare shifts until they couldn't be mended anymore.

She felt like she wasn't wholly the girl she'd been before, or the woman she'd become, but damned if she had any idea who she really was. And she blamed Xander for that feeling.

She'd been fine before he'd walked back into her life. She'd been at peace with her choices. And now he was demanding so much from her. So much more than she ever thought she'd have to give to anyone.

"I thought perhaps I had seen a ghost." She looked up and saw Xander standing there, his shirt open at the collar, his tie and jacket discarded.

"That's how I felt the day I saw you at the convent."

"I'm sure."

"What are you doing down here?"

"I might ask you the same thing."

"I am…brooding. I think that's what this is called."

He sat down next to her. "I'll brood with you."

"Brooding is best done alone."

"Doesn't that get tiring, though?"

"What?" she asked.

"Being alone."

She looked out across the water, at the moon reflecting on the waves. "You're never alone, though, are you? I mean, you've never had to be. You've basically been at a giant party for the past few years."

"I've been surrounded by people, yeah. But it's amazing what a hell that can be."

"I doubt you've spent one night alone when you didn't want to be alone," she said, feeling bitter now. Because all she'd had was an endless void of alone. In that huge house without her family, with only a couple of servants to help her with things. Making sure she ate, making sure she didn't overdose on her pain medication.

Locking up her pain medication. And then, when they'd taken her one bit of solace, they'd felt like her enemies, not her allies. Even though she knew differently now.

Xander truly had no idea how isolating her life had been. How low she'd gone. How dark it had been. Because he'd walked away. Because he hadn't stayed. When things had gotten hard in his life he'd left her there, but there had been no way for her to unzip her damaged skin and crawl out of her own body. There had been no way to escape her pain.

"I'm sure getting smashed in a casino was terrible for you, but while you were doing that, I was by myself in my parents' old home in a prescription drug haze, so excuse me if I don't feel that sorry for your plight."

"Layna…"

"No." She stood up. "I wasn't going to tell you this, and for what? My pride? What pride have I got? No, you should know. You should know because you should have been there, Xander. You should have been there with me. I…" A sob broke through, tears spilling down her cheeks. "I needed you…" The words were torn from her, pulling at any thread of dignity she might have had, but they were the truth. A truth she'd never even allowed herself to think before, let alone voice.

She wiped a tear from her cheek. "Do you have any idea... Sometimes I just wanted to be held and there was no one there. And it should have been you. You were supposed to be my husband, you weren't supposed to leave me."

"I won't leave again," he said, his voice rough. "Though...I don't know that I would have done everything for you that you hoped I might."

"Anything would have been better than being alone. My days just kind of blended and...I got addicted to my pain medication. It was so much nicer to be out of it than it was to feel. And the medicine helped with that. Helped things seem nicer. Without them it was just endless despair and... and I would think things like...if I walked out to the beach and went out into the ocean and just...kept walking until the water went over my head, would anyone care? Would I care? Or would everything just stop hurting?"

He swore. "Layna, I'm sorry."

"Why couldn't you help me? Why couldn't you think of anyone but yourself?"

"Because," he said. "Because I killed my mother, Layna. Because my father looked me in the eye and told me he believed it was my fault, and my brother thought so, too. Because I couldn't stay here and face that. And I might never have thought of walking into the ocean but everything I've done has been about seeing that I shorten my days in a very spectacular fashion."

Her chest felt tight. And for the first time she really thought about him, and his loss. Not just her own need. "Did they really blame you?"

"Yes."

"That's not fair, it was an accident."

He nodded slowly. "But we were arguing. And no one

knows that but me. I was angry, and so I wasn't paying attention. I looked up and there was a truck cutting across the line and I swerved and hit the side of the mountain because I panicked and overcorrected. They were my mistakes, and they were brought about largely by my anger. Because I didn't take the time to pull the car over. Because I let emotion take over and I behaved… I was stupid. And it was my fault." He looked at her. "Maybe I should have stayed for you. But I don't think I could have been the man you needed. I know I wasn't the man that you thought I was."

"I've never told anyone before," she said. "I've never told anyone about wanting to…about having trouble living. I don't even like to remember it but…do you know what's nice?"

"What?"

"Even when I told you, even when I let myself think about it, I can remember how bad it was, but it doesn't make me feel the way I did then."

"The convent is what changed things for you?"

"It gave me a purpose. I didn't know what to do with myself. I didn't have you. The marriage wasn't going to happen, I wasn't going to be queen. No other man would marry me. My friends, who I took such delight in cutting down behind their backs, wouldn't see me. No one invited me to parties, and I wouldn't have wanted to go if they had. Everything changed for me and all of that combined with my depression just made me…I was just drifting. But after talking to the Sisters after my last surgery, about the work they did, about the life they led, I thought maybe the answer wasn't trying to go back, or even making myself want to go back, but to find something new."

"That's sort of what I did. Only without the altruism or chastity."

"How so?"

"I changed everything. Because things were too different to be who I'd been before."

"That's sort of how I feel right now," she said, turning to face him. "Too different to be the girl I was fifteen years ago, and not quite the woman I was a week ago when you found me again."

"I am sorry," he said. "I'm sorry I've uprooted your life again. And that you were alone. It's funny," he continued, "you're right, I never spent a night alone unless I wanted to. But it's a strange thing about sex. For a moment, there's this clash of heat. A connection of some kind. Ten minutes of euphoria, and then, in the end, you can be skin-to-skin with someone, inside of them, and feel more alone than you ever have in your life." He stood up, hands in his pockets. "There's nothing more terrifying than that. Because it's moments like those where you realize how far beyond human connection you are."

"Is that how you feel?" she asked, the picture he pained cutting a swath of pain through her heart.

"It's just not in me anymore. To love someone. To feel all that deeply. I care about the country, but what I do...it comes from my head."

"Is that a warning?"

He nodded slowly. "Maybe. I don't want to hurt you, it's clear to me that I've done that enough for one lifetime. But we will make a marriage, a real one. We don't need love for that. And...I will be faithful to you."

"You said that already."

"I did say it, but I'm not sure I meant it. I do now. Because I gave it some thought, and what it comes down to is that I know the kind of pain infidelity causes. Even if one party never finds out, there are always consequences."

"What else is there, Xander?" she asked. Because she

could sense, somehow, that there was more he wanted to say. That his pain came from somewhere even deeper.

"There isn't anything."

"Really?"

He shook his head. "It's not important." He cleared his throat. "Tomorrow we're going to go and see my father."

"Both of us," she said, confirming it.

"Yes."

"I was going anyway. For my part, Xander, you're not going to be alone anymore. And neither am I."

CHAPTER TEN

HE COULDN'T HIDE the headlines from her forever. But he would do his best. He had expected…something triumphant. Something about Layna's bravery. About her beauty, at least her inner beauty, to grace the pages of the newspapers. But he was disappointed.

There were before and after photos. Layna, young, radiant and golden, and Layna as she was now. With the scars that had changed the landscape of her face.

And they asked would she now be the face of the nation. And suddenly…suddenly they were acting like he was a saint. Honoring past commitments in spite of present circumstances.

Isn't that what you wanted?

His blood boiled. Rage spiking through him. At the media. At himself. He had used her. He had exposed her to this.

And he would protect her from it as long as he could. Because he needed her. Of that he was certain. He had no idea how he would rule without her.

He couldn't dwell on it now. Today he was seeing his father. Today, he was facing the hardest part of his past.

At least Layna would be beside him.

His father was an old man. That was his first thought when he walked into the hospital room and saw the man he'd always thought of as so imposing, hooked up to all the machinery.

He was asleep. Or maybe he was unconscious. Xander wasn't sure. He wasn't certain he could get close enough to find out.

Delicate fingers wrapped around his hand and he looked down at the top of Layna's head. Shocked that she was there. Shocked that she was touching him.

"I told you," she said. "You aren't alone."

"You don't owe me anything, Layna."

"I know. This isn't about owing you. This is about getting you through."

"I didn't help you get through."

"And I didn't help you. But that was then. And we're both here now."

He wanted to tell her he didn't need any help getting through, but the words stuck in his throat. "What do we do exactly? He isn't awake."

"Talk to him."

"I would feel stupid."

"King Stephanos."

She approached the bed, small and regal. Yes, it was she who belonged in this position while he…he was not sure he had a place in life much less in Kyonos.

"It's Layna Xenakos. And I'm here with Xander. He's home. He's here for you. For Kyonos."

She turned back to face him and the sun caught in her hair, catching the deep golds that were woven in with the browns. She was practically glowing, and he had a feeling he couldn't even blame the sun. She seemed to glow from the inside. "I don't feel silly."

"No," he said. "I can see that. But it's been longer since I talked to him so…"

"Yeah, like a week longer." She reached out and grabbed

his arm, squeezed it. "I understand, though. I know you left on poor terms."

"Understatement there."

He looked at his father and tried to find one part of himself there. Because part of him had always hoped his mother had been wrong. But he could see nothing of himself in the old man. Eva's stubborn chin, so many of Stavros's features. But nothing of himself.

The king wasn't his father.

He'd never for a moment believed his mother would lie about his parentage, but he had hoped off and on that she might be mistaken. Denial was a beautiful state. The one he chose to live in.

Suddenly, the room seemed too small. The beeping machines all too loud and antiseptic burned his nose. "Let's go," he said, undoing the top button on his shirt. Damn. He couldn't breathe. "I have to go."

He pushed through the curtain and out into the halls, gasping for air. It was a luxurious environment for a medical center. The sort of place you sent kings, of course. But no matter how comfortable, it couldn't ease him now.

He walked down the hall with long strides, pushed open the doors and went out to the parking lot, leaning forward with his hands on his knees.

"What happened, Xander? I know he looks sick…he's your father and…"

"No…Layna…" He couldn't say it. He could barely think it. He could barely think at all. So instead he did what felt right. And it felt right to take her arm and pull her up against him.

He stroked her cheek—the undamaged side—and he really couldn't see the point in holding back on what he wanted. Not now. Not when everything felt terrible and he just wanted to lose himself again.

Before he'd run. From Kyonos. From himself.

He couldn't do that now.

And there was only one other way he could think of to lose himself completely.

He leaned down and took her mouth. And he wasn't gentle. Because this wasn't for her. Madonna or whore, it didn't matter to him, all that mattered was the feel of her lips on his and what it did for him.

And oh, *Theos*, what it did.

It set him on fire. The flames so hot he could feel nothing else. Nothing but his desire. Nothing but this. He coaxed her lips open, sliding his tongue against hers as he delved in deep.

Yes. This was what he needed. He could drown in this. In her sweetness. She didn't know how to kiss him back, her rhythm a step behind his, her fingers curled into the front of his shirt like little claws.

And it was the most wholly erotic kiss he'd ever experienced in his life.

"Where is the car?" he asked, feeling beyond himself. Unable to think straight.

"Over...over there," she said.

He took her hand and led her over to the limo, which was parked near the front doors. He must have passed it on his way out of the building. He honestly couldn't remember it, though.

He jerked open the back door and got in, pulling her in with him, reaching across and closing the door behind him, with her half on his chest, her leg draped over his lap.

She had no makeup on today. Her dark hair was loose around her face, and she was back in one of those unflattering dresses. He needed to take her shopping. But he had no time to concern himself with that. Not now. Not when her touch, her lips, were so perfect.

He made sure the divider between them and their driver was up, and then he pulled her to him, kissing her deeper, harder than he'd done outside. He poured everything into the kiss. All of his anger. All of his desire. Everything.

He breathed her in, and he found he wasn't suffocating anymore.

He could forget himself like this. Because a woman like her would never kiss a man like him and that meant that it was easy to pretend he was different. A different man, in a different time and place.

But he knew it was Layna. He knew it when he cupped her cheek and brushed a thumb over her rough scars. When he lightened the pressure on her lips and felt the hardened tissue by one corner of her mouth with his tongue.

Layna, who the media called ugly. Layna, who he wanted more than anything. To possess, to protect. He wanted all of it. Everything.

He put his hands on her hips, bunched the thin fabric of her dress into his fists and pushed it upward. Her body was a treasure. Full, round hips, a slim waist and those breasts…the ones that had haunted his dreams since he'd seen them in that gown of hers.

He needed to see her again. All of her. Now.

He pushed her dress up farther and she pulled back, breathing heavily, her eyes wide. "What are you doing?"

"If you have to ask, clearly I've done something wrong." He was so hard it hurt. And his lungs felt tight now. Being deprived of her lips was like being deprived of oxygen. He needed her. He couldn't explain it, but he did.

But he would never let her know.

She shifted and moved away from him, tucking her hair behind her ear. "I mean, I know you were…that you were…"

"That I was about to make love to you?"

"Well, that. But we're in a parking lot. Our driver is just behind that divider and I seriously doubt these windows are that tinted."

He frowned and looked outside. "There's no one around."

Layna felt like she'd been underwater for too long. Her lungs were burning, her head was fuzzy and her body ached. Though it ached in very pointed and telling places. How was she supposed to think when he was kissing her like that?

He'd essentially devoured her. In a parking lot. She'd never been devoured by a man in her life, much less had it happen while she was in a parking lot.

It was scary, how he managed to steal her control, her common sense. How he made her lose sight of everything. That they were in public, that she was inexperienced. That she'd been about two minutes away from losing her virginity in the back of a limo.

Yes, he made her lose sight of a lot of things.

But when he'd run out of the medical building, his pain had been palpable. Coming off him in waves, a deep hurt that she knew he wouldn't share. One she knew he'd had to exhaust by kissing her. For some reason.

"It doesn't matter that there's no one around. People don't just…do that."

"I do," he said. His posture readjusted. To this sort of slouched position in the seat, a half smile on his face. Gone was the desperate man of a moment before, replaced by the Xander character that he was so very fond of playing.

"Well, I don't. So that's something you'll have to deal with being married to me."

"You're a prude?" he asked.

"Practically a nun," she answered.

"Touché." He straightened and pushed the intercom

button that fed into the front half of the limo. "Back to the palace, please."

"Are you going to tell me what happened back there?"

"It's not important."

"You can just tell me that you aren't going to tell me. It's more honest than saying it's not important. Don't say things that affect you that deeply aren't important."

"Well, it's unimportant in terms of you and I."

"I see."

"You can't act like a miffed fiancée, Layna, not when you don't act like a fiancée when I need you to."

She frowned and looked at him, ignoring the kick in her heartbeat. "What do you mean by that?"

"If you were my real fiancée, and by that I mean, if you were with me for some reason that extended beyond the desire to heal the country and protect them from my wickedness," he said, his tone dry, "then you would have lifted your dress for me and given me the thing I really needed."

"What is that supposed to mean?" she asked, her voice tight.

"That it wasn't talking I needed, baby. It was f—"

"Stop it," she said. "Stop turning into a horrible…beast every time you encounter territory that wounds you. Whatever happened between you and your father isn't my fault. In fact, I've suffered enough due to all of those events, thank you."

"Why don't you take a little pleasure out of it?"

"Can we stop? Can we stop with this shallow, ridiculous nonsense. You aren't telling me what's really going on. And I'm not going to let you…not here."

"Still sticking with your wedding night plan?" he asked.

"Yes." Although it was more for self-protection now than anything else. To prove that she could wait. To prove she wasn't helpless against this thing. This…this attraction.

"Then I suppose we won't have much need of each other over the next few weeks. What I would like you to do is coordinate with Athena, my father's personal assistant. She has all of the information regarding Kyonos, the budget, various charities and so on. Make that your project. And I'm going to be sending you a new wardrobe. You're not allowed to turn it away. Burn those dresses you've been wearing."

"I'm donating them," she sniffed, irritated by his high-handedness. But she wasn't about to argue because what he was proposing meant that she got to avoid him.

"Do as you like, but you aren't wearing them anymore."

"No, I have a better idea," she said. "For every one outfit purchased for me, two new outfits—new—will be donated to a battered women's shelter."

"That is your affair, not mine."

"If I'm going to get something out of this arrangement I intend to start now."

He looked at her, dark eyes molten, and an answering heat started in her core. She knew challenging him was a bad idea. But she didn't really care. Something about him made her feel free. Made her feel like she could say anything. Made her feel like she was no longer bound up by a bunch of safe parameters.

She wasn't sure she liked it at all. Though, goading Xander had its merits.

"I will make sure you get something out of this marriage, *agape mou*," he said, his voice rough. "Several times a night if you're a very good girl."

Her cheeks heated. The bastard. "Perhaps I will endeavor to be a bad girl then."

A slow smile curved his lips. "Even better."

True to his word, Xander avoided her over the course of the next two weeks. And she kept busy. Athena had a lot of useful information and between the two of them, they had endless ideas for more efficient and helpful social programs and ways to help fund various charities.

It was the big picture of all she'd done at the convent. There, she'd been on the ground, physically handing out clothing and food, and it had been wonderfully rewarding. But this was like flying over Kyonos in a helicopter, being able to see every bit of it at once.

And even better because she had the resources to help.

The sad thing was, though, that she was unhappy not seeing Xander. Darn him. She should be glad to get a reprieve. And yet she wasn't.

She'd grown accustomed to his presence. To not feeling alone.

She missed riding. She would have to do something about that eventually, but she'd honestly been so busy. But then, she supposed that was the trade-off. Going from a life of service, reflection and meditation, to a life of high-octane service, balls and luncheons.

There were ever so many luncheons and she'd been invited to all of them. But people were shockingly nice to her.

It made her feel like she might be able to weather it after all. And the makeup artist Xander had hired to help her get ready for big public events didn't hurt. Neither did the new wardrobe that suited her figure so nicely.

She managed to look polished at the very least.

She glanced into the dining room and saw Xander sitting at the table, an expression of doom on his face, papers spread out in front of him. Her heart jolted. She hadn't run into him at all in days, and there he was, just sitting there.

"Hello," she said, coming into the room. She wasn't going to avoid him. He was her fiancé after all, and it would be silly.

He pushed the papers together, stacking them oddly,

his frown intensifying. "I would have thought you'd be ensconced in an office with Athena."

"We're done for the day. Athena had to go home and see to her sick child. Why are you glaring daggers at the headlines?"

"It is nothing," he said, waving his hand. "Just…the news is never good, is it?"

"I don't know. I've spent so much time cut off from it." She wandered over to where he was sitting and he shifted his elbow, like he was trying to hide something from her view.

Buried beneath the top pages, she saw the edge of what looked like her dress from the ball. "What is this?"

"It is nothing," he repeated.

"Then I can see it." She reached down and jerked the paper from beneath the stack and his arm, holding it up, her stomach sinking as she saw the headline and the accompanying photo. "The Zombie Princess," she said. "Oh."

"I will not have this," he said, his tone dark. "I will take steps to make it stop. I'll…"

"Abolish the freedom of the press?" she asked, feeling dizzy. "There's nothing you can do. They…they can think what they want and write what they want. After all. It's only…it's nothing. Vanity."

"You told me to stop pretending like the things weren't important." He took the paper back from her, throwing it down on the table.

"Yes, well, you didn't follow my advice, did you? Why should I follow yours?"

"Because this is garbage. They've hurt you. And I will not allow this to continue."

"It's clever. A joke. An old one. Because I look a little undead. All things considered there were worse things to be called, though."

"Name one."

She put shaking hands on her hips. "I…I can't think of any but it doesn't mean they don't exist. It could be Zombie Drudge, so…you know…Princess is better than that."

"I didn't want this," he said.

She took a deep breath. "I know. And now it's happened. The press did what I thought they would do. They took the easy route and insulted my looks. But that's not actually very surprising. It's what they do. It's how they operate. I can't exactly get upset about it." As she said it, a tear slid down her cheek. "Ignore that. I don't know why that happened."

Except she did. It was like being pulled from her shell, a defenseless crustacean exposed to the elements and scrubbed raw by the sand. This whole experience had been like that. Being with Xander, being back in the world. She'd lost her protection and it left her feeling wounded and fragile.

"Bastards." He picked up his cell phone and dialed a number. "This is Xander Drakos. I want you to track down the owner of *National Daily News* and let him know that if he likes his pants, he'd better print a retraction for his recent article featuring my fiancée. Otherwise, I'll sue them off of him." He hung up. "There. I feel better, I don't know about you."

"It wasn't necessary."

"Oh, come on, there's no point in having power if you don't abuse it a little."

"I take back what I said about you being perfect for the job," she said.

Xander stood, looking down at her, his dark eyes intense. For a moment she thought he might pull her into his arms. Thought he might kiss her again like he'd done yesterday. And she found she wanted him to.

"Can I see the rest of the article?"

"Why?"

"Please."

He handed the paper back to her and she skimmed the article. One thing that had changed about the tone of the articles was the way the press seemed to see Xander. He was being hailed as a man who had changed. As evidenced by his willingness to marry her.

"Well, they seem happier with you," she said. "That's good."

"Is it?"

"It's what you wanted."

"They seem to think I've reformed," he said.

"Have you?"

"I'm not sure."

"Are you going to run again?" she asked, arms crossed under her breasts, her chin tilted up, defiant. If he was, he'd better tell her now.

"No."

"Then you won't screw it up. Because I don't think it's in you to fail. You have to walk away from everything entirely in order to slack off last time."

"I'm not going to run permanently," he said slowly, "but I might need a day off. Do you want to come with me?"

"Where?" she asked.

"The beach. I think I need a day at the beach."

For the beach drive, Xander chose that ostentatious sports car rather than the limo. This moment really did feel like it was from another time. Strangely light. Strangely happy. The Zombie Princess headline lingered in the background, but right now, the mountains were green and beautiful and the beach was a glittering jewel. The windows were rolled down and the wind whipped through the car, smelling of salt and sand and sun.

"Now, this reminds me of the past," she said. "But in a good way."

"Me, too," he said, looking over at her briefly before putting his focus back on the road.

"There's that little window of life where you don't worry about much of anything. I think being seventeen was my favorite. I could drive and could do things I wanted with friends. But I wasn't quite to my dynastic engagement with you, so there was nothing too serious happening. Just parties and trips to the beach."

"I never had that. I mean, I was always raised to be the heir."

"You always seemed happy, though. Like you were having fun at life's expense."

"Yeah, well, I sort of was at that point. I always knew my responsibility, but I liked to have fun. Because, that's the flip side of the heir responsibility. I was assured of my place. Of my divine right to become the most powerful man on the island. How can a young guy not get off on that?"

"I suppose it's impossible."

They rounded a corner and she noticed Xander's knuckles get white on the wheel. She looked up at him, at the hard expression on his face.

"What?" she asked.

"Nothing." She could see his chest, rising and falling hard and fast as he struggled to breathe.

"What's happening, Xander?"

"I'm so stupid," he said, his lips white as his knuckles now. "I didn't realize where I was going."

She really thought he might pass out on her now. "Pull

over," she said. "Just up here, there's a place with beach access."

He nodded slowly and pulled the car into a gravel turn-out on the side of the road, killing the engine. There was silence except for the sound of his breathing and the crashing of the waves.

"What happened?" she asked.

He got out of the car without saying anything, the keys in the ignition, the door open. And he started down the stairs that led down to the beach.

And all she could do was stare after him.

She wondered what pain hurt so bad that he couldn't bring himself to speak about it. It was related to what had happened to him yesterday with his father, she was sure of that. She unbuckled and got out, following him down to the beach, white sand sifting into her sandals, piling into a warm ball beneath the arch of her foot. She kicked the shoes off and ran ahead to where he was.

He started walking into the ocean. She remembered telling him how she'd longed to do that. To disappear beneath the waves and never come back up. And then he dipped his head beneath the water, and Layna couldn't see him anymore.

CHAPTER ELEVEN

"Xander!" Layna shouted, following him out into the waves.

The waves were hitting her at chest level. She gave up on walking and tried to tread water, even though she could touch the bottom. But the waves washed her backward, away from him. "Xander!" she sputtered, water going over her head. She let the water draw her back toward the shore and stood hip-deep in the surf.

He came back up then, his dark head breaking the surface. A wave pushed him back so that he was near her.

"Are you trying to drown yourself?" she asked, feeling half-drowned herself. She knew all the beautiful makeup that had been put on in an effort to de-zombiefy her was gone.

"No," he said, his words heavy. "Not that. Just…I felt like there was blood all over my hands and I thought maybe I could get them clean."

She moved closer to him and took his hands in hers. And without asking why, without asking for an account of his sins, she held his hand up. "I don't see any."

"It's there."

"Tell me," she said.

"I couldn't go any further," he said. "I'm sorry."

"Don't apologize to me. Explain. Explain all of it. Yesterday, today. Something hurts badly enough that you have to run when it catches up with you and I want to know what it is."

"We were going to have to pass the accident site to get to the beach I had in mind and for some reason I didn't realize until we went around that last corner. It reminded me of that day."

"Oh…no, Xander I'm sorry."

"I'm sure it's horrible to watch someone die," he said, a shiver racking his body, "even if they're a stranger. But to watch your mother…to watch her get white, all of her color bleeding out of her, onto your hands…there is nothing worse." He met her gaze, the demons behind his eyes raging now, lashing him from the inside out. "I couldn't do anything but sit with her until help arrived and by then it was too late. But they couldn't get me to let go of her. The last thing she ever heard from me was anger. Those were the last sounds she heard on this earth. Me yelling at her. Swearing at her. I was…so angry with her, Layna."

"About what?"

"It doesn't matter," he said. "It doesn't change anything. It doesn't change what happened. It doesn't change the last moments of that relationship. I can never fix it. Can never apologize for the words I said. I can never go back and decide not to get angry. Decide to pull the car over. Decide not to go out that day. I can never go back and tell her that no matter how angry I was back then, I would have gotten over it and we would have been okay."

He shivered again. "Get on the sand," she said, "out of the water, and wait for me."

She scrambled back up the stairs, up to where the car was parked and took the keys from the ignition, fished a blanket and food out of the trunk, then closed all the doors before heading back down to where he sat.

She threw the blanket over his shoulders. "There. And I have sandwiches."

"I don't think I could eat," he said.

"Then we'll talk."

"Trust me?" he asked.

"Not really."

"Probably a good thing. But if memory from my misspent youth serves me, there's a cave over here. We could get out of the wind. And not have anyone stumble across the heir to the throne shivering and on the cusp of a mental breakdown."

"That might be for the best."

He kept the blanket on his shoulders and led the way down the beach and away from the water.

"This is all a little too perfect, Xander," she said, walking into the small stone alcove cut into the mountain.

"My break with reality and emotional meltdown?"

"How many women have you seduced in here?"

"Oh, this was my much younger misspent youth. Not my teenage years."

"I never really knew if you'd dated much before we were together."

He winced. "I didn't date so much as take advantage of women who liked the idea of getting dirty with a prince."

"I see."

"I take it you didn't?"

She blushed, but thankfully, in the dark she knew he couldn't see it. "I come from a political family and my mother was very blunt with me early on about what nets you a good husband. Purity, or at the very least the illusion of it, is quite important. Princes and the like don't want a lot of tabloid articles going around about their future wife's wild years."

He laughed. "I was expertly snared, wasn't I?"

"We both knew what our marriage was supposed to be. But yes, I did work to make my image one that would fit in with the Drakos family. I worked to be suitable."

"You did far too much for me," he said. "I never deserved any of it."

"I didn't do it for you," she said. "I did it for me. I don't think you fully grasp what a shallow little power grabber I was."

"You were far too pretty for me to care."

"Yes, and when life took that I had to work on developing my character a bit. A harsh wake-up call, and I resisted it for as long as I could."

"I'm still resisting it," he said. He put his hand on the rough stone wall and looked up. "I know a little bit about those hazy years, you know."

"Do you?" she asked, her throat tight all of a sudden.

"Yes. I was so high for the first couple of years after I left I could barely remember my reason for taking off in the first place. It was a lot harder to remember what it was like washing my mother's blood off of my body, too."

"It's terrible to live like that," she said. "Half alive."

"I tried to use things like sex and drugs to make myself feel. But in the end, it doesn't work. It's fleeting and the aftermath is so bad you wish you would have just stuck with empty."

"When did you stop?"

"The drugs? Probably twelve years ago. The drinking and sleeping around? It's been a couple of weeks. I've been walking with my favorite crutches for a long time."

"It's funny. I've been in a convent and you've been in a casino, but I think, at the end of the day we were doing the same thing."

"I think you might be right."

"I'm sorry about what happened. And I'm sorry I was

so angry at you. I didn't really stop and think about how you must have felt. All you must have gone through. My own tragedy overshadowed yours in my mind."

"I don't blame you for that, Layna. You were put through hell."

"We both were."

"Yesterday when I kissed you," he said, "I just wanted to lose myself. To forget who I was. Where I was. To forget that this was my life. That my father, who I haven't spoken to in so long, was unconscious. That he's dying. Another person I'll never reconcile with. When I kiss you it's hard to think about any of the bad things because…I just want you."

"Kissing me really works that well?"

"Yes," he said.

"The Zombie Princess?"

"I don't have time for people like that. They're idiots. They don't know what it's like to kiss your lips, or feel your curves beneath their hands. They know nothing."

She was really blushing now. "It's hard for me to think when we kiss, too. I didn't think I would miss touch. I thought I could live without being with a man because I didn't want to deal with the fact that I could be rejected for my looks. Or that any man who was with me might be with me out of pity. But when you kiss me, I care less about how you feel because I'm too focused on what I feel."

"I make you selfish?" he asked, moving closer to her.

"Yes. For that. For what you can give me. I've…never actually been kissed by anyone else. And the one thing I always regretted, in spite of myself, was that the night in the garden, you know what night I mean, we got interrupted."

"I regretted that, too. I tried not to think of you after I left, Layna, but I did regret that. I regretted you. If my life hadn't have changed, you would have been my future, and

I was always content with that vision. The life I've had has never been as beautiful as that dream. As that certainty I had for those few months we were engaged. I could see it all, you as my wife, us ruling Kyonos, and it felt right. Maybe that was really why I came to look for you after I returned. Because I hoped that somehow it wouldn't be too late to have some of that."

"And look what you came back to."

He put his hand on her cheek, a move he made often and one she didn't think she'd ever tire of. He was so comfortable touching her, even her scars. "But the feelings are the same. It's amazing how much we've both changed, only to come back to this point." He put his hand on her other cheek and lowered his head, kissing her, deep and long. "I do want you. As badly as I ever have. More even, I think, because I know how bitterly I've regretted the fact that I didn't claim you before. I will never make that mistake again."

She looked up into his eyes. They were still so bleak, so haunted. She could see it even in the dim light of the cave. "Do you need me?" she asked. "Do you need to forget?"

She did. She was wounded and hurting. For her, for him. For everything they'd lost. For the years of pain. For the years they suffered alone when maybe what they should have done was cling to each other.

"Yes," he said. "Please."

She kissed him then. Slowly traced the seam of his mouth with her tongue, asking for entry. He gave it, and with a growl wrapped his arms around her waist and held her tightly against him as he let her take the lead on the kiss.

She knew she was a little clumsy at it, but he really didn't seem to mind, his erection hard against her stomach, an air of desperation coming from him in waves.

She could feel it reflected in her, deep in her core. The need to feel like she wasn't alone. He'd said that he'd been inside of a woman before and felt utterly isolated, but somehow she knew that wouldn't be true with them.

Because they both knew rock bottom. And it seemed like they deserved to reach for the heights, even if it was just for a few moments.

He took the blanket off his shoulders and laid it down on the sandy floor of the cave. "I have never seduced a woman in here before," he said. "I know I told you that already but it feels like my current actions might make that assertion seem suspect."

"A little bit, but I don't really care," she said, blinking back tears. "I've been cold for a long time," she said.

"Because you were in the ocean."

She laughed and shook her head. "No, I've been cold inside for a long time. I feel like you could make me warm. I need you to make me warm."

"You deserve better than this," he said, kissing her again, cutting off any response she might have made. "You deserve so much better than this, but I don't have the strength to give it to you, because all I can do is take this for myself."

His desperation fed hers, the need that wrapped itself around his voice was like balm for the scars inside. She might be the Zombie Princess, but right then, the beautiful, damaged prince wanted her.

They were both broken. Barely limping through life. But maybe if they held on to each other tight enough they could hold each other up. Maybe she could be strong enough if they were braced on each other.

He swept his hand over the line of her back, a wave of sensation crashing over her. How long had it been since she'd focused on her body? On what she felt physically.

She'd been training herself to deny physical desire. To deny cravings of any kind. Of specific foods, rest, sex. Because it was important for a woman with her aims to deny herself.

But right now, Xander was making it impossible to think of anything else except what she felt. What she wanted. He was making her need, a deep, aching need that she couldn't possibly let go unanswered.

She wouldn't let it go unanswered. She knew what he meant now. Because she knew what she should do, too. She knew she should ask for a bed and soft sheets, and for him to be slow and gentle because it was her first time.

She knew she should demand marriage vows, because it was right.

But she was beyond that. None of it mattered. The cave floor would do, the commitment they had would have to as well.

She had a feeling that, if she had met him again and he hadn't offered marriage, they would be in the exact same position.

Because this was unfinished business. This was the chance to either bond her and Xander together for good, or to at least have him lose some of his power over her by answering some very important questions. The chance to turn regrets of missed chances into mistakes made.

She was honestly okay with the idea that it might be a mistake when it was over. Because she was short on those. Or maybe not. Maybe her life had been one long, steady, low-key mistake.

That sent a jolt of panic through her, spurred her on, made her kiss him all the more desperately. Xander made her feel so much. So many things she thought she'd let go of, and he brought it all roaring back, or to life for the very first time.

He pushed his hands beneath her shirt, repeating his earlier move, this time over bare skin. She moved her hands to his stomach, tugging his shirt out from his pants and slipping her fingers beneath. He was so hot, so hard. So very different from her.

She would have been shocked by her boldness in other circumstances. But not now. Not when they were in the dark. In this place that almost seemed removed from reality. Not when they were holding each other up.

Not when they were helping each other forget by filling the present with so much pleasure the past couldn't exist anymore, and the future couldn't be a concern.

He pulled his lips from hers and kissed her neck, teeth grazing her sensitive skin, his tongue sliding over her flesh to soothe away the sting. He knew just where to hit, just when to stop and suck at her skin, when to inflict pain. When to give pleasure.

He tightened his hold on her and drew her forward, raising his other hand to cup her breast through the fabric of her damp top. He moved his thumb, finding her nipple with ease, finishing the work of the cold water and tightening it to a painfully hard point.

A low growl rolled through his throat and he propelled her backward, pushing her against the wall of the cave. He pushed a thigh between her legs, then took advantage of her widened stance, his arousal coming into contact with the most intimate part of her.

There were layers of clothing between them but she still felt it, so devastating. So erotic. So unlike anything she'd given herself permission to want or feel for far too long.

She'd told him that she was a woman, and had been long before he'd walked back into her life. And it was true. But she'd suppressed an amazing part of what it meant to be a woman, and only now, with his lips on her skin, his hands on her body, his hardness against her softness, did she realize that.

She angled her head and caught his lips, kissing him deep, tasting him, reveling in the slide of his tongue against hers. For too long she'd had hazy. Gentle. Life on a near flat line with barely a blip, and now she felt like she was going to explode with the intensity of this encounter. With the rawness of it.

The rock at her back, the man at her front, the sound of the waves just outside the cave walls. It was sensory overload in the most perfect way. An infusion of sensation, bursts of flavor on her tongue. Years of bread and water dissolving into a sensual feast that she didn't think she would ever get enough of.

He forked his fingers through her hair and tugged, hard, guiding her away from the wall, down onto the blanket, his body covering hers, his lean hips settling between her legs. She bucked against him, chasing the promise of release that sparked through her with every touch of his body against hers.

He pushed her dress up, tugged her panties down to her knees, his hand at the apex of her thighs, thumb deftly finding the sensitive bud there. She didn't have time to be shocked or embarrassed, didn't have time to do anything but simply revel in the pleasure he knew how to give.

"You want me," he said, his voice feral, his words barely intelligible.

"Yes," she said, kissing his neck. "Yes."

The blanket was bunched up underneath them, only offering a partial shield between them and the ground, but she didn't care. It added to the intensity, to the depth of it all.

He slipped a finger inside of her and the wholly foreign sensation rocketed her to the brink of orgasm.

"You're a virgin, aren't you?" he asked, his voice hoarse.

"Yes," she said, pleasure rocketing through her as he slid his thumb over her clitoris again.

"And you're sure this is what you want?"

"I need it," she said. "I need you. I need it like this."

"It's not going to be romantic," he said, abandoning her body, reaching for the closure on his pants and unbuttoning them, then tugging his shirt over his head. "It's probably going to be fast."

"Are you trying to talk me out of it?"

"*Theos*, yes. Because if I have a soul left, this will damn it for sure."

She shook her head. "No. It won't. How could that be true? How can that be true when I feel like if I don't have you I'll die?"

He kissed her lips, gentle, searching, at odds with the ferocity of the moment. "That's absolute proof that I'm right," he said. "I'll try not to hurt you."

The blunt head of him probed at the entrance to her body and she tensed for a second before he started to push inside. The farther in he went, the more she relaxed. It didn't hurt. It just felt...new. And wonderful.

He put his hand under her bottom and lifted it, thrusting into her all the way. A harsh sound escaped from his lips, along with a curse that sounded more like a prayer.

He pushed her dress up higher, exposing her breasts, lowering his head and sucking a nipple deep in his mouth as he moved inside of her, driving her higher, faster than she'd imagined possible.

It seemed natural, having him like this, moving with him, finding her pace. She locked her legs around his lean hips and arched against him, meeting his every thrust, nails digging into his shoulders.

He lowered his head, his movements harder, faster now,

pleasure sparking in her, each thrust bringing the bursts of white heat closer together, turning it into a continuous flame that burned through her whole body, threatening to consume her as he ravaged her, pushed her to a point she hadn't imagined possible.

Xander growled, teeth closing down on her shoulder, his pelvis hitting hard as he froze above her and shuddered out his release. The pain ramped her pleasure up higher, the overflow of sensation an utter shock. Beautiful. Blinding.

And when the fire burned out, it was only the sound of their breathing echoing off the walls of the cave.

A chill stole through her blood, a slow trickle of ice that replaced the heat that had come before. And it hit her that she was lying on the floor, outdoors, kind of, almost, with Xander on top of her.

Her dress was still on, his pants only pushed down just past his hips. That she'd let him—no, begged him—to take her like this. When they weren't married. When they hardly knew each other. When they certainly didn't love each other.

He moved off her, standing and tugging his pants up, his movements fluid as he dressed. It all spoke of his experience—experience he'd gained with other women.

Anger curled in the pit of her stomach. Anger she had no right to feel because she knew his past, she knew something of his experiences, and she'd just benefitted, mightily, from those experiences. It had been…amazing. Physically.

Emotionally she felt…an empty, crushing weight in her chest. The kind he'd spoken of. They'd just been as close as two people could possibly be and she felt alone. More alone than she'd felt in ages, with him right there, the scent of his skin still on her body. It made no sense.

Sex without love.

Yes, that had to be it. Lust. Empty lust that meant nothing.

But it had all seemed substantial in the moment. It had seemed necessary. Now she felt singed inside. Like she'd been burned, hollowed out.

No wonder she'd spent so many years content with… contentment. Happy to feel no brilliant highs so that she could avoid the lows. So that she could avoid this level of emptiness and confusion.

"Let's not talk," she said, scrambling into a sitting position and trying to put her clothes back in place. "Let's just…not."

"Why?" he asked, doing his belt and the final few buttons on his shirt.

"Because there's no point. I don't want to…I don't want."

"Do you regret it?"

"I don't understand it."

"What's not to understand? We wanted each other. We acted on it."

"Didn't I just say I don't want to talk?"

"Hiding?"

"Why not?" she asked, feeling like she was on the verge of tears. "It's what we're both best at. We hide from our pain and our issues and from anyone who might hurt us or ask anything from us, right?"

"Sums it up," he said, his tone hard. "And that right there is my favorite method of running. You have to admit, it's a lot more exciting than hiding in a convent."

"It was more *something*, but I haven't decided if I liked it or not yet."

He grabbed her arm and pulled her forward, kissed her hard on the mouth. "You liked it."

"I did?" she asked, keeping her voice monotone.

"You came pretty hard, baby, you can't hide that from me. I could feel it."

Her face heated. "Don't."

"Don't because you want to pretend that you're just a sweet, good girl? We both know you aren't."

"That's where you're wrong, Xander. Assuming I care about being good. I don't. I never have. I just cared about hiding. I've never needed to be good, and I think if I had, I wouldn't have given you my virginity on the floor of a cave."

"Then maybe our marriage will be a success, *agape*, because if neither of us care about being good, then we might have a lot of fun."

"More fun like that, you mean?" she asked, her tone disdainful.

"Yes," he said, "that's exactly what I mean." He hauled her against him for a kiss, his lips hard on hers. "And don't play wounded maiden with me. It doesn't suit you."

"What? All my wounds aren't convincing enough for you?"

He released his hold on her. "Whatever the hell your problem is? Get over it. I expect sex in my marriage and since you don't want me to have it with anyone else, I'll damn sure have it with you. Unlike you, running off into celibacy isn't my style."

"You are…you are…"

"Sexy?"

"Your ego is…"

"Yeah, I know. But I don't need ego in this instance. I know just how much you enjoyed that, so let's just skip this part."

She gritted her teeth. "I believe I'm the one who suggested that in the first place."

"So we'll continue with it then."

Layna dressed, careful not to look at Xander as she did, then headed out of the cave and into the sunlight. It was shocking that it was still midday. Shocking that the world seemed so normal outside while everything inside of her was rearranged to the point where she couldn't find a damn thing!

And, yes, damn again. She blamed Xander for her expanding vocabulary. Not that she hadn't known the words, just that she hadn't seen fit to use them until he'd come back into her life.

"For what it's worth," Xander said, his voice coming from behind her, "I do feel better."

"I think I might find that offensive."

"Don't," he said. "Because usually I feel worse when it's over, and I don't. Even after we've had a fight. Actually, I think I like that we had a fight."

"Why?" she asked, incredulous now.

"Because we talked. And I don't want to leave it on a fight because sometimes, you never get a chance to repair it when it's over."

Her heart squeezed. "I suppose that's true."

"A truce, then?"

She didn't really know how she felt about a truce with the man she'd just had sex with. She didn't know how she felt at all.

He stuck his hand out, as though she was meant to shake it and all she could do was stare. "A truce?" she repeated, sounding dumb.

"It's better than fighting, don't you think?"

But not very honest. Not when she felt all jumbled up. "Okay." She extended her hand and wrapped her fingers around his, shaking it slowly. This was silly, but it meant she was able to stop and collect herself. Shore up her defenses. It meant neither of them had to be particularly honest.

She was quite comfortable with that.

"Good," he said, releasing his hold on her. "Now, let's go. I think we both agree that a day at the beach has been had and there's no need to go any further."

No need for him to pass the site of his mother's accident. No need for them to confront what had passed between them. No need for them to talk about why he felt so dirty. Why he'd felt the need to walk into the ocean to get clean.

"Yes," she said. "I think I'm quite ready to go back."

He smiled, and she knew that he knew, as well as she did, what they were both doing.

Hiding.

"Excellent."

CHAPTER TWELVE

XANDER COULDN'T GET his tie right. And who the hell cared? He hated all of this. Hated that he had to dress for dinner because Stavros had invited heads of state and all other manner of dignitaries Xander could care less about.

Not when he was highly concerned with his feelings for his fiancée. Or rather, how his fiancée had felt when she'd been naked underneath him. Being with her yesterday had been a revelation. He swore succinctly and tossed his tie down onto the bed.

She had been... There were no words for the blinding flash of perfect oblivion and clarity he'd found when he'd pushed inside her body.

And wasn't that a damned funny thing? He'd always known sex had power. It had the power to wipe his worries from his mind. The power to make him feel. To bring his life, the emptiness of it, into sharp perspective the moment the buzz from his orgasm faded.

But this was different. He hadn't felt alone when he'd been with her.

Maybe it was because they were both so very much the same, though he doubted she would ever admit to that.

He looked down at the tie and frowned. Then picked it up.

He could call a servant, but he hated that nonsense. He

probably needed a valet or some such, no doubt his father had one.

But that wouldn't serve his purposes for the moment. Sure, it would get his tie on straight, but it wouldn't serve his purposes.

He flung his bedroom door open and stalked down the corridor. The servants were very good at ignoring him and his moods. But then, he supposed that was part of earning their salary.

He opened the door to Layna's room without knocking, hoping he might find her there. He was not disappointed.

"I need help," he said, his tone as stern as the walk he'd used to bring him here.

Layna frowned from her position on the bed. "You have a very bad habit of barging into my room."

"Since when does a fiancé need permission? And I have now seen all of your body, so let's not even pretend that your modesty is offended."

"Just because you've seen it once doesn't mean you have ongoing permission to see it whenever you like," she said.

"Of course it does." He sat down in a chair by the bed, one leg out straight, his arms on the rests. "I am to be king. I will see what I like when I like to see it."

She arched her brows. "Has being in your childhood home caused this regression or do you just always behave like a recalcitrant boy?"

"I need help putting my tie on," he growled. He was not going to dignify her question with a response.

"Then why didn't you call someone?"

"What the hell is the point of a wife who doesn't want me to see her naked and who won't tie my damned tie for me?"

"I'm not really sure, actually. Maybe it's the time for you to rethink your proposal."

"I won't." He stood up and walked toward her, draping his tie over his shoulders. "Fix this."

She let out a long, exasperated breath and gripped both ends of the tie. "It's been about a million years since I've done this. I did it for my father a couple of times. He felt it would be a good skill to know."

"For such a time as this, I should think."

"Clearly, yes, the idea was for me to be able to serve the every whim of my crabby husband. But you are not my husband yet, don't forget it."

"I made you mine in every way that counted today."

"Indeed," she said, her tone frosty.

"You don't agree?"

"Does every woman you have sex with belong to you? If so, we should start partitioning off a wing for the royal harem."

He pulled away from her and started working on the tie on his own again. "You need to dress for dinner."

"And the subject has changed."

"It bloody well has."

"Are you always such a horror after sex?"

"No, but I am always such a horror when I have to put on a tie and perform at some…state dinner I have no desire to partake in."

"So I should expect a lot of this then?"

He sat down again, his hands folded, his chin braced on his knuckles. "I have to get over it, don't I?"

"What?"

"The fact that I don't like this. Or want it. That I don't know how to do it anymore."

"How is it that you managed to lose all of what you were raised for? How did you lose so much of who you were born to be?"

Xander shifted in his seat. And he wondered if it was time she knew. "Because it's not who I was born to be."

It was too late to take it back now. There was no pulling back from a statement like that. She would never let him off the hook now.

"What do you mean?" she asked.

It didn't mean he wouldn't make her drag it out of him since just saying it seemed too hard.

"The way the system works here in Kyonos, it's almost as if our bloodline gives us some divine ruling powers. I mean, Stavros's children can't be in line for the throne because they're adopted, because they don't descend from our great and noble lineage. Are there magic powers in it, I wonder? I've always wondered that, even when I was a boy. Wondered how I'd been so fortunate to be born with such blood and the divine right to rule that came with it."

"No wonder you were so insufferable."

"Yes, it's no wonder at all when you're born believing that the simple act of your birth puts you above the common folks." He took a breath and looked out the window, at the slice of blue sky just barely visible. Not for the first time, he thought he would rather sail into the horizon than deal with all of this. But he'd made a promise.

He'd made a promise to Layna.

He wouldn't run again.

"But I found out…that I was not born with that right at all. I have no royal blood, Layna. I am not my father's son."

"What?" He had succeeded in shocking her. Her eyes flew wide, one eyebrow raised, the other, paralyzed by scar tissue, still managing to convey her surprise.

"That was what my mother and I were fighting about. She told me, on our trip to the beach that day that I was not of royal blood, but the product of an affair she had with her bodyguard. Ironic, considering Eva's marriage. But my sister had the courage to walk away from her arranged marriage when she decided Mak was the one she wanted. My mother made a different choice. She went ahead with the marriage to my father, knowing she was pregnant."

"What? How…"

"She seduced him quickly, is my understanding, and it was no hardship to convince him I was born just a few weeks early."

"But she's certain?"

"So she told me. She was already pregnant when she slept with my father for the first time."

"And the bodyguard?"

"Sent away with a grand payoff. She never took a test of any kind, and that was, in the end, why she told me."

"What do you mean?"

"She'd been getting increasingly paranoid, with the way technology was progressing. She was starting to fear that someday my DNA might be used against me. And so she begged me not to ever undergo any sort of analysis of my blood. Or to ever let my children undergo such a test, when you and I were married."

"But why would she…?"

"I think it was long-held guilt, starting to eat at her, making her see shadows where there were none. But the thing was, the economy had been having issues already and with the state of political unrest she was concerned for me."

"But if… Why couldn't Stavros rule then?"

"My father didn't know. She didn't want him to know. She loved him by then, you see? She hadn't loved him when they'd first married. So lying to him hadn't seemed so bad. But later…she wanted to keep it a secret. For her. For him. And for me. In her mind, I was her firstborn son and I deserved the honor. I think in some ways, I was her favorite son because of my real father. Because he was her first love. Because she had gone to such great lengths to protect me and ensure I was the heir."

He shrugged.

"I've had fifteen years to think this over. And I have. High, drunk, sober, alone and in the arms of a woman, I've thought about this. About what it meant. About what my responsibilities were. She did so much to ensure I could be named the heir. But the fact remains that I'm not."

"And that's why you left?"

"That. And the fact that I do blame myself for her death. I was so angry, Layna. I could hardly see straight and I was yelling, I just drove faster and…"

"You made a mistake. You didn't do it on purpose."

He shook his head. "I didn't. But it was a hell of a mistake. There are mistakes you can come back from, but then there are mistakes you make that someone doesn't walk away from, and those are the hardest ones to deal with. The hardest ones to seek forgiveness for. From yourself or anyone else."

"Tell me about the day you left," she said, sinking to the floor in front of him. "Tell me about what happened, now that I know everything."

"My father had called me into his office. Stavros was there, too." He could picture them both—his father ashen, angry and grieving. His brother, so young and sullen. A teenage boy still. "And then he proceeded to tell me that he found me responsible for the death of his wife. And how he had no idea how I could possibly be his son, when he would never have behaved in such a manner. And I had no argument. For I felt he spoke the truth. And I had just learned I was not his son. So there was no lie in what he said."

"And Stavros?"

Xander cleared his throat. He hated that the memory had this much power over him, even now.

"He looked at me and said he would always hold me responsible for the loss of his mother. His mother, as though she were no longer mine because I had taken her from the world. And remembering the words I'd yelled at her before the car hit the rocks? Where I had said she was no longer a mother to me? I couldn't argue with that statement, either."

"And you had nothing," she said, her voice a whisper.

"In one moment, I lost all my family. And I knew I had no real claim on the throne. I saw no reason to stay."

She rose up, planting her hands on his thighs, and kissed him on the mouth, the touch sweet, sincere. He raised his hands and gripped the back of her head, his fingers sinking deep into her hair, holding her tight to his mouth. He needed this. He needed her. He needed her so badly he was shaking with it already and it had been less than twenty-four hours since he'd last been inside her body.

He tugged gently on her hair, tilting her head back, exposing her tender throat, then he lowered his head and kissed her, slowly. She moaned, encouraging him, spurring him on. He bared his teeth, scraped her delicate skin and reveled in the raw sound she made in response.

She liked this. His little innocent. She liked him unrestrained. She liked to be at his mercy. Which naturally put him at hers. To have a woman on her knees before him, allowing him this kind of sensual feast? He might have the physical power, but she was holding the leash.

Keeping his hand in her hair, he reached down to his belt and undid the buckle, freeing himself from the confines of his pants.

She looked up at him, angelic eyes wide, her lips in a shocked *O*. There was something about that face that turned him on even more, and it shouldn't. He knew it shouldn't.

"You know what I want from you?" he asked, his voice strangled.

She nodded slowly and he tightened his hold on her hair. He watched the color in her cheeks rise, from arousal, not embarrassment. The flush spread down to her neck, her chest.

"Suck me," he said, his voice rough.

She leaned forward, guided by his hand, the tip of her tongue touching his rigid length.

"More," he said, tugging gently.

But she didn't comply. Instead, she just ran her tongue along his shaft. And he could do nothing but sit helplessly, let her have her way. She shifted then, taking all of him into her mouth, and he leaned back in the chair, a harsh breath hissing out through his teeth.

He swore, short and to the point, but it only seemed to encourage her. She wasn't shy. She seemed to have no qualms about tasting him, touching him, boldly changing the rhythm or stopping altogether, squeezing the base of him with her hand, pushing him to the brink.

"Careful," he groaned, when her tongue brushed the sensitive skin just beneath the head of his erection. "I don't want it like this. I don't want it over too soon."

The look she gave him was wicked, reminding him of Layna Xenakos as she had been. Confident. A minx. A flirt. A woman who had a sensual air about her, and an innocence, too. It had all called to him even then.

She had always called to him.

She lowered her head again and he tugged her hair. "No," he said, his voice sharp. "I want to be inside you."

She stood then, lifting her dress and tugging her panties off. He reached for her, hooked his arm around her waist and tugged her onto his lap, bunching her dress up around her hips, squeezing her bare butt before giving her an open-handed slap. Nothing too hard. Just enough to draw one of those sweet sounds from her lips.

Then he gripped her hips tight and positioned her over his body, testing her with the blunt head of him, finding her wet and ready. He starting to pull her down, sliding into her by inches. Her head fell back and he couldn't resist another nip on her throat.

When he was inside her all the way, she rested her head against his chest, her hands on his shoulders. "Yes, Xander," she said, and he knew she was still with him.

A relief, because he'd been so lost in his own need it would have been easy to forget her. To forget that she might not be ready for this. But she was. She was right there with him.

"My dress," she said, panting, "would you—?"

He tugged it up higher, pulling it over her head and throwing it to the floor, then undoing her bra with unmatched speed, exposing her breasts. "My pleasure," he said, lowering his head and sucking one rosy bud between his lips.

She arched against him, her internal muscles flexing around him. It was too much for him. But he'd already taken too much from this and she needed hers. He needed to watch her face as she came for him.

He reached between them, sliding his thumb over her clitoris as he thrust up into her.

Her fingernails dug into his back and for a moment she lost herself. But he didn't lose her. He held her the whole time. Watched as her lips parted, her eyes closed, her forehead creased. The way the scar tissue by the corner of her mouth folded, and how one brow never did match up with the other.

It was all her. No one else could have made this moment. No one else could have coaxed his darkest secret from him and then taken him to heaven on its wings.

She squeezed him tight, and the world exploded, his blood turning to fire and swallowing him whole while his orgasm burned through him, clearing out all the pain, all the regret, all of who he was and who he'd been, leaving him desolate in its wake.

And when he came back to himself, he was in her arms. And he wasn't sure who he was. Or why he'd cared so much about a tie only a few minutes ago.

"When is dinner?" she asked, her voice sleepy.

"Eight," he said.

"So we have five hours," she said.

He nodded and somehow, in spite of the fact that his legs felt like jelly, he managed to lift them both from the chair and carry her to the bed. He pulled back the covers and laid her down, then got in beside her, pulling her body up against his. He buried his face in her hair and took a deep breath, the air filling his lungs seeming all the fresher because it was infused with her scent.

"I should have done this after the first time," he said.

"What?"

"Taken you to bed. Held you close. You're so soft." He let his hand drift over her curves. Her hip, her thigh. "You are beautiful, Layna. I saw it just now. With that look on your face as you came. The most beautiful thing I've ever seen."

"You don't have to say those kinds of things."

"I know. But it's true. And you asked me only last week if I could say you were beautiful, and I said no. But I was wrong then. I know so much more now."

"A week to obtain wisdom. I wish I had that gift."

"Not wisdom in all things. But wisdom in how magical it is to watch you lose yourself in pleasure. To see the light catch your hair and pick up the hidden gold strands that always remind me of the past. Only the good parts of the past," he said, laughing. "And I don't know quite how I missed just what an incredible thing your smile is. Because you still have it. Because life has been cruel to you and you still smile."

"So do you," she said.

"Yes. But you mean it."

"You don't?"

He shook his head. "I already told you. I think we took different paths to accomplish the same goal. I tried to pretend everything was fine. I hid behind my smile. Behind artificial highs. So that I could pretend I felt something when I simply didn't. When I couldn't go back and face all that I needed to face. The only thing to do was never look at the past, and pretend everything was fine in the present."

He felt her nod, her body shifting slightly against his. "Yes. That sounds about right. I mean, I understand that."

"And you?"

"In my case, I thought if I could focus on other things, not myself, for a while, I would be okay. If I could have some purpose beyond living in a darkened mansion floating around like a tragic, gothic heroine, then maybe none of it would hurt so bad."

"Did it work?" he asked.

"Yeah. It did. I…I love helping people. And I was able to surround myself with women who had no love for clothing or fashion. I lived a life where outer beauty was a trap because it could lead to vanity. To pride. And since I had none…" She laughed. "In an odd way I suppose I soothed my pride that way. Because I was clearly the least in terms of looks, so I was starting at a greater advantage, and I could be proud of that. That it wasn't a challenge for me to avoid the mirror or to not long to spend ages on my appearance. So…I guess what I really did was try to find a new place I could be the best. But I wasn't that good at it to be honest. I had—I *have* faith. I believe. But I preferred to ride horses and not meditate indoors. I love food, and it was always hard to fast. But it was quiet. And easy to be content and nothing more. Nothing less."

"You always use that word to describe it," he said. "You never say happy. Content is the one."

"Because happiness is too big, I guess. Unlike you, Xander, I haven't been searching for the big emotional high. A return to feeling. It hurts too much to lose everything. And if you care…if you care then it's almost impossible to recover from. Not only did I lose everything, I had an audience. And the moment when I was attacked I had no control. I just stood there. Screaming and screaming, the pain…I can't even describe the pain."

He felt a tear splash onto his arm and an answering ache echoed in his chest.

"And I just let them all have it. Every drop of it. The protesters, the media, everyone. I never want to be like that again. I never want to feel so much. But I think…I think just having contentment doesn't work, either."

"You don't think?"

"I was starting to feel a little dry. Brittle. Does that make sense?"

"Like you needed to be watered," he said. "Like you would fade to nothing if you didn't have something new and fresh added to you."

"Yes."

"It makes sense, because I felt it, too." Nothing was real or substantial in his world, nothing truly passionate in hers. And for people like them, it was a recipe for death.

"I think that's why I like the way you are with me," she said, turning her face into his arm, muffling her words.

Heat assaulted his face. A strange thing. Almost like he was embarrassed, which was ridiculous. "The way I am with you?"

"Yes. The way that you're…rough. I know this isn't how it is for everyone. I understand that the way I like it isn't the way everyone does."

"No," he said, his blood rushing south, "it's not."

"But I think the reason it works for me is that I spent so long filled with nothing but this sort of bland steadiness. And you… You fill me with sensation. Pleasure and pain so sweet I can't bear it. It lifts me up from contentment and takes me somewhere else entirely." She turned over to face him, her expression serious. "But it's only physical, so it feels safe. Does that make sense?"

"Yes," he said, ignoring the uncomfortable tightness in his lungs. "Yes, that makes sense."

"I don't shock you, do I?"

He had to laugh at that. "You shock me? Until yesterday you were a thirty-three-year-old virgin fresh from the c—"

"Convent, I know," she said, sighing, sounding exasperated. "But look at it this way: I've had a lot of years of nothing more than fantasy. A lot of…desire building up inside me and all. And it was sort of by accident I discovered I liked a bit of rough. I blame the cave wall."

"Do you?"

"And you. I think you're corrupting me."

He laughed again, but this time not because it was particularly funny. "I'm afraid that might actually be true."

"I'm happy with it." She shifted against him. "So, what are you going to do?"

"About?"

"You aren't the heir."

"I know," he said. "And for years I was deciding to just not be the heir, but Stavros's circumstances and Eva's wishes have changed that for me."

"I understand that."

"But you don't approve?" he asked.

"It's not that I don't approve. It's just that I wonder if your father needs to know. If your family needs to know."

He tightened his hold on her. "I can't do that."

"Why not? Because you might lose your place?"

"Because I might…I won't have…"

"You won't have your family."

The tension released from him slowly. He was glad she'd said it and not him. "Silly, I know, considering I hadn't spoken to any of them in ages."

"But they were there. I understand that. My family is there, even though we don't really speak."

"Why is that, Layna?"

"It's easier not to. For all of us. I should think you would understand that."

"I do."

"Why don't we sleep for a while," she said, yawning. "Then…then maybe I'll do better tying your tie, and we'll have a hope of being on time for dinner."

CHAPTER THIRTEEN

THE PLAN TO make it to dinner perfectly pressed and on time didn't exactly go off without a hitch. Halfway through tying Xander's tie for the second time, Layna found herself tangled up in him, and the bedsheets, again.

That put them behind schedule by a good twenty minutes, and by then, she hadn't been able to have her makeup artist coat her face with all the paint she needed to begin to cover her scars, which meant she was rocking a much more natural look for the dinner than she'd intended.

But Xander didn't seem to mind.

And he'd called her beautiful.

Something bloomed inside of her, like a flower that had found the sun after a long battle with the clouds. And she wanted badly to crush it herself. But she couldn't bring herself to do it.

It was frightening, how much his words meant to her, and yet she found she wanted to hold them close, even knowing that doing that might be too costly.

She didn't know how today had happened. All that nudity, and not just in bed. It had been real honesty that had passed between them.

And their lovemaking was… She felt her cheeks heat even as they walked into the dining room together, where ten dignitaries were already seated. Yes, their lovemaking was explosive and far beyond anything she'd ever imagined.

If she thought way back to when she'd imagined she might have a sexual relationship with a man, then she remembered having fantasies about Xander. But she remembered them as being quite calm and hazy. Certainly not with her loving the bite of pain from his hands in her hair and rough demands issued from his lips.

She tried to look casual as the past few hours replayed in her mind. This was not the time. This was a formal dinner. Stavros and Jessica were seated near Eva and Mak, and the head of the table was empty, as was the foot. And just like it was choreographed, she and Xander parted and he walked up to his chair, while she moved down to hers.

It was choreographed, she supposed. From a time long passed, but even so, they both knew the steps. They were steps ingrained in them from years ago. It was the position they'd trained for. The marriage they'd trained for.

So strange to be here now, after she'd let go of it all. So strange to have it be so much the same to what she'd imagined and also so different.

They both had scars now. They had the kind of passion that had nothing to do with a bored, disinterested worldview. They might even be better people now than when they'd first been poised to slip into this roll.

"In the absence of my father," Xander said, "I will be acting as host."

"And how is the king?" One of the politicians to Xander's right posed the question.

"He is as well as can be expected. I would hope he makes a recovery."

"But of course we can't plan for that," Eva said, looking bleak.

"We can't plan for the worst, either, Eva," Xander said.

"We can prepare for it, but why not do that and then plan on a better outcome?"

She smiled. "I like that idea better than mine. I tend to be a catastrophist."

"I think this family has had enough catastrophes," he said.

Layna looked down the table at Stavros, who was looking at his older brother with an expression that was... almost like approval. It made her heart do strange and wonderful things. Because she found that she cared about what happened with Xander and his family. It made her ache for him. Made her appreciate how truly difficult things were for him.

Because he felt like he had a smaller foothold on the Drakos family than he should. Because he wasn't truly a Drakos at all, but the child of an unnamed man he would never know.

It made her want to go to him. Made her want to hold his hand. But that wasn't the proper thing to do. So she would help him by being everything a royal wife should be. She wasn't his wife yet, but today she was acting the part. It was what she could do for him, so she would do it.

The conversation turned to unchallenging things. No one questioned Xander on his years away, no one asked about her scars. No one compared her to a zombie. All in all it went very well.

And when it was over, Xander, Stavros and Mak adjourned to Xander's study—and it killed Layna not to follow and act as support—while Eva and Jessica stayed behind with her.

"We can take coffee in my study," she said, gesturing for them to follow her. She felt like a bit of a fraud considering Eva had lived in the palace until a couple of years ago, and Jessica was a frequent guest, where Layna was just learning the layout of everything.

Both women smiled graciously and followed her, and Layna waited until they were seated before settling herself in one of the armchairs that was positioned by the fireplace. It was lit and roaring already. She was used to having to see to things like that herself. But she wasn't going to complain.

"He's doing well," Jessica said.

Eva smiled, a kind of special smile a little sister has for her older brother. "He's brilliant."

"And both of you are happy?" Layna asked. "With the order of things, I mean. Jessica, I understand that when you married Stavros it was with the idea that he would rule. That you would —"

Jessica shifted in her seat, her red lips pursed. "Neither of us have ever really wanted it. He would have done it, because he believes so strongly in doing his duty. But he loves his business, and frankly, I love mine."

"Are you still a matchmaker then?" Layna asked, having been briefed on her future sister-in-law already.

"Yes. We both work less now that we have the children. Lucy and Ella take up a lot of time, after all, but we're both still heavily committed to the companies we've built. Stavros is so interested in bringing more business to Kyonos and he's thrilled to have more time to focus on that. And more flexibility for the girls. It would have been a hard life for them. Raised with the strictures of being the king and queen's daughters, with no hope of ever taking the throne. They would be considered second forever, because of their blood." Jessica's eyes glittered in the firelight. "The idea of that…I can't stand it. I'm so glad they were spared it. I had no idea how hard it would be until we were faced with the reality of what it would mean for them."

"I hadn't thought of that, either," Layna said, looking down at her hands. "How terrible it would be for them." And Xander, how terrible it would have been for him. To be the oldest child in the household and not be the heir. In some households, the matter of blood could be forgotten because love forged the bond. But in a royal house it was different. In a royal house blood was so much more important.

She swallowed and looked up at Eva. "And you, Eva? What about your children? Do you want this for them?"

Eva shook her head. "I've always chafed at what was expected of me. I don't see why my children would be any different."

"And Eva would be bored with palace life," Jessica said. "It's no wonder she had no desire to marry a prince."

Eva smiled. "Or perhaps I just liked what the bodyguard had on offer."

Jessica winked broadly and crossed her legs, her tulle skirt fanning out around her. "The prince does all right."

"Thanks, Jess."

"Oh, come on. Don't get prudish on me now, Eva. You didn't get that baby bump by eating a watermelon seed."

Eva sniffed. "How very American of you."

Layna laughed, genuinely enjoying the interplay between the two women. Between these women who would now be her family. And it was a relief to her to hear they didn't want the throne anywhere near them.

"Yep. I'm totally American like that. Another reason I probably shouldn't be the queen of anything," Jessica said.

It all made Layna appreciate the impossible place Xander was in even more. The reason he'd run. The reason everything had felt so hopeless.

It wasn't enough to have your father look you in the eye and lay the blame for your mother's death on you. He'd had to experience it knowing that the man wasn't really his father. That there was no magical bond between them. Not a blood bond.

And in a family like this, blood was everything.

"How about you, Layna?" Eva asked. "Are you all right with being in this position?"

"There is nothing holding me to the position. Nothing forcing my hand."

"Except for your relationship with Xander," Jessica said, her eyes narrowed.

She and Xander did have a relationship now, and she couldn't deny it. Not after they'd been together so intimately. Not when she felt this need to protect him.

"Xander and I have an understanding, based on our desire to see the country succeed. It has always been our goal. We were just derailed for a while."

The back of her neck prickled and she looked up—Xander was standing the doorway.

"Forgive me if I'm interrupting. But I'm ready to retire. I had thought you might come with me, Layna?"

There was something strange in his eyes. A raw, wounded look that she could see behind the careful facade he had in place.

She always saw through those walls, and sometimes, she wished she didn't.

Sometimes she wished she could go back to simplifying him. To not seeing him. Or at least to seeing him as nothing more than a playboy. Now she saw all of his wounds. Now she saw he was just as scarred as she was and it made it hard for her to hold onto her anger. Hard to keep her shields up.

And she needed her shields. Because when they were down, it burned like acid. And she knew, better than anyone, just how that felt.

Because she couldn't deny him now, even if she should. Even if they needed distance from today so that she could make sure she felt shored up again.

But she couldn't deny him. And she wouldn't.

"Of course, Xander." She stood and looked back at Eva and Jessica, who were giving her saucy raised eyebrows. She wanted to tell them it wasn't what they thought. Except it was what they thought and she knew it. Xander needed her, and if he needed her, it would be her body he required.

And she would give it.

She made her way to the door and took his arm, allowing him to lead her up the stairs and down the winding corridors until they were at his bedchamber.

"I had a maid send your things," he said. "I didn't see any point in pretending things weren't like this between us."

"Of course not."

He started to undo his tie, the one she had done earlier. It was a strange thing, to be a part of both rituals. The dressing and the undressing.

It made things feel very serious.

"I suppose you want—" She was going to say "sex" but he sat on the edge of the bed on a heavy sigh that seemed to demand silence.

Then he tented his fingers in front of his face, staring sightlessly ahead. "I feel like it's wrong not to tell them."

He wanted to talk? That really did shock her. More than that, it wasn't what she wanted. It was too much. Too challenging.

"Maybe you should think on it. You'll feel better after—" Again, she was going to say "sex," but he pressed on.

"Stavros is well-suited to the position. Listening to his thoughts on the economy I found myself quite humbled.

I am not uneducated in these matters, but he's a man who has examined the way things function on every level. From the workforce to the day-to-day running of things. Stockholders and traders, different kinds of industry. He's truly a man now and not the boy I often see him as. He makes me feel like the stupid boy, to be honest. He's been here holding everything up while I've been..." He paused and looked down. "Layna, I've done less than nothing. I didn't even have the decency to get employed somewhere, I gambled for room and board. And Mak...he's not royal and yet he's got a core of steel. Nothing would ever break him. His children, his and Eva's, would be well-suited to taking the throne one day."

"But they don't want it," she said.

He nodded slowly. "I know it. And I find myself in an impossible situation where I feel I must become a better man to make up for the fact that Stavros won't be the one on the throne, and I don't know how to be better."

Her heart ached, her throat tightening. This was too much. He was making her feel too much. Not in the delicious pleasure-pain way that came through sex. This was all in her heart. A heart she'd kept protected for so long that every lash of emotion felt like being hit with a battering ram.

"It doesn't seem like something we can solve tonight. Maybe we can—" She was going to say "have sex," but this time he cut her off with a kiss. And when he swept her into his arms, and into bed, she could focus on that.

On the sensations he created on her skin, not beneath it. The smooth and sensual, the rough and hard. And she let it all fill her. Until she was conscious of nothing more. Until the pain in her heart was overshadowed with sweeter physical pain, and much sweeter physical pleasure.

And when it was over, they didn't talk. They held each other until they fell asleep.

Layna's last thought before drifting off was that it was very strange not to be alone.

This was the second time in his life that Xander Drakos had woken up with a woman in his bed. The first time had been the previous afternoon, when he and Layna had napped after their pretty intense sex session.

And now, here it was, morning. He'd slept with her all night long, with her curves pressed up against him, his arms tight around her. Very tight. Like he was afraid she might escape.

But she wouldn't. Layna was so constant. So faithful.

If anyone could teach him how to be a better man, it was her. She didn't have royal blood and she was the epitome of steadiness and temperance. Well, maybe not really. But she did a wonderful job of acting like she was and maybe that was enough.

All he'd had practice at was indulging his more selfish whims.

Layna had spent years denying hers.

Perhaps he could learn something about restraint from her.

He shifted and looked down at the top of her head, at the golden highlights he could see, revealed by the shaft of sunlight breaking through the drapes.

"Layna," he said.

"What?" she mumbled sleepily. She wiggled against him then startled, drawing back to look at him, blinking like a mole who'd just come out of her burrow. "I forgot you would be here. Or that I would be here. With you."

"I was quite surprised to wake up with someone myself, but I find I don't mind it."

"You've slept with lots of women," she said.

"I've had sex with a lot of women," he said, heat bleeding over his cheekbones. "I don't sleep with them."

"Oh. Well."

"They never mind. They're usually staying in the same hotel."

"That's right. I forgot you didn't have a home."

"And if I had, I wouldn't have brought them to it."

"You are quite something, you know?" she asked.

"That's the thing, Layna, I do know, which leads me to what I was going to ask you."

"Which is?"

"Make me better."

"What?"

"I need to be…better. I have to be able to justify the fact that I'm the one taking the throne and not Stavros."

"No," she said, "you don't. You don't have to justify anything. Not to me. I talked to Jessica and Eva last night and they explained very clearly why they don't want it differently. Eva doesn't want her children raised in this environment and Jessica can't stand the idea of her husband being king while his children can't inherit because they're adopted. There. You're absolved."

"No, Layna, I'm not. Because that's not what ruling is. It's not being comfortable or making everyone happy. It's doing what's best. Stavros knows this. He would accept it if I were to leave."

"You said you wouldn't run," she said. Not accusing, just a fact.

"Is it running if you're simply trying to protect your country? Your people."

"What is it you need to do to feel like a better man?"

"I guess it's too late for me to join the church."

She blinked. "A bit. If you still plan on marrying me."

If he left, he would have no reason to marry her. Which drove home the point that he had to stay. Whatever happened. She was too important to him, and he didn't want to stop and examine why.

But she was changing him. Just being near her was changing him, and he needed that. Needed to be with her. Otherwise, what was there? Nothing more than that endless haze of neon lights and booze. And the idea of going back there now felt like the equivalent of walking into hell of his own free will.

He held her tighter. "And I am planning on it," he said. "You have my ring and my word."

"I've had both before."

"The man I was," he said. "Not the man I am now. And I'm vowing to change."

"So you'll stay."

"Yes. And does it matter to you so much that I do?"

She frowned. "I want you to have a place in the world, Xander. Everyone should. I don't want you to go back to the life that you were living. I don't want you separated from your family."

"And you tell me, since I imagine you know more about this than either of us, where is truth in all of this?"

"I don't know, Xander. Maybe there is no place for it."

"Seems like that might be heresy."

"Maybe. But isn't all of this? Life dealt us both an impossible hand. We either fold or we cheat. I'm becoming convinced of that."

"A gambling metaphor. You know me so well."

"Well, you were asking about the church, I thought I'd bring in the casino."

"Since we're aiming for heresy?"

She sat up, the blankets clutched to her chest. "Not exactly aiming for it." She pushed her hair off of her face.

She didn't seem so self-conscious of her scars around him anymore, and he found he quite liked that.

Especially since he didn't see them the same way he had at first. When he'd first seen them they'd looked like they weren't real. Like they were a mask over the face he remembered. Now it wasn't that way. He saw them as a part of her face. They didn't bear extra notice, not more than those mesmerizing eyes, or the shape of her nose. The stubborn set of her chin.

They weren't an intruder on his eyes or on her beauty. They were a part of who she was, what she'd been through.

Sometimes looking at them hurt, because it was a reminder of how much she'd been hurt. It was a reminder of her pain. But also a reminder of her strength.

"You're staring," she said, her eyes narrowing.

"Because I like to look at you." He let his eyes drift down lower. "But I do wish you'd drop the sheet. I could compose poetry about your breasts. And I don't even like poetry."

She surprised him by letting the sheet fall to her waist, her full, rose-tipped breasts on display for him.

He smiled. "Damn. I'm glad to be a man."

"That's the best you have, Drakos?"

"Shall I compare your nipples to a summer's day?"

"Okay, you can stop now."

"I don't think I can. Not ever."

She let out a long breath. "Xander, I don't know what I'm going to do with you."

Stay with me.

It was the first thought in his mind. It was the thing he wanted above all else.

"Reform me," he said, his throat tight.

"Sometimes," she said, looking away from him, "I'm not really sure I want you reformed."

He pulled her close and kissed her for that. And then more. Until everything faded away. And when they were done, Xander wasn't alone anymore. He was with Layna. And he felt it all the way through.

And he had never felt more alive. He had never felt more.

"Actually, Xander," she said, her voice a whisper, "I think you're already the best man I've ever known. You make me...you know you make me feel like I just might be...beautiful."

Light burst through him, bringing pain along with it. Like the sun hitting his face after a night of hard drinking. Only this didn't feel like stale regret. It was hope. It was something bigger, better than he'd ever known before. He didn't want to hide. He wanted to push off all the layers of rock and dirt, everything he used to hide himself, his secrets, from the world, to protect himself from the painful truths in his life, and emerge the man he was supposed to be.

But he could never do it, so long as everything was covered. He could never be free until he cut the ropes that bound him in the darkness.

With Layna by his side, the idea of it didn't seem so impossible.

"I have to tell him."

Layna looked up from her lunch and at Xander, a strange sense of dread filling her chest. "You what?"

"I have to tell him."

And she didn't ask who or what, because she knew. Somehow she knew what he was thinking without him saying it.

"But why, Xander?"

"Because he's my father. Or, he thinks he is, and for all

intents and purposes and everything that matters to me, he is. And moreover he's the king, and he has the right to choose who his successor is. With all of the information given to him."

"Xander, don't do this. He won't have a choice—"

"There is always a choice, Layna, and this is the thing I've been hiding from. It was horrible to lose my mother, but I couldn't fight against my father's anger, I couldn't stay because I was far too afraid that the truth would come out and then things would be…then they could never be fixed. I have to tell him everything, all of it. So that I can have forgiveness. So that I can have my life. So I can be free."

"But, Xander," she said, a desperate fear clawing at her now and she didn't know why. Didn't know why this was so terrifying. Only that it was making her feel like she was clinging to the ledge of a cliff, her hold slipping with each passing moment. "If you do this, he might send you away. He might…you might never be king. You won't even be a prince. You'll be the royal bastard."

"I'm the royal bastard whether anyone knows it or not," he said, his voice quiet. "And I can't keep hiding behind a lie. Because that's the key, I think. To reforming. To… to changing and being a man who's actually worth something. I have to stop hiding. And that doesn't mean leaving Monaco and returning to Kyonos, clearly I've done that already."

"It means taking less than you deserve because you've had a sudden attack of conscience," she said, shocked at the words coming out of her own mouth. Shocked at the vehemence behind them. She didn't know why she cared so much. Why it felt so vital and frightening.

"I can't argue with you about this."

"Why not?"

"Because I can't change my mind."

"You're just running," she said, anger and fear swirling in her and making her panicky. "You're running again."

"No, Layna. I've finally stopped."

Xander got up from his seat at the table and walked out of the room.

His father was awake this time when he went to see him.

"Xander?"

"I suppose you didn't hear that I was back," Xander said, standing in the doorway.

His father lifted a hand. Strange to see King Stephanos like this. So diminished and pale. But he was awake. Perhaps he would recover. Then, at least, the need for Xander, or Stavros to rule wouldn't be so pressing.

Then, at least, he might have some time left with this man. Time he'd wasted in fear.

"Are you back?" his father asked, adjusting his position in the hospital bed, fiddling with the lines from his IV.

"Yes. I am. But…and I know that this is a bad time to drop bombshells on you…."

"Xander, from where I'm sitting, there may be no time. I'm only glad you're here."

"You seem better," Xander said.

He nodded. "Better. I can speak again. Though it took a while. It was a bad stroke."

"I know."

"So say what you need to," he said, "and then I'll tell you what I need to say."

Xander took a breath. "It's about me. And mother."

King Stephanos closed his eyes and nodded. "Yes, we need to talk about that."

"Not the things you might think. There was a reason

for the crash. And that is that we were fighting, and I was reckless."

"Xander…"

"No, I need to finish. It was my fault, but I could never truly explain it to you. Not when the circumstances…not when I felt I couldn't tell you the truth of the matter. It seems cruel to tell you now, and if it weren't for the way things work in our family, if it weren't for the importance of royal blood, I wouldn't. I found out that day that I am not your son. She was certain of it."

King Stephanos nodded slowly. "I had suspected, of course. You were born quite early and yet quite healthy."

"You suspected?"

"Yes. But I was hardly going to accuse my new bride of faithless behavior. In truth, Xander, ours was a marriage of convenience. In the beginning. I do think we grew to love each other very much."

Xander nodded. "She did love you."

"There is no reason to condemn her for a sin that's thirty-seven years old."

"I'm afraid I didn't feel that way at the time."

"Of course you didn't. How could you?"

"You understand now why I had to leave," Xander said.

"You had to leave because of me," the king said, his voice heavy with regret. "I was hurting and I said things to you… I was not a loving father."

"But you aren't my father at all," Xander said.

King Stephanos frowned. "Xander, no matter what, you are my son. No matter the revelations, or the years that have gone by, or angry words that passed between us, you are my son."

Layna hung up the phone, her hands shaking. She had no idea how the reporter had gotten her line here at the palace. No idea why he'd felt the need to call and tell her they were doing a story, why he'd needed to recite the ugly things being written about her.

That they had photos of her, standing on the balcony off of Xander's room in a thin nightgown, her hair pulled back revealing the worst of her scars, no makeup on her face. And that they were publishing the photos.

Does he make love to you in the dark?

That was when she'd hung up. Her fingers had felt numb.

She hated this. Hated the way they were exploiting her. The way it made her feel. At first, she'd helped Xander's reputation, but was she helping him now?

He said he needed her, but when his rule was taken over by gossip about her looks, about their marriage, how would he feel then?

She sat down in her office chair and tried to catch her breath, failing as it dissolved into a sob.

What would happen when he didn't need her anymore? When he knew he didn't? When he could have any woman, why would he want her?

And he'd gone to confess all to his father. If that lost him his spot on the throne…he would never keep her with him. Never.

Despair washed over his as every word, every insult from the media, from now and fifteen years ago, played back through her mind.

Xander might not leave her now, but one day…

She'd survived losing him once. She couldn't do it again.

Xander walked into the palace with a strange, buoyant feeling in his chest. He felt lighter. He felt like he could breathe for the first time in fifteen years. And more than that, this felt like a place he could live. A position he could have.

Because his father, the man who would always claim him as his son, had said that Xander was the man he wanted on the throne.

The truth truly did set you free. Interesting. He wondered if Layna would be amused by his epiphany.

Layna. He needed to see Layna.

He needed to have Layna. With none of his walls between them.

He prowled through the halls and opened her bedroom door. She wasn't in the suite of rooms that were set aside for her. He walked out and continued on, toward the place she was using as her office.

He found her there, sitting behind a desk, staring off into space. She started when the door hit the wall.

And as soon as he saw her, every thought left his head completely. He'd forgotten why he was there. Where he'd just been. He forgot everything.

He could only stare at her, at her eyes, her high cheekbones. The extra fold by her mouth where her scar tissue was thick, a fold that deepened when she tightened her lips, like she was doing now. At her asymmetrical brows and her neat, feminine hands.

At Layna. All the pieces of her that combined to make the woman that had changed him on every level. That had changed him in a fundamental way he could neither name nor deny.

And he needed her. Needed to be close to her, inside of her, right now. Needed to affirm what he was feeling. To have her brand his body with her touch the way that she had branded his soul.

To brand her body, so that she would feel it, too.

"Layna…" His words evaporated on his tongue. He didn't know what to say. Or how to say it. He knew how to flirt, knew how to throw practiced lines at women and get them into bed for the night. But he'd never learned how to keep a woman with him for two nights, much less forever.

But he had to try. He had to try.

Because he'd gotten everything today—acceptance, forgiveness. And still things didn't feel finished.

"Layna," he began again, "you have been missing from my life every day since I walked away."

"Xander, what are you talking about?"

He went over to the desk and rounded to her side, hauled her up into his arms and kissed her. Then he kissed her cheeks, the damaged corner of her mouth, the winkled line of skin that ran along the bridge of her nose.

He pressed his forehead against hers. "I've been wandering in the desert for fifteen years. I have had no home. No one to call a friend. And I was okay with that because I didn't want anyone to get near me. I came back here, it was supposed to be the promised land, so to speak, and I didn't feel anything. I didn't feel home. Until I saw you."

"Xander, please…don't do that, I don't need it."

"I need to tell you."

"How did your meeting with your father go?"

"That isn't what I need to talk about."

"It's what I need to hear about," she said.

Layna tried to calm the wild beating of her heart, tried to do something to quell the panic that was racing through her. She didn't know what to do with this. With his words, his ferocity and sincerity, with such strength that it burrowed beneath her defenses and started pulling them down. Left her feeling raw and exposed. Reminded her of how it had been to lose it all, all of her control, all of her beauty, in front of hundreds of people.

To care so much and have it all torn away…

Zombie Princess. Does he make love to you in the dark?

She closed her eyes and kissed him. She didn't want

to hear him speak anymore. She couldn't hear more, not now. She could do this. They could kiss. They could make love. They could get married and live together and have children, and rule Kyonos.

So long as she could keep pieces of herself hidden, so that if the world ever fell down around her again, she wouldn't be left with nothing.

But she had to keep him from saying things like that. He could touch her skin, but she couldn't let him keep on touching her heart.

She couldn't risk it.

"Layna," he growled, kissing her deeper, longer.

It was working. He was focusing on her body now, his hands roaming over her curves. This was what she needed. This overwhelming tide of physical sensation that only he could make her feel.

Because it blocked out the other feelings. The ones that surrounded her heart and pushed at the walls. The ones that she'd made to protect herself.

When he'd said he was going to talk to his father her world had ended for a moment. When he'd made it clear he was willing to take a step that might end what they were building here, and it had made her feel like the earth had simply run out, and she was standing on the edge of a cliff waiting to fall, she'd known she had to shore up her defenses.

And now he was here, and he was saying things. Romantic things. Things that had nothing to do with sex or convenience or honor, and she couldn't do it. She couldn't handle it.

This she could do. This was all they needed. He just had to remember that. She would make him remember. That this was good. That it was enough.

"Take me," she begged against his lips. "Hard. Now."

But he didn't obey. He kept kissing her, his lips so tender and sweet it made her ache. She didn't want to ache. She didn't want to care.

She didn't want to love or be loved. She didn't want to care about anything. About whether or not they called her the Zombie Princess, or if Xander thought she was beautiful. If Xander stayed with her forever or only for a few months.

She didn't want to care about any of it.

It was too frightening. It asked too much.

"Stop it," she said, pushing against his chest, pushing him against the back wall. "Stop being gentle. Kiss me like you mean it." Like there was nothing else. Like the press didn't exist. Hard enough that he could made her forget, long enough that she wouldn't be able to breathe. That she might drown in it. In this.

She kissed him again, and she felt his fingers lace through her hair, and he tugged hard, drawing her head back. Yes. This was what she wanted.

"I have to look at you for a moment," he said. "You're lovely." He traced her ruined lips with his thumb, holding her still with his other hand, forked deep in her hair.

She shook her head. "I don't need you to lie."

"It's not a lie. Any man that misses your beauty is a fool."

"He's a man who has eyes, Xander." The whole world had eyes. And they didn't like what they saw.

He kissed her hard, a punishment for her talking back. The kind of kiss she wanted. The kind she reveled in. "You should know this, Layna," he said, his voice rough. "Beauty, the kind on your skin, is terribly vain."

"Inner beauty, Xander? Is that what we're talking about?"

"No. For the love of God, woman, do you honestly believe that a rough patch of skin takes away who you are? Takes away your allure? Your beauty? Your lips…your hair and eyes. *Agape*, they are worthy of any man's praise."

She could feel the cracks in her defenses widening. Could feel herself, her resolve, weakening.

"But I don't need praise," she said. "I need you, here and now."

"Sex is all you want?" he asked, a strange note to his voice.

"Sex and a partnership. Anything else is gratuitous."

He tugged her hair harder, kissed her throat. "I can show you gratuitous if you really want."

"Yes," she said.

He leaned down and picked her up, carrying her over to the desk, which was quite clean—and she had the vague thought that it was a good thing it was—and set her down on top of it, stripping himself of his clothes as quickly as possible. "Take them off," he said to her. "All of them."

And she obeyed. From her position on the desk she stripped off her top, pants, underwear and shoes, and stayed perched on the edge while he positioned himself between her thighs. He braced his hands on her hips and slid slowly, making her aware of every inch of him as he entered her.

He lifted one hand and gripped her chin. "Look at me," he demanded.

"No." She didn't know exactly why, but she couldn't.

"Look at me, Layna," he said, thrusting hard into her.

"Xander, please…"

Her eyes flew to his, shock preventing her from doing anything else. From thinking it through. And the minute she saw him, really saw him, her heart started to feel too big for its cage. She looked down again, squeezing her eyes closed.

"Don't shut me out," he said.

"Xander…"

"I love you."

"No," she said, shaking her head, closing her eyes tighter, a tear tracking down her cheek.

"Layna, I love you." He kept moving inside of her, his thrusts matching the terrified rhythm of her heart, as he drove her to the brink with his body while his words delivered fatal damage to the walls surrounding her heart.

"No. Don't love me. Don't ask me to love you."

He cupped her face and kissed her lips, moving hard and deep within her, his mouth covering hers, swallowing her denial, and the cry of pleasure that followed it as her orgasm crashed over her in a perfect storm of agony and ecstasy.

Just like everything with Xander.

Perfect pleasure. Perfect pain. Perfect misery mingled with joy.

When she came back to herself, his arms were around her, and he was holding her tight against his chest. She realized she was shaking. Sobbing.

Because of him. She pushed away from him.

"Xander, I can't…"

"You don't love me?"

"Why do you think you love me?" she asked, even though she didn't want to know the answer. Didn't want to hear any more. "No. Don't answer that. I can't…I can't breathe, Xander. I can't." She started hunting for her clothes, tugging them on as quickly as possible.

"Why not?"

"I thought I could…" She was gasping now, panicking. "I thought I could do this. But do you know why I cling to my contentment? Because at least if I don't…if I don't love anything, if I'm never excited, or overjoyed, I can't go back to the low place again. If I don't care about my looks then I can't be destroyed when people call me names. If I don't love you I can't fall apart when you leave. I can't fall into depression, and that…fog, Xander, that horrible fog. I won't do it again."

"I'm not going to leave you, Layna," he said, walking forward, gripping her arms. "Ever. I made a promise. And I will keep it."

"You didn't mean it, though. You still went to your father and told him the truth, even though it might mean you would lose this. Lose me…"

"I don't have to be king to have you, but I do need you to be a good man. I need you. You don't understand."

"That's just it! So what happens when you don't need me anymore? And you run."

"You don't trust me at all, do you?"

She wrapped her arms around herself, trying to hold it all, hold herself, together. "I don't trust in anything. Not you…not…"

"God?"

"Don't. You don't know what it's like. Fine if you have a trauma, you just get to run and run. But the rest of us are left with nothing. I couldn't run from my pain, Xander it was in me. And you don't know what that is!"

"Oh, I don't?" he growled. "Because throwing my life away on drugs and drinking and sex wasn't a horrible existence? It was, Layna. It was. It was every bit as dark, and every bit as rock-bottom."

"I don't suppose you ever thought about killing yourself. Because I did. I thought about it a lot."

"I never thought about it," he said. "I just assumed that running toward death at full speed like I was would eventually amount to it. One day you drink too hard, you take too much of the wrong thing, and you don't wake up again.

I was sort of hoping for that day, just too much of a coward to pursue it with any kind of real dedication. Or maybe it was the ties here. But for whatever reason, I didn't. Still, I know that place you're talking about. I know that kind of darkness. But I walked up out of it for real today and I want you to do it, too."

She shook her head. "I can't. I can't do it again, Xander. And I'm sure you think that I'm weak. And maybe I am. But I used up all my strength already and I can't possibly put myself at risk like this again. I can't just…put myself out there. All of me, and risk being pushed down into the darkness again."

Xander looked down at the desk. The desk where they had just made love. He was still naked. And he didn't seem all that concerned about it.

"My father told me that I was his son. No matter what the paternity test might say." He looked up at her. "He's my father no matter what."

"I'm happy for you. I'm happy for…you don't have to have a wife now, do you? Not one like me. You're accepted and your people love you. And I'm the Zombie Princess. You don't need me, Xander."

He hauled her against his chest, holding her to him. "I *do* need you, Layna."

"No, Xander, you don't. And more than that? I'm starting to hurt things for you. At first…at first maybe people loved you for sticking with me, but now I'm just a burden. An embarrassment. It's going to be…I'll be ridiculed by the world. Kyonos will be."

"Whether the people approve of you, or me, or not. I need you because you are the only woman for me. Because I love you beyond words. Because you have reached down deep inside me and shined a light on the real me. Made me look at myself and see who I am, and who I want to be. Because back when I was a selfish, entitled, wreck of a man, you were the only woman for me, and no matter what life has thrown at me in the meantime, at the end of it all, you're still the only woman for me."

"I can't be the woman for you." She pulled out of his hold, and he let her go. "I can't live like this. With…with the press closing in around me all the time. They took pictures of me, Xander. And a reporter called and…"

"What?"

"He asked if you made love to me in the dark."

"Layna…"

"So even if the people love me. Even if they love you being with me. Even if I don't end up embarrassing the nation I can't…I can't do this to myself. They'll never leave me alone. They'll harass me. Forever. For all of my life and I can't…do it."

"And you don't love me?" he asked, his tone flat.

She shook her head, the walls around her heart strengthening, folding in around it like a concrete blockade. "No."

"I see."

"I'm going to go."

"To your room."

"No. Away from here. Just…away from you."

"You're running?" he asked, his tone even, deadly. "I thought we agreed we weren't going to do that anymore. I thought we promised."

"No, Xander," she said, her voice a whisper. "You promised. I didn't. I don't want any of this. I don't want to be in the public eye, I don't want to be under scrutiny like this. I don't want your love."

"But you have it. I want you to want it all, Layna, I want you to have it all."

"How dare you?" she screamed, angry now, cracking apart inside. "How dare you take my safety away from me!

How dare you pull me from my home, from my quiet life and bring me here! You said we would be partners, you didn't say you would demand my soul."

"Nothing less, *agape*. Because you have mine."

"Well, you don't have mine. And I'm going. Goodbye, Xander. I wish you the best of luck in ruling, and in finding your future queen. She won't be me."

"What can I do?" he asked, a desperate thread in his voice that seemed tied to her heart, squeezing her tight, making it impossible to breathe.

"Show me the future. Show me nothing will happen. Show me that if I choose to want again, to feel again, to need again, that I won't have it all ripped from me. Prove to me you won't leave, you won't cheat. Prove to me that things will be well. Show me. Show me that when you don't need me anymore, when your reputation isn't helped by me, you won't want someone else. You won't regret me."

He ran his hand down his face, looking so impossibly tired, so defeated. "You of little faith," he said, laughing bitterly.

"I don't know how you can say that to me."

"I don't know how you can claim to be anything different. You spend fifteen years in a convent, pretending to be a woman of faith when you don't have enough to feel an emotion that transcends anything more than basic contentment. You're afraid to take a deep breath, Layna Xenakos, afraid to make a ripple for fear God might notice you and strike at you again. Afraid to live."

"I'm not. That's not it...."

"The hell it's not. At least I can do this. At least I can put the past behind me and walk forward. You don't want to go back to that hell you were living in, but you keep one foot in it to remind yourself. You keep yourself afraid. You keep yourself from ever feeling happiness. From ever feeling love. What's the point of protecting yourself if all you're protecting is a life half-lived?"

"Tell me why I should trust you," she spat, "when all your history proves that when things get hard, you'll leave. You haven't earned my faith, so don't stand there and talk about how I don't have it."

He jerked back like he'd been slapped. But he was only stunned for a moment. "I haven't earned your faith?" he asked. "All that I have given you, all that I have promised you, my body, my soul, and I have not earned your faith? Think of what I promised you before I ran the last time. Nothing. Engagements end, which happened with ours. I had not made vows to you, I had not promised undying love. I hadn't even promised you undying lust. I promise it all to you now and then some. I give you my word, my vow, that I will never leave you, no matter what comes. I give you everything I am. I'm laying it at your feet here, Layna. But now you tell me I have not earned your faith."

She looked at him, at his eyes, blazing with anger and hurt, burning inside her so that she had no choice but to look away. Because what she'd said was worthy of anger. Insults he didn't deserve.

She took her ring off. Shaking, she put it in his hand, forcing his fingers to close around it. "This is the second time I've returned a ring to your family. Maybe…maybe don't offer me one again."

"Is that really what you want?" he asked, his voice strained.

She nodded, trying to keep the tears from falling. "Yes. It is."

She walked out of the office and ignored Xander shouting her name. Ignored the sound of his footsteps behind her as she ran to her room. She looked around, at all the pretty things. And decided she didn't need any of it.

She wouldn't stop running again until she'd reached safety. Until she could feel safely hidden from the wall of grief that was threatening to overwhelm her.

CHAPTER FOURTEEN

LAYNA RODE UNTIL her thigh muscles burned and her lungs ached. Across the fields and up to the highest point on the hilltop, where she could look over the ocean. The wind was blowing her hair everywhere, her horse shifting his weight beneath her.

The drunken gambler didn't think she had faith, it would make her laugh if she didn't feel like she was cracking apart inside. Stupid man. Stupid, stupid man.

She closed her eyes and inhaled deeply, the salty air burning her throat. Mother Superior hadn't blinked overly much at her return, but this morning she'd called Layna into her office and told that she would have to make a choice now.

Either she would take her vows, or she would find somewhere else to go. The abbess hadn't been unkind, but the simple fact was, Layna's room had been filled and she'd been off living…well, unchastely. That was the truth and she couldn't deny it.

This wasn't a place for her to hide, while she was free to have bouts of going off and doing what she wanted. It wasn't fair. Or right.

Damn Xander. She had no idea who she was anymore. *You of little faith.*

It wasn't fair. He was asking her to have faith in him

but she didn't have a guarantee. She couldn't be sure that she wouldn't lose everything again.

That she wouldn't be left stranded at rock bottom alone.

For we walk by faith, not by sight.

Well, that was just inconvenient. She got off her horse and looked out at the ocean, over the rolling, gray waves. Everything seemed to have been leached of color to accommodate her mood and she appreciated it. At least something was working in her favor.

Suddenly she was hit by a wave of sadness so strong it crippled her. She went down to her knees, the moisture from the grass bleeding through her dress.

He was right. She had no faith. It took no faith to hide. You didn't need faith when you were safe. Didn't need it behind the walls of a convent, where you were protected from the world. When your every need was met daily and you were never challenged, you didn't need faith.

You didn't need faith when you were a novice who'd spent years managing to not take vows. Not taking the leap of faith and committing the trust it took to go wholly into that life, not having the faith to go back into the world and try to live.

She'd condemned herself to a halflife in exchange for safety. It wasn't the press that scared her. It was what he made her feel.

He made her feel so exposed. He didn't accept her excuses. Didn't let her scars keep him at a distance. He wanted it all. Worse, he wanted her to have it all.

And wasn't sure she was brave enough to ever take that risk again.

If ever there was a time Xander wanted to run, it was now. From the searing pain in his chest. From the burning in his eyes, from tears, damn it, and not because he was hung over.

He hadn't had anything to drink since she'd left.

It was like he'd well and truly changed. Fancy that. Change didn't feel all that rewarding when you were sober and you didn't have the woman you loved.

A pain shot through his chest. Yes, he did love her. He wondered now if he always had. If he'd been a shallow boy, in love with a shallow, beautiful girl. Until their world shook apart and he'd gone off licking his wounds.

He'd come back a man changed, to find her a woman changed. And to find that everything that had been there between them from the beginning was still there. That the tragedies of life had reshaped them, so much so that they fit together now even more perfectly than before.

And she was too afraid to see it. Too afraid to reach out and take it. To trust him. To be with him. She was choosing to be unhappy so that she wouldn't be devastated and that killed him.

Unless she just doesn't love you.

Well, that was always a possibility. But still, with him or without him, she was choosing fear over happiness and that ate at him. Because it was what he'd done for so long. Because he was an expert in empty, meaningless things. In pursuits that were vain and useless.

In turning away from everything pure and strong, and hard and wonderful, so that he could simply find some shelter from reality.

He was done with that now, though. He loved her. More than the throne. More than his own life.

So he could sit here and brood soberly, or he could go after her. Make a fool of himself. Again. For her love. And if he couldn't have her love, he would beg her to let go of all that pain and live the life she was meant to live.

Not shut herself away from the world, but shine in it.

Of course, he would beg her to be with him first. She could shine with him. Failing that, he would let her shine alone. But dammit, she would shine. Scars and fears couldn't keep her hidden anymore.

She was beautiful. She deserved everything. And he had to make sure that she knew it.

"Why don't you go for a ride? Or a walk?"

Layna turned toward Mother Maria-Francesca, feeling distinctly ashamed just looking at the other woman. She shouldn't still be here taking up valuable space and sulking. Though, sulking seemed like too weak of a term.

"That's probably a good idea."

"Where will you go?" She detected a hint of concern in her voice. Probably afraid Layna would do something dire since she looked like a specter of death.

But she wouldn't. She couldn't honestly say she wouldn't. "Just up in the hills. To get a view of the ocean. My favorite place."

"Will you take Phineas?"

"No. I need the walk. I need to move slow. I have a lot of thinking to do."

She folded her arms beneath her breasts and walked out of the church building and out into the stormy weather. Wind was blowing in off the waves, rain threatening to fall from swollen gray clouds.

Layna lowered her head and started up the hill, not thinking, just feeling. Just letting her emotions wash through her.

She felt like she was drowning even while she was standing there breathing air. But the strangest thing was, she didn't feel like she was losing herself.

She scrambled to the top of a grass-covered hill and

looked out over the ocean, tears blinding her. She hurt as much as she ever had, her heart smashed to pieces, shards embedded in her chest, but she wasn't fading into the mist.

Maybe it was because Xander's face was too strong in her mind. Maybe it was just because she had something, someone, to care about now.

Maybe it was because she finally knew who she was.

She wasn't a party girl with spoiled looks. Wasn't a princess who would never be crowned. She was Layna Xenakos, whatever her circumstances. Whatever her face. She was strong. She had run through hell and caught on fire along the way, left with scars that were inside and out, but she'd run through.

She had lost her faith, but for one blinding moment, she felt like maybe she'd found it.

Because this was that place again. That rock-bottom moment. But she wasn't alone.

She closed her eyes and tilted her face up to the sky, a raindrop landing on her cheeks. No, she wasn't alone. And she was strong.

A lump rose in her throat, a sob breaking through.

It didn't matter what happened. She could trust herself. She could trust Xander.

Oh, Xander.

She needed to go to him. Because she loved him. Because he was the one she wanted to be with, that was the life she wanted.

She had to get down and beg for his forgiveness if that's what she needed to do. To ask him if he would take her, as she was, so broken and scared, when she'd been so horrible to him.

To tell him she feared nothing. Not pain, or love, or the media, more than she feared a lifetime without him.

She turned and her heart nearly stopped when she saw

a dark head come into view, cresting the top of the hill, followed by a familiar face, and a heartbreakingly familiar body.

"Xander," she whispered.

And she ran to him.

Layna threw her arms around his neck and held him close to her, tears falling, her hands shaking. "What are you doing here?"

"I lied to you," he said, voice rough, his fingers forked through her hair, his face buried in her neck.

"You did?" she asked, pulling her head back so that she could look at him.

"I told you no more running. But I'm running now. To you."

She laughed as tears rolled down her cheeks. "Well, you're in luck because I just stopped running. So it looks like we're finally standing in the same place."

"It's about time," he said, kissing her lips. "It's about time."

"I love you," she said. "I was so scared, Xander. So scared to say it, or hear it, or feel it. But I found my faith. I found it and now I'm not afraid."

"I still can't give you your guarantee. Not as far as anything in life is concerned. But with me you have one. I'll always stand with you. I'll always stay with you. You will be my wife. The mother of my children. You're the only woman for me, Layna. Now and always. There are many uncertain things, but not my love."

"I don't need a guarantee. Not now. Faith is all about walking without sight. I don't need to see ahead, I just need to see you."

"You have no idea how glad I am to hear you say that."

She laughed. "About as glad as I am to say it?"

"I need to tell you this. I need you to understand—"

"I believe you, Xander, you have nothing to prove," she said, cupping his face and kissing him again. "I'm sorry I made you feel that you did. I'm sorry I doubted you. I'm sorry I let fear win. But it won't. Not again."

"But you need to hear this. I have walked down so many dark paths. I've chased pleasure in all its forms, and oblivion. I've tasted hopelessness. There was nothing there. No satisfaction. No answer. But with you, I find I am the man I'm meant to be. I find I'm the man I should have been all this time. You gave me the strength to face my father, to face this. I had to come and find you right away because somehow I knew I couldn't do it without you. I felt it."

She took a deep breath, of the sea and of Xander.

"I feel like we're standing at the beginning again. But better. Because I know so much more. I've been down those paths, too, and I know how dark they can be. So I know now just how important it is to always reach for the light. I know how weak I can be, but I also know how strong I can be."

"Very strong," he said. "You are so very strong."

"I wouldn't go back," she said, another tear spilling down her face. "I wouldn't take it back now. Because this is who I need to be. This is when we need to be. Not fifteen years ago when we would have made each other more vain and selfish, with equally vain and selfish children. But now."

"Now that I'm a broken-down playboy and you're a scarred novice? You are still only a novice, right? You didn't take vows, did you?"

"Nothing half so drastic, don't worry. But, yes, the scarred novice and the broken-down playboy with no pedigree. That's exactly who we needed to be."

"It was always going to be us in the end, wasn't it?" he asked.

She nodded. "I think so. How else would we survive all of this if we couldn't hold on to each other?"

"We wouldn't," he said. That simple. That certain.

"I'm just glad we got to become better versions of ourselves before it happened."

"I'm just glad that we're finally together."

"So am I."

"And we're together because of how much I love you, because of how much you love me. Not for Kyonos. Not for appearances. Not for any other reason."

He picked her up, and spun her in a circle, rain falling in earnest now, soaking them both. She flung her hands wide and let it fall on her, let it wash away the years. The regret. The pain. So all that remained was love.

"You know," she said, "I always felt the most free when I was riding my horse. But now I just feel that way. I just feel free."

"We both are, Layna. We both are."

EPILOGUE

Fifteen years later...

"HE'S GOING TO outlive us all." Xander sat down on the edge of the bed and looked at his wife. He was exhausted from the ball, a sort of "coming out" affair for Jessica and Stavros's oldest daughter. His own daughters had been so excited about it they'd been driving him mad for weeks.

Now they were feverishly planning their own, even though it was some years off. Mak and Eva's oldest son had reacted to the entire thing with the same sullenness of his father, and nothing his squealing cousins had done to entice excitement from him had worked. The same had been true for Xander and Layna's son, who had copied his cousin's practiced disdain. They had succeeded very well in annoying the girls, which Xander privately assumed was their goal.

He sighed. How he'd become the father of two teenage girls and a sullen preteen boy he didn't know.

"Entirely possible," Layna said. She was standing by the vanity, all long elegant lines. He was always fascinated by the way she removed her jewelry. The way her fingers moved, the way she stood.

But then, everything Layna did fascinated him. Now and always.

"Can you believe the way he moves around the palace

in that motorized cart of his? It's…well, it's the funniest thing I've ever seen."

King Stephanos had firmly denied both death and doctors and was a very crotchety old man. Xander was the acting ruler at this point, his father not able to perform most of the functions required by the position, but that didn't mean he wasn't still acting the figurehead. With gusto.

"It's that Drakos spirit," she said. "You're all too stubborn to be defeated."

He smiled. "True enough." Ever since that day he'd reconciled with his father he'd felt like a Drakos, unquestionably. "I still hate wearing ties to these things," he said, tugging the black scrap of silk off and letting it fall to the floor.

Layna smiled and walked over to him, planting her hands on the bed on either side of him, leaning down for a kiss. "The torture you're subjected to," she said, smiling that special smile of hers.

He kissed the crease by the corner of her mouth. "I know it."

"So tell me, Xander Drakos, heir to the throne, have you ever regretted coming back?"

"Not once. I would wear a tie every day of my life so long as I spent those days with you."

"Now that was the right answer."

"I'm getting pretty good at this husband thing."

"You've been good at it for a while," she said.

She kissed him again, deeper, more passionately. And then he was lost. As he always was with her. Years hadn't diminished their need for each other, their love.

Much, much later, Xander held his wife against his chest, threading his fingers through her hair, stroking her scar-roughened cheek.

"Layna Drakos, you make me very glad that I stopped running."

* * * * *

MILLS & BOON®

Mills & Boon have been at the heart of romance since 1908... and while the fashions may have changed, one thing remains the same: from pulse-pounding passion to the gentlest caress, we're always known how to bring romance alive.

Now, we're delighted to present you with these irresistible illustrations, inspired by the vintage glamour of our covers. So indulge your wildest dreams and unleash your imagination as we present the most iconic Mills & Boon moments of the last century.

Visit **www.millsandboon.co.uk/ArtofRomance** to order yours!

MILLS & BOON®

Why shop at millsandboon.co.uk?

Each year, thousands of romance readers find their
perfect read at millsandboon.co.uk. That's because
we're passionate about bringing you the very best
romantic fiction. Here are some of the advantages
of shopping at www.millsandboon.co.uk:

* **Get new books first**—you'll be able to buy your
  favourite books one month before they hit
  the shops

* **Get exclusive discounts**—you'll also be able to buy
  our specially created monthly collections, with up
  to 50% off the RRP

* **Find your favourite authors**—latest news,
  interviews and new releases for all your favourite
  authors and series on our website, plus ideas for
  what to try next

* **Join in**—once you've bought your favourite books,
  don't forget to register with us to rate, review and
  join in the discussions

Visit **www.millsandboon.co.uk**
for all this and more today!

MILLS_WEB